100 PROOF STUD

A Teenage Sleuth Thriller

A. J. LAPE

100 Proof Stud

A.J. LAPE

To my readers...thank you for being patient; I would be nowhere without your loyalty.

Chapter One

CRUEL AND UNUSUAL PUNISHMENT

No one was perfect, but some sure did appear to have the corner on the market. In my meager sixteen years, it had been my experience that even the "perfect" had secrets. But secrets sucked. Secrets could kill.

...I should know.

My name's Darcy Walker. I may not operate on perfection, but I did operate on a lot of secrets. Some were mine. Some were others', and some remained nameless until the nosy in me pieced them together. Maybe at one time I had a perfect life, but I felt like one of those little snow globes, and someone came along and shook things up. Things all of a sudden looked different. *I* was different.

I watched the hot dog on the greasy roller and wondered if I was bound for Hell...or a bullet.

It was Saturday night, a cold and blustery Cincinnati December, and I stood zombified in Belinski's Bookstore. When I rolled into work, a Plexiglas hot dog case sat on the checkout counter, revolving with dogs as the freebie of the day if customers purchased a book—a marketing ploy I could appreciate. So I purchased a book for breakfast, lunch, and dinner. My palate wasn't all that sophisticated.

I was "in a period of reflection." A fancy way for saying grounded. I'd done naughty things like broken curfews, hotwired a car, and roamed my neighborhood after hours, spying on my insanely weird neighbors. In Darcyville, those were benign incidents, but my father thought they warranted a two-week sabbatical on anything fun.

Murphy is my father, and I'd addressed him by his first name since I turned six months old. Crazy? Sure. But we did crazy like Al-Qaeda did terrorism. It was a congenital defect. Example? When he found me gallivanting at midnight, he met me outside with a frying pan. I wasn't sure what he thought he'd accomplish with a thirteen-inch skillet, but when I dumbly laughed, he looked at me like I had too much "North" running through my veins...and anyone from the "South" would get it. Whatever the case, he'd stripped me of my verb status, relegating me to a lowly noun.

The killjoy...he'd nuked my party girl reputation.

I licked my lips as the hot dog rolled over, saying, "Free?" to my boss, Castro Belinski.

He grumbled, "Buy another book, and that dog is yours." I fished around in my purse and pulled out a twenty-dollar bill, buying a pocket book on the migratory pattern of the cuckoo bird.

After I plunked the cash down on the countertop, I opened the grease-splattered case, picked up the tongs, and dropped the dog on a bun. I slathered on mustard and relish, closing my eyes for prayer. I wasn't sure I had a direct line to God, but I did always manage a food prayer. *Dear Lord*, I prayed to myself. *May you not clog my arteries or kill me from food poisoning. Thank you Jesus, and God bless America.*

I demolished one-third in my first bite.

When Mr. B saw me reopen my eyes, he made the sign of the cross, muttering, "Long live Poland and Cuba."

"Long live Poland and Cuba," I agreed, toasting my dog in his direction. I guess if I liked communism.

Mr. B was half Polish and half Cuban with an overabundant love to his two homelands. He was heart-attack-round at three hundred pounds, hygienically challenged, and dressed like a hillbilly. His standard uniform consisted of bibbed overalls with a tan blazer one-size too small. Sometimes he wore shoes. Sometimes he didn't. At any given time, customers could catch a panoramic view of him doing one of three things: marking up merchandise, eating a high-calorie snack, or enjoying the Christmas spirit. Not in the traditional sense, but in the liquid sense.

Mr. B had a proclivity toward liquor.

My guess was he might've been tipsy when he decorated the place because we worked in a neoclassical time warp. On the ceiling, he paid homage to Michelangelo's work at the Sistine Chapel. Customers didn't see replicas of angels and King David though. They got a load of Mr. B's chubby face transferred onto bodies that belonged in *Playgirl*.

My days consisted of helping customers find books, ordering books, and reshelving books. Wasn't hard to do because only five rows anchored the store. Granted, they were long rows, but once again, The Double-B (as customers called it) wasn't about variety. It was about the bottom line—his.

Mr. B thrust his palm in my face. "That dog'll cost you one dollar and fifty cents."

I burst out laughing, wiping my mouth with a napkin. "The sign says it's free, and I just bought my fourth book of the day on the cuckoo bird!"

He narrowed his stingy eyes. "It *is* practically free. That ten-pack of dogs cost me ninety-nine cents."

Not in the mood to argue, I motioned to the change he pitched on the counter and watched him count out a dollar fifty, placing it in the register. He took a minute to finger-count the ones in the drawer and then fish-eyed the remaining customers in the store. The Double-B was only a little more than the walking dead. I worked with three other females, but each had plans for the evening, so Mr. B (in the Christmas spirit) let them make their exit early. As a result, I'd been fated to pull a twelve-hour date with boredom since I had no boyfriend, nothing planned, just eyeballing the books that no one ever bought.

Mr. B opened the case and likewise constructed a frankfurter. He popped the cap on the ketchup, squirted on a streak, and then grabbed the glass jar of relish, emptying the remainder onto his dog. A glob of ketchup splattered on the top of his balding head. I considered telling him, but his stingy butt deserved a condiment head.

Stuffing the remaining two-thirds in my mouth, I watched a dollop of relish tumble to my black "Belinski's is the Bomb" shirt (karma, probably). I quickly untucked the hem, pulled it to my lips, and licked it clean.

Swallowing the last bite, I zeroed in on the remaining six. "Can I buy another one?"

"Sure thing," he grumbled. I plopped down another one fifty as he snatched it up and placed the coins in the cash register. "Are you thirsty?" he grunted. "I can grab you a Coke from my secret stash in the back. It's next to my juice."

He had no juice. His juice was vodka. Mr. B was splotchy-faced and a little more glassy-eyed than normal. A field sobriety test fail. I made a mental note to chuck the vodka down the drain and hide his car keys.

When I gave him a smiling nod, he moseyed back toward the break room, his bones creaking and moaning like a rusty door hinge. Figuring I had a good ten minutes, I pulled out another dog, cradled it snugly between a bun, and glopped on ketchup.

While I balanced it between my teeth, I rang up a customer and gave him a freebie hot dog in an attempt to keep us clean of false advertisement. Bundled up in a down jacket, he looked so plump and bulgy it was hard to discern his body type. All I could make out was a thin smile beneath his droopy white toboggan. Toboggan was as big as my father. My father, however, was massively good-looking. Toboggan had sub-humanoid properties. His face was too puffy, pimply, and weirdly angular. Let's just say if Frankenstein and those hyenas from *The Lion King* had a lovechild, the spawn would be Toboggan Guy.

One creepy teenage boy followed. I couldn't tell if they'd come together, or if he merely finished his just-looking gig too.

Creepy Teenager stood about an inch shorter than me with an Abe Lincoln beard. He was scarecrow skinny, wearing jeans that hung lower than Justin Bieber's. He smelled emotionally unstable, his laugh like a mad scientist. Both guys were sketchy and seemed to be strange for strange's sake. They'd paced all night, perusing sections that didn't fit what I would've guessed as their reader profiles.

Like Toboggan, Creepy Teenager scored high on the perv scale. I bent over—he focused on my rear end. I reached for a top shelf—

his eyes glued to my chest. I smiled at someone—he licked his lips and looked like he wanted to eat mine.

Douchebag. Thank God, he wasn't the hot dog type, but I still had to deal with Toboggan.

When I dropped the hot dog in Toboggan's hand, he brushed my knuckles long enough for his intent to be clear. He wanted a piece of Darcy Walker, and he didn't strike me as the type above using force. The moment I talked myself out of his forward advances, he opened his mouth and removed all doubt.

"You've got a killer bod," he muttered lowly, taking a bite of hot dog. I ignored him, cringing at the thought of his hands anywhere on me. "Did you hear me?" he asked. "You've got a killer bod."

The way I saw it, I had two options. Ignore him (um, no), or confront his sick innuendos (heck, yeah).

I hitched my chin up, giving him my patented eat-dirt-and-die face. "When you decide to be a douchebag, you're all-in, aren't you?"

Toboggan didn't respond, but Creepy Teenager threw his head back and laughed, maniacally.

Normally, crazy people fascinated me, but I wanted them gone... like yesterday...maybe last week. "You should leave," I said quietly.

"It's a public place," Toboggan refuted.

"So?" I countered.

"What's your name?" he asked.

"Dontspeaktome Walker."

His thin lips tilted upward. "Long first name."

"Yeah, you ought to hear my middle."

"Which is?"

"Youdoghumpingmothertruckingponkey."

Toboggan and Creepy Teenager let that string of words sink in. Especially the last one—*ponkey*. It was Darcyspeak (my own made-up dictionary of terms), but there was no doubt in the message.

Get. Out. Now.

I went back to cleaning the green countertop, surprised when I finished that they both still did the staring thing. "Hmm," Toboggan muttered, wiping his mouth on his sleeve. "You have a strange look on your face. What're you thinking?"

I braced both hands on the countertop and blurted out the truth. "I'm thinking middle finger."

Yup, I went ghetto.

Creepy Teenager dispensed more of the mad scientist laugh, and I glanced toward the break room, wondering how long it took to get a freaking can of Coke. Not that Mr. B would be much help, but a girl could hope.

"I like a girl with spunk," Toboggan said, chuckling in a pervy voice.

I never changed my stance, only reiterated myself. "Take your ponkey self out the door and kiss off."

"Only if you tell me what a ponkey is."

Like an idiot, I obliged. I'd learned a long time ago to not give psychos what they wanted. It empowered them and weakened me. But the guy rubbed me the wrong way, and I dumbly put one more coin in his psycho bank.

"It's Darcyspeak, you idiot. There are punks, and then there are donkeys. For those in life who pack the double whammy—where the punk in you makes a donkey out of your ass—I refer to them as ponkeys. You, my friend, are one of the biggest ponkeys I've ever run across. And I mean that with all due respect," I lied and batted my eyelashes sarcastically.

I actually said the ass word. I never cursed, but perv was worth the sin.

"Darcy," he said with a grin, acknowledging my name. "I like that."

Once again, something lewd crossed his lips, giving me a bad case of the heebie-jeebies. I threw him a dirty look—the environmentally acceptable alternative to live grenades. At the last minute, I pulled out my iPhone and clicked on the video, shoving the screen right up into his face.

He went ballistic. "What are you doing?" he barked.

It was my turn for the smile to go wicked. "I'm taking a video of you and your dumb-butt friend. You're giving me a weird vibe. If I wind up dead, I want the po-po to come after you specifically as a person of interest."

At that, he and Creepy Teenager quickly headed for the door, waving goodbye with less than five fingers. I quickly replayed the video, depressed as heck when I realized a piece of hot dog had been stuck to the camera lens.

Ugh, all I got was pork on a neck.

Massaging my forehead, I negotiated with my brain. I couldn't shake the feeling I'd been watched lately. Every little peep spooked me, and every headlight that shone on the building made me dodge imaginary bullets. I mumbled to myself, "Your imagination's working overtime, Darcy. You've been bored too long, and this is what happens."

The effects of being vertical all day played nasty games with my lower back. As the clock ticked closer toward nine p.m., I jumped on my orange RipStik and rode a path around the store, trying to realign my spine. I straightened the snowflake holiday decorations dangling from the ceiling and dusted off the mistletoe hanging by a red velvet ribbon in the main aisle. For a brief moment, I thought about the mistletoe. It was a vibrant, earthy green and had seen occasional lip action—but for me personally, it was simply a twig. Mr. B, however, saw it as a vehicle for a true love match. A romantic at heart, he always looked for an opportunity to get his sexy on.

Perhaps that was why there were so many holiday parties. Parties meant more opportunities for a love connection. It was that "peace on earth, goodwill toward men" sort of thing permeating the air. Breakups became makeups and differences were set aside to celebrate the holiest time of year, the season of faith. But oftentimes, even if someone found a connection, the love was temporary. Every holiday season came to an end.

The holidays at my home were bittersweet. Sure we were happy, but ache tugged at my heart when I thought about the empty chair at dinnertime. I tried to be emotionally numb and go through the motions, but it didn't always work.

I felt everything...

After two 360s around the store, I parked my RipStik next to the space heater. The Double-B felt colder than the Klondike. Mr. B had bought a heater at Costco that threw off enough BTUs to fry an egg, but the heat still hadn't reached my bones. Taking a second to warm my hands, I swiped the countertop one last time, scooting the breadcrumbs into my palm, tossing them in the trash.

I was tired...not just physically, but mentally.

In my brief life, I'd been shot at, shoved into the trunk of a car, had a knife pushed up against my carotid, not to mention seen dead bodies and appendages without torsos. Just thinking about the things I'd experienced made me ponder the loose ends in my life. The biggest being my quest to find the man who'd shoved me into the trunk of his car (more on that later).

Right then, my cell phone vibrated, millimeters from teetering off the counter. A look at the screen showed the brooding mug of one of my besties, Jon Bradshaw. My hands were so cold the screen on my iPhone didn't recognize me as Homo sapiens. I waved my index finger all over it like an idiot, giving up and using my nose.

I hit the intercom, mumbling, "Speak."

"I need a girlfriend...STAT," he grumbled. "But you have to keep the desperation on the DL."

I rolled my eyes so hard they nearly fell out of my head. Every time he called, I heard a Taylor Swift song playing in my brain. His relationships never went anywhere, and then I was doomed to hear of their demise anytime he opened his mouth. "Give it up, bud," I said laughing. "No one is dumb enough to consider you their HEA."

"HEA?" he repeated, confused.

"Happily ever after, you moron."

"Come on, Walker. I'm as single as a dollar bill and tired of it."

"You're preachin' to the choir, bud. You're preachin' to the choir."

"Then show a brother some love."

I'd rather snag him with a cattle prod, but I was thinking that was illegal.

Nicknamed Grumpy because the guy never smiled, he was one of my closest friends and inducted first into my top-secret brother-hood. He'd been extra clingy in the past four months. Well, clingy for him since he was the emotional equivalent of a wet towel. Why the extra need? He and I almost died in a car crash on the first day of school, both of us spit out through the passenger side window and windshield respectively. In fact, Grumpy *did* die in the ambu-lance. They jumpstarted his heart, and he didn't once see the light (cough, Hell bound, cough). All he remembered was a big, black hole of nothingness when he woke up with a broken nose, arm, and facial lacerations. Maybe that was why I put up with his woe-is-me sob stories. It was my opinion he had bigger problems than not being able to land a significant other.

As if I should be anyone's spiritual advisor.

After a few "sures" and "okays," I took a timeout from the convo and touched the three-inch scar on the back of my head. My head had been shaved, and the ER doc was kind enough to buzz a lightning bolt into my scalp before he stapled me shut. The scar hadn't healed nice and flat. It was a rigid bump that'd be there for the rest of my life.

When I catapulted through the windshield, I landed spread eagle on my back on the pavement. My head split in two with the force. As I drifted in and out of consciousness, the man who hit us hovered overtop me, and that was when I realized he was the crony of Turkey Cardoza—a mobster associated with my best friend's detective grandfather. He'd struck the Suburban we rode in on purpose. After initial impact, our SUV skidded into oncoming traffic and looked like an accordion, coming to rest between two cars.

Grumpy and I were the worse for wear. Finn Lively, who'd also been in the backseat, only had a slight concussion (a fact I attributed to him wearing my lucky hat). And Dylan Taylor, my best friend, had a few bruised ribs, a black eye, and a cut in his hairline complements of the only airbag that'd deployed. Later, authorities discovered the rest had been deactivated—the second clue someone attempted to manipulate our lifespan. Dylan's grandfather was still hellbent on bringing Cardoza to justice.

It hadn't happened yet.

The accident still caused me problems, especially with my best friend. I could be one hundred years old with dementia and never forget the sound of Dylan's head hitting the steering wheel. The horn's continuous beep still rang in my nightmares—I laid there and feared he'd died. You see, my hands weren't completely clean. I'd meddled in his grandfather's work, and even though Dylan and his grandfather adamantly claimed "a detective's family always has a target on them," I considered that an elementary summary of the situation. Dylan, Grumpy, and Finn might not have entered the picture of possible victims if I hadn't involved myself—or the Fates hadn't involved me. While I'd chased my latest obsession this past summer, I had a chance encounter with the Cardoza crime family gunning for Lincoln Taylor. Had I been the intended target during our car crash? If I'd minded my own business, it wouldn't be a consideration. But such was the bane of being a verb: I acted first and considered ramifications later.

But guilt was a killer...

And I'd found myself pulling away from Dylan.

Problem was, at the time of the accident, Dylan had resurrected a conversation about us becoming a couple...as in couple-couple...or best friends dating. Can you just say, *Friendship wrecking ball?* Our relationship had evolved through four stages: best friends, flirting, him acknowledging his true feelings, and then me running like an illegal immigrant across the U.S. border. Ahhhh, Dylan. We were almost a couple...*almost.*

But I'd blown our love boat right out of the water despite the fact he'd given me the hottest, most toe-curling first kiss imaginable. In fact, up until then my girl parts had never experienced a single jolt of pleasure. I'd all but convinced myself I was asexual, needing hormone rehab.

I stupidly recapped the kiss amongst Grumpy's incessant rambling.

The setting was Orlando, on vacation. I'd snuck into Dylan's bedroom for a late night chat. We exchanged a few whispered words, but before I could say, *Hold on lover boy*, his lips found mine —slowly moving, taking, and demanding. After a few seconds of OMG, it was though someone else entered his body because the tempo abruptly shifted. The kiss became hungry, frenzied, and so savagely impassioned I actually crawled out of the dang room because my legs forgot how to work. I could confidently say that last type of kissing was why the Earth was overpopulated. And I feared if it happened again, I'd get pregnant from saliva alone.

The thought made me shivery.

Dylan and I never spoke directly of the kiss, but after the accident, it hung in the air like a sexual humidity. The heated gaze in his eyes told me he'd actually been conscious for it. A part of me wished he hadn't—that he'd been dreaming, and I was merely the conduit to a hormonal fantasy. Problem was, I *felt* something which—shall I put diplomatically—lay in that dark, forbidden nether region Murphy Walker forbade me to speak of.

We still remained best friends. Wild animals couldn't tear us apart. In fact, he dropped me off at opening and then drove to Ohio State University to visit his sister, due to pick me up at closing. First off, I found it odd he drove to Columbus for the day, merely to turn back around and pick me up that evening. Secondly, when he was hush-hush about the reason for the trip, I didn't push. But he called an hour earlier and said a tractor-trailer dumped a load of animal fat all over the freeway, leaving him stuck in bumper-to-bumper traffic.

Suuuuuure. Riiiiiiiight. All I wanted to know was if the bumper fit the four-wheeled or two-legged kind. Chances were she was the 36-24-36 model.

That left Claudia Gonzalez, my Puerto Rican nanny, to perform taxi service. Right on cue, the moment I disconnected with Grumpy, Claudia bounced through the door dressed in a Hawaiian flowered muumuu. She stood five feet tall with inky black hair, big lips, big boobs, and big hips. Claudia never—and I mean *never* wore a coat. I think it was because she'd been gifted with so much insulation upstairs.

The door caught a gust of wind, floating through the vertical blinds on the windows. I shivered and hugged my arms to my sides.

Claudia grabbed my hand across the counter like she tried to catch a runaway train. "Vamoose!" she eeked, wanting to get out of Dodge quicker than the cast of *Gunsmoke*.

Why? Mr. B had a crush on her. As in an I'm-going-to-knock-you-up-soon crush.

It couldn't have been scripted better. Mr. B maneuvered up the aisle with a Coke in both pockets of his blazer and a leg of lamb in his hand. When he saw Claudia, his eyes went loopty-loo, and a long pause hung in the air. He thought it was destinies hooking up. Claudia felt she was dodging a cow patty.

"Vamoose, vamoose, vamoose!" she nervously gasped again. She grabbed my purse from the counter, hooked it over her shoulder, and had one booted foot in the doorway when he appeared at her heels.

Turning her around by the elbow, he pointed the leg of lamb in her face. "You, woman, are going to be my porkin' Jezebel by Christmas. Pork," he grunted, "you're one hot chiquita."

I felt the need to laugh but shockingly squelched it back

"Castro needs to clean up his mouth!" she snapped, slapping his head. "Or my niña quits! Do you understand this 'porks'?" she said, turning to me.

I didn't want to plumb the depths of Mr. Belinski's brain. Talking with him was tantamount to reading the King James Bible —the words didn't always make sense. All I knew was he made the word pork a curse word—when in reality, bacon might be the eighth wonder of the world. When he grinned even deeper, she slapped him harder, her flowered muumuu swaying like a tropical palm. Mr. B's head snapped, and he rocked back on his heels, dropping the leg of lamb. When he moved to catch it, he flat-backed in a decibel that rattled the foundation. Heck, it probably rattled the world.

His chubby hand palmed his jaw. "I like a woman who takes what she needs."

Ugh, that statement made me feel dirty. I squatted down, miraculously pulling him to a standing position. As he continued with the goo-goo eyes, I quickly unplugged the hot dog case, switched off the space heater, and grabbed the silver down-filled jacket I'd slung over a chair. I then jogged back to the break room and "lifted"—I marked in quotations in my mind—Mr. B's car keys. I'd return them tomorrow once he slept the vodka off in the store.

Claudia and I left him standing and stepped out into the gusty night air. The cold wind bit into my face like an angry dog as I hurriedly stuffed my fingers inside my gloves. Cincinnati sucked in the winter. Come to think of it, *everything* sucked, and my boredom just added to the suckery.

Snow blew in my face, and while I swatted it away, I kerplunked my new Adidas sneakers in a mud puddle. Kicking the snowy slush free, I glanced across the street to the neighboring strip mall comprised of Schomberg's Dry Cleaners, Nowacki's Videos, Walgreens pharmacy, and Turn-and-Burn Tanning Salon.

I leaned up against a column and retied my shoe, pausing to glance down at the curb. Holy Moses, it was a criminal's dream. Lying in the snowy gutter were two dirty Visa check cards and one social security card. I blinked twice for the image to register. Snatching them up, I shoved them in my coat pocket and pulled my zipper to my chin. I felt the buzz of my new iPhone in my back pocket. Since Murphy considered an iPhone electronic overkill, I worked to upgrade to a newer model all on my own. This month's ringtone was "Grandma Got Run Over by a Reindeer." I fished it out and realized the caller was my Uncle Shepard, AKA Rookie Johnson. "Hey, Rookie," I greeted.

Rookie possessed one of those deep voices that woke up every cell in the body. He worked as the Hamilton County Prosecutor—the head honcho responsible for bringing criminals to justice. For future reference, that could come in handy, but so far I was on the recreational side of his personality. "Hey, Darc," he murmured, "are you on your way over?"

I was spending the night with him while my father and little sister were out of town. Overnights usually meant ice cream for breakfast, but it also meant he'd grill me on the particulars of my love life. I had no love life. The thing with Rookie, he'd let me express my opinions with impunity. Lawyer talk for no judgment...at least not verbally.

"Yeah," I answered, sunshine in my voice. My cell beeped again, alerting me another call was on deck. I sighed deeply when I clocked on the number.

"Hold on a sec. It's time for my daily Dylan Interruptus.'

I heard Rookie chuckle when I clicked over to my best friend. I wanted to say, "What's her name, Romeo?" Instead, "Hey, D, I missed you," tumbled out of my mouth. I hated when my mind and mouth didn't work together, and frankly that was the majority of the time. But Dylan's mere presence deluged me with too many emotions to count. The biggest being attraction. We had a cat-and-mouse game going that'd grown old.

Something had to give...and give soon.

"Talk dirty to me, sweetheart," he murmured.

I rolled my eyes to his occasional greeting. "Nuclear waste, Wall Street, Congress," I muttered. "That's all the dirty I've got today. Let me call—"

"Ah-ah-ah," he said, chuckling staccato. "Not so fast. I've missed your voice. My watch says your shift is over, so whoever you're talking to can wait." I didn't like ultimatums. In fact, they made me want to do the opposite, but when Dylan issued one, it sounded sort of...*well, hot.* "Let's go to dinner, sweetheart. I'm about thirty minutes out."

I lived on impure thoughts—food was kind of an afterthought.

"Nah, I'm good. Listen to this sound...*beeeeeeep*."

"Don't hang up," he said quickly. "That's cruel and unusual punishment. I didn't know you were into kinky, but it's not like I'm objecting."

"I'm into a lot of things. Just not with you."

I added a diabolical *bwahaha* laugh.

I could hear Dylan frowning. He breathed...I breathed. I shook the ice out of my shoe again, but when Claudia laid on the horn, it shocked me back to reality...or my default setting.

To risk another frown on an otherwise perfect face, I sighed and said, "I'm teasing, and I missed you."

Blah, blah, and more codependent blah. I succumbed to another laugh and then looked to the right while I stepped off the curb. I briefly wondered if we'd still meet up and barely realized a small part of me—unfortunately, the smallest—screamed I was danger bound.

Chapter Two

FATAL ATTRACTION

*I*t was like we'd been frozen in time.

My head slowly shifted to the left when I realized I'd stepped out in front of a moving vehicle. Sometimes people said they had out of body experiences, where their mind actually stepped outside their physical entity and observed the world around them. I think I had one right then. I'd slipped outside my skin and watched myself spill to the pavement and splat like an egg. My phone crashed several feet ahead as my right hand took the brunt of the fall. I even threw in a forward roll before the car squealed to a stop. Somewhere in the distance, I heard rapid Spanish and the ground echoing with frantic footfalls. I landed flat on my back, spinning and facing the car with half my body underneath. A different series of bumpity-bumps hit the air, and I didn't know if my brain rattled around or another part of my body broke in two.

When I made an effort to stand...God help me, I tumbled down.

Down, down, down, into what I quickly surmised was an open manhole.

Holy shiiiiiii-, I almost cursed. I screamed my I'm-Jamie-Lee-Curtis-and-Michael-Myers-is-after-me scream of *Halloween*. I was freaked way the heck out because my guess was...

I was dead.

All I could hope for was they spelled my name right on the

tombstone because God knew I'd been misrepresented before. Last summer, I went undercover and helped the Orlando Police discover the whereabouts of a little boy who'd been missing for six months. I had a knack for solving problems or seeing things no one else saw, and when I read of his plight, I inserted myself into the details of the case. To make a long story short, I used a code name of Jester. I liked to think Jester was the bad girl, not Darcy Walker. Call me the Queen of Rationalization, but it was the way I made peace with my impulse control issues. To the best of my knowledge, Jester was still only known by a handful of people, but when the newspaper credited things to Darcy Walker (successes that came via Jester), I'd erroneously been listed as Darky Walton.

I mean, get it right, or leave me out altogether.

Mofos...there went my fifteen minutes of fame.

I mouthed my name twice, carefully enunciating the syllables, throwing in the correct spelling. Trouble was, no one was around to hear. I heard another squealing stop and what sounded like a car door slamming shut.

I laid prostrate in the bowels of the city's sewer. Gutter trash. As I dragged myself up, it felt like I swam in an oil slick. My hands were slippery with white, peppery slush, and the cold water drenching them cut like a bee sting. A full moon filled the round hole I'd fallen through, and the first thing to register was a flashlight and a pair of legs, dangling until they dropped down beside me in a coordinated jump.

When our gazes connected in the sewer, I concluded those legs belonged to a guy—he was emotionally distraught, screaming toward the open manhole to call 911 to a male shadow who had accompanied him. I grabbed my head with both hands because his words came at a rapid-fire pace like a machine gun. Dropping to my knees, I curled into a ball and closed my eyes. Yup, dead. Off to the Sweet By and By. No one wanted to die in the sewer in front of The Double-B, but it looked like the method of my demise as I met my Maker.

I heard, "Niña, niña! Rise!" Oh God, it was Claudia...or Satan must be Spanish. Claudia had been schooled at some weird school in Puerto Rico for spiritualists.

Her supposed claim to fame? Raising things from the dead.

I opened one eye and trained it on her voice. She'd bent herself and one boob in the hole, training another super-powered flashlight on me. The guy in the manhole with me squatted down, and my other eye went to his body like a magnet. Taller than average, he had coppery-colored hair, a square-cut jaw, and intensely focused silver eyes. He wore a brown leather bomber jacket zipped to his chest with a white button-down shirt...starched, just like his khaki pants. Immediately, I knew he was one of those boys who left tongues hanging and drool-dripping girls falling in a heap at his feet. My eyes took the slow boat to China as they slid up to the manhole. The guy huddled next to Claudia held an outstretched hand for us to grab.

I could do without more metaphysical mumbo-jumbo in my life —I had enough of that with Dylan—but I found myself memorizing the lines of Silver-Eyed Boy's face. Like they'd magically been made indelible in my brain. His hair fell in long layers, his bangs lying slightly past his brows. As he shoved them off to the side, I caught another glimpse of silver. It was one of those times I felt like I had my television—or in that case, my ears—on mute. I couldn't hear anything above my own heartbeat. He squatted down to see if I was breathing. But my eyes were open...*weren't they?*

His lips moved.

I opened my mouth, but my voice went bye-bye. I wasn't sure where. It just packed up and made me look like a moron. I fought to catch my breath before trying to sit up, but when the world swam in crushing waves, I laid back down.

"Easy there, angel," he murmured softly. "I'm so sorry I hit you."

Angel. No one had ever called me angel in my short, trouble-filled life. My answer came slowly...then I realized it didn't come at all. After a few more wordless seconds, "Shoot," finally came out of my mouth while a whole lot of expletives rattled around in my brain.

No shiz, I sounded like an idiot.

The frigid air blew so brutally that the breath coming from his mouth was a visible, white air. I sucked in a big gulp, trying to catch it as if my life depended on it. Did I have bad breath? I'd had five hot dogs, for God's sake. I probably smelled like a gas station vending machine.

Gently pushing my hair off my face, his smile quirked up cockily at one corner. "And who, pray tell, are you?" he asked.

His voice robbed me of speech. He had a slight British accent that rang smooth, pouring out like a steady, warm stream of sanctuary. My heart did a cartwheel, and it felt like a herd of wild horses bucked uncontrollably under my sternum. I wanted to kiss him. Sweet Lord Almighty, I wanted to kiss the guy who nearly killed me with his car. Maybe I was depressed about the holiday season. Maybe I was depressed about my best friend and his probable date. Maybe I was depressed I'd never had a boyfriend, and sweet sixteen had come and waved its depressing butt goodbye. Or maybe I had a major case of the stupids going on because it was the second car accident I'd had, and I longed to kiss the guy who ran me over.

Before an answer came, he took my right hand and placed it in the outstretched palm of the other guy hanging through the manhole. I grabbed ahold, and in a one-handed strength, he pulled me up to where I promptly sprawled out ungracefully on my arse. My yoga pants hung below my hips. I felt cold air on my butt cheeks. The blood drained from my face as I quickly yanked them up, telling myself not a doggone person saw a thing. That brought up a huge philosophical debate: if you're not humble in life, then life will thrust humility on you. Been there, done that, even had the T-shirt. Falling on my arse after I'd been hit by a car and fell into a manhole was humbling.

I'd had my fill.

Next thing I knew, Silver-Eyed Boy squatted next to me and slid my matted hair off of my face again. Before I could say a word, the door to the bookstore blasted wide with Mr. Belinski walking fast. I wouldn't actually classify it as running—a turtle ran faster than Mr. B—but he motored nonetheless.

"What the pork!" he screamed, acting like a badass mofo. Then he abruptly stopped, staring in dumbfounded fear, as he slowly registered what'd happened. Once Mr. B saw Claudia's sweating brow, he bellowed like a walrus during mating season. But his violent outburst—and believe me, it *was* violent—only amped her up more. She began praying double time. So fervently that one of her boobs fell out.

But wait...it gets better.

It didn't just fall out. It bounced up and down like she jumped on a trampoline. You see, Claudia sometimes fell out of her clothes. People did that when they refused to admit they needed a larger size. Not only did she need a dress two sizes bigger, but a bra that'd house the hooters of a hippo. I coughed and pointed, but Silver-Eyed Boy didn't even notice. Mr. B, however, thought he'd hit the mother lode.

Whatever. Who cares. The woman tried her best to grab my soul out of Death's hands.

"Oh, God, let me help you up," Silver-Eyed Boy gasped, like he'd totally forgotten his manners. My trembling hand reached forward, but as soon as our skin touched, he stumbled backward as if he'd been branded with a hot iron. I fell back onto my rear end, again with a thud.

Gee, how romantic...

The other guy sprang to my side, barking, "Dude!"

First impression? Total opposite of Silver-Eyed Boy. That guy's torso seemed thicker, older, but with curly, black hair, and a hoodie sweatshirt. Where Silver-Eyed Boy had a playboy look about him, the male accompanying him seemed more sensitive and quiet.

If I didn't know better, I'd swear Silver-Eyed Boy wanted to bolt. What was the look he gave me? It held a grave look of concern punctuated with something else. The cocky smile fizzled out in a snap—as though he felt he'd done something wrong—or better yet, wronged someone else.

He stepped back even further, running into the bumper of his own car. "I'm sorry," he apologized. "I just felt something I don't understand."

I'll tell you what *I* felt...a whole lot of mother-trucking embarrassment.

A swell of emotion took me by storm, and before I collected my thoughts, I blinked back a rush of tears. Oh, my. I hated to cry, and public crying was even worse. I'd done the public thing a few times during school, and it never ended well. Girls either helped someone hide or they gossiped and made it worse. Guys tried to remain oblivious. It was easier to ignore what they didn't understand.

He glided forward like he had the weight of the world on his shoulders. I fixated on his burgundy penny loafers, noticing they'd been scuffed around the edges. Thing was, they had dimes in them. Even if he needed to make a call from a payphone, he couldn't—not with twenty cents.

Private school pedigreed.

I should sue...

He bent down on one knee with a brutal groan. "Oh, please. Don't cry."

"I'm not *crying*," I whispered.

"You're *crying*," the other guy said and sighed.

My hands fisted into his jacket as he pulled me up. My legs edged closer and closer. I didn't mean to...he didn't mean to...but somehow our bodies molded together like Velcro. Wow, he felt strong...lanky, but fit and strong. My brain had already registered I found him attractive, but there it went and did it again. In fact, my brain said he felt pretty dang incredible. Somewhere in the back of my mind, reason told me to try and get my dignity back, but I figured that possibility had long gone.

He whispered into my hair, "You're going to be okay." He then paused, murmuring, "I promise."

Only if you're with me, I begged in my brain. My guess was I'd be a prime candidate for a head transplant if it were ever AMA approved. Mark my words, I'd be embarrassed tomorrow, but it was like some sort of fatal attraction.

I mean, shouldn't we talk things over? Get the finger pointing out of the way and come to a conclusion exactly who was in error? My eyes bounced over to his car. The headlights shined on us, capturing the shadow of sleet flying through the blowing wind. The temperature had dropped significantly. When sleet happened in Cincinnati, it usually meant the bigger flakes were on their way, but then again, it could be part of a weird weather pattern that'd decided to hang. Cincinnati's weather was one big tease. My eyes trailed to the hood to see the make of the car, a brand new Audi A4 in metallic beige...spotless. No Darcy-dents anywhere.

I laughed, not able to escape the irony. Most girls my age were holed up with their girlfriends, confessing if their boyfriends had made it to first or second base (whatever that was). But noooooooo. Not me. I'd gotten hit by a futher-mudging Audi.

I slowly worked my eyes up to his, stuttering out, "I'm s-ssorry."

I said a few more unintelligible sentences. I was pretty sure of it because they all looked at me like I had two heads. Silver-Eyed Boy smiled and wrapped his arms around me, rubbing my back like someone would comfort a child who had a bad dream. I wanted to tell him he felt like a succulent baby lamb. But my pride leaked like a sieve as it was. I might as well keep my mouth shut and not release it like a broken dam.

He, Claudia, and Mr. Belinski ooh'd and aah'd over red scratches on my right hand. There weren't many, but they made me flex my fingers countless times to see if they still worked. Then Silver-Eyed Boy squatted down to check my legs. My black yoga pants had shredded at the left knee. After I performed a few deep knee-bends, Mr. B palmed his greasy hand over the back of my head. The guy pulled his cell phone from his back pocket, saying something again about 911. I wish I understood what they said, but all I heard was "blah, blah, blah...pain." When he kept pushing the issue and Mr. B chimed in, it was like Claudia got hit in the head by a two-by-four. She quickly switched back to English and emphatically stated the cops weren't necessary. Whenever someone mentioned any sort of official vehicle, Claudia, I think, had visions of being deported and singing Viva Puerto Rico. Murphy explained over and over that Puerto Ricans were U.S. citizens, but sometimes her behavior didn't add up. Inspiration hit me to sing School House Rock's "The Preamble." God only knew why because that actually was kind of stupid. When my audience deduced that was only possible with a functioning brain, that, in itself, kept me from the whole lights and sirens gig.

The evening hadn't ended as under the radar as I would've liked. Wouldn't you know Levi Schomberg saw the whole deal from his dry-cleaning shop across the street? Right when I made it to Claudia's GMC conversion van, Valley's fire truck showed up. Granted, I fell in a stinking manhole, but who in the heck needed a fire truck? The city of Valley must've been low on action, so the EMT vehicle accompanying them shoved me on a gurney and took my vital signs: blood pressure, pulse, check for dilated eyes, and more Good

Samaritan overkill. Since I'd had a tetanus shot during my car wreck four months earlier, thankfully their final assessment was to go to the ER if I developed any unusual drowsiness.

The policemen on the scene—who automatically followed an issued 911—concluded it had been my fault. Of course it was. My body was hidden behind a pillar, putting my shoe on, when I stepped out in front of a moving vehicle. Major moron behavior. Rookie didn't take the accident well via telephone, especially when a partially coherent Claudia attempted to explain the particulars. When I informed the officers who my uncle was, they finally stepped up and got scarily formal, describing the scene down to the diameter of the manhole and shape of the snowflakes.

One found my iPhone.

Complete with a fractured screen.

Cue the tears.

Trouble was, once it was all over, Claudia and Mr. B both had epic meltdowns, talking about the fragility of life and how'd I'd been given a second chance to make a difference in the world. My word, all I had were a few abrasions, and they wanted me to be the next go-to missionary. More than likely God would veto the nomination. I looked at the brothers who'd hit me (yes, they were related) and mouthed a desperate, "Help me." They both choked back laughter, but other than that, there was no time for conversation. The only formality was the exchanging of names and telephone numbers. True to my unpredictable self, I gave them fake digits. I didn't know if that was genius or mistake. I was probably nothing more than an afterthought anyway because chances were I'd never see them again. They introduced themselves as the Ryan brothers...the out of town Ryan brothers. Silver-Eyed Boy named: something. Brown-Eyed Boy named: something else. For the life of me, their names laid on the tip of my tongue, but I couldn't spit out the sounds.

They never said why they were in town, so to speak, but I got a feeling their presence was business-related. Cincinnati is the land of the transplant citizen. General Electric, Procter and Gamble, Macy's, and Kroger were a few companies whose home offices were based here. So if someone had a parent trying to move up the corporate ladder, chances were he or she would eventually do a stint in the Ohio Valley.

Silver-Eyed Boy inked his number on my palm, but I'd loofah'd it away once I stepped inside the shower. I felt like the little girl at the fair denied the pony ride. I saw something that represented fun and excitement, and then someone made me go home early. But I liked him. Maybe it was part delusion—or perhaps desperation.

I slipped out of bed in the pitch black, my path illuminated by the moonlight of the home's many skylights. It glowed with a wonderful spooky factor, and fortunate for me, I didn't spook easily.

I pulled the lapels together on my white, fluffy robe and walked like I tiptoed over broken glass into Rookie's office. Rookie trusted too easily, or perhaps he thought things were safe in his own home. Normally they would be, but I was on the premises, which threw a whole new variable in the mix he probably wasn't prepared for.

He had one of those miniature refrigerators built into the bookcases, covered in the same mahogany wood. I flipped open the little door and cracked open a can of Coke, settling down to business. I had insomnia, plus a thunderclap headache with Silver-Eyed Boy's name all the heck over it. Caffeine was my wonder drug. It could relax my mind or arm me with a power pack. Right then, I needed both.

I took a burning swig and slumped into the burgundy leather chair behind the desk. Rookie lived in Indian Hill, which was big bucks in the real estate market. His house—which used to be the one he shared with my mother's twin—was überluxurious, but Rookie was common. He hailed from South Dakota and practically grew up in a barn. Rookie himself was meticulous though—well groomed, nothing ever out of place, even the knick-knacks were perfect on their shelves. But his desk looked like a twister had touched down. Piles of folders, unopened letters, and a magazine for an upscale New York boutique (my aunt's mail) littered the top.

His relationship with my aunt was stagnant of late, but they still seemed awful coupley to me. They'd been married and divorced four times—the last time for a year—wherein she briefly worked with a PI firm in the interim. Somehow Rookie wooed her back into his office, and they successfully worked together.

But he pined away...and that killed me.

I tapped the mouse on his laptop, activating the screensaver. When I received a few rays of light, I held up a personalized letter, but the paper was so thick nothing could be deciphered. I flipped through a few files and sifted through photographs of what my gut told me were local riffraff. I knew more than the average teenager about criminals by eavesdropping on conversations. In my limited knowledge, local riffraff never saw much time if the offense was minor. Oftentimes the prosecutor's office used them to reel in bigger fish.

Rookie's cell phone lay charging by the printer. It rang with an unfamiliar number, and at two something in the morning, no doubt it was important. Number one, I could ignore it; or number two, I could answer and pass myself off as someone Rookie was working with on an all-nighter. Guess which one my nosy little self picked? I wasn't a freshman at that sort of offense—I'd answered texts on Dylan's grandfather's phone last summer, passing myself off as an LA detective. Thing was, I watched a video of a man whose head fell off during the impersonation. I wasn't sure I'd ever top that.

"Hello," I answered quickly.

"It's about time, darlin'. It's Tito Westbrook. How's my favorite redhead?"

Oh. My. Good. God. Tito Westbrook was the go-to crime reporter for *The Cincinnati Enquirer*. I'd followed his work since I could read *Green Eggs and Ham*. Apparently, he thought I was my aunt, Tabitha Arthur. I didn't know he and Red (her nickname) were close enough to be in the darlin' phase, but their paths obviously crossed more often than not. I quickly decided to leave him on speakerphone, hoping the long-distance sound of too much air would throw him off.

I pulled on my sleepy voice. "I'm good. Tired but good. What do you need?"

Tito laughed in a southern drawl. "Rookie called *me*, darlin' in a bad case of phone tag. Sorry it took so long to get back to you, but this was the first chance I've had."

I drew a blank and bit my bottom lip hard enough to taste blood. I decided to throw out every bit of crime lingo I could think of. I coughed out, "What are we looking at? Drugs, gangs, ragers, the latest knife attacks, or shootings?"

He immediately answered, "No, darlin'. Let's focus on me only. I feel so violated it's indescribable."

"I can understand that," I said, still not tracking the conversation.

"Tabitha, I wrote that story on what happened to me, and now this guy apparently wants to take me down."

"Explain," I pushed.

There was a short pause where he took a breath. "It's like my story said. My rent check bounced."

"You still use paper?" I asked shocked.

"Okay, darlin', I'm showing my age here, but I do. So when I went to the bank to see what'd happened, the branch manager printed out a list of transactions. We found a bunch of activity that happened locally. Activity made with my bank account number, but not by me. We immediately closed the account, but the damage had already been done."

"Meaning?"

"Meaning this person is still trying to bleed me dry. I know I'm operating in paranoia mode, but from best we can tell, this person is taking this to an even bigger level. After a fraud investigation, we discovered more activity under my name."

"How?" I asked.

"He didn't only steal my bank account number. This person somehow gleaned personal information about me and tried to buy a house in Brunswick, Maine. He produced two other forms of identification, down payment using one of my personal checks, had credit references, all to bring to a closing on a new home. Even though the bank froze my account, it wasn't before the impostor had all of this other stuff rolling. Anyway, he got spooked and stood everyone up in Maine. Heaven knows when he'll surface again. I mean, he has my social security number, darlin'. I'm standing in the crosshairs of a rifle."

Sure enough, on Rookie's desk was a newspaper clipping with Tito Westbrook as the byline. I scanned the first paragraph that summarized everything he'd just said. But why did he think Rookie and Red could help?

"Did you get the picture I faxed over?" Tito asked. "Are you going to share it with Cookie? My source says this guy is from the north side of town, perhaps in Valley, right in Cookie's backyard.

The source also claims he's a teenager. I've contacted Cookie, but she's not big on returning calls to the press."

Question answered.

Cookie, or rather Charlotte Veronica Harper-Stark, was Rookie's counterpart in Mack County—the county in which my township, Valley, was located. She took Reese Sanders's job when Reese abruptly quit right before election time and moved to New York. From what I heard, Reese passed on her unrequited love torch to Cookie because Cookie drooled after my uncle like a dog in heat.

Procedurally, Rookie occasionally shared information with other county prosecutors when they felt their crimes overlapped. So it sounded like he thought he could aid Tito by asking Cookie if she'd provide a name of the person. I pivoted around, rifling through paper in the fax machine, until I reached a picture of someone who looked like an extra in a mob movie. His hair was greased back with what resembled real motor oil. His eyes were deep-set and brown, one slightly lower than the other. His thin, pursed lips made him appear permanently ticked off. The fax coversheet said *The Cincinnati Enquirer, Tito Westbrook.*

Booyah! It didn't get any clearer than that.

I swallowed down another drink. "Yup, got it right here. Unfortunately, no name is listed."

"Darlin', if I had a name, then there would be no issue. Does he look familiar to you? As far as I can tell there's no known association to anyone."

"Never seen him before."

Insert nervous laughter.

Tito didn't say anything for a while. I panicked and immediately started negotiating with my intestines. "Tabitha, perhaps we should talk tomorrow," he finally added strangely. "You sound tired. Either that or you're stalling."

No! I shouted in my brain. I really needed to learn to control my energy bursts because the chair tipped back, and I splatted onto the hardwood floor. I lay there like a fat tick on a dog, waiting to hear Rookie barrel through the house with a gun. His house was armed with a state-of-the-art security system. When nothing happened, I righted the chair and sat back down, propping my mismatched blue and white knee socks on top of the desk, trying my best to act like a know-it-all redhead. I calmly declared, "Let me see what I can find out from Rookie, Tito. I know this is your personal business, but you're going to have to be patient and allow us to color within the lines."

Major Pinocchio moment (I think), but the words sounded logical once they left my lips.

My brain and gut started arguing as usual. My brain said to keep up with the charade. My gut said he was on to me.

Insert a collective sigh where we both considered our next move. Tito buckled first. "Now why don't you give me your real name, darlin'? Tabitha's always on, no matter what the time. And she *never*," he emphasized with half a laugh, "waits to clear anything with Rookie. Exactly *who* are you, and *why* are you answering Shepard Johnson's cell phone?"

I croaked. I'd died on the spot and was pushing up daisies. He'd caught me red-handed answering Rookie's cell phone. Why he called him Shepard, though, I had no idea. My uncle had been addressed as Rookie since he put a serial killer behind bars at the tender age of twenty-six. Maybe he merely tried to catch me off guard.

At that moment, something unexpected happened. Bells and whistles went off, sirens rang, and a choir of heavenly angels sang a chorus. I practically belted out, "Jester."

Yup, I'd gone total moron.

"Jester," he repeated. "And who is Jester to Shepard Johnson?"

I looked to the heavens, hoping it would supernaturally meet the need. I got nothing. From my perspective, I was screwed six ways from Sunday. But if I had anything to do with it, things would *not* blow up in my face.

Hopefully, Tito wasn't the type to nurse a grudge. "Let me put it this way, Tito. People like me are journeymen. We get around. I work the north side of town and heard what happened to you."

I abso-FREAKIN'-lutely had lost my mind.

Tito stepped up the questioning. "So you didn't even see a faxed photograph, huh?"

Oh. Shoot. I had to say no. Otherwise I'd be admitting I was in Rookie's home. "No, I just wanted to talk to you."

"How did you get his phone then? Did you do something to him? Where is he?"

I opted for the truth. "He left it some place where I now am."

"That doesn't sound like something he'd do."

"Check with him tomorrow. He was unbelievably distracted." Okay, that was a little bit of the truth interspersed in the lies, and even the densest of criminals knew it wasn't enough to press charges. Besides, what was the crime? Impersonating my aunt?

Big sigh on Tito's part. "Okay, Jester. Let's play. How old are you?"

"Old enough."

His voice lowered an octave and lost all of the southern charm. "Am I to believe you truly want to take down an identity thief, Jester? What exactly do you want? The reward?" Well, I didn't know a reward was posted, but since he'd dangled the carrot, I'd take it plus some recreational activity, I suppose.

"I didn't know about a reward, Tito. How much green are we talking?"

"Ten grand."

I nearly peed my pants.

Nervousness took over. In ten seconds flat, I managed to organize Rookie's desk, files in straight alignment, unopened letters in a neat pile by his laptop. "I'd be a fool to say ten grand wasn't appealing," I finally admitted, "but I'll only work with you. I need protection. If you bring either prosecutor's office into our arrangement, you'll never get what I know."

Tito was quiet. I heard a breath deep enough to leave him underwater for days. "Here are the rules," he dispensed. "I hate email and texting. I'll never risk blowing your identity because it's just too risky. I'll check in with you every couple of days, and you let me know immediately if things get dicey. Where can I contact you safely?"

Nowhere actually. "Okiedokie, no email or texting," I reiterated, "but it's better if I contact *you*. And no one can know of Jester's existence...ever."

More of the silent routine. My guess was he didn't like me writing the parameters of our agreement. Heck, I wasn't even sure I understood our agreement yet. I didn't know a lot about reporters, but I knew enough that sources were usually in the driver's seat. Reporters wanted them happy or as happy as possible.

"Okay," he eventually grunted, "we'll go with your plan."

I didn't have a plan. I just hoped I fell into a whole lot of luck.

I felt his balk and laughed. "Do you want me to prove how good I am beforehand?"

Tito didn't respond. I took that as a yes.

After he gave me a number, I heard a click-click-click and then the proverbial dial tone. Seconds later, Rookie's house phone rang. I jumped out of my skin, flying to bed faster than a Peregrine Falcon. Tito was checking up on me—and the gig might be over before it even started.

———

I needed to prove I could hang, but the depths I'd have to navigate to do that would be pretty darn tough. Tito was no blockhead, so it wasn't like I could schmooze him into liking me. But guess who found two credit cards and a social security card of three different people before a car hit her?

How fortuitous for me.

"Finn," I whispered when he picked up. Finn was my go-to guy. He could find dirt on just about anybody.

"Chica," he groaned sleepily. "Do you know what time it is?"

Finn Lively's accent of the day was South of the Border. Very rarely did he operate as just Finn: hot white boy, resident geek-slash-genius, from Valley High. Whatever his persona, he wore the look well. He burned hotter than fricking Mercury.

My iPhone said three twenty when I pulled the three cards out of my coat. Two were the Visa check cards of Lindsee Maroni and Kelley Lowder. The social security card was of a male named Lucas Aaron Carlton. "I need to know what you can find on these three people," I told him after I gave him the names. "Anything would be good. In fact, make it *oh-mazing*. It has to be quick though. I've got to find these owners before what little conscience I have starts eating away at me. Do you need to write this down?"

"No," he muttered and killed the call.

Chapter Three

DONKEY KONG

I felt like I'd spent the weekend in a Mexican jail.

On Monday, I was still stiff and limping with a faint aroma of gutter. As far as I could tell, my brain operated on an all-systems go, but I had to wonder after the stunt I'd just pulled. Uh, Tito Westbrook? Why did I think a seasoned investigative journalist needed someone as unseasoned as *me*? The way I saw it, I might as well shoot for the stars even if it meant they might fall on top of me.

Best I could tell, Tito hadn't mentioned Jester when he phoned Rookie. Once Rookie assured Tito he breathed on this side of the dirt, Tito gave him an abridged version of what went down. How did I know that? I stumbled into Rookie's bedroom, acting as if the house phone had wakened me—seriously, it was Oscar material—and listened to Rookie say he must've left his phone at McDonald's since we'd eaten there that night as a midnight snack. Normally, Rookie would be all twenty questions, but he must've been off kilter when he heard someone had used his phone and posed as his ex. Instead, he politely thanked Tito for the concern, claimed a psycho stalker (didn't know he had any) could be playing pranks, and ended the convo.

May I just say I couldn't have orchestrated a better ending? Tito seemed satisfied with the explanation and set up a time where they'd discuss his specific case later. Plus, when we began the "search and recovery" for Rookie's phone, all I had to do was beat him inside the golden arches and drop his cell in the booth we'd sat in.

Case closed...*I hoped.*

And to help it "close," I erased the history of Tito's and my call altogether.

I was riding cloud nine, feeling like I'd duped the undupable... until Dylan strode through the door. Then I was stunned into submission by pheromones that had me as the target.

I got my license on my birthday—aced that sucker, although I do admit to some massive flirting with the instructor to seal the deal. Since I still had no wheels, he'd been my ride to school all year...we were alone.

Biiiiiiiig problem.

Murphy and my little sister got back into town the night before, and he drove her to school bright and early. Apparently, she'd been placed on the naughty list for talking too much in class. He wanted to get to the bottom of who she'd been talking to, what they'd been talking about, why she wasn't being challenged, and so on. In other words, why it wasn't her fault. If anything, my father was loyal. But Murphy's emotions rolled like a nuclear reactor, and he was due a Chernobyl moment.

Dylan stopped dead in his tracks, massaging his heart. Like he'd seen the most beautiful thing ever created and had to convince his heart to keep pumping.

Moron...

I had dishwater-blonde hair and almost green eyes. At five foot nine, I was definitely model-tall, but since I packed around one hundred and thirty pounds, I didn't try to stand next to skinny people. Maybe I was skinny for my height, but my size twenty-seven jeans in a high school of zeros made me the longest-living Neanderthal on record. Plus, my curves were few and far between, and what curves I did have...well, let's just say my lady parts weren't symmetrical.

A tough pill to swallow.

Standing beside him didn't help my self-esteem either. Dylan looked pretty dang amazing with his clothes on. Underneath, I would guess was that much better. He had the body of the finest athlete and the kick-butt and take-names attitude of the strongest of warriors. I started calling him Big Man last summer when he went off and left me heightwise in the course of two months. He towered at six two with two hundred and twenty pounds of Greek real estate.

As usual, he looked impeccably irresistible—dark-washed jeans, expensive sneakers with an unzipped black leather jacket overtop a slate-gray sweater. His eyes boiled like melted butter that had an affair with toffee, and his thick-cropped hair was pitch-black.

Three words? Mah. Ve. Lous.

While he lazily leaned against the kitchen counter, I swallowed my last bite of SpaghettiOs, ran the bowl under the faucet, and stacked it in the dishwasher. Brushing my teeth in the kitchen sink, I poured a second cup of coffee in an insulated travel mug. I made out with number one fifteen minutes earlier. Why? I was sixteen years old and had kissed a guy one time. One time, and it was the passionate type where people got sweaty and felt guilty later. But I was off men. Off Dylan, specifically. My coffee cup, I guess, was my unofficial boyfriend.

While I balanced the mug in my teeth, I slid my arms through my coat and slung my Jansport copper-brown backpack over my shoulder. Our home was your standard single-family abode. The study and dining room were in the front with a kitchen and den in the rear. When I stood within inches of Dylan, his testosterone worked like a tractor beam. We had to touch. The moment our hands collided, it felt like I'd been tasered with 50,000 volts.

Siiiiiigh.

The chemistry was un-freaking-deniable.

He pulled my hand to his lips, and the warmth rushed up my arm and straight to my hiccupping heart. "You look beautiful. How's my girl?"

I gave him half a shrug.

I sported my I-don't-care look. Black Burberry glasses and pony-tail with only lip gloss and mascara. Occasionally, I added the triplet of blush, but the routine always consisted of those first two to give the assumption I cared a little. As for threads, I wore my favorite pair of Seven jeans tucked into tan UGGs with a skin-tight black turtleneck. "I don't care," I said, shrugging in explanation.

He came at me in a PDA mood, hugging me to his side "Dare," he whistled out. "I love your 'I don't care' look."

"Boys are supposed to be repulsed by 'I don't care' looks."

"I don't think it's possible for you to repel men," he murmured grinning.

Dylan was smooth...*soooo smooooooth*. A fact that made me feel like a million bucks but also question his sanity. Thing was, I felt out of my league. If his face wasn't perfect enough, the hot boy gods gave him two dimples that imploded when he was happy.

"I love it when you're stupid," I said with a laugh.

Stupid was my favorite word, and in my opinion should get top billing in the dictionary. It could be a noun, an adjective, or an adverb dependent upon the way it was phrased in a sentence. At one time or another, I'd embraced all those parts of speech. Right then, Dylan embraced them all.

He glanced around the house, his chest heaving with something probably best we didn't put a name to. "Are we alone?" he asked suspiciously.

Oh, boy, I knew what was coming next. "Uh-huh."

He held his arms wide, like a perp did when he was being arrested. "Come on, sweetheart, frisk me. Make sure you don't miss anything either."

Dylan always had flirty banter—banter that made it increasingly difficult to keep my hands to myself. Oh, the conundrum. (A) I could learn to be a 'ho and have my wicked way with him; (B) I could eat a box of cookies and die of a sugar coma; or (C) I could shoot him. Shooting might be the best option, but then I'd wind up in prison orange outrunning Big Bertha.

Repeat after me, I told myself. *Dylan is bad. He's like two-boxes-of-Twinkies bad.*

Mid-mantra, the tiny part of my soul that didn't give a darn about a mantra decided to make a point.

It was on like *Donkey Kong.*

Murphy kept a glass jar on the counter he called the Stupid Jar. I'd toss fifty cents inside it when I did something stupid. I dropped two quarters in the bottom with a clang, manufactured some bedroom eyes, and painted a pouty look of seduction on my lips. Slinking closer, I said sultrily, "Spread 'em, Big Man."

I wasn't sure if Dylan coughed in shock or giggled. "Yeah?" he verified, his voice thick.

"Yeah," I dared him.

Dylan turned with a low chuckle and spread both palms on the wall, legs squared as wide as his shoulders. Now I'd seen my fair share of cop shows, so I'd make sure he got the full-bodied treatment. Threading my fingers inside his, I let them linger for a beat and then slowly ran them down his arms, spanning the breadth of his shoulders and sliding south to his tight waist. Next, I slowly—and I mean slooooowly—traveled the muscled circuit of his legs and back up between the thighs, ending at his hips. Feeling Dylan in his entirety—those muscles on top of muscles—I might've had my first religious experience. I crossed myself even though I wasn't Catholic, and I didn't know if that was in confession...or thanks.

Dylan gasped and growled, "You're evil."

I swallowed a laugh, thanking the hot boy gods that I'd copped a free feel. Thing was, I wasn't through with him yet. I leaned into his back and whispered hotly in his ear, "Now it's my turn." Another growl. "You're killing my buzz here, D. I'm going to take that as confirmation that I've won this round."

Dylan. Didn't. Move.

Smacking him on the rear, I grumbled, "Spoilsport," and zipped my jacket to my chin, shoving his catatonic body out the door.

I live in Buffalo Trails Country Club in Valley, Ohio. Trouble is, there's no Club. When your community's name is BTCC—and there's no "CC"—you practically were the trailer park *within* the trailer park. We started out with the best of intentions, but the developer ran off with the homeowners' money. The 'hood looked stupid with a sign that bragged BTCC and four measly golf holes.

I lived only a few miles from school, but sometimes Dylan came early so we could take the long way through town. We'd stop for coffee at United Dairy Farmers—my favorite coffee—or we'd grab a danish at Servatii's in nearby Voice of America Plaza. At the moment, he was tardy. He'd phoned and said something had gone wrong with his mother's car, and he had to help fix a "ping." I found that odd, especially since they had five cars on their property. Why obsess over the one that was sick? I frowned at my own thoughts because I didn't understand why my unquestionable trust in him had faltered lately. It was like I expected the worse, and a decade's worth of memories and unwavering loyalty was being snuffed out by something I couldn't see.

One word when I stepped outside? *Brrrrr*. Single digits cold. Not what citizens wanted to wake up to, but reality was like a cold shower on your back in Cincy. One of the major differences between Dylan and me was his blood ran volcano-hot, while mine ran ice-cold. So as he casually strutted to the car, I did a full-out sprint to his black Beemer and dove inside. Once settled in the heated leather seats, we backed out of the neighborhood.

"I'm sore," I complained. My hand felt like I'd dipped it in acid, and my left knee still oozed pus like a corpse that was mid-rot. Just the mention of the accident, however, and Dylan wanted to go bull-dozer on the Ryan brothers. He tensed up, his fingers briefly grip-ping the steering wheel tightly. He reached out an arm. "Come here, and let me love on you."

Dylan's idea of "loving on you" was so provocative I felt like I needed to be behind closed doors or have a priest absolve me. My word, we were best friends, but lately I'd heard the Indy 500 phrase: "Gentleman Start Your Engines," accompanied with a black garter belt and fishnet stockings. I didn't know what it meant but had a pretty good idea it spelled too much HBO and hormones on overdrive.

He noticed I was somewhere else. "What's wrong?"

My explanation spilled out in a nervous giggle. "I'm thinking too hard, I guess."

I laid my head up against the window and regurgitated my mantra: Dylan is bad, two-boxes-of-Twinkies bad. That time I was determined to mean it. No frisking. Nothing that would FUBAR us any more than we already were.

Pushing the thought of him aside, I sighed deeply, thinking how my quest for significance continued every school year. Unfortu-nately, my failures were followed by a kaleidoscope of excuses. Trouble was, they weren't really excuses. They were explanations. I was one of the many diagnosed as having ADHD (attention deficit/hyperactivity disorder). So it wasn't only hard for me to pay attention, but to sit still. According to my father, I tested at genius level, but a 160 IQ didn't do any good if I had one idea and my body had another.

We had a little over two weeks before Christmas break. I was on target to make the C-List, but a few Ds were possible, and God knew if they gave out conduct grades, mine would be in the crapper. Plus, I was vaguely depressed because I had no money for Christmas presents. The only cash I had was a wad of ones I'd found in the dryer. Money didn't buy happiness, but it sure as heck could rent it.

And by God, I was in the renting mood.

"Darcy?" I heard.

"Mmm, yeah?" I muttered, sliding an eyeball over.

"I said you need to hug me," he murmured lowly with more force.

I debated the wisdom of that but then quickly crawled into his space, brushing my cheek against his. Our version of a kiss. It wasn't easy having a best friend as a boy, but dang, it sometimes had its fringe benefits. Dylan wrapped my ponytail in his fist, holding me to him as he kissed the top of my head. "I've missed you," he murmured, leaving his lips at my forehead.

All I could do was sigh. Heck, maybe it was a moan. After a few seconds of nuzzling my cold nose into the curve under his chin, I scrambled back into my seat, ignoring how yummy the boy smelled.

Besides, I was Darcy Walker. Single. Ready to Mingle. Bleh.

"What do you want for Christmas?" I asked, changing the subject.

Dylan grinned, showing his dimples. *The* dimples. That always meant complete and utter trouble for my independence. "Just you," he answered. When I groaned, he finally answered, "How about some new music, sweetheart. You know what I like."

Actually, there was a new Apple iPod on the market Dylan would kill to have. Trouble was, I'd need to sell a kidney to get it...or find a stripper pole and a very indiscriminating clientele.

I stared at the radio.

Dylan winked, pitching his chin toward the buttons. "Knock yourself out, Darc."

After scanning through a few channels, I made a decision. A heavy metal satellite channel. I needed to find my wake button.

"How about you?" he murmured.

Leaning forward, I grabbed the dash and bobbed up and down with the screeching. I was hyper and prayed to wear myself out by first period. I tried to think of a good answer. The one thing I wanted most no amount of money in the world was ever going to buy. I gave a resigned sigh, settling on my standard response. "Bigger boobs, better grades, the Bengals in the Super Bowl...the usual."

Dylan knew my biggest desire more than anyone but decided to smile at the joke. Smart man. "Come on, Darc," he murmured chuckling, "give me something."

"Cell phone charger?"

Dylan burst into deep laughter. "Nothing says intimate like a cell phone charger. Besides, you've got about ten already."

"True, but I just like having one in every room so I don't have to go searching for one."

"Practical, but I'm not buying you a charger. How about I surprise you?" He brought the car to a stop at a red light, turning to me winking. He always winked as a way of promising things would be okay. Maybe. Or maybe I'd learn to live with disappointment another darn year.

"Okay," I muttered.

Dylan grinned a smile that made a girl want to do bad things. "Did I tell you that you look beautiful today?" he murmured.

Welcome to my world, bro. No wonder I couldn't dodge a crush on him. But Dylan only buttered me up when he wanted a hug-fest or was fishing for information. Predictably he followed with, "Explain to me again what happened when you got hit by a car."

I gave him a watered-down version, the same one I'd given him too many times to count since he broke his freak-out meter when I dropped his call. "I was in a blind spot and stepped off the curb. Honestly, I'd always given that a difficulty rating of about a two, but maybe it was like a nine or something. But you've got to admit the addition of the manhole was priceless. The universe won that round." I stopped to shake an angry fist at Heaven. "You can't make this crap up."

Dylan had a deep baritone voice, but when he was happy, he sounded like a preschooler, complete with a giggle that owned my soul. "Do you feel better at all?" he murmured, still chuckling.

Kind of, sort of, I guess...not really. I finally just shrugged.

He narrowed both brows. "Don't front with me, Darc. Ever."

I produced generic shrug number two. "I'll live."

Dylan was charming and spiritual, thinking a purpose existed for everything. He probably thought a deeper meaning laid in what happened if I cared to ask. I suppose that was because he viewed the world in black-and-white. Dylan's tendency to see things in B&W carried over into his personality. His personality ran paradoxical, however. He was tenderhearted, intelligent, and even-tempered, but other times he was immovable, too simplistic, and as hotheaded as Murphy during rush hour.

Those last times found my straitjacket-crazy crap as the root cause.

As soon as we pulled into the school parking lot, Jagger Cane, school Lothario, pulled beside us with Ivy Morrison—his longtime (not exactly paragon of virtue) girlfriend and my arch nemesis.

Our school was like most other schools. When they're big, students were given a designated parking space number. The parking lot gods hadn't smiled on us because Dylan had been assigned number 405 while Ivy was assigned 406. Not far enough for my taste, but then again, I didn't think Valley High had spaces in Middle Earth.

Ivy stepped out of the car right as I did, scantily clad as usual.

Ivy was Valley's Barbie doll wannabe from fifth grade. She had on white patent leather boots and white corduroy booty shorts overtop snowflake tights. A knee-length white fur coat hung loosely at her shoulders. It was the most bizarre, flamboyant expo of BLECH I'd ever seen (and a dress code violation). About one hundred and fifteen pounds of pure witch, her hair was parted straight down the middle and even though she was a natural blue-eyed blonde, she'd colored it to be as white and cold as frost.

Ivy's parents stupidly pandered to her every whim. Where most got an early Christmas gift of new pajamas or socks, hers was a white MINI Cooper.

I wanted to douse her in pig blood...seriously.

She hadn't been behind the wheel—Jagger was. Jagger coasted around six feet with spiked, coffee-colored hair, and razor-sharp, black eyes. I guess if Ivy was my arch nemesis, Jagger was Dylan's. Jagger played all sports, but he had one thing that'd always hold him back—he had a tendency to be lazy. He was constantly suspended from teams for lack of participation and bad attitude, and he'd beg and weasel his way back.

As he turned off the ignition, he met eyes with Dylan first, painting on a cocky smile. When he punched his door wide, a cloud of cigarette smoke rolled out and smacked me in the face. I didn't think either of them were regular smokers, but I *did* think they were the type to try anything at least once. The sky was so thick with cold that the reed of smoke froze for a second, like it ran into a wall, before gradually intermingling in the December air.

In one smooth move, he strutted over to me, twining a strand of my ponytail around his finger. As usual, he threw off an I-know-I-look-good vibe—dark jeans, expensive tan loafers, and a black wool coat that fell to his thighs. Definitely easy on the eyes, he unfortunately had the desire to copulate 24/7.

"Hello, babe," he murmured.

Hello Satan. "Jagger," I coughed out. "What an unpleasant surprise."

I waved away the smoke, yanking free of his grasp.

Jagger immediately reached for my hands. I quickly shoved them in my pockets, but Jagger boldly slid his hands inside my coat too. Jagger was a *fastard*. That was Darcyspeak for bad boys who moved a relationship at warp speed, only for the girlfriend to find out they had several other girls on the sly. He longed to make me one of them.

Hell would freeze over first.

Dylan barked out a few expletives and slammed the Beemer's door, making his way to my side in four long strides. I hoped a fake smile defused what could easily escalate into a physical altercation. Thing was, Jagger had absolutely no respect for the person he dated or the person he hit on. And lately, his jabs had gotten worse.

I was used to it. Dylan never would be.

Dylan's face took on the appearance of a storm cloud when he growled a low rumble. "Remove your hand, Cane."

Jagger stupidly replied, "Nu-huh."

Dylan threatened again, "Remove your hand, or I'll break your fingers."

Jagger ignored him and gazed at me, smiling seductively. "You're my type."

The moment I removed my hands from my pockets, Jagger went at my ponytail again, twisting it between his fingers until it stopped at my ear. I tried not to think that whatever mannerisms Dylan had with me, Jagger seemed to mimic. That insinuated a little too much observation for me to be comfortable with. I attempted to back out of his clutches but stopped when I felt a chunk of hair straining at the roots. Dang, the fastard, he didn't know the difference between pleasure and pain.

"And what type is that?" I ridiculously wanted clarified.

"Gorgeous, funny, and slightly damaged."

Juuuussssst beauuuuutifullll.

That statement set a fire under Dylan's behind. He unwound Jagger's fingers and twisted his arm behind his back until a small *umpf* fell out of Jagger's mouth. Dylan had a dark side. For some reason, it was a major turn-on. I'd debate that later.

A shocked Ivy stood beside Jagger, no clue what move to make next. It was one thing for your boyfriend to be a lowlife cheat— another for him to rub the indiscretion in your face.

"Cool your jets, D." I said, nervously giggling. "It's all part of my allure. Low self-esteem, childhood trauma, self-destructive tendencies, etcetera, etcetera, etcetera."

Jagger chuckled. "Listen, I'm here for moral support. Day...or night." Yup, he was stupid. "What are you staring at, Taylor?" he said, exhaling as Dylan released him.

Dylan smoothed down his jacket, like he was bored. "Not much. Just sizing up the enemy."

Right then, Jagger took a turn at acting bored. "Is that a threat?"

Dylan laughed a humorless laugh. "Believe me, I'm not threatened."

Jagger leaned over, whispering something in his ear. Dylan growled something in return, giving him a no-trespassing look. Normally, Dylan wouldn't care what anyone said, but it was almost as if a secret existed between them. Dylan raked his hand through his hair, something he always did when he tried to compose himself. For a moment, he seemed paralyzed with fear.

Jagger sneered. "Why do you constantly act as if you and Darcy are more than friends? You're overly affectionate with her to the point of nausea, but we both know it means nothing. She's single, and so am I."

My eyes immediately darted over to Ivy. Her chin shook with shock.

I made a fist, angrily punching Jagger in the shoulder. I didn't like Ivy. In fact, she was one of Valley's biggest cancers, but he wasn't going to use me to be mean to someone else. "You're mean," I hissed. "And I'm thinking bad words about you."

Dylan tag-teamed, "You're an ass, Cane. You just made your girl-friend cry."

Jagger snorted. "That's a double standard, Taylor, if I ever heard one."

Listen, I didn't fall off the turnip truck yesterday. And I had a gut-wrenching feeling that statement meant something I wouldn't like.

The tendons in Dylan's jaw and neck drew together like taut cables, ready to snap. I tugged on the sleeve of his jacket. "What does he mean by that, D?" Dylan's face remained masked and unreadable. When he hitched his chin higher, I tugged again. "Dylan?" I pushed.

A sigh left his chest as he decided to answer. By the look in his eyes, I could tell he was going to wax poetic. Trouble was, poetry was sometimes the subjective stuff that no one could understand. He murmured, "It's between Cane and myself, Darc, and there will never be a relationship I have that doesn't put you first. Does that clear up anything?"

Not really...I mean, *duh*.

"Pinky swear?" I promised. Dylan's and my pinkies had been participating in profanity since age eight. It was the way we kept our relationship pure and unadulterated to the ways of the world. I'd been operating under the assumption that when we twined our pinkies together, we had unequivocal honesty.

Right then, I wasn't so sure.

Dylan sounded hoarse, like a boulder sat on his chest and he wasn't breathing well. He tenderly ran his knuckles down my cheek. "It doesn't and will never affect you," he murmured again. "Please, just trust that." Spoken like someone with secrets. If the roles were reversed, he would've held me down until I answered the specific question. The double standard was definitely alive and well.

The wind picked up, and the first flakes of snow floated down like a blanket. I blew a few off my glasses before they smeared. Dylan held his key fob out to the Beemer, beeping it locked as we left Jagger and Ivy to makeup or breakup. He threw his arm around my shoulder, the incident all but put behind him. Surely, he knew I'd want a more detailed explanation, but doggone it, I had to turn around. Nothing shocked me more than to witness Jagger and Ivy kissing. Like really, really kissing. It was "the rockets red glare, the bomb's bursting in air" kind of stuff. Her hands were in his hair—his hands were...*well, everywhere*. PDA overload. Um, yucky. After watching their version, I concluded what I knew about the art went right out the door.

Was that a goodbye kiss? God only knew what a hello looked like.

Chapter Four

KICKED OUT

*C*hristmas cheer, my a-s-s.

Some people were definitely more cheery than they were the other days of the year. Others were mean SOBs, mowing people over at the Black Friday sales. Sort of like VHS. Some were friendly. Others couldn't wait to make like Elvis and leave the building.

My Christmas cheer was on blackout, and sitting in junior science with Herman Himmel, Ph.D. at the helm, morphed me into Ebenezer Scrooge. I'd already made it through math, health, and career development and had hoped the world would end in a fiery ball before fourth period.

It hadn't...

Can you just say...crap?

And crap again. Um, CRAP.

Herman Himmel. The name alone made my underarms sweat. One would think time would help me outrun bad teachers, but alas, that wasn't the case. I'd had Mr. Himmel in grade school, and he made it clear he had no patience for my particular ailments. I failed tests. I stared out windows. I chattered too much, plus I had a myriad of other issues I preferred to remain nameless. But that was the ADHD. Some days were great. Others, I couldn't even remember if I should be upset about my predicament. There also was a period of time where I missed a ton of school. Mr. Himmel wouldn't offer extra help in any way, shape, or form...no matter how hard Murphy begged.

Little by little, it chipped away at my soul.

By some twist of fate, there'd been a shakeup in the educational system, and he taught at the high school level. Wouldn't you know I'd have to study under the man who caused me to chug Pepto-Bismol for an entire year? He gave me a serious case of PTSD, and my body produced a weird physiological response every time I neared him. My stomach churned, my nose ran, and I could never tell from which end the nausea would appear first. Usually, I ran to the restroom to cover all the bases.

Mr. Himmel wasn't exactly what I'd call attractive either. He had short, graying-blond hair and stood several inches shorter than me (like troll height), with a scaly-red face that belonged on *Jurassic Park*. He always dressed in brown, matching his beady, soulless eyes. He droned away in the kind of voice that sounded like fingernails on a chalkboard. Painfully annoying, and the only way for it to go away was for someone to cut his tongue out.

I glanced around the room, housing twenty-one students, trying to locate something to inspire me for the next fifty minutes or so. It was devoid of decorations...a stark, sterile white reminding me of an insane asylum. Most teachers made an attempt to be festive during the holidays, but his room was so boringly bland I wasn't sure how anyone was ever inspired to get an A. Just my opinion, but Mr. Himmel didn't believe in anything other than his ability to beat the shiz out of his students' self-esteem.

I wrote a post-it note and slapped it on Grumpy's back for a little extra help. The note said, *Sit still, be quiet, and don't get up.* Then I kicked my UGGs off to help me relax.

Grumpy had a stocky build with wavy brown hair and eyes, generously listed at six feet tall. Like me, he mostly wore jeans and T-shirts because he ranked low on style. He knew I'd done something but couldn't decode the specifics.

Laughter spilled out of my mouth when he started to squirm. I cleared my throat to cover it. Cleared it a second time. When I decided to go for a third, I held my breath until a twitch entered my left eye.

"Miss Walker?" I heard Mr. Himmel say.

In between hypothetical shots of tequila, I voiced a prayer to be invisible, but when Heaven wasn't used to me calling, I wasn't sure it felt obligated to answer. The conversation had only one place to go —in the crapper. "Yup, Mister Himmel?" I mumbled. I was the only student who didn't address him as "Doctor." Hand to God, I didn't mean it disrespectfully. I'd done it before as a joke, but the habit was so ingrained I'd had difficulty breaking it.

His bushy unibrow bounced up. "It's *Doctor* Himmel, Miss Walker. Are you paying attention?"

"Darcy," I heard Dylan coach behind me.

There goes my dramatic silence...

My answer was a long time in coming. "Can you rephrase the question in a way that I won't have to lie?" I said and grimaced. A chorus of eeks immediately filled the room followed by a whole lot of nothing. Everyone wondered how I could be so blatantly stupid. Frankly, so did I.

Mr. Himmel leaned a hip up against the blackboard, crossing his arms over his barrel chest. "Well, aren't you the comedienne," he grunted.

"I do what I can for the planet."

Mr. Himmel barked a few more sentences at me—accompanied with a scowl so acidic it could melt the flesh from my bones. I carried on the entire conversation covering my left eye. My nervous tics sometimes surfaced when I had energy that needed to go somewhere. When Dylan saw my hand over my face, he cursed under his breath, murmuring diplomatically, "We were all a little distracted, Doctor Himmel, but I promise it won't happen again."

Mr. Himmel slowly rapped the fingers of his right hand on his left elbow—pinky to index, pinky to index, pinky to index. He repeated that sequence four times. "You weren't addressed, Mister Taylor," he fumed.

A caustic and confrontational groan escaped Dylan's chest. It wasn't readily clear whom he was angry with—Mr. Himmel or me— but the deadly atmosphere made a few chairs squeak in terror.

"Miss Walker—" Mr. Himmel continued, eyes glaring at mine.

Dylan sidled up to where his lips hovered right underneath my ear. "Darcy," he whispered, "this is where you're supposed to say, *I'm sorry, Doctor Himmel. This is my favorite class, and I'm happy to be h*ere."

In other words, I needed to lie. Problem was, I couldn't lie if I lived in a compound for sociopaths. Being truthful or at least semi-truthful would help my chances with the universe. But then again, my reasoning abilities were clearly a little skewed. I took a deep breath, knowing things wouldn't end well but hoped I at least got a happy-ending December 25th.

"I'm sorry, Doctor Himmel," I said sighing. "This class is a snoozapalooza, and I guess there's some place else I'd rather be."

Mr. Himmel angrily slammed his chalk in the tray. It bounced to the floor and split in two with powdered smoke staining the floor. Most teachers would pause to deliberate the degree of mercy they'd dispense. Mr. Himmel paused to deliberate the degree of pain. But guess what, he had the magic word in Teacherland: tenure. And wasn't that a total suckfest for the rest of us.

He stalked forward and hissed in my face, "This attitude of yours is going to catch up with you sooner or later, Miss Walker."

"I figured as much," I mumbled, "and with my luck, that might be on the soon part of later."

"Well, figure this. You're out of my class for the rest of the week. And if I had my wishes, you'd never return. You'll never make anything of yourself, Walker. You're still the same kid you were when you were younger. Nothing has changed."

And there you have it. All of those times he made me feel icky weren't the products of an imagination fueled by negative thoughts. Those words were confirmation he hated kids with problems. Why did I say that? I'd never participated in his class one time—even when I knew the answers—because I feared what would come out of his mouth. Right then, he made me think lying would've been an appropriate response.

"Oh goody," I stupidly said out loud.

He narrowed his eyes into snake-like slits. "Make that two weeks. No," he amended, "you're not back until January."

See, that was where I sometimes liked to push back. Categori-cally dumb, but dang it, no one wanted to publicly be made an example of. I blinked my uncovered eye, hoping to go Superman and laser vision him down to a lump of clay.

I tried. No dice.

"I'm sorry," I whispered, suddenly aware he'd humiliated me more than anyone had in a while. "Please, forgive—"

Mr. Himmel waved me off like he would an annoying fly. "Leave, Walker."

Dylan forcefully cleared his throat and cursed in my ear. Then he halfway stood out of his seat, exasperation coloring his voice. "Doctor Himmel, that's not fair. Not to mention your comments were flat-out rude, unprofessional, and uncalled for. Can you not think of another more appropriate punishment? We have a test coming up and a science experiment due before Christmas break."

Mr. Himmel carefully placed one gray orthopedic shoe in front of the other, thundering up the aisle like he had plans to drop a six foot two boy dead to the ground. I'd advise you to take a seat, Mister Taylor, or you'll be joining her."

Dylan stood his ground, looming like he'd eat Mr. Himmel's head off if he could get his mouth to open that wide. With the addition of my hand to his arm, the threat eventually chased him back down into his chair. My eyes brimmed over with desperate tears. I didn't always care what happened to *me*, but I always cared what happened to *him*. While I made a mental note to get my inner idiot in check, I gathered up my books, shoved my feet back in my UGGs, and gave a quick nod in Dylan's direction.

He grabbed my hand, stroking it under his thumb. "Sorry, D," I whispered, tears spilling to my cheeks. "I just didn't want to lie."

And you know what, I didn't care about the audience. I parallel parked myself alongside him, leaned into his chest, and gently brushed my face against his, leaving it there until I could collect myself. I went on autopilot. Something I'd learned to do ages ago when I'd been embarrassed. "Pardon my French, but I'm such a screwup," I said, sniffling in his ear.

Yep, Dylan could always pull my emotions out...even when he wasn't trying.

He was one heartbeat away from going gonzo. When I stepped back, his eyes softened, hardened, and then turned mushy one last time. "Aw, sweetheart," he solemnly muttered. "You're beautiful. Don't allow his words to make you doubt yourself. I'll somehow salvage this and work it out."

File that under *I'm An Idiot*.

Subcategory of *Common Knowledge*.

After I did a jaunt along the school's interior, I ended up crashing on the bleachers in the gym. I'd made two new acquaintances. One guy told me his girlfriend dumped him for the fifth time. Another asked if I'd like to ditch school altogether and run away with him. He wasn't half bad looking—I considered it for three point five seconds until I realized he had massive BO.

Total mood kill.

Finding Eminem's and Rihanna's "Monster" on my iPhone, I shoved an earbud in one ear while I explained my situation to the school's basketball coach. Seriously, I didn't have a leg to stand on, but the thought of more "good student" rhetoric made me want to cry...or puke...depending on the person delivering the lecture.

I sighed. "I had a shift in schedule."

"A shift in schedule," he repeated frowning.

"I sorta got kicked out of class."

"Himmel?" he said gruffly.

I preferred the Antichrist, but properly identified him. "*Doctor* Himmel. Evidently, he doesn't appreciate my style."

"Aw, Walker," he groaned. "Perhaps you should try."

"I *do* try. His expectations are merely outside of my comfort zone."

"That's the spirit," he muttered, rolling his eyes. "Whatever the specifics, Himmel needs to be fired. Follow me. I've got some time." It was no big secret the staff didn't like Mr. Himmel. I was guessing kids like me were a common occurrence.

Coach Munk Wallace skimmed a little over six feet with a solid, oak tree kind of build and paunch in his gut. Don't let anyone ever tell you gym teachers were in shape. Occasionally, they had too much time on their hands making laps to the vending machine. With balding ginger-colored hair, he didn't embrace his balding status either. He tossed and teased so much it accounted for a two-inch lift. He also rocked the same look, regardless of the weather. It consisted of athletic shorts, golf shirts or hoodies, and dirty glasses.

Coach led us to a small office tucked away in the corner, practically in another zip code. It didn't even have a door. I took stock of my surroundings. Two students, one guy and one girl, gave small waves as we walked inside. They did homework at desks—he looked familiar, she didn't. A silver metal desk sat against the back wall with state championship trophies on shelves behind it. A coat tree anchored the left corner, weighed down with at least four different coats. Cardboard boxes had been stacked atop one another by the desks, holding empty pizza boxes from LaRosa's. Add a computer from the Dinosaur Age, and he just might be the next episode of *Hoarders*. But lo and behold, a Mr. Coffee coffeepot percolated on a credenza behind the desk.

My day just got better.

Black folding chairs sat in the middle of the floor. I parked myself in one while Coach pushed his body behind his desk, collapsing into a worn black, leather high back. Call me a lot of things but a fool wasn't one of them. I had a captive audience, and by God, I would make the best of it.

I pulled the photograph Tito faxed Rookie out of my purse (I'd made a copy), sliding it across the desk. "Do you know this guy?"

Coach Wallace gave it half a look. "Weird dude, but no," he muttered. That didn't mean anything. As far as we knew the photograph could be last year's look. Tito didn't divulge if it was up-to-date, and I hated to admit I wasn't firing on all cylinders at the hour or wise enough to ask.

"Are you sure?" I pushed.

Apparently teachers—or Coach, at least—kept files on the criminals of tomorrow. The ones probably truant and delinquent on homework who courted trouble in and outside VHS's four walls. Bracing his left hand on the desk, he pulled open a right-side drawer and removed a thin manila file, flipping it open. Stopping to blow the gunk from its surface, a cloud of dust mites invaded the space, and I immediately sneezed.

As I grabbed a tissue from the corner of his desk, he took a harder look at the photograph, comparing it to a quick thumb-through of his folder's contents. He lifted one out and shoved it beside my photo for comparison, shook his head, and then rifled through a few more. Once again, he said he'd never met my guy, not even asking why I cared. With a weary sigh, he closed the file and slid it to the side. God willing, I'd get my hands on the file before I blew the joint.

Something was wrong with Coach, despite the fact he harbored me (and two others) who couldn't get with the program. I pulled a two-year stint in counseling (you know, childhood trauma), and if I'd learned anything, it wasn't wise to leave people in a desperate state.

The coffee pot burbled, and I took it upon myself to pour us both a drink. Stained dirt-brown, the pitcher probably hadn't seen a wash in months, but beggars couldn't be choosers, and I was deficient on caffeine.

I filled two Styrofoam cups with a liquid resembling swamp water. "What's wrong?" I asked, trying to get my psychobabble on.

Immediately, he thought I'd referred to the file. He blew into his cup as I slid back into my seat. "Bad childhoods for the most part. Some make it out with a good support system. Others wind up liking the constant rollercoaster. All I know is I have them over and over in the school's detention program. Maybe that's all they know."

If I had the time, I'd think about that rollercoaster and myself, but Coach swiveled around and looked at an itty-bitty photograph on the side of his desk, stealing my attention. It had been displayed inside one of those clear plastic frames with no border. So I not only saw the front, but the back. A quick look showed a hand-written caption on the rear: *Jacinda Olivia Jemima Opal and me.* One heck of a long name.

My nose started itching. "Who is she?"

He glanced up with a deep inhale, exhale. "Ex-wife." First of all, if someone were *my* "ex," the last thing I'd want would be a daily reminder in my face. But consider Rookie and Red. Their relationship was so dysfunctional I couldn't even term it.

Emotions slashed across his face. And even though he appeared troubled, he handed me the photograph as if it was a priceless heirloom. I drew the photograph up to my eyes. He was his usual coachy looking self, but she had a ditzy bimbo look about her. Big, bleached-blonde hair with too much makeup.

I gave him my spill-it face.

"Divorce was final in June," was all I got.

June was six months earlier, so why the extra pain? Anniversary, the upcoming holidays, a torch he couldn't extinguish? I pulled my shrink back on, but the mood was broken by someone loudly clearing his throat.

I heard the funeral march in my head.

A grin painted on Coach's face, but soon enough, he acted like someone had him by the *happies* (er, testicles) and squeezed. "Taylor?" he sort of coughed.

The guy and girl doing homework coughed too.

Dylan's voice murmured, "I'm here to chat with my colossally idiotic best friend." My hands gripped the desk, my right leg motoring like Jagger Cane's libido. I should've known he'd find me, but I was never prepared for the way his presence made me feel. I was practically fibrillating. "What can I do to fix this, sweetheart?" he asked.

You can kiss it and make it all better. I laughed hysterically to myself.

"And would that be so bad?" the girl muttered.

Where's a stun gun when you need it...

Evidently, I'd said that out loud.

A current sliced through the air from Dylan's direction, charging the air with electricity. "God help me," Coach groaned after he swallowed.

Coach and I met eyes, him frowning deeply at my R-rated thoughts.

Dylan murmured, "Darcy..."

Oh, boy, when he addressed me by my first name that meant I should fall in line before he resorted to some friendly force. I caved and dutifully got out of my seat, shuffling over to stand in front of his begging-to-be-mauled body. His left shoulder leaned against the doorjamb, right ankle crossed over the other.

Good enough to eat, I thought.

Dylan had a body built for bad things. I let out a heavy sigh, wondering why my best friend was better looking than the day before, knowing I'd repeat the same confusing phenomenon tomorrow.

When my attempt to get a smile fizzled, I lifted his stubborn jaw. "Hey," I said, adding a tiny grin.

He stared.

I stared.

Then I knocked him flat...on...his...gorgeous back—figuratively, of course.

"I need prayer, D. Even *I* know you shouldn't fib at Christmas, and I'm trying to live a clean life."

Dylan had that look like he'd fallen off the wagon train and got his jeans caught in the hitch. A gutsy move on my part, adding God to the mix—still, I glanced heavenward for a lightning bolt. Dylan repeated what I'd said, actually stuttered on it, looked to the ceiling, but gave up and dropped his jaw. We stood there for a few seconds while he tried to assess whether I'd formed a relationship with the Creator of the Universe or reached an all-time low. See, Dylan was a good Catholic boy—Mass, Lent, all the stuff that showed he truly cared about his final destination. I wasn't anything except trouble.

With a sigh, he reached for my hand.

Coach muttered from behind, "Do you two always act like there's no one else in the room?"

The girl to my left sighed dreamily, saying, "Yes."

Who in the heck *was* that chick?

Dylan released a devilish grin, which instantly turned naughty. I had no idea what he thought but found myself fanning a blush. Coach suddenly stood near us, throwing his arm around Dylan's shoulder, steering him out of the room like he removed a boiling pot from an open fire.

The bell jingled for the next class, and I knew I had to act quickly before they pulled the plug on my plan. In matters of sin behavior, I was lucky. Things fell into my lap. Seeing the file seemed too much of a coincidence to be coincidental in my world. At least, that was the story I planned to tell my conscience when it woke me in the middle of the night.

Realizing he who hesitates is lost, I grabbed my things and shoved Coach's file into my backpack. My next steps were vague, but they involved a little meet-and-greet with the people in the file. My instincts on the guy Tito faxed over to Rookie were bone-deep. If he was from Valley, as Tito's source claimed, he was either in the file or chances were good others in the file knew of him.

Smiling at Dylan who'd turned around with a wink, I knew I'd done something I couldn't undo.

Chapter Five

THE LITTLE ENGINE THAT COULD

*E*very once in a while the planets lined up in your favor when you walked into class. The teacher told you to read for the entire hour. She wasn't going to bug you, discipline you, or rat you out to higher authorities. She was simply going to let you find your personal zen and veg. That was what happened in English literature.

Collette Reynolds had been subbing for our regular English teacher for the past three weeks. She was early twenties and a sex-crazed substitute who always wore a G-string and a skirt three inches too short. Frankly, she deserved an award for defying physics and it not riding up her butt. Whatever the case, she appeared under the weather. Slumped over her desk, her ash-blonde hair had been pulled up in a messy bun overtop one of those red holiday sweaters with a Christmas tree on the front. Making love to a jumbo cup of coffee, she popped Jolly Ranchers and cough drops like she ended a forty-day hunger strike.

Can we just say, *Ba-da-bing, ba-da-boom*, problem solved?

As soon as Coach's folder was in my possession, I contemplated how I'd get the time to pore over it before school ended. Right then, the sub had given me carte blanche to do as I pleased. My plan was to look at it, memorize the details, and return it while it still fell under the auspices that I'd "borrowed" it.

When I clued-in her mind was elsewhere, I opened the file and grouped students by grade, offense, and time they'd actually spent at the county jail. Believe it or not, his file had an asterisk by those who'd been in the Mack County Juvenile System.

God love the organized people. Made my job easier.

I narrowed the list down to two, possibly three. All three had theft on their list of offenses as well as credit card offenses. Number one was Slapstick Wilson. Wilson reminded me of Hercules, so huge it was like his momma fed him steroids in his baby bottle. He stood around six and a half feet tall, and for a boy who was still a teenager, that height was on a plane of bizarre people didn't see often. His black hair was thick and fell at his shoulders, pushing the limit of what the school deemed acceptable. His hazel eyes were deep-set with a crooked line on a nose that'd been broken, but it didn't detract from an otherwise appealing face. Slapstick was hiding one fine-looking body by not having the outer package society said made a guy marketable.

I'd heard the same thing about me (via Ivy). I laughed to myself.

According to the file, one felony offense was stealing his neighbor's wallet two years earlier and going on a spending spree at the grocery store. The judge let him off easy with community service because the neighbor ultimately didn't want him to see time. Other offenses were misdemeanors like vandalism and disorderly conduct on the Fourth of July. Misdemeanors normally didn't carry jail time, but there was another felony offense listed of carrying a knife in public. My guess was the judge wanted to send him a message because the charge involved a deadly weapon. Consequently, Slapstick did a short stint in juvie the past summer.

Potential number two was Damon Whitehead. Once again, a felony offense of burglary and check forgery (he stole his uncle's check card and bought a bicycle). Listed as a senior, Damon's file said he'd endured several broken bones in foster homes, but they hadn't been attributed to abuse. Not at least to what had been proven or what he'd admit. Whitehead was like a circus carnie, literally running along rooftops and performing death-defying feats for the heck of it. Sometimes he made it. Sometimes he didn't. He'd been in juvenile detention for vandalism and smoking marijuana...in Target, I might add.

Sort of impressive.

Then came prospect number three. Coach had spilled coffee on the lower half of the paper that listed his name. As a result, I had to peel it from the sheet in front of it, which unfortunately left his jawline murky. Because of the obscured photograph, my memory meter registered zero. He didn't look familiar. His right eye was swollen shut, but darkness still resided in his gaze. Something was gone inside. Snuffed out too soon, perhaps. Like the others, he had the common thread of theft. He didn't look exactly the same as the photo Tito faxed Rookie—this guy had dirty-blond hair—but the beating he took made it impossible to tell for sure. I blew out a sigh. The task before me made *Where's Waldo?* look easy.

I closed the file and thanked the Milky Way Murphy was a clean-living man who came home each night. All of us had problems, but the file told me those three lived with a different set of circumstances than I did. Perhaps it was who they were, no matter their surroundings. Or perhaps they gave up and simply walked in the world they'd been born into. I'd learned the fine art of selective blindness when I was a child too. It was easy to shield your eyes from the painful if it was a matter of survival.

———

I'd done something baaaaddd.

I left class a few minutes early and jogged to Coach Wallace's office to return the file. Except when I arrived, the two students inside earlier were back again and all over each other. I. Mean. All. Over. Each. Other. Now I didn't know a lot about making out—only what I'd read in romance novels I hid under my mattress—but when I saw the young girl's tortured face, it was only by the Grace of God, I didn't hurl the pork rinds I'd found in my locker. The guy was giving her stand-up CPR. Ahem, hands where the Good Lord didn't intend for them to be for those who needed a definition. I concluded pretty darn quickly he was the type that didn't understand that no meant *no*.

I went cuckoo for Cocoa Puffs—wrenching my way between them, punching, pinching, and name-dropping that Dylan would kick his evil rat fastard butt. I even closed my eyes and lunged for the family jewels but thankfully came up with air. He went tribal on both of us, grunting and pulling our hair, until he abruptly stopped and sprinted out of the room. By the time I caught my breath, my clothes were as askew as the girl's. Shifting my undergarments back into place, the small brunette had the top of one boob showing. No lie. She stood there mouth agape, no move to cover her lady bits. I closed my eyes and did my best to shove her back in her bra, but when I squinted one eye open, she merely stared as though she tried to tell me something. Something, by the look on her face, was melodramatic and possibly an episode for *60 Minutes*.

When I said, "Just say it," she grabbed her things and bolted for the door.

I thought that went pretty well...all things considered.

I was stuck with a real dilemma. As much as I tried, I couldn't pry the file out of my own stinking hands. I decided to keep it. Anyway, a hot glue gun lay on Coach's desk along with his wallet and stopwatch. The glue gun was still plugged in, still a fire hazard, and right there for me to abuse.

After a quick glance behind, I pumped out a stringy glob and glued his stopwatch to the desk. Surely it would come off, but then again, my impulses didn't always afford me the luxury of thinking. Once I'd performed the deed, I boogied to the parking lot where Dylan was supposedly patiently waiting.

Except he wasn't just waiting, now was he.

He was seated in his car, motor running, being entertained by Brynn Hathaway who'd pulled her black BMW convertible beside him. Heck, they practically had matching his-and-hers cars. Her car door slid open, and she bounced over to the driver's side window like she was fueled by too much pep and sugar. Two things happened at once. My gag reflex kicked up a notch, but then I saw the distraction as opportunity. The opportunity? I could tell Brynn to her face I had a coffin with her name on it.

Let me take a little hop down memory freaking lane here. Called Brynn-baby by the guys who crushed on her, she'd had a thing for Dylan before his first whisker even made an appearance. She tried extra hard to make sure he noticed her too. Sporting dark jeans so tight it was a wonder they didn't rupture her butt, she'd paired them with thigh-high black leather boots and a black leather blazer. Not cold weather threads by definition, but Brynn dressed more for effect than practicality. Her build was fit and petite with wavy, chestnut-brown hair and bright blue eyes. And check out her résumé: cheer captain, homecoming queen, and nationally ranked gymnast.

That last one, I think, made guys fantasize about her flexibility.

Mere feet from his car, the unspeakable happened. She moved her upper body through Dylan's window, her well-manicured nails touching his face...her lips dangerously close to his mouth. The tightness in my chest kicked up a notch.

I do not like this. Not at all.

I let out a belligerent, "D!" hotfooting it their way. But when I witnessed him give her The Dimples, my courage went down the rabbit hole. I stopped, mouth ajar. They were two beautiful people, laughing and enjoying life. It was a picture meant for a dang greeting card. Dylan didn't appear overly exuberant, but Brynn was the girl-next-door—her family's home within walking distance of his. Maybe their convo was something they'd pick up later. When she gripped his arm tighter, he was definitely Dylan: smooth, mannerly, with a body gifted by Jesus.

I called fate the B-word before being jarred from my thoughts with a screaming, "Walker!"

I swallowed and spun around.

Don't let anyone ever tell you an overweight man couldn't find a few moves when he was so inclined. Coach Wallace booked it toward me like a bank robber out of a blaring alarm.

Jeez, guess he figured out it was me. Shocking.

I smiled and blew him an air kiss as I darted for Dylan's car like a cheetah with its fur on fire. Dylan and I always felt we were connected metaphysically. Perhaps he heard Coach yelling, or perhaps he felt my heart in his throat. Whatever the motivation, he blew Brynn off like yesterday's news, cranked his door wide, and shot halfway up out of his car.

With a naughty giggle, I yelled, "Move out of the way, Romeo! Like *now!*"

He didn't move fast enough.

With a huge leap, I dove headfirst into the driver's side door, taking him with me, banging my head on the center console. Dylan caught all my weight with an, "Ugh." Somehow my foot hit the chair release, and the door slammed beside us. If that wasn't bizarre enough, as embarrassment would have it, my bum landed right smack in the middle of his face when we tumbled into the back seat.

My backpack slid off my shoulder with a bump-bump-bump.

I didn't move.

I didn't know what to do, really. But sometimes wisdom was out on a smoke break when you needed her. All I knew was outside wasn't safe, and inside...well, it felt hotter than the Devil's pitchfork.

Dylan was vintage Dylan, letting out a flirty moan. "Sweetheart, I've wanted to get you in the backseat of my car for some time, but I would've preferred it being dark and a little more secluded."

"Seriously," I said, giggling and wriggling toward the front. "I thought your fantasies involved barnyard animals."

"Like I said..." he said with a chuckle.

The jackwagon...I walked right into that one.

Dylan ran his hands up and down my hips, treating my body like the happy hunting ground. I froze. Did. Not. Feel. A. Freaking. Twinge. Maybe I had a hormonal imbalance because most women would give their right ovary to sit where I was sitting. Did I need testosterone? Estrogen? I'd only recently discovered hormones, and right then, they'd shriveled up like a spider when it died.

I crawled overtop his backpack to the opposite side but felt someone pull my UGG out the driver's side window. My legs scissored in the splits.

"Crap," I mumbled.

Dylan rose up in an ab curl. "Aw, sweetheart, I don't have a dog in this fight," he murmured.

Coach barked, "Walker, get out!" Only an idiot would get out. When I didn't oblige, Coach turned his attention on Dylan.

"Taylor," he bellowed, flailing his arm through the window, "you're in more trouble than she is!"

Dylan giggled. "Holy Mother, what did you do?" he asked me. *Better yet, what did* you *do?* I thought. Brynn Hathaway was one step from needing a drool bib. A cursory glance showed her gone...smart girl.

I kept kicking at Coach while Dylan attempted to tug me back inside. Sometimes it was easier for me to talk about personal things when Dylan and I were otherwise occupied. And Brynn Hathaway was definitely on the *Must Address List*.

As Coach pulled my boot off, I spit out, "Brynn wants to go out with you." *And by the way, I stole Coach's file and impersonated my aunt this weekend*, I omitted.

Dylan slowly dropped my leg, lounging back in the chair, looking thoughtful. Turning me around, he pulled me onto his chest and literally put his mouth to mine...but he didn't kiss me. He whispered into my lips, "I know. We've had this talk before, Darcy, but you know it means nothing to me...unless you *want* me to date her?" he finished as a question. Lips still on mine, he cocked a brow, waiting for my answer. Heck, *I* waited for my answer, but nothing came out but a tiny moan. I mean, his lips were still on mine!! I inhaled his scent mixed with the leather and knew I needed to find the exit.

And side note: I DID NOT NEED ANY FREAKING HORMONE REPLACEMENT.

"Gosh, your eyes are amazing," I whispered.

His grin quirked up, showing me his dimples. *The* dimples. "Focus, sweetheart." Frankly, my mind blew a few circuits, so tracking the conversation had proven rather difficult. Especially when his lips felt bizarre, scary, and life altering all at the same time. I remembered what kissing Dylan was like. It was wonderful, forbidden, and titillating to each cell in the body, but I spent a good deal of time trying to figure out if I was alive when it was over. My God, he might be capable of killing me. As tenderhearted as he was, I had a feeling that branching out and evolving our relationship into something else would be like the untrained playing with a Bunsen burner. But why did that burn sound so gosh-danged exciting? "Do you not know what's going on here?" he whispered into my mouth.

As God as my witness, he then nipped my lower lip with his teeth!

What.

The. Freak.

Was.

That.

In my defense, I was ADHD. The whole thing would take some time for me to grasp. I blinked in morbid shock. Dylan and me? Let's face it. He'd be slumming. When I readied to say, *No, it would kill me, and I don't want to share you*, I was jerked so hard out of the car I popped the button on my pants.

"You're grounded!" Coach shouted.

Wasn't the first time I'd heard the phrase, but I had to say it was the first by a gym teacher. "What did I do?" I said, feigning ignorance. I reached underneath my silver down coat, resnapping my jeans, trying my best to look like a concerned citizen. Dylan slowly opened his car door, not even asking what'd happened as Coach dangled half the stopwatch in front of my face.

Holy cow, what did he do? Smash it with a crowbar?

After a few more phrases of me acting like I hadn't a clue what'd upset him, all three of us realized how cold it had grown. A look to the sky showed nimbus clouds. Snow was expected. Three to five inches. In Cincinnati, if you had a good nose, you could smell it in the air.

All at once, Coach looked as if he'd grown twenty years older. I had the distinct feeling whatever bothered him earlier had inflated tenfold.

"I'll replace it," I blurted out.

"Take me to my car," he muttered to Dylan. I jumped in the back, and when we circled around the side of the building, nothing could've prepared me for what we'd see. Your parents always warn you to not laugh at others' misfortunes, but sometimes the joke was so hilarious the body couldn't help but be a smartass.

I laughed so loudly I snorted like a pig. Dylan did some sort of strangled cough and bit his lip. In tie-dyed letters on the back of Coach's white Honda Civic was painted "Coach Wallace is a Wanker." There was the start of a few expletives, but thankfully whomever the artist was either ran out of paint...or nerve.

"Maybe you should cut back on this wankering thing if it's so upsetting to people," I joked.

He and Dylan sat there, mouths agape. When I rambled on about the weather and how the rainbow of colors made a nice, whimsical pattern, Dylan reached back and flicked me on the top of the head.

Well, *he* wasn't saying anything...

After a few more beats of nothing, Coach leaned his head back against the headrest like his life had officially ended. He let out an exhausted sigh. "Walker, find out who spray painted my car. Unless I can get the person to pay for their crime, I'll have to drive the thing around until I can pay my thousand dollar deductible."

My father was in the insurance business. I'd rather take a fork to the eye than follow in his footsteps, but Murphy spewed his travails so much, I could probably ace a training class.

"That's a pretty high deductible," I said.

He muttered, "This isn't a first time occurrence."

"Seriously?" Dylan added.

"Three times before and one of them was Vinnie Vecchione," he grumbled. "Granted his was washable, but still."

Ah, Vinnie...

Vinnie was a full-blooded Italian with a prominent nose and lamb chop sideburns. Never short on a girl, Vinnie was the type of guy who oozed "something." A something which made the most gorgeous girls imaginable fall for a guy about fifty pounds over-weight...with moobies.

Dylan and I exchanged worried glances. As far as we knew, Vinnie still lived at Ohio State University. He played football with Dylan last year and received a college scholarship as an offensive lineman. I doubt Vinnie had anything to do with Coach's car, but I owed him a phone call anyway. Vinnie was on retainer with me, so to speak, and the association definitely upped my street cred. When I was abducted and thrown in the back of a car last spring, a man in a yellow Dodge Charger was the offender. When he yanked me out of the trunk, I wasn't met with a chainsaw. Instead, I received a lecture on how to stay alive doing the things that made me Darcy—wow, er, no other word to describe that kind of ripple effect. Problem was, I hadn't seen the man since. Vinnie had a large net of informants across the city who'd been playing lookout. We had several confirmed sightings, but when we investigated (behind Dylan's back), nothing ever panned out.

"Why me?" I asked with a giggle.

Coach finally laughed, although it might've been at my expense. "You cut your teeth on being nosy, dollface. God knows you roam

the hall enough, and you did a fine job with that gang last spring."
Okay, I did roam a little, but the roaming helped bust up the Northside 12 from infiltrating our school. When all was said and done, the
Northside 12 had a rap sheet of assault, drug trafficking, murder, and
attempted murder. I learned something about myself then. Once I
put my nose to the ground, my bloodhound instincts rarely led me
wrong.

Graffiti could be random or premeditated. The premeditated
usually were personal. Looking at his car, premeditation seemed
obvious. Sure, someone could've happened onto a can of paint and
felt creative, but random occurrences more than likely would've
involved more cars. Furthermore, logic said his car hadn't been
parked in its current space. He was in the teachers' parking lot,
positioned near a security camera. A crime perpetrated in that location was asking to be caught.

Someone knew his specific car and where to find it.

I said, "Someone was after you specifically. So where were you
parked because I know it wasn't here."

Dylan's dimples imploded, like he knew where my mind was
headed.

Coach pivoted around, one eyebrow raised. "You deduced that
from one glance at my car?"

I did my shoulders up and down in an exaggerated shrug. "This
wasn't random, Coach, or other cars would've been hit. And it didn't
take place in the teachers' lot because there's a security camera right
next to your car. It would've documented the whole thing. I could
give you more, but I need to know who your enemies are first."

He rattled off the usual...

Disgruntled athletes who didn't make the basketball cut, angry
students he'd failed in gym, and his recently divorced wife who...
jackpot...vandalized his car twice during the year already. Huh, I'd
just found out he had a wife, let alone she was the artsy type.

A glance to Dylan said he'd known about the revelation. Dylan
had left his car idling. I leaned forward between the seats and thrust
both hands forward toward the blowing heater. My hands were
numb, and my fingers felt past the resuscitation phase.

"Obviously things didn't work out, Coach, or there wouldn't
have been a divorce. Who threw in the towel? You or her?"

He scratched his head, debating a reply. A look crossed his face like he felt bad talking about her without her present to defend herself. Whatever she did must've been pretty crummy, or he wrestled with overwhelming guilt and regret.

When he didn't respond, I touched his shoulder. "Tell me what I'm working with. Did she hit you, rob you, cheat on you, or poison your dog?"

"Yes," he answered.

"Which ones?" I shrieked.

"All of them."

The animal lover in me yelled, "She poisoned your doggie?"

"All right, maybe not that, but I didn't want the divorce. Besides, I'm sort of talking to someone else."

"Oh, yeah? Who?"

"It's new," he muttered. "We hooked up on Facebook. Haven't met in person yet."

"Well, that definitely has the makings of something everlasting," I mumbled.

Dylan yanked my hair.

The three of us sat there listening to Dylan burn away more gas. I'd never rubberstamp a divorce, but oftentimes circumstances warranted the break. I knew Dylan agreed with me. Catholics were more no-no on divorce than Murphy was, and my father was his own brand of Holy Roller. Dylan was uncharacteristically quiet. He not only knew of their marriage but of details he hadn't divulged in our late night soul-baring chats. Well, guess what, it was only a matter of time before I pulled those suckers out of him.

Dylan finally graced us with a comment. "No video footage of anything?" he asked. That question was actually next on my list. But dang it, I hadn't been hired yet.

Coach answered, "No. I'd parked in space 270. Some huge SUV parked in front of me, and we got nothing but the black silhouette of a Nissan Armada when Security and I went through the tape. All I know is it happened between the time I pulled into the lot and right before first period because I discovered it when I ran out to the car to grab my whistle. Just my luck," he mumbled to himself.

"Why had you parked there anyway?" I asked. "Whose space *is* or *was* it?"

"That space is always open, and I just took advantage. I was running late and didn't work out this morning, so I pulled into 270 and sprinted to the door."

"Dude, you burned a whole two calories. Good for you," I said with a giggle. I held my hand up for a high-five, but he left me hanging.

Dylan reached over and flicked my head again. Coach ignored me, still caught up in his personal problems, I guess.

I wasn't the type to beat around the bush, but if he wanted my services, it'd come with a price. I glanced at Dylan who gave me a wink. I smiled and said, "Five hundred dollars."

Coach snorted in laughter. "You're going to charge?"

Hellooo, my budget was bleeding. Of course, I'd charge.

There wasn't much room between the seats, but I managed to cross my arms in protest. "You're asking the best to solve a problem, Coach. That's actually my discounted rate."

Dylan giggled behind his wrist.

"How about half?" Coach countered.

Dylan peeked out from behind his hand, with an eye roll, shaking his head.

"Five hundred," I declared, holding my head higher.

"Three hundred," he said frowning. When I returned a deeper frown, he muttered, "I'm a teacher for goodness' sake! That's practically my paycheck!"

Yeah, well, I was a poor student. We were even. "Look at it this way, Coach. If you don't pay me, you'll force me into a life of ill repute. I'm broke, man. And you weren't going to turn it into your insurance company anyway. Your wife—"

"Ex-wife," he interrupted with a frown.

"Right," I said, grinning bigger. "She got artsy before, correct? All I can say is if you reported two acts of vandalism this year, one more time and your rates will skyrocket."

I picked at my nails as Dylan coughed to keep from laughing.

Coach glared, like he negotiated with a viper to crawl back in its hole. "You're vicious, Walker," he grumbled.

"I'm a businesswoman," I explained professionally. "Pay me, or pay your insurance company."

"I'm still out my five hundred dollars and haven't paid for a paint job."

"It's the season for giving," I said, grinning big.

"It's the season for scams," he grumbled.

"It's the season for miracles," Dylan said chuckling. "Give me all of your estimates, and the man who handles my father's fleet of cars will beat it. You won't have to turn it in at all." Dylan moved toward me, winking and running a finger down my nose. "Don't you like to win, sweetheart? I so like to win."

I gave him an even bigger grin, cooing, "Winning makes me feel special."

Before we called it a day, Coach showed us the videotape of the offense. I was sure it was against school policy, but when we walked into Security and no one manned the shop, the tape sort of turned itself on (wink, wink).

Cameras rolled 24/7, and at seven o'clock, Coach's Honda Civic was a dirty arctic white. The cameras definitively documented the time of him driving into the parking lot, but like he said, he made a C-turn and popped into space 270 where cameras didn't have a full-view. By seven twenty, the bumper had been tie-died like a darn rainbow with WANKER in all caps. Holy guacamole, I didn't even know what a wanker was. Whoever painted, painted fast. We viewed the tape from seven o'clock up until school started at seven fifteen and noticed nothing out of the ordinary. We didn't see anyone congregating around the area other than a white van that paused for a minute to chat to a few students. No one was bowled over with laughter in the nearby spaces or aisles. What did that tell me? People either had no clue what went on around them or I needed to see who'd been listed as tardy for the day. A few minutes late to class could mean all the difference in the world.

After Coach gave me the names of the students he considered possibilities—unfortunately, none I recognized as listed in his file— he opened his door and turned around with furrowed brows. My word, he looked at me like he looked at a creature underneath a microscope. "Do you really think you can do this?"

It didn't take a lot to galvanize me into action. Tell me I couldn't do it, and I'd die trying.

"Call me the little engine that could," I said and smiled. "And by the way, that guy and girl in your class earlier? Don't leave them alone again."

"Why?"

"Let's just say he was having trouble keeping the beast in check."

Dylan shifted uncomfortably in his seat. Coach still hadn't caught my drift. "Dumb that down for me, Walker," he grunted.

"You heard me, Coach. He doesn't know when *no* means *no*."

Coach dropped his chin, his eyes going wide like a hoot owl's. "Please tell me that doesn't mean what I think it means."

"It does," I said with a snort, "but don't worry. I took care of it."

Dylan cut him off, slaying me with his gaze. "And how exactly did you take care of it?"

"Well, I didn't have a stake for his heart, so I made do. In fact, my retaliation was so brutal I think I sprained my own hand."

All the air rushed from Dylan's lungs. I pounded on his back.

"I'll look into this," Coach said, sighing heavily. "Thanks, dollface."

"I'm going to need his name," Dylan hissed low in his throat.

Heck yeah he needed it because my girl bits might need protected, and I was positive I gained a new enemy in the process.

Chapter Six

100 PROOF STUD

"*I* worried, Mister Murphys. Death is coming to your life."

For the past forty-three minutes (yes, I actually counted), Claudia, frantically mirrored Murphy's every move, telling him to skip work or take the bus, or heck, quit working altogether and embrace government assistance. She spoke through a crack in the bathroom door, pulled him out of his car, and even helped stir the pot of chili he'd been cooking on the stove. Murphy, his usual uncomfortable-with-emotional-displays self, patted her awkwardly on the shoulder grunting, "I'm good."

Claudia wasn't so convinced. She'd bolted us in nice and tight and shoved a chair up against the front door, an ottoman against it. Claudia believed in her powers over any voice of reason whatsoever.

When she was thirteen, Claudia walked through the streets of Puerto Rico when a fruit truck backfired and a load of produce fell off the bed. She said she saw the Virgin Mary in the spray of tomatoes. Ever since, Mary or Baby Jesus would occasionally visit her. Last spring, she saw Jesus on a Keebler cookie—a cookie that I accidentally ate.

Yeah. Mazel tov.

Claudia'd just picked up Murphy's briefcase and saw Death, whatever it looked like, on a file folder with the words "Dumbass Kansas Account" hand-scrawled on the header. First off, Murphy *never* cursed, so the account must really be stupid for him to immortalize it on company property as such. We'd just finished eating dinner, and he fell into his recliner, finishing up a recorded episode of *The Young and the Restless*.

As Claudia chanted a voodoo spell of protection, I scrounged around for dessert. I had bad eating habits and referred to my snack cuisine as the 3Cs: a coffee, Coke, and a cookie. I'd since added a fourth—the churro. Claudia had just baked a batch, and I jumped up on the countertop, eating two of the remaining three. That was how I wanted to die...I wanted to die falling face-first into a plate of churros. In about eight bites, my slobber switch turned off, and I was left with a mouthful of food I couldn't swallow.

While I downed half a Coke with a burp, Claudia bounced over in a hot pink muumuu. It looked like a shower curtain wrapped around two inflated beach balls. File that under another episode of *Bathroom Commercial Gone Bad*.

She smacked my hand, pointing to the last churro I'd licked and placed back on the countertop. "Did you do?"

I shrugged. "My lips sort of fell on it. Sometimes that stuff happens."

She cocked her head to one side, debating the chances, but gave up and sang a Spanish song about baby angels. When *Y&R* ended, Murphy switched to the six o'clock news right as a live-streaming camera showed Nowacki's Videos—the latest establishment to fall victim of robbery and vandalism—and what the reporter claimed was "...already a case of confirmed identity theft."

That could only mean the crooks cleaned him out, stole information from his personal accounts, and then divested him of his assets. Quick movers, if the press already had confirmation, which insinuated a high level of organization.

Nowacki's Videos geographically lay across the street from Belinski's Bookstore—where I found the three ID cards. Furthermore, that was one too many instances of vandalism and identity theft for me to not cry foul. Coincidence? I think not.

"Was anyone hurt?" I asked, jumping off the counter. Mr. Nowacki never left the place until ten o'clock. Windows had been broken and glistened like diamonds on the front sidewalk. A cleaning crew wiped down what appeared to be profanity because the news station blocked the words from viewership w.th white rectangular boxes.

As the anchor reported the incident happened after hours, he touched on other incidences in the area while my mind tugged at me with the promises I'd made—a promise to Tito for information on the person who stole his identity, and a promise to Coach to unearth who'd painted his car. Add those together and I talked enough money for Christmas (hello, $10 G reward), plus the beginnings of a substantial savings account. In my little corner of the world, I'd be freaking rich.

Needing a starting place, the only person who could point me in the right direction was Tito...but I didn't want him to have my real number. I could use my phone and *67 the call, but I'd recently heard there were ways around the code for people who knew what they were doing. That might be a truckload of BS, but Tito seemed like he'd know the skill if it held merit.

About that time, my little sister, Marjorie, walked into the room with—thank my lucky stars—the disposable phone Murphy purchased to basically shut her up.

The Lord works in mysterious ways. I smiled to myself.

She had almond-shaped brown eyes and wavy hair colored fire-engine-red. Marjorie had been nicknamed M since she was a baby, for obvious reasons. Who wanted to learn to spell an eight-lettered name? But my little sister was smart. She'd mastered it by age two and made all the other parents feel like they'd birthed morons.

"Did you have a good day?" I asked, smiling down at her

She frowned, and the freckles on her nose scrunched together. "Well..." she pouted. Ugh, not a good sign. Starting a sentence with "well" never ended in a condensed version. It was more like a dissertation.

My patience was wearing thin, so I blurted out, "Let's switch phones for the night. You can play on all my apps and buy new ones without getting approval. Here's my password to the Apple Store."

I recited it with a huge smile.

By the way her face lit up, you'd think I'd offered a lifetime supply of naked Barbies. Finn had given me my life back. When my iPhone screen spider-webbed on Saturday, I bought a repair kit on

Amazon, had it overnighted, and Finn replaced the glass in less than fifteen minutes after basketball practice.

As Marjorie skipped over to sit on Murphy's lap, I stole away to the bathroom, punched in Tito's number, and sat on the toilet, my legs pumping like they ran on a treadmill. I'd never once considered he wouldn't pick up, but on ring number four, it felt like a boxer wailed away on my gut. When he finally muttered a "Tito," I said, "This is Jester, I've got two names who might be your guy. Get ready to be impressed."

Huh, his silence led me to believe he hadn't taken me seriously. *The nerve.* I laughed to myself. He was quiet—bordering shock, no doubt—and repeated, "Two names."

"Two names," I verified. He paused, probably wondering if I was an idiot. I paused, hoping he'd never get definitive proof. "I need to know what kind of connection they have," I told him, "because it was something other than all the bad apples being found at the bottom. And let me tell you why. Did you see the news tonight, Tito? My guess is these guys vandalized Nowacki's Videos, and to already have cleaned out his bank accounts, signifies an overwhelmingly organized operation."

He released a jagged sigh. "There's theft and vandalism all over the city, Jester. What makes you think this is *my* guy?"

My gut. "Deductive reasoning," I answered confidently. "Anyone can rob a place, but to systematically wipe out the owner's account like the reporter suggested? That's a little too close to your situation without investigation. Listen," I paused, "I get it. You don't trust me. Blah, *bl*-blah, blah, blah. But you're out nothing, and this ain't my first time to the rodeo, cowboy. I know how to get things done... take that to the bank."

"So if I get this information for you...*Jester*," he paused, slightly sarcastically, "then you'll provide me with information on who stole my personal identity?"

A mirror hung in the three-by-five foot hardwood bathroom surrounded by two wall sconces that gave off as much wattage as the North Star. I gazed at my reflection, reminding myself Jester and I were one and the same. If I wasn't careful, I could lose sight of myself and the still small voice of reason that occasionally surfaced. In my mind, I sang, *I think I can, I think I can, I think I can.*

"If I promised," I declared, "then I'll deliver. Here are the names..."

———

Whoever said the eyes were the window to the soul knew exactly what they were talking about. If someone took the time to look—or more specifically if he or she was allowed to look—they could figure someone out. The eyes rarely lied, and the truth appeared even more pronounced with my father. In one instance, his eyes could be warm and sensitive, and in another, they could leave a grown man girl-screaming like his cojones were in danger. Murphy was either all up in my business playing drill sergeant, checking cell phone logs, auditing the history on my computer, or he was so hands-off I called the shots in my own personal disasters. That lack of pretense, however, was the only predictable thing in M's and my world of uncertainty. Even though we knew he was a teddy bear at heart, it was hard to get past his tough bear exterior to find the "teddy" part. And all of the toughness was due to the fact he was a man still desperately in love with one woman.

I sighed at the thought.

Life sucked...and Christmas didn't always bring miracles, now did it.

Murphy was seated at the foot of my white wrought-iron bed while I stood in my closet, staring at my clothes. He'd dusted my painted white desk and chest of drawers, absently scrolling through the channels on the VIZIO flatscreen mounted on the wall. We weren't rich. Like everything else, I'd saved my money and then increased the annual sales of Costco.

Murphy and I met eyes, and my beating heart told me to brace myself. "So I got a call from Dylan today. He was dribbling a ball at practice, kid. What on God's green Earth did you do at the Valley of the Shadow of Death now?"

Murphy called Valley High, the Valley of the Shadow of Death... how freaking apropos.

My guess was Dylan went into disaster mode and gave Murphy a heads up about Mr. Himmel. Murphy had two rules: try your hardest, and tell the truth. Sounded simple enough. Trouble was, that last one came back to bite me in the bum. In order to save time, I spit out the facts. "I told Mister Himmel I didn't want to be in his class."

Murphy gasped, "Shouldn't you have lied? And for the love of God, call him Doctor Himmel. You don't disrespect someone's wishes and tell them you don't like their class followed up with an 'oh goody,'" he said sarcastically.

Well, well, well, when Dylan gave a recap...he certainly gave one heckuva recap. Point for him, however, he knew I would probably skip over the whole incident and hope for the best.

I thundered out of the closet, giving him a belligerent, "It's Christmas, Murphy! Lying on Christmas is like Biblical plague stuff." And I needed God to answer my prayers for two miracles even though I wasn't sure I ever really prayed.

Murphy snorted loudly. "Your sense of rationale, as always, is without equal, kid. What about this science project?"

"I'll come up with something."

"You'd better, but I'm calling him tomorrow...*Jesus*," he muttered.

"You're calling Jesus?" I said giggling.

"Doctor Himmel," he grumbled. "Jesus I'm going to talk to tonight about how I can get Doctor Himmel fired."

When he finished, I mumbled, "He won't change his mind."

"Jesus?" Murphy asked.

"Mister Himmel," I told him. "I mean, Doctor Himmel. He doesn't like me."

"Well, I can assure you Doctor Himmel's going to *hate* me." No kidding. Murphy loved hard...hated even harder. By the time Murphy was through with Mr. Himmel, he'd probably like an infestation of bed bugs better.

Murphy dropped his head, clasping his hands in prayer. He mumbled, "Sweet, Lord. Please do something miraculous with my firstborn child."

I wasn't sure what I was supposed to do. Pray along with him? Tell him it was futile? Mr. Himmel made people think they were stupid. Plus, I was pretty sure if we shaved his head, the Devil's mark might be in his crown. In my opinion, outing Himmel as a jerk fell under the premises of a community service project.

When Murphy ran out of gas, he stared off into space. A good chance existed I would've failed the semester anyway. At the moment, it was all but an eventuality.

While Murphy stalked off, I fed my lovebirds, Churro and Chimichanga (my latest impulse purchases), which were probably two more headstones for the pet cemetery in my backyard. God help me, I'd killed every pet I had. Afterward I collapsed on the side of my bed. I felt like I'd been skydiving and the ground was coming up quick...what was the next move? My to-do list was seven continents long. One, I needed to find out who spray painted Coach's car. Two, I needed Tito to consider me the Messiah. Granted, I'd already given him the names of Slapstick Wilson and Damon Whitehead, but embarrassingly, I couldn't give him the third because it wasn't legible in Coach's file. And three, I needed to return the social security and bank cards to their owners before I died of guilt. Question was, how would I get information before the first bell? Additionally, I could add a number four. I still needed to speak with Vinnie about any leads he had on the guy in the yellow Dodge Charger.

Crawling under the covers, I rolled over and checked my phone one last time. No texts. No voicemails. Nothing but a picture Vinnie had sent of the crease in his forearm...it looked like a hairy butt crack. That was five days earlier. Vinnie had been unusually quiet, and it made me want to crawl right out of my skin. I loved Vinnie. The love was different from what I had for Dylan, but it ran just as deep. He was beautifully flawed and neurotic and had as many cuts on his heart as I did.

"Call me, V," I muttered when I got his voicemail. "You're worrying me, buddy, and you owe me an update. And I want to know if you had anything to do with spray painting Coach Wallace's car today. I know it's a stretch since you're out of town, but I've got five hundred dollars riding on finding the culprit. So let your fingers do the walking and make nice with Jester."

Pitching my iPhone back to the nightstand, I pulled the down comforter to my chin and lay on one of many white pillows. My down comforter was so comfy, it begged a person to dive in and lose yourself. It was ten o'clock. Normally, I didn't fall asleep 'til somewhere between eleven and midnight, but my eyes grew heavier than a lead weight.

I dozed off into never-never land only to be jolted awake by my cell phone blasting. I fumbled around, brought it to an eye, and saw Dylan's smiling face. I didn't even say hi, hello, or hey. I think he got a grunt.

"Talk dirty to me, sweetheart," he said and chuckled.

"Scabies," I mumbled.

An even naughtier, deeper chuckle. "I tried to SKYPE, but you must've fallen asleep. I received a text that the team has a six-thirty meeting tomorrow morning. Do you want to come early or grab the bus?"

Occasionally, the cosmos threw a person a bone. If I tagged along, I could stakeout where Coach parked to see if the perp returned to the scene. Maybe there'd be a correlation. Maybe that was wishful thinking. No matter what, I had to do something.

I decided not to blast him for ratting me out to Murphy. His intentions had been good, and right then, I needed a ride. My voice purred, "Wouldn't miss it for the world." God love him, he assumed the purr was because I couldn't be without him after the sweet nothings I picked up through the phone.

I mouthed, "Thank you" to Heaven, wondering if I really should be thanking Hell.

"Where the freak have you been?" I hissed. It was five a.m. Tuesday when Vinnie returned my call. I wasn't sure why I snapped in a beeyotchy voice—either because he'd blown me off or the fact my body fought through some sort of shock at the early hour.

"Dolce, you're never going to believe it, so I'm going to jump right in. I'm an actor." Vinnie had called me "Dolce" for years (Italian, for sweet), because of our mutual love of sugar. My over indulgences so far hadn't caught up with me. Vinnie's, however, gave him a permanent spare-tire gut.

"What do you mean you're an actor?" I said, adding a worn out sigh.

"You know, hit your mark and smile for the camera. I've been filming an indie flick when I'm not in class." Vinnie gave me the particulars, and I seriously smacked myself to make sure I was awake. Evidently, he'd filmed a low budget flick called *100 Proof Stud* (instant classic, I'm sure) and was living off fifty large.

"Someone gave you fifty thousand dollars to be the love interest in a movie called *100 Proof Stud?*" I said, snorting with laughter.

"100 Proof," he flirted.

"Subtle."

"My middle name."

Only Vinnie could find instant success in a low budget film, but I knew he'd blow through the cash by the end of the year. Whatever the proper responses were in life, Vinnie's were the opposite. Socking some cash away for a rainy day probably had never entered his mind.

I attempted to rein him in. "Okay, V. We'll talk about that later, but right now you need to get your head out of the clouds. First off, did you vandalize Coach Wallace's car today?"

Vinnie took a beat to let the accusation take shape. "No," he eventually answered, expelling a big, roguish laugh. "I was making out with a redhead, and we..."

La-la-la, I sung to myself. Vinnie's words were the most descriptive, disgusting, play-by-play of what males and females did together —things I called the shama lama, ding-dong. I attempted to bleep him out, but a few choice scenarios seeped through. I found it best to not pass judgment since I harbored the stolen identities of three different individuals. Individuals probably scared poopless over their lost cards. I'd return them once I made it home. I'd give them to Tito, show him I had a fountain flow of information (which I didn't), and salve my morally bankrupt self at the same time.

I spoke above his laughter. "What about the yellow Dodge Charger? I need to know who he is. He acted like he *knew* me, and I have a feeling it means something in the circus I call my life."

Vinnie's voice took on a serious tone. "Rome wasn't built in a day, Dolce. I'm home this weekend for a short trip, and I'll get back on it."

The moment I think Vinnie put the "D" in dumb, he spouts out an idiom about Rome. Problem was, my nerves traveled the speed of light whenever I thought of Dodge Charger Man. Let's hope I found him before he found me. I had a dark feeling I needed to be one step ahead.

————

Tito and I had a conversation first thing at ten minutes until six o'clock. Two cups of coffee later, he claimed Wilson and Whitehead had done time together during the summer in juvenile detention. They also lived in the same foster home for two years when younger. Can you just say, *Ding, ding, ding. Darcy won the first round?* Get this, their foster parents were in the printing business. Aaaaah, things kept getting better and better. Maybe they learned some tricks of the trade and could manufacture look-alike ID cards.

My working plan was to hang out in the library, Coach Wallace's office, or any other place that'd make me appear anonymous. I had plenty to think about from a recreational point of view, but from an academic point of view? Even my subconscious tried and failed to work out the mess. The night before, I'd dreamt I played Red-Rover, Red-Rover with Mr. Himmel and the Mother Mary. Mr. Himmel had on a ratty bathrobe, and the Mother Mary wore a football helmet along with a low-cut shirt that said "Equal Rights for Women."

Leaving that to incubate, I shut off the shower and quickly pulled on black, lacy boy shorts and my matching Miracle Bra. The Miracle Bra promised a cleavage for every unfortunate soul who bought into the hype. One look in the mirror made me want to take up the whole miracle concept with the Creator. My boobs were flatter than the plains of Nebraska.

Why the black lace routine? In several moments of stupidity, I couldn't stop thinking about that kiss with Dylan. I wanted to feel girlie. And desirable. And sexy girl underwear was supposed to bring out the vixen in me. Next were gray cable-knit tights, a jean miniskirt, and long-sleeved T-shirt with four Native Americans holding rifles on the front. Caption was "Homeland Security, Fighting Terrorism since 1492."

Obviously, I had an identity crisis.

I swiped my lashes with mascara and combed my tangled hair, covering my damp head with a gray toboggan that had a big white pompom on top. Not my usual commando-black gear for sleuthing excursions, but by God, it was daylight, and I needed to blend in. I hopped down the steps pulling on sand-colored UGGs, lifting Murphy's binoculars and compact camera from the hall closet.

As I munched a doughnut, I stole a look in the hall mirror reminding myself time was my enemy. But I was prepared. Binoculars? Check. Toboggan? Check. Camera? Check. Maniacal laugh? Check.

The sky was battleship gray, fog-heavy, and spitting snow like a ticked off camel. I shielded my eyes and jumped over a slushy puddle in the front yard, making my way to the Beemer, butchering the song "Jingle Bells." When I opened the door, Finn popped out and slid in the backseat, allowing me to ride shotgun. Finn was a blue-eyed Scandinavian blond, about six feet tall with a wide receiver's long and lean body. He was the type girl's dreamt about but didn't dare touch because they would incinerate with the heat. He had chin length tousled hair and thick black eyelashes with that Mumford & Sons thing going on—tweed pants, a white oxford rolled to his elbows, and a matching tweed vest. Bowler hat.

Finn was suddenly single as of the night before. His blink-and-you'll-miss-it relationship with sophomore, Gucci Grayson, was kaput. Finn happened to be fickle, so a longtime relationship for him ran about five weeks. All I knew was Dylan said he'd be riding with us *indefinitely* because something had *accidentally* scratched Finn's black Kia Forte. My guess? Gucci's ego and/or car keys. But what did he expect? The girl's name was Gucci.

"Bonjour, mon amie," he whistled out, a naughty grin on his face —and that was the problem. He was a ladies man and part of the appeal was a different accent each day. Apparently, right then was au Francais.

"Nasty," Dylan murmured, glancing at me from head to toe.

Nasty was one of those words in teen vernacular that could be good or bad. It ranked right up there with the word sick. I slid into the seat with a "Gracias," wondering if he meant it good or, God forbid, I smelled like trash.

"You look cute, sweetheart," Dylan added, leaning over to kiss my cheek.

I swear to God, I grabbed ahold of his jacket and yanked him over like a wild horse I wanted to break. While I tried to figure out what the freak came over me, Dylan said, "I love you, too, sweetheart, but I'm going to need to sit behind the wheel if I'm going to get us to school safely. But hold that thought, yeah?"

He cupped my face in his hand, and like an idiot, I turned into it and kissed his palm. Errrgh! My feelings betrayed me. I even started breathing heavily. Dylan's gaze grew heated, and something passed over his face that made my insides quiver.

He upgraded his grin to the Jason Derulo talk-dirty-to-me stare.

"In case you didn't get the message yesterday in the backseat of my car," he said, adding a flirtatious wink. "Our conversation is far from over."

I metaphorically stabbed myself...

Dylan was jock-juicy: letterman jacket, worn-out jeans with a small rip in the right knee, and his favorite Under Armour black and gray sneakers. The black coat clung to his chest and biceps like it'd been painted on, his jeans straining around the width of his thighs. I considered thanking him for the view but concluded it wasn't the right time or place, let alone proper.

I was the best friend.

Best friends hated each other as much as they loved one another.

Yup, Dylan and I totally found one another repulsive (NOT).

While Dylan answered a phone call from his mother, Finn leaned up and whispered into my ear. "You two have to work this thing out, mon amie. It's like the longest, most exhausting game of tennis I've ever watched."

I took a breath in through my nose. In the past four months, there had been conversations between Finn and me regarding my particular status with Dylan. I think they remained confidential, but Finn pushed the boundaries of loyalty. I swore him to secrecy—he swore he'd have my back—but I also knew how determined Dylan could be if he wanted something. And I ultimately didn't possess the things that bonded guys together...the 'nads.

I refused to think of Dylan and me together and changed the subject. "Do you have something for me?" I whispered back.

"Mon amie," he said more sternly. "Do you call him countless times a day?"

No answer.

"Do you hug only him like he's the best thing in the world?"

Still no answer.

"Do you seek only *him* when you're sad?"

Ugh, he had me.

"Do you want to break the Ten Commandments with him, mon amie? Answer. That's a big one."

I couldn't help it, but I broke into laughter. Dylan slid his eyes over like I'd lost my ever-lovin' mind. First off, I thought the Ten Commandments talked about adultery, and Dylan and I weren't married. But I didn't want to point out Finn's lack of sound theology since he probably knew of some obscure Hebrew text anyway. "You're not working that blond-headed mojo on me today, Finn," I whispered over my shoulder. "Maybe we can discuss things later when we're deciphering the mysteries of the world," I paused, "but now? No way."

Finn tucked a letter-sized, sealed envelope inside the crack between the seat and door. I knew immediately it contained the information I'd asked him to find. Information on the three IDs I'd found outside of The Double-B. Finn and I operated under a don't-ask, don't-tell policy. How he unearthed what he did was beyond me, but I wouldn't bite the hand that fed me.

Quickly stuffing the note in my backpack (hard to do since Dylan still held my left hand), I decided I'd read it during first period. Right then was stakeout time. The crime happened between seven o'clock and seven twenty. My hopes were the criminal had the same late habits of getting to school.

Next thing I knew, my ADHD grabbed ahold, and I'd stationed myself on top of the stinking building, facing Valley Lane. Thankfully, the fog hung so thick I could virtually cut it (*ding, ding,* point for my corner), because God knew I wouldn't get points for being discreet. Discretion didn't always cooperate when someone was a verb. How did I get here? While Dylan and Finn disappeared down the hall, I jogged to the second floor, shimmied my way up the downspout, and made like a statue.

Before I could blink, it was six forty-four. Oh. My. Freaking. Gosh. What was I thinking? My fingers were stuck to my gloves, my teeth chattered, and my butt cheeks had all but iced over. Pulling the miniature pair of binoculars from my coat pocket, I zipped my coat to my chin and hunkered down, not having a darn clue what in the heck—or *whom* in the heck—I was looking for. Cars slowly streamed into the parking lot like a bunch of elephants holding tails. Normally, I couldn't sit still. My legs bounced all day, or I twiddled my thumbs to the point of exhaustion. But right then, I had purpose. Purpose could make someone endure a lot of things the brain said was impossible.

My eyes were peeled on the spot where Coach's car had been parked (and right then again) in space 270. Still tie-dyed, still with WANKER, in all capital letters. If I had the time, I'd laugh. But the air was cold, and laughing felt like it'd hurt at twenty degrees. I'd requested he park in the same spot simply so I could see the reactions of those around him. Trouble was, I could barely see anything past my own breath.

It had grown colder. My nose hairs had fused together, and a quick glance at my watch showed the time at seven o'clock. I'd been outside for over twenty minutes and had run out of knuckles to crack. I was a Darcycicle. I should've worn jeans and peed one last time. My three cups of coffee had snuck up on me, and when I tried to think warm, happy thoughts all I did was picture the bursting of the Hoover Dam.

A whistle hummed through the air followed by a gale-force gust of wind from the west. It screamed like little girls on the front seat of a rollercoaster, ridiculously loud and then scary-soft like I had one foot in the grave. I slid forward three feet and almost flat-faced off the building. That seemed like an überly bad idea except two cars pulled into the empty spaces on the left side of Coach's car, my guess in spots 271 and 272. One guy exited a red Mustang. Another pulled the key from his silver Chevy Colorado extended cab and joined him. They circled together, pointed and gaped. Maybe they enjoyed the graffiti, but then again, maybe Darcy just got lucky. Trouble was, the fog was so thick I could almost cut it. All I could make out was brunette hair color on one of them, a black baseball cap on the other. Average height and builds, both wore jeans and dark down coats with hoods. Soundwise wasn't much better. All I heard was laugh, laugh, laugh...rib, rib, rib. Not enough to raise a suspicious hair on a Doberman.

When I stepped to the right for a better angle, a white van pulled alongside the Mustang and Chevy Colorado. The owner left it idling and then got out, performing two gimpy laps around Coach's car. He hobbled forward and high-fived one of the guys. Well, huh...that was as confusing as a darn Rubik's Cube. If I could only get to the ledge, I might snag a better look. Taking a few gingerly placed steps, I lifted the camera draped around my neck and clicked four pictures off in a row. But the guys weaved in and out of my view, at least a view I could safely have without falling over the ledge.

Before I knew it, I yelled, "Stand still!" Honestly, I think I shocked my own body. My heart pumped frantically...then skipped a few beats. Next thing I knew, the weather sirens sounded, signaling imminently bad weather. Those things were annoying enough when people were safely tucked inside their homes. Outside in the elements, perched in a crow's nest, was something else. I tumbled forward until I hung on the downward incline of the roof.

No, sirreee...this was not a setback.

I quickly crab-walked backward and couldn't hear a darn thing overtop the siren's blare. Once the wind picked up, it was though Divine Will had other plans. I literally fell-slash-scooted down on my butt, two feet from bouncing over the side. Jesus, Mary, and Joseph. I heard that song, "Do, Lord. Oh Do, Lord. Oh, Do Remember Me." I figured if I would go out at the tender age of sixteen, I might as well go out singing a gospel hymn. Hanging onto the ledge with one hand, I shakily picked the binoculars up in my left, staring at the van and two cars. The gimpy guy motored back to his van, still chatting over his shoulder. While I strained to decode his words, all of a sudden I heard a frantic, "Darcy!"

Well, I didn't know if frantic was the right word. Maybe it was feral.

Who knows how, but Dylan sniffed me out. Wind whipped underneath his jacket, and his black hair was in motion like he stood in the eye of a storm. Even though it took an Olympic effort to stay upright, he gradually pivoted around and saw me dangling mere feet from multiple broken bones and internal injuries. He slowly brought both arms up, leaving them clasped behind his neck.

He stared at me, I stared at him, and then he had a moment where the light bulb blinked on over his head.

That would fall under the category of *Darcy Will Be Darcy*.

After his what-the-heck moment ran its course, he started to yell but then figured I might fall if my ears took in one more decibel of anything. He then made some ridiculously stupid hand motions I interpreted as get the freak down. Slowly and methodically, I made my way south on the downspout, wiggling twenty feet until I met the second-floor stairs. I jogged down the flight into Dylan's waiting arms. There was no tear-filled reunion or "how was the view?" He yanked me inside the building so fast, my feet barely touched the ground.

Since freshman year, our lockers were beside one another because locker assignments were the same until graduation. Once we stood in front of numbers twelve and thirteen, he pointed an angry finger in my face. He opened his mouth to speak, closed it, and opened it again with more conviction.

"Stop," I said, holding out a hand. "Is what you're planning to say patient, loving, and kind?" After a violent heck-no shake of his head, I added, "Then you shouldn't say it, D. Besides, I'm wearing black lacy underwear. A thong. Well part thong because it's a little more than a piece of thread. Don't I get points for that?"

Dylan wasn't fazed...didn't even suck in a breath...a response more depressing than my lack of a love life. He placed his palm against my chest, backing me up against the locker until my head banged.

"You've got to be frigging kidding me," he barked.

I stifled a giggle, knowing full well it'd only make things worse to laugh in his face. "Walkie-talkie?" I dumbly asked.

"Walkie-talkie," he mouthed, but even that resonated like blood and thunder.

Oh. God. Walkie-talkie was his name for a lecture. The lecture ranged from bearing the outside elements, to dying-before-my-time, to the shama lama, ding-dong because someone could've looked up my skirt. I appropriately agreed, looked sad at one interval, and then somehow managed a tear. I guess I saw the error of my ways, but maybe my calling in life was to be a statistic of what not to do... or how to get killed.

Chapter Seven

IT GIRL

The setting was third period, career development.

Most days I listened to students talk about their dream jobs—doctor, lawyer, professional athlete, yada-yada, whatever. I never heard anyone dream of working sixty-hour weeks at minimum wage. High school was the time where teachers planted those seeds of hope: *if you do abc, then xyz's going to happen.* In other words, if I studied hard and tried my best, the Fates would reward my hard work. Occasionally, that rang true. Others, I was left wondering, *Why me?*

I paused for a few moments, listening to my teacher promise the world. Meh. My brain shut down. I believe it was one of those survival things.

My world turned upside down when I was nine years old, which happened to be the last Christmas season my mother and I spent together. I vaguely remember what she smelled like: sort of like coconut cream or lemon meringue pie. And if someone was a self-professed sugar junkie like me, she was an epicurean delight. I used to mock her facial expressions, throwing my head back with her belly laugh when I was alone in the bathroom. I'd hide in her closet, walk in her shoes, and apply her makeup until all I had left were empty containers. Over and over, I told myself if I could get a fraction—a zillionth of what she had—then maybe things would be fine...for both of us. But I found out the hard way wishing things to happen didn't always make them a reality.

Another Christmas had come, and she wouldn't show up under my tree.

In times of desperation, I caught a glimmer of a thing called hope. I suppose hope was what got me through the day. Unfortunately, hope didn't hang around long. What usually worked in times of hopelessness was to go after the impossible and make it the possible.

That's me: Darcy Walker, hope-bringer to the masses.

You're welcome, America.

Case number one: who stole Tito Westbrook's identity? Since Tito's source claimed he was a teenager from Valley, my hunch was he might be in Coach Wallace's file. So interviewing those three was key. Case number two: who painted Coach Wallace's car? Even though the weather and Dylan cut my stakeout short, all things considered, I had some things to think about, i.e., Mustang and Chevy Colorado, white van, pictures to download, what was the connection...?

Bottom line, would it mean anything?

Dependent upon the sky and season, sometimes we would go to school in the dark and return in the dark. Looking outside, the light flurry of snow swirled into something more fierce, blowing sideways into wind shears, rattling street signs, and overturning trashcans like the first stages of a tornado. Cars traveled at a snail's pace, and like earlier that morning, a weather alert pierced the air. With a loud crack, the sky lit up like a Roman candle.

Simultaneously, the overhead speaker sounded with Principal Grim Ward calmly requesting we get in disaster mode. Disaster mode came ingrained in my DNA, people. Whenever I entered a building, I checked emergency exits first and decided which windows I'd break if I got backed against a wall. Well, let's just say I *tried* when I didn't fall victim to my ADHD, but everyone didn't think like me. There were a lot of Chicken Littles on the planet... namely Ivy Morrison.

While the teacher waved her arms to get control of the class, I pulled the photographs out of my file, along with the names from Finn, and shoved them up under my Homeland Security T-shirt.

Leaving our things at our desks, we single-filed into the hall in a semi-orderly manner. Before I could mutter Susan B. Anthony, the bulk of the females grabbed onto the nearest male.

Seriously, that set the feminist movement back by a decade.

Ivy, the biggest wuss, had plastered herself to Finn's side, batting her fake eyelashes against her fake-baked face.

Finn and Grumpy were in my class, and both were charter members of my secret brother society. Jon, er Grumpy, was brother number one, yet he might be the most reluctant. We became blood kin when we wrecked on his dirt bike freshman year. We didn't physically share bodily fluids. We held up our mangled limbs in a sign of mutual solidarity with the commitment of 'til death do we part. Gradually, I added other kindred misfits into my brotherhood, and I became Darcy Walker, AKA a teenage godfather. Finn was brother number two because he was...well, Finn. A brainiac whose skills I occasionally needed. The rule of our commitment was simple. Loyalty. We lied for one another. We spied for one another. And in Grumpy's case, I spied on his crushes. He'd been infatuated with Ivy Morrison, Trudi Hatchett, and Clementine Miriam Rabinowitz since freshman year.

Clementine seemed sweet and showed he had good taste. Ivy and Trudi confirmed he was a freaking moron because Ivy was pure witch, and Trudi was a minion with man-hands. Like Clementine, she had dark hair and eyes, but her features weren't as refined and sculpted symmetrically. Her body was disproportionate with a big nose, big hips, and hands that belonged on Goliath. Thing was, she had money—and a good stylist could camouflage where your mother's and father's genes screwed you.

Grumpy was smiling, the equivalent of seeing little green men. He had Clementine on one arm, Trudi on the other. That left me bringing up the rear, staring at all of their butts. Trouble was, when I made my way down the hall, I got shoved into a group from a different class. We huddled on the floor, shoulder-to-shoulder, sneaker-to-sneaker, and butt-to-butt. Realizing I was in a race against the clock, I ripped open the sealed envelope from Finn.

He'd typed up a detailed report that rivaled a brief from the FBI. The social security card of Lucas Carlton belonged to a baby boy, six months old. His mother had left her purse in her shopping cart unattended at Meijer and reported it stolen weeks earlier.

The second victim, Kelley Lowder, lost her Visa during a wedding party weekend at The Horseshoe Casino. She had no clue she'd been violated (the bride and groom paid for all expenses) until she'd returned home and discovered the thief spent one thousand dollars at the nearest Coach store, bought curly fries at Arby's, several Caffé Americanos at Starbucks, and pumped gas.

The third victim, Lindsee Maroni, had her check card eaten by an ATM at Speedway. The station manager returned it to her, and she thought she would be fine, but unbeknownst to anyone, the ATM had a machine called a skimmer attached to it. A skimmer was camouflaged to look exactly like a component of the ATM, but in actuality it was a small computer storing the data from each card once the card was slid through. As a result, the user's bank account, social security number, password, address, anything else the bank had on the card's magnetic strip was free game. The thief would then simply detach the skimmer and take it home. That particular thief had the capacity to manufacture cards because when Lindsee discovered her bank account had been cleaned out, her bank contacted the merchants in question who had actual credit card receipts...new receipts...and a signature eerily similar to Lindsee's.

So the thief not only skimmed her information but also made an entirely new card containing the same data, with a practiced signature.

The fact Finn had successfully exposed that information was absurd.

The fact I'd asked him to do so was even more absurd.

Pulling the three photographs from under my shirt—along with the faxed photo from Tito—I resolved to use my time wisely by interviewing the poor fools next to me.

I got a lot of, "No, never seen him...big guy...he's weird...what did they do?" But there was nothing definitive from a credible source. Then I heard a voice—a voice that'd be burned into my brain eternally as nothing more than Beelzebub's brother.

Oliver "Bean" Anatoly was the biggest ponkey who ever walked the earth's surface.

"Walker!" he shouted. I swear to God, if there were a beach around, I'd dig my way to freaking China.

I shifted my weight and slid farther down the wall. "Walker!" he screamed louder. Bean had a loud voice—possibly the biggest ever placed on a human's head—but he somehow found an even higher pitch. "What were you doing on the roof this morning?" he finished.

When I gave him a surprised, who-me look, he laughed hysterically. "You're so stupid."

He got a takes-one-to-know-one stare. I didn't particularly like Bean. Maybe it was because I saw in him what reminded me of *me*—unstable, unpredictable, with a mountain of OCD quirkiness. Bean could be the poster child for *Things That Can Go Wrong When You Never Read a Fashion Magazine*. He had glasses two inches thick, hair balding at the crown, and wore all blue with a pocket protector and gel pens. What hair remained had been styled in a bowl cut he'd been rockin' since second grade.

How did Oliver get the nickname of Bean? In third grade, he stuck a lima bean up his nose to see how long it'd take to germinate. The answer? Four days. Sure enough, a little green sprout was seen when we shoved a flashlight up his nostril during classroom changes. Forever after, he was known as Bean, the kid who shoved a bean up his nose. Unfortunately, I became known as the kid who dared him.

I was thinking he held a grudge. "Nice to know you're still a ponkey," I mumbled.

"Ponkey?" the boy beside me asked.

I explained ponkeys were a cross between a punk and a jackass. At least, I got a laugh.

While teachers paced up and down the hall, Bean wriggled over the tan linoleum, army-style, and squeezed in on the opposite side. He pulled a folded-up sheet from his back pocket.

"What's that?" I asked, pitching my chin toward the paper.

"Voting ballot. It's that time of year for the It Girl election." I raised a brow. "Yeah," he continued. "The guys from the in-crowd," *believe me, I stifled a huge laugh here*, "decide who is this year's It Girl. Then we rank the runners-up."

"Runners-up?" the guy to my side wanted clarified.

"Yeah, we call them Hot Girls," Bean explained. "Last year, you were a Hot Girl, Darcy. Actually first on the list. Although there might've been problems with the balloting. At least, that was the rumor."

Well, excuuuuuuuse me.

I choked down the overwhelming urge to spit on him. "I'm sure the balloting was fine," I said self-righteously. "So who was I behind?"

"Behind Brynn Hathaway, there's a list of nine other girls."

My ears started to bleed. Of course it was Brynn. That was like saying grass was green and dogs hated cats. That stuff was written in the stars.

"So am I number two again?" I asked hopefully.

Bean looked like someone shoved him in front of a moving car. "Um...no. Geeky girls are out. Brains are in."

I shot up to my feet, shoving my arms on my hips, defiant like a mule that refused to move. I didn't care who saw me, and I didn't care I was supposed to be hunkered down like a good little girl waiting for a storm to kill us all. "I've got brains," I said snorting. Bean glanced up, raising a brow. "I do!" I shouted and then articulated all of the things I did where I showed my smarts. Eh, the list was small. So be it. I asked, "What does it take to go from last year's It Girl—"

"Runner-up," he corrected. "Runners-up are Hot Girls."

"Last year's runner-up Hot Girl," I repeated sarcastically, "to not even blipping on the radar?"

Someone yelled, "Sit down, Walker!" and when I spun around, I tripped over Bean's boat of a foot and took a header—my legs twisting painfully in the scorpion over my back.

God hated me. He really, really did.

"And that's why you dropped out of the Top Ten," Bean mumbled as explanation. "I'd tell you it's an honor to be nominated, but I stopped lying a year ago. All that matters is making the list."

I found it weird that I crawled back to a sitting position, like making a fool of myself was as expected as a sunrise. Maybe that was why I tumbled from the list. I was too weird to date.

"Who is the It Girl this year?" the guy on the other side asked.

"Of course, Brynn is number one," Bean said, almost drooling. "But Rudi Morgan is number two, by only one vote. Just you wait.

She's invading the school. And I'm going to take her and the rest of the list on a date before the year ends."

A smile crept up my lips, quirking all the way to the sky. Rudi *deserved* to be the It Girl. One of the few girlfriends I had, she was a colleague of mine at The Double-B and teeny-tiny at barely five feet and less than one hundred pounds. She had big brown eyes, cool Ben Franklin glasses, and brunette hair styled in an asymmetrical chin-length bob.

If I were a guy, I would've voted her number one. Trouble was, she was deaf and dirt poor. She could speak in an underwater-muffled sort of way, but she preferred to sign, lip read, or have someone interpret. Being the almost It Girl would make anyone think she'd have plenty of dates—she'd didn't. Not only did she have to fight a language barrier, but also the fact she was just too good.

Most guys found good a foreign concept.

"I don't think we've talked this much since counseling," Bean said to me. "Do you remember?"

That would fall under the category of *There Are No Words*. Bean and I saw the same therapist, and as much as I tried to avoid him, we ultimately wound up on the same weekly rotation. After two years, I'd sprung the joint, and I briefly wondered if Bean ever had. Bean suddenly snagged all four photographs from my hand, pulling them up to his eyes. I feared he'd blow the lid off of my plan but instead of decking him, I flat-out lied.

I took a deep breath, jutting my jaw out with confidence. "School contest," I fudged. "Just like yours. All of them have come into some money, and it's my job to track them down."

No one questioned or even cared. That was one of the benefits of a school the size of VHS. Contests, raffles, and split-the-pots were constantly in play. Last I remember, Bean ran with a seedy crowd. Maybe that was destiny speaking. I adjusted the wattage on my smile and started the twenty questions. "Do you know them, Bean?"

I fluttered my eyelashes flirtatiously, choking down the vomit that reminded me Bean was Grade A ponkey.

Bean flipped through all four photographs, stopping to wipe his nose on the back of his sleeve. "Detention," he said when he was finished. "They're part of the Saturday morning crowd. These two," he muttered, pausing at the coffee-stained photograph and the one Rookie was investigating, "I've never seen before."

That stripped the wind right from my psychotic sails. When I debated a sob, Bean slid them across the hall to an equally geeky friend of his. My palms started itching, and before I could get my fingers back on those photographs, they'd gone through about ten people. What the heck, I went for it. I cupped my hands over my mouth in a loud whisper, "Could you write on the backs of the pics if you have classes with any of them?"

There was no protest. Interested folks simply took the pink gel pen Bean pitched, jotting down notes like it was a classroom assignment. While the sky cracked with angry sounds from Mother Nature, Assistant Principal Vance Unger scurried up and down the hall like we were one foot from the grave. It reminded me that no matter where a person came from, at the end of the day, everyone was one and the same...no matter what we had in our brain or what number we were on the It Girl list.

AP Unger stopped directly in front of me with a frown that'd scare the hair off of Sasquatch. "Walker, you can't wear a shirt to school with guns on it."

I glanced down, totally forgetting I'd worn my "Homeland Security" T-shirt with Native Americans, proudly holding their rifles.

I grinned and said, "I'm celebrating my people." Murphy had Native American roots. One could see the chiseled features all over his face. My skin was darker than normal, but the rest was watered down by European influences.

"You're advertising terrorism," he said, frowning deeply.

"No, I'm advertising Homeland Security which *combats* terrorism. Sounds to me like you're discriminating against my people and culture. Or maybe you're a liberal. Liberals believe we can love people into good behavior. Murphy will straight up tell you that's not possible. He's tried and failed—and has the battle wounds to prove it," I said, adding a giggle.

"Oh. My. God," he groaned. "You've given me a migraine."

AP Unger and I had a tempestuous relationship. In fact, when a gun-wielding student chased me last spring, he took a couple of bullets as he ran in hot pursuit. I rushed to his side when he fell, triaged as best as possible, and took his cell phone to call for help under the alias of Jester. He had no memory of giving me his phone, and I accidentally chucked it in the water when said student breathed down my neck like a fire-breathing dragon on drugs. In fact, AP Unger barely remembered getting shot—only that he woke up in the hospital a week later.

Jester, my alter ego, was safe...for the moment.

By the thank-you-God look on his face, we were destined for an early dismissal. There were no two sweeter words in the student language than "snow day," but right then, that spelled disaster. He gave me his we'll-discuss-later frown and hotfooted it down the hall.

Bean propped himself up, his body falling into mine. "Can I help with your project?"

Bean acted like we were in this thing together. I woke up in the morning thinking I was best friends with Mr. Do-The-Right-Thing (um, Dylan), and then I find out I'm running deals with ponkeys. I had to admit it was an exceptional idea.

When I did nothing but choke on my own spit, Bean pushed for an answer, "Yeah?"

I looked at Bean. He wasn't going away. In fact, he acted like a stray dog that'd finally found a home.

"Fine," I heard myself saying. "But this is only between you and me. One slip up, Bean, and you're out."

Bean excitedly nodded up and down, already giving advice. "Why don't you give everyone your cell number and have them call if they find anything out?"

I reluctantly returned Bean's nod. He had a point. I could look for these guys, or I could really be stupid and have them come looking for me.

Chapter Eight

POLITICAL FOOTBALL

*E*veryone that jotted down so much as a pencil smear got my digits. I tacked on the request to feed information on anything they'd hear about Coach Wallace's car too. My deal with Coach didn't stipulate I had to fly solo, and even if it did, I wasn't above bending the letter of the law. Against my better judgment, I confessed to Bean that a school contest was merely a front. I didn't say the front was actually to out an identity thief. I allowed him to believe the front was simply to find out who'd wronged Coach. When he continued to act all Dr. Watson to my Sherlock Holmes, I commissioned him to interview two students Coach thought might have motives (Owen Lancaster and Wyatt Brown). I realized I'd have to sift through a lot of Beanisms to get to the truth, but my gut wasn't leading me toward those two anyway.

Buses had been called to school early, and after a quick check-in at homerooms, we were released to the pick-up line or parking lot. Finn, Grumpy, and I took off toward the gym to meet up with Dylan, our ride home. Grumpy complained, or should I say *mumbled*, how Clementine Miriam Rabinowitz needed to date his Gentile body. Grumpy could have his finger lopped off, and he'd barely crack a wrinkle. But Clementine brought a whole herd of mumble I'd never experienced.

He ran a hand through the tangled mass on his head society called hair. "I want to date her, and get her a nice Christmas gift, or

Hanukkah, or whatever," he said to whomever would listen. "I don't know what Jews do. What do Jews do, Walker?"

Finn and I never slowed our gait. Grumpy didn't want a response, and the wallflower in me sure as heck didn't know how to advise him. While he fretted over his private life, I worried about the promises I'd made. Like a gift from Heaven (or elsewhere), I got the bright idea to tap into the school's database. Due to Bean's suggestion (and the notes students scrawled on the backs of the photographs), I had a "semi" idea of the days of Slapstick Wilson and Damon Whitehead. What I needed was their full schedules, which would up my chances of bumping into them. Then I could stake them out. See how weird or unweird they seemed.

So whose computer to use? Since we were on our way to the gym, Coach's computer seemed as good as any. But let's face it, I wasn't sure it'd work, or if I was smart enough to resurrect what should've been put down decades earlier.

My iPhone belted out "Grandma Got Run Over by a Reindeer," and a glance at the number showed Murphy's frowning mug. Whenever there's an early dismissal, the school sends a robocall, informing parents their kids were being sent home, unattended. For most, that was not a worry. For Murphy, it was like finding out a fox was in the hen house.

"Hey, Murphy," I greeted.

"Hop on your broom, kid, and hurry home."

I took a second to laugh. "Finn, Grumpy, and I are meeting up with Dylan. Then we're going to smoke pot, rob the liquor store, and make naked snow angels in the front yard. Not necessarily in that order."

"Watch out for frostbite," he grunted. "And hey, tell Finn I think your toaster has some sort of toaster virus. I could swear it said, 'Mmmmmmm, girl, your butt looks good in those jeans' when a waffle popped up."

I repeated the message to Finn who gave me a devilish wink as Murphy unloaded a dial tone.

Finn invented a talking toaster as a gift for my sixteenth birthday. If a Pop-Tart was set on the lowest setting, it whistled out an, *Oooh, that feels good.* The hottest growled, *Oooh, baby. Gimme more of that burn.* Anything in between was so off-color it made me feel like I'd lost my virginity.

That got me to thinking. If I wanted to tap into school property, who better to assist than someone smart enough to do it with as little of a conscience as me?

While Grumpy scouted around for Dylan, Finn leisurely tagged alongside me, sawing logs even though his eyes were wide open. No kidding...I too felt school was a snoozefest. I blurted out, "I need to break into Coach's computer."

Finn was a little too street smart to try and manipulate. He knew something was up, and when I put my finger to my lips in a, "Shhh" manner—mimicking a six foot two posture with bulging muscles (ahem, Dylan)—he grinned, mouthing in French, "Oui."

We quickened our pace, juking around stragglers, taking a left at the water fountain and freshman lockers. The gym provided a quick cut-through to any side entrance, and it was occupied enough for us to slide by Coach Wallace undetected. He moved a portable wheeled cart around the floor, picking up basketballs and other items left haphazardly in the rush.

While Grumpy aimed for him, Finn and I stole inside Coach's office, immediately getting down to business. He picked up the computer, looking on the back for a serial number as if he searched for gold. I dug down in my purse and pulled out a new stopwatch I'd bought to replace the one I'd destroyed. I left it on Coach's desk with a big note in red lipstick that said, *Love, Darcy*. I didn't use paper, people. I scrawled it on the wood.

Ask me if I cared.

When finished, I staged myself as lookout and explained what I needed.

That little work of sin meant nothing to Finn, and if it did, he was smart enough to know it wasn't the time for questions, let alone explanations. He slid into the black leather chair, ravaging the school's computer like a raccoon does trash. After a few keystrokes, lo and behold, a screen popped up that said Valley High School Registrar.

I heard Beethoven's Fifth Symphony in my mind.

Da-da-da, dum. Da-da-da dum...

Taking one last glance toward the gym, I watched Grumpy

scratch the back of his neck and wonder how in the world the two of us fell off the grid. Dylan paced next to him with a deep frown, pulling his cell phone out of his pocket.

Immediately, I clicked mine off, attempting to do the same with Finn's, but I found his wasn't even charged. "Hurry," I said, giggling out an order. Finn typed a little too leisurely for me to feel comfortable. At the risk of feeling stupid, I decided to take his ease as a good thing and picked up the photo of Coach's wife. It was turned upside down and backward, an angle different than the day before. I strode over, dusted it on my leg, and then set it aright.

That made me think of the future...

...and the girl-next-door to Dylan.

I said to Finn, "Can I ask you a question?" Finn nodded, still looking at the screen. "Have you heard anything about a relationship with Dylan and Brynn Hathaway? I know they went out this past summer. Dylan told me. He even said it didn't mean anything. But honestly, I've kind of found myself pulling away since our car accident. All I know is I bring trouble along with me, and I don't want Dylan or *you*, for that matter, to be on the receiving end of the crap I conjure up. And look at Grumpy. He seems to be more traumatized than all of us. He's a walking mood machine."

Finn aborted the typing and narrowed his blue eyes into glaciers. He then opened his mouth and snapped it shut. With a headshake, he finally murmured, "No one wants to be strung along, but there are some things you need to understand about Dylan. Number one..."

"Walker!" That from the door.

I didn't even have time to form a response. All I could do was turn around, hands up in surrender.

It was Grumpy...no Dylan present.

Thank God for the little things.

"What are you two doing?" he barked. "Taylor's going bonkers probably turning over every car in the lot."

"Merde," I heard Finn say...no kidding.

Grumpy schlepped in and fell down in a black folding chair. He didn't push for an explanation. His mind was elsewhere—wondering, my guess, if he needed to convert to Judaism.

But oh, I thought the coast was clear too soon. Seconds later,

Coach Wallace followed, expecting to find nothing but an empty office, but instead found his own personal effects being raped and pillaged. He went beet-red, all his energy focused on me instead of Finn who couldn't have cared less if a raging bull was headed straight for his gut. Coach's voice gruffed like an angry bear. "I would be tempted to say this was the Nerd Squad," he said, "but that'd insinuate there were three brains in this room."

I felt a laugh building but somehow managed to look offended. I strode forward, hoping to shield Finn's indiscretions. "I have confidence issues already, Coach. My therapist wouldn't like your phrasing."

He bobbed his afro'd head from side to side, attempting to peer around me toward Finn. "What are you up to, Lively?"

Finn ignored him, typing in names, and hitting the print button.

"There's nothing in here but us drifters," I told him.

Coach shook his head slowly, his frown growing more conspicuous. "Drifters or grifters?" he muttered. "Because I'm sure your pretty little smile swindled these two upstanding players of mine to do something they know I wouldn't approve of. And what exactly would that offense be?"

What we were doing was barely legal. All right, it wasn't legal at all, but when I had a job to do, sometimes I had to rationalize the crap out of my assignment. I opted for a version of the truth, telling him I had a brainstorm regarding who painted his car (um, no), and how I planned to catch them, not mentioning Finn dug through school records on possible identity thieves. I then went for broke, being overly dramatic about how I needed money, or I'd be forced into a life of walking dogs and picking up their poop.

I actually sniveled.

Luckily, Coach didn't care because he pulled his buzzing cell phone out of his hoodie pocket , glanced at the number with a smile, and exited the room.

"Facebook girl?" I yelled to his backside.

He ignored me with a snap of his hand...holy crap on a cracker. Was the Milky Way about to collapse?

Grumpy leaned back in his seat, his eyes brimming with laughter. "Did I hear this correctly? You're trying to figure out who painted Coach's car? You couldn't catch a fly if your big mouth was a Venus fly trap," he said with a chuckle.

Grumpy had a deep scar in his right eyebrow where he'd head-butted Finn in one of those guy moments where they tried to act cooler than they actually were. His eyebrow came out the loser. It was puffy with a dozen imperfect dots, appearing to have been stitched together by the guy who finished last in medical school. I got so angered at the insult I hauled off and smacked him twice in the scar.

"Use your words, Walker!" he bellowed.

I didn't have time to use anything because the guy that I beat up earlier (well, slapped around because he accosted the other girl) jumped me from behind, pulling me out the door by my hair. One moment I laid sideways on the tile, the next I laid on my back and was so shocked-out I feared I'd have a stroke. Once through the door, I somehow made it to vertical but not before he grabbed me by the hair and shoved me face-first up against the gym wall, banging my forehead so hard my teeth crunched and rattled.

"I'm going to kill you!" he barked.

Here was the thing. The guy was shorter than me. And maybe even weighed less. Problem was, when a guy was mad, testosterone always overpowered estrogen. It was an oversight the powers-that-be should've thought through during creation.

With every ounce of fiber in my being, I elbowed him in the gut, turned, and...spit on him. Yeah, that felt good.

"You...*blankety-blanking, blank-blank-blank*," he cursed. I'd heard a lot of cursing in my life, but that guy took the cake, and I'm pretty sure Heaven just struck his name from the "maybe" list.

In what had only been a few seconds, Grumpy tore through the door like a bat running out of Hell, aiming for the guy I referred to as Jerkwad. True to a real brother's personality—you know, I can talk about her, but you can't—Grumpy went ape poopoo and dove into the fight.

He pounded him once.

Twice.

And would've gone for a dozen more, if time permitted.

After a few headshakes, I realized Grumpy wasn't in control of the fight. As much as he'd been dishing out, the other guy was meeting and occasionally exceeding. That was odd because Grumpy packed a mean punch. Made me think Jerkwad was fueled by something other than anger and food. I dove back in the middle, not having any kind of form or end game in mind other than for Jerkwad to shut the freak up.

My bra strap ripped, my tights got a hole in the knee, and God Bless Native Americans, but the ponkey tore the shirt of my people. The lace of my black bra peeked through the tear, right there for everyone to see it was padded!! Ugh, the nerve! My instincts said to bite him, but I read somewhere cannibals could get some sort of brain disease. Instead, I chose the happies. Murphy said a swift shot to the groin would down any man.

Unfortunately, that message didn't make it to the execution part of my brain. So I just swung. I swung for the moon but got nothing but air and Jerkwad's butt in my face.

FYI, I stunk at fighting. It was almost embarrassing.

Grumpy's eyes had gone wide, and he had both thumbs trained on Jerkwad's eye sockets. Oh crap. Oh, crap, oh crap, oh crap. I heard Dylan's running gait thunder across the floor. Dylan had a presence, like energy flowed off of him. Sometimes it was good. Sometimes it was so bad only a moron wouldn't be scared. I peered through my hair that had flipped over my face and crawled out of the pile. My scalp hurt. Scratches marred both arms and legs. And I felt cold air on one of my boobs. All I could hope for was that Jerkwad didn't carry rabies.

When Dylan got closer, his face paled and his gaze went wide, giving my body a once-over like I was one step from a medevac. He went breathless, his chest not even heaving, eyes blinking from stark, cold fear to undeniable fury. I'd found when Dylan was really angry and wrestling with adrenaline, he was almost statue-like. As if his body conserved energy for one burst of power that'd be cataclysmic.

Dylan literally picked Grumpy and Jerkwad up by the scruff, but Jerkwad squared his stance, shoved his hand in his back pocket... and pulled out a knife. Popping the six-inch blade to an up position, he brought the crazy and took a swipe at Dylan's gut. Dylan jumped back with a curse.

Dylan clenched and unclenched his left hand, taking one methodical step forward. Not worried in the slightest.

Grumpy bent at the waist, trying to retrain his lungs how to breathe. "He beat the crap out of Walker, man. He came at her first...and slammed her head up against the wall. Do something."

OHHHHHH. CRAAAAPPPPP.

Another step. And another. "Let me take a guess," Dylan said lowly. "You're the asshole who Darcy stopped from molesting that girl."

Jerkwad squirmed.

Hemmed and hawed.

Dylan glanced to the ceiling. "Well, thank you, God," he seethed sarcastically, "because I'd scheduled a little meet-and-greet with you anyway. Now it seems like you've been delivered up to me instead."

"I *do* want to kill her," Jerkwad hissed, adding a psychopathic laugh. "And by God, I *will*."

Dylan dove (jaws and fists clenched), and took Jerkwad out in a rib-cracking explosion. The knife skyrocketed, arcing up into a "U," and coming to rest point-side down underneath the basketball goal. Jerkwad writhed for two-point-something seconds (probably a reflex) and then flattened like he'd gotten trampled by a herd of angry elephants. Dylan pushed up on his hands, his I'm-going-to-play-with-you face grinning. But before he got off a shot with a fist, Finn met him in a full-bodied tackle, and they slid across the recently waxed floor like stones in a game of curling.

Dylan immediately scrambled to his feet, but Grumpy lunged at him with his eyes closed. Guess he expected pain.

Dylan got knocked on his butt twice, trying to get to Jerkwad, which only made him angrier. Coach Wallace instantly appeared, distraught, quickly surmising Finn and Grumpy merely tried to keep Dylan's beast on the chain. He wrenched his way between them, tailed by an even more distraught Principal Grim Ward.

Can you say...W. T. FFFuuuuuuudddGE!!

Grim Ward ran the place, and by goodness, we barely knew what the man looked like. I'd always thought he was of the mole genus because he rarely saw the light of day.

Coach blinked rapidly, pointing a shaking finger in Grumpy's face while he bent over and angrily snatched a still-wrestling Dylan and Finn off the floor. "What in God's name happened here?" he barked.

Grumpy served up an explanation.

He raised his shirt, spitting blood into the hem, furiously pointing to Jerkwad who laid there, still not able to reclaim his breathing. "He hit Walker, Coach!" he barked back. "He claims he's going to kill her, but I'll kill him first. I want his dead body to lie on the pavement so the vultures can pick away at it."

And that was why I loved Grumpy...

We all heard something. Maybe it was Dylan breathing. Maybe it was Dylan's heart beating. Whatever the case, the six of us took pause. Like people do before they go down one of those shark tanks and find their teeth look bigger than they initially thought. There was a flash of speed, and that time, Coach and Finn brought Dylan down in a body slam.

I needed to barf.

Did they not know they'd asked Dylan to willingly castrate himself?

Finn had one swinging arm and Coach had the other. Both were flung around like ragdolls in an angry dog's mouth. Coach's glasses went airborne, and he caught an elbow to the jaw—Finn took one to the cheek when he dodged Dylan's headbutt. They made no headway at corralling Dylan until Principal Ward wormed his way between them. Principal Ward was a large man—head and shoulders above most—but he was no match for Dylan when his Darcy-switch had been flipped. His comb-over began to flap, this way and that. Last I saw him, he didn't even have a comb-over. Once again, the mole thing.

Finn, Coach, and Principal Ward frantically locked on my gaze, begging for an assist. Pure unadulterated fear froze my body in place. After a few breaths, I fearfully tripped forward and braced both palms on Dylan's chest—an effort to calm but push further away if need be. "I'm good," I whispered.

"He hurt you," he growled. Fat tears immediately spilled down my cheeks, and I was pretty sure I had raccoon eyes from the sweaty brawl. When Dylan saw them, he clenched his teeth so hard it was a wonder he didn't crack a molar. Dylan was *thisclose* to doing permanent damage. I watched in tense anticipation, knowing he could flatten the whole place if he so chose.

Pinky swear, his eyes demanded.

I searched for a pinky swear loophole and came up empty-handed. I gave him a subliminal I'm-good face, but by the heavy emotion crackling between us, I got the impression he didn't buy it. I should've lied. At that, Dylan's anger revved again, and after a few shoves and words students shouldn't say in front of their principal, Dylan eventually heeled enough for Principal Ward to demand a reason for the rumble.

Coach verbally stumbled around, but as I brushed imaginary dust from my clothing, I calmly dispensed the details. "Jerkwad here fondled a girl yesterday, I stuck up for her, he came at me like a spider monkey, Jon defended me, we all started punching, he pulled a knife on Dylan, blah, blah, blah, it got ugly."

I made an exaggerated switchblade movement of decapitation, promising I'd find my girl cojones if he came at me again. Well, at least I planned to find them. Then I dumbly added—and let me emphasize the *dumb*—"You'd better find a safe house, Jerkwad, because I'm not through with you yet."

Then I giggled.

Giggled, I say. *Who giggles when your boob is practically hanging out?*

Principal Ward mulled those words over so long it began to make me nervous. Slowly, he walked underneath the basketball goal and pried the knife from the hardwood where it had firmly planted itself, pointing north. Once he flipped the blade down, with one slow blink, he drilled his angry brown eyes into Jerkwad, then to Grumpy, and ended on me. "Detention," he snapped, "all three of you!"

Well, well, well, words escaped me.

I slid my eyes to him, painting on a flabbergasted face—letting him know, point blank, he'd blown it. He'd blown it by incarcerating the kids who were the heroes. AP Unger and Murphy were friends—as in "real" friends. In fact, they dueled in *Ruzzle* almost nightly. That didn't always bode well for me, but I could promise AP Unger would've handled the situation differently. Principal Ward and Murphy didn't have a relationship. In fact, he'd just guaranteed Murphy would be his mortal enemy.

Pardon me, but the lousy, donkey lovin', sack of shiz deserved it.

Dylan's words rang like a gunshot through the room. "No frigging way," he hissed, turning to him. "Some guy hit my best friend— a girl—her clothes are visibly damaged, and you're okay with that? The guy has a knife. He took a swipe at me, for God's sake, and should be expelled because of what he would've done with it had I not jumped out of the way."

The record player screeched in my mind.

I'd cheated the Grim Reaper...AGAIN...how much longer could I outrun his scythe?

I buried my head in Dylan's chest, and God love him, he kissed the top of my head. "I'm going to leave this world early, aren't I?" I mumbled into his shirt. "And this was my best bra. Black and lacy, the recipe for sexy according to last month's *Cosmopolitan*." Good grief. I'd lost my mind. I said that out loud...right there in front of God and everybody. I glanced up into his face, tears stinging the backs of my eyes.

Dylan rubbed circles around my back.

"Please, don't punish them," Dylan begged Principal Ward. "Darcy and Jon are like brothers and sisters. They fight, but if someone else messes with the other, we get involved. This guy hit a girl and practically molested another. Doesn't that count for something? You should be patting them on the back, not punishing them for having character."

Principal Ward didn't consider us all bros. He wanted blood.

My hands shook a little—maybe that was shock. Maybe for the first time in my sorry life I had a normal freaking reaction until...

I got to thinking. Detention wasn't such a bad idea. Maybe detention was where I *needed* to be. Bean said Slapstick Wilson and Damon Whitehead were practically founding members. While there, I could also throw out random questions about Coach's car being someone's art project.

Simple math.

At that time, Finn sidled up alongside Dylan, giving me a nod that said, *I got the information, and my genius powers gave you something a little extra*. He threw his arm around Dylan's shoulder before Dylan could dislocate Principal Ward's. "It's a lovely day, n'est-ce pas?" he asked him.

Dylan blinked at the statement.

Blinked like the whole thing was so preposterous it had to be an optical illusion.

Grumpy held his chin high, blatantly daring Principal Ward to throw him in the school's boot camp for losers. "Listen, if that's how you want to play this thing, then go ahead and put us in lockdown. You're screwing up, Principal Ward, and you're going to know it by the time everyone's parents get an earful of what happened here."

Yeah, it'd be Valley's next political football if I had anything to say about it.

Principal Ward didn't appreciate Grumpy's choice of verbiage. Even told him to point blank, "Shut up."

Jerkwad had wisely kept his mouth in check, but Principal Ward bore a hole in his face (should've been his crotch) that said discussions with him specifically were far from over. He then unloaded a similar look on Coach Wallace. Coach was being blamed for not being present, I sighed, and all he'd wanted was to talk to his Facebook girlfriend.

"Can't the man have a girlfriend?" my inner-idiot whispered in his defense.

Assuming I should be in tears, Coach gave a silent assessment of me, trying to figure out what made me tick and whether it was worth trying to un-tick.

Well, guess what? He hired me, and the road to success ain't always pretty.

Chapter Nine

HANUKKAH HELL

*H*anukkah started the past weekend, and it was tradition for Marjorie and me to celebrate with Rookie. Rookie was a proud half Jew, but in truth, he only half observed the holidays. Partly because my mother's twin, Tabitha Arthur, I think, was the one thing he truly worshiped.

Hanukkah held many traditions like exchanging gifts, spinning the dreidel, receiving gelt (a coin-shaped piece of chocolate), and eating fried foods. Rookie's tradition at the moment, however, was the usual—a knock-down-drag-out fight with Red.

"Shalom, Rookie. Thanks for the jeggings," I said when he picked up his phone. I'd had my eye on jeggings at Hollister for months, and a new pair was lying on my doorstep in a UPS box when Dylan dropped me off after school. My guess was Red bought them online and had them mailed to me as Hanukkah gift number four.

Rookie didn't have a clue what constituted a jegging but murmured, "Shalom, baby, and you're welcome" anyway.

Rookie always wanted particulars of my day. *Did I have any tests? Did anyone pick on me? Did I have a good night's sleep,* and so on and so forth. I opted against telling him what Jerkwad did for fear of his reaction. It was election year, and if Rookie went badass-mofo-prosecutor on people, then he might need to beef up his burger-flipping skills. Instead, I told him I believed I'd made headway in uncovering who painted Coach Wallace's car. As a testament to his despair, all he gave me was an, "Uh-huh."

Murphy hadn't been such an easy sale. When I gave him each depressing little detail, he'd gone psycho, opting to phone AP Unger first who talked him down from charging into Principal Ward's home and beating the holy bejeezus out of him. Things that included—pardon me for the visual—ripping his balls from his groin and feeding them to him. Problem was, Murphy had two beefs with VHS...make that three. Mr. Himmel, Principal Ward, and Jerkwad who smashed my face against the wall. Murphy made headway with Mr. Himmel. No, he didn't get him fired, but he *did* get my assignments, including permission to turn in an at-home science experiment. Word was mum on what would happen to Jerkwad, but my guess was he'd get slapped with assault and battery by the time Murphy was through with him.

Believe me. It was better than Murphy's fist.

Rookie murmured, "I feel like rebelling, baby. I lost a case today. Get ready, and let's go grab a hot dog at Gold Star."

If you live in Cincinnati—AKA Chilitown, USA—you'd better develop a taste for hot dogs. Trouble was, our chili joints delivered the pork version. A Jewish and Hanukkah law-breaking no-no.

He explained, "I didn't take her advice, and we lost. I've heard enough of her mouth to last a lifetime. Plus," he paused, "*he* called. God," he muttered, sighing in prayer, "I hate what that man does to her, and I hate it even more when I let her tell me."

Ahhhh, Boyfriend Zero—the guy who started Red's love train in motion.

Never met him. Red never spoke of him. But we all knew he existed.

Cue the violins. "Sorry, Rookie."

More of the no noise thing. "It's okay," he finally said, worn-out. "So you'll go?"

First thing I did when I clocked into HQ that afternoon was to drop the credit cards and social security card in a padded envelope —addressed to Tito Westbrook—and then leave them in our mailbox for pickup. Second, I attached Murphy's camera to the computer to evaluate the photographs. In short, they sucked. As a result, I hoped to flow-chart what I'd learned, following an information trail if one materialized.

But Rookie was beat...and I couldn't leave a good man down.

"I'm in," I answered. While Rookie paused to say something to someone in his office, I pulled ripped Rock & Republic's on and a ribbed, red turtleneck. I rounded out the outfit with new black UGGs, Hanukkah gift number one. I stepped inside my bathroom and coated my lashes with mascara and rolled on Go Glam! clear lip gloss. Looking ghostly pale, I kicked things up a notch and added pink blush.

Let's face it, folks, I needed all the help I could get.

Once Rookie and I ended the call, I texted Rudi and told her the good news—she had been named first runner-up (a Hot Girl) by only one vote, after (gosh, I hated her) Brynn Hathaway. Rudi was profusely embarrassed, but after I convinced her it was a good thing, she said she'd heard of my latest project. She then confessed she had sixth period study hall with Slapstick Wilson.

Yahtzee. I'd take it.

I clocked in with Tito next. Trouble was, Tito wasn't there, so I made nice with his answering machine and told him I'd mailed something über important and to keep on the lookout. Worried he'd find out I was Darcy Walker, I'd used Claudia's cell phone. Claudia only answered if she recognized the number, I would be as safe as safe could be.

Padding over to the corner window, I pulled the curtain aside and peered through the blinds. It was a stormy, tempestuous night. But even though the wind whipped and whistled violently, nothing became of the early morning weather alert. We were sent home due to someone's panic attack. One inch had fallen, and the subsequent gusts blew it all away.

Rookie and I left Murphy and Marjorie eating fried chicken, and where I figured we'd go to the nearest Gold Star Chili—only a few miles away—Rookie drove downtown to the one closest to his office...where Red supposedly burned the midnight oil. I wasn't a fool. His frustration had evaporated if not totally disappeared. I mean, he even blasted Christmas music in the car. I got it...that was love, I guess. But I'd experienced too much disappointment for one lifetime to think love always saved the day. An unrequited love—or love that sucked a person dry—wasn't something I was interested in.

And Dylan, I think, would suck the marrow from my bones.

Rookie pulled up to the side of the road, maneuvering his silver Mercedes SUV to a stop. A vertical line marked the space between his eyes that had Red's name all over it. Rookie massaged the area, mumbling how Tabitha would give him a heart attack one day soon.

I wasn't a patient person, people, especially when I had an empty stomach. Once the hot dogs were in front of us, I destroyed my first cheese coney slathered in sauce, onions, and mustard in barely one bite. Rookie's was in two.

Rookie always had that boy-next-door thing going on. Thing of it was, his brown bedroom eyes milked it for all it was worth. Rookie was sharp, calculating, and as ruthless as a Wall Street broker...and pretty much anatomically perfect. He sported a dark gray suit and gold tie, and when a man stood six foot four with big shoulders and narrow hips, he was a commercial for *Please Be My Baby's Daddy*. So why was my aunt so stupid? The cute brunette manager sure as heck wasn't.

She wanted to bathe in his saliva.

Early thirties, she was painted into a Gold Star orange long-sleeved shirt, wearing tight jeans and a Santa Claus hat. Her nails painted a candy apple red.

A television was mounted in the corner of the room. Rookie apparently didn't like the news station because he pushed out of our red vinyl booth, asking if the channel could be changed, pacing like a caged critter.

"Of course," the manager replied with a toothy smile. She strolled over to our booth, squatting at my side, pointing to Rookie who had the TV control in his hand. "Red or Tabitha?" she whispered jokingly. Apparently, it was no secret Rookie only uttered Tabitha when he was angry.

"Tabitha," I whispered back. "They had a fight, and it was a whopper."

She frowned. "They eat in here all the time, but he always makes an effort during Hanukkah. You must be her niece. I must say, you're practically identical."

Similar, but not *identical*. Everyone said I inherited my aunt's looks. People at the grocery, and next-door neighbors paused to stare. Even her housekeeper was struck dumb by the similarities. We had the same dimpled chin, truck driver laugh, and legs up to our armpits. Hers fit together nicely with a body that went va-va-va-voom. My body was a car crash of limbs that belonged on an inbred cavewoman.

My cell phone pinged with a text when the manager excused herself. I pulled it out and choked on my tongue:

Hello, angel. Did you think I wouldn't find you?

The text had been signed with a smiley face emoticon, followed by the name Ben. Oh, jeez...I felt like I ran into a concrete wall. That was Silver-Eyed Boy's first name: Ben...Ben Ryan. Ben. Ben. Ben. The epiphany hit me as soon as I saw the letters linked together. Should I ignore it? Delete? Claim he had the wrong number? Ask him how in the heck he got my number in the first place? I decided to return a frown face and be done with it, but my body had some sort of weird systemic reaction. It felt like I'd been struck by a car all over again. My arms and legs went rigid, like a tree about to snap in the wind. Only one other person ever incapacitated me like that, and he pulled me off the top of the building earlier and practically spanked my behind (here's to wishing).

Rookie finally sauntered back, collapsing in the seat and loosening his tie as I received another text. That time from none other than Kyd Knoblecker, a friend who lived in Serendipity Country Club in Orlando where Dylan's family had a summer home. My finger's cramped up. Kyd thought I was the girlfriend kismet ordained he should have. But Kyd was model-handsome and a fastard. It was wisest to stay away from guys better looking than me and notorious cheats. I had enough hang-ups. Worrying a boyfriend might trade-up wasn't one I wanted to add to the mix.

No freaking thank you.

Miss u, the text said.

I sent five gun emojis in a row and avoided conversation. Surely to God he got the message. Rookie opened his jacket and removed his cell phone from the side pocket, checking to see if anyone had called him. After he scrolled through a few emails, he turned it off with a grunt.

I downed my drink, knowing the clock ticked away. "Rookie, I think there are a group of people at our school stealing peoples' identities. You know, check cards, social security cards," I explained.

I immediately shoved three fries in my mouth, acting as if I merely made conversation. Rookie squirted a stream of ketchup on the side of my white oval plate, helping himself to a pile of fries. He gave me a despondent and bewildered head shake. "Sad, isn't it? The world's just sad."

Oh, boy, major case of melancholy.

I mumbled, "I know." Rookie stuffed three more fries in his cheeks and held up two fingers to the waitress, motioning for two more dogs, fully-loaded. I grabbed my second hot dog, rethinking my attack. As plans went, my trip seemed pretty rudimentary. Get in the car with my uncle, have dinner with my uncle, ask my uncle questions, and voilà I had answers.

His grief had piped down the plan.

My phone belted out Grandma's woes. At least, he laughed a little. Thing was, I didn't even look at the number. Just muttered into the receiver, "This day sucks."

"Where are you?" the caller demanded.

"Dylan?"

You know, if a person could predict when an earthquake was going to happen, I was pretty sure I felt a premature tremor. It wasn't Dylan. The voice breathed out, "Jagger Cane, beautiful." Well, shoooot. A phone call from Jagger brought a whole new level of sucking.

"I'm at Gold Star, Jagger," I said, "chowing on a hot dog. I'm on the road to self-actualization."

"You're on the road to heartburn," he said, chuckling loudly. No, I was on the road to serenity and full-bodied awareness. Put a hot dog in my mouth, and I was standing nude in the middle of Utopia with no secrets to hide. Okay, probably an overstatement.

"Do you speak Utopian?" I asked, slurping down a drink.

"Absolutely. Does the person you're *with* know Utopian?" he asked suspiciously. No, I was pretty sure Rookie stood in Hanukkah Hell at the moment. I didn't know what their particular language was, but I was positive it included profanity and rotting promises to Yahweh.

"What do you need?" I asked.

"Listen, I heard about what happened after school today and wanted to check in. I hear Bradshaw and Taylor roughed him up, but stay away from Nico Drake, babe. I heard he got expelled permanently, complements of Dylan's father, but I also hear he's not through with you."

GRRREEAAAATTT.

Even stranger, who would've *thunk* Jagger would care?

Regarding Colton Taylor, the fact his words held weight didn't surprise me. Dylan's father was a big wig at Go Glam! Cosmetics and a huge benefactor at VHS. His word—or *wallet* I should say—was gold.

"Thanks for the heads up," I muttered.

Rookie took a long swig on his drink, raising a brow, holding his hand up for the check and saying rather rudely to me, "Who is that?" His bad-boy detector was definitely spot-on because he sure as heck hit the nail on the head with Jagger.

I placed my hand over the phone, "Boy from school," I told him. He lowered his eyes, and my stomach flip-flopped.

"That's your third contact with whom I assume were males in the past ten minutes, Darcy. Do you answer every text, and would I approve of them?"

I found it odd it was raining men, and my sheepish smile pretty much summed things up. Teenagers answered every text they got. Even from people they didn't like. Made them feel indispensable, I guess.

He motioned for me to disconnect. I told Jagger, "Hey, thanks again, but I gotta run. See ya tomorrow."

I shut down the convo before Jagger could protest. Funny who you'd run into in Hell, wasn't it.

———

Rookie took a phone call from Shoshanna Goldstein as we piled into his Mercedes. Shoshanna was Jewish, about a decade younger, and if Charlotte Veronica Harper-Stark ruffled Red's feathers, Shoshanna gutted her like the English gutted William Wallace. She was dark and tiny and such a mild-mannered lady she made Red look like a prison inmate with anger management issues. Throughout the conversation, Rookie's demeanor changed. He relaxed and melted into his seat, like a healing balm washed over his weary body. Four divorces would insinuate that Red shouldn't care—but she did. And if she was in the dark with the turn of events, then it was my duty to tell her to wake the H up.

Rookie wouldn't wait forever, and frankly, it seemed unfair to ask him to.

Rookie's plan had been to pop in the office and get a file—where Red was—but that was before Shoshanna called. From what I could tell, they made some sort of Hanukkahish plans, so he walked me to the door, said I could have a short visit, and went off to reconsecrate himself or do whatever a person did to get back in Yahweh's good graces.

"Hello, Ebenezer," I said, giggling and striding inside.

"Bah, humbug to you too," she said, chuckling in a naughty voice. "Rookie was eating all-meat hot dogs? He's such a bad Jew." Red was shoeless, wearing a black pantsuit tailor-made to fit her tiny waist. She stood five foot ten, one hundred and twenty-six pounds. Red didn't walk...she percolated. But she was a redhead, people. Percolating was mandatory. Her hair was pulled back in a ponytail with an expensive-looking ivory barrette. Her skin was creamy, and the shade emphasized the small beauty mark on the right side of her dimpled chin. Her hair color right then was blonde like mine, not the rich auburn hue Rookie loved.

Sitting behind a dark oak-stained desk in a black leather chair, her emerald-green eyes were intently focused. Christmas carols blasted high, the television set mounted to her wall turned low. She'd been watching the weather report. A warm front supposedly moved in—probably the reason for the lightning show that sent us home. As the meteorologist said temperatures were expected to rise, Red drummed her fingers on the desk. I looked down at her hand. She wore an ice skating rink on her finger, an early Christmas gift from her Hanukkah-observing *ex* (I think) husband. Go figure. Murphy said Rookie gave it to her during the weekend, wrapped in nativity-themed paper, complete with a smiling Baby Jesus in a manger.

"Nice rock," I said, grinning big.

She frowned while she gazed at the stone. "Rookie can kiss my ass." *He probably wants to,* I almost said.

Red's favorite word was a-s-s, the donkey word. She said it was in the Bible. Therefore, it was okay to say. Made sense, I guess. Still, most parents went bat-poop crazy when their kid picked up the slang. Made them feel like they'd done a royally bad job at the parenting game.

She smiled and said, "Kisses," pointing to the mistletoe hanging above her head.

I walked across the navy carpet, leaned across her laptop, and pecked her lips. Then I collapsed in one of the two black leather chairs in front of her desk. I gave her desk a once-over. It had your usual telephone, laptop, notepads, and pens and pencils. On the credenza behind her was a little red mitten, a snow globe with a mermaid inside, and a picture of her and my mother when they were seventeen on their way to college. On one wall hung undergraduate and law school certificates. On the other was a corkboard adjacent to a standing dry-erase easel.

"Murphy phoned. Are you all right?" she said and frowned.

Ah, I assumed she referred to whom I knew as Nico Drake. "Yeah," I said shrugging. "The worst thing that happened was he destroyed my Miracle Bra."

"Hmmm," she said. "Next time someone destroys your Miracle Bra in a fit of passion make sure you have a ring on your finger, baby."

And that was the extent of my good girl lecture for the night. "Please tell me you didn't tell Rookie," she said and grimaced.

"I thought better of it," I answered.

She nodded, relieved. "Listen, baby. I respect why you found yourself in this situation, but if you're going to continue to fight the good fight and go all guardian angel on the masses, then make sure you're in the company of your best friend."

"Point taken."

With a sigh, she threw a file on her desk and out popped the photograph of the guy Tito faxed over Saturday night. Same greasy hair, same deep-set eyes, one eye lower than the other.

It was a miracle...nothing short of Jesus walking on water.

I spit out, "Who's the guy?"

Red was one of those people that her Christmas cheer spilled over onto everyone else. But not with this case. Her face leaked radioactive byproducts. We briefly went over what'd happened to Tito (I acted unaware) with Red pointing out that next year was election year. What I knew from election year was that candidates better have their ducks—or cases—all lined up in a row, solved, and ready for the archives.

"Cookie Harper-Stark needs to solve this case," she murmured. "If she doesn't, her career's over. I *want* it to be over, but I'm afraid if she doesn't solve it, then Rookie's good heart will find her a job here. And I find it odd she won't speak to Tito—who is directly involved as a victim—and there's only one reason that makes sense. She's stalling. She's stalling even though her district needs it solved. And that, my dear, is simply because she wants help from Rookie. I love that about him, and I hate that about him. Anyone else," she said with a shrug, "I wouldn't care, but Cookie," she sneered, "wants my husband." I raised a brow. "Well, he's not really my husband," she amended, "but Cookie can't have what's mine."

"It's not only Cookie who wants him," I said, sort of smiling. "He just met up with someone else."

Red narrowed her eyes, all judicious. "Who?" she demanded.

I picked at my nails, propping my feet on her desk, crossing them at the ankles. "Shoshanna," I said quietly.

She slammed a fist on the folder. "Ah, hell to the no, no, no!! That's the little pipsqueak, Jewish princess of his dreams!" she spat, marking the words with venom. She frantically picked up her phone, dialing her ex-husband's number.

No answer. Went to voicemail.

Two more times...voicemail again.

"Apparently, I'm going to have to act like I still love him," she grumbled.

"You do," I reminded her with a grin.

"Shepard," she seethed, calling him by his first name, deciding to leave a message. "Answer your phone before I ram your yarmulke up your ass." I snorted so loudly I slammed my hand over my mouth. "Watch this baby," she said with a wink. She held up her fingers, counting down the seconds. "Five, four, three, two, one..."

He never called back. But she didn't look angry.

"Okay," she muttered to herself. "I've really upset him." I caught up on *Dumb Ways to Die* on my iPhone as she punched in his number again, her face saying she'd go for a softer approach. "Rookie, baby," she begged tenderly. "Pick up. I'm sorry." She held up a hand again but got nothing but voicemail, looking one step from going postal and shooting up the place. "What an ass," she mumbled, dialing yet again. "God, you've got to help me here," she added with a begging look to the ceiling. She pushed away from the desk and paced over to the window, flipping the blinds back to peer outside. "Shepard, I'm standing here half naked, prepared to show you how sorry I am, but if you don't pick up the phone, I quit!"

After some bone-chilling silence, the phone rang. "That always works," she murmured and laughed.

Trouble was, it didn't...

Murphy was on the line, wondering when I was coming home to do the homework he was "gosh-danged certain I had." Before we knew it, thirty minutes melted by, and Rookie was so MIA, Red thought it was issue-an-APB time.

She had her elbows resting on her knees, one hand clutching her cell, the other worshiping a Dr. Pepper like it was the last cup of water on Earth. I told her to stop dialing because it made her look desperate, immature, and like a teenage stalker. When she heeded my words, I used the time to pick her brain.

"Who is he?" I asked, nodding to the faxed photograph of whom I referred to as Motor Oil Hair.

Red went back in lawyer-mode. She sat down on the couch across from me, pulling on her three-inch black leather boots that made her well over six feet tall. She was frustrated and broke a nail yanking the zipper up too fast. "This kid is called The Ghost," she said with a sigh, deciding to bite the hanging nail off. "If I had a name, then we could simply tail him and find out who he's associated with and what all he was up to. Tito's source," she said soberly, "swears this kid is the identity thief on your side of town. But Tito's source didn't give us a name. Only a picture. We have a few good cops looking out, and normally I don't get involved, but I need this done. If I can get it done, then Cookie will be out of Rookie's life and my nightmares."

"Are these cops good?"

Ask and ye shall receive because she answered, "Not as good as Tito. You ought to read the stack of notes he gave me."

You know what, I intended to. I tried to look innocent, but the nosy part of me chomped at the bit. "Like what?"

"The Ghost has some distinguishable characteristics."

"Such as?" I asked again.

"He cracks his knuckles non-stop and has to hold something in his hands at all times. He licks it and stuff," she shuddered. I burst out laughing. "Yeah," she groaned. "That really sets him apart, doesn't it? How in the world can't you identify the scum of the earth who makes-out with things other than people? These guys all crawl out of the same holes. Someone either isn't looking down the right hole or the guy truly is a ghost. Evidently, he's in and out like the wind. The things you've been involved in before pale in comparison to this guy's setup."

She referred to me solving who murdered the body I found in a dumpster and helping find a kidnapped child last summer.

"All of that was child's play if this guy is as evil as we think," she explained.

"How evil?" I asked confused. "He steals identities, Red. Granted that's bad if you're the vict—"

She cut me off. "From what we suspect, murder is in his background. I have two bodies who fit the personality profile of Tito. People that tried to find this guy and wound up dead. The medical examiner claims a bullet killed both men, but both had also been stabbed long after their heart stopped beating. So we've got a killer who likes to use his hands, who more than likely enjoys a little bit of torture. Those kind bother me the most. And baby, we both know murderers are bad. Smart murderers, the worst."

I barely had enough headspace for identity theft...add a murderer, and my brain was almost tapped out. "Does he go to my school?" I pushed.

She didn't directly answer or issue a denial. She directed the questioning back to me. Smart woman...she knew what I'd do if I had more information. But Tito had already told me he was a teenager, and Valley High was the only high school in Mack County.

"Does he look familiar?" she inquired.

"Never seen him before," I lied, "and if I don't know someone personally, I at least recognize the face."

Finn had truly worked a miracle. He'd provided the names of who was tardy on the day Coach's car had been painted. Plus, he printed a list of who'd been in detention—not one year, but two years out—all with their student ID photographs, class schedules, and home addresses. Coffee Blot Boy—what I'd nicknamed the guy in Coach's file—did not appear to be in the photographs, but granted, he'd been beaten to a pulp in his picture. What was interesting, however, was that Motor Oil Hair (Tito's faxed photograph) looked an awful lot like a guy named Brantley McCoy.

A guy who was mysteriously unaccounted for when I combed through the past six years of school yearbooks.

"Cookie is going to post a reward," she explained.

I licked my lips.

She shoved his picture back into the file, and my guess was that was all Cookie would get from Red's energy reserves at the moment.

Red recited the reasons for all four divorces, clearly rattled. I nodded, riding her downward spiral into despair, trying to sympathize and rationalize her actions. While she paced the floor, erasing the contents of her dry-erase board, I succumbed to temptation and dumped the file's contents into my black Coach tote bag, Hanukkah gift number two. I had to give accolades to Rookie. He sure as heck could give good gifts. I'd never be able to purchase a Coach bag and had always settled for some pleather knockoff.

There was a good, solid knock at the door. We both looked up at the brass clock hanging from a wall. Eight o'clock.

Red yelled, "Come in if you have dinner because I'm famished." I thought that to be a little dangerous, but hey, who was I? It could be anyone considering the time of night—a crazed custodian, or heck, an out-on-parole felon with a pizza.

But in walked Rookie, a ballsy move perhaps, because Red was hungry and the look on her face said Rookie was food. He carried a takeout bag from Izzy's, a homegrown restaurant that specialized in corned beef Reubens with sauerkraut and swiss cheese on rye. *Red's favorite*. I smiled to myself.

Anger—that morphed into an even deeper despair—washed over her, followed by an instant relief he was present. Still, she fumed, "Why didn't you answer my calls?" He stared. Not dignifying it with a response. Only Red would get upset Rookie didn't answer her call but instead graced her with an in-person visit. "Answer me," she demanded. She was stuck in Attorneytown.

Rookie gave her a benign smile as if she had no effect on him whatsoever. He leisurely removed his jacket and pitched it to the leather couch, pausing to wink and make eye contact with me. After the unspoken niceties, he turned to her. "Drop the cold-shoulder, Tabitha. Remember who signs your paycheck."

It was game-over, lights-are-down-on-Broadway stuff going on in his eyes.

They truly were a romantic comedy: girl meets boy, girl loses boy, girl gets boy back and apologizes for her stupidity. If I had a car, I'd be out of here. Intimacy oftentimes made me uneasy. Maybe it represented a familial unit, or maybe it represented something missing in my personal life.

"Don't mind me," I muttered. Rookie gave half a nod because Red then had both her arms wrapped tightly around his waist as he pulled the ivory ponytail holder out of her hair. She even shook her fake blonde tresses out like women do in shampoo commercials.

One of life's little mysteries. I sighed.

Fishing my phone from my back pocket, when my thumb hovered over Dylan's speed dial, Finn's words rang ominously. I *did* call him when I needed a hug. Well, everyone deserved a dumb day. Unfortunately, I had more than the average person. "Hey, Darc," he answered before I even said anything. "Dad and I stopped by to check on you, but Murphy said you were with Rookie. I've missed your face, and I'm still tortured by what happened. I died a little inside this afternoon," he said on an exhale.

"Don't worry, D. It's just another day in Darcyville: rated-NC-17 for violence, raunchy humor, and indecipherable language."

"I just worry," he said, sighing like he'd aged a few years. "Tell me you're fine."

Now I am, I thought, but I wasn't good for him. My life had an expiration date...one I knew instinctively was about to shorten even more.

It is thought a disgrace to love unrequited. But the great will see that true love cannot be unrequited.

—*Ralph Waldo Emerson*

Chapter Ten

POETIC JUSTICE

*R*ed's file contained more juicy tidbits than bathroom recaps of Jagger's infidelity.

Inside, I discovered general information that helped to paint a clearer picture. Other than stealing a purse or wallet outright, some identity thieves discovered a card's password by doing something called "shoulder surfing." They'd stand too close in the checkout line and watch someone input his or her password. Then, when the time was right, they'd discreetly nab the vic's purse or wallet. A man dialed 911 who had that exact thing happen to him by a "scumbag teenager" at the self-checkout line at Walmart. When he went Lone Ranger on the teen, the teen bolted and the man went rage crazy, continuing pursuit. Thing was, the man was found dead a week later. Gunshot and stab wounds. The coroner estimated he'd been dead for some time, so a good chance existed he died on the day of the confrontation. During the time he was missing, the thief emptied the man's bank account over a series of four days.

If that sounded hairy, try the next case on for size. A man had his mail delivered to two locations: his office and home. Someone intercepted a credit card that the bank had sent him when his old one was about to expire, activated it, and had several thousand dollars charged to his name. Last thing heard from the victim was that he knew "exactly who the effer was" and attempted to bloodhound him out. Er, it didn't go well. He was found with a screw-driver to the chest under one of Cincinnati's overpasses. A bullet was also dug out of his gut. Authorities interviewed everyone in his office but walked away with no leads.

And like Red had said, both bodies had been stabbed after being shot—almost like the perpetrator wanted to play with the victim. The real friendly type.

Once finished, I flipped on Murphy's printer and copied the contents of Red's file. Then I placed the originals in a FedEx overnight envelope Murphy had on hand and marked it for delivery tomorrow. My note to Red? *Oops*. I'd cover my lack of creativity later if it came back to bite me.

It felt crazy to put all my eggs in one basket with detention because it'd either end with answers or I'd be SOL and back to square one. There was no choice but to embrace it and cross my fingers those on my hypothetical payroll would uncover something useful. What I didn't expect was for the payroll to include Bean. I'd given him the assignment of contacting Owen Lancaster and Wyatt Brown—the two Coach mentioned might nurse a grudge—thinking it would be futile and sate his OCD tendencies for days. Shock of all shockers, he called the night before, job done. Owen Lancaster reportedly "cried like a girl" he'd even been considered, and Wyatt Brown set up a play-date to watch *The Lord of the Rings* trilogy.

And Coach thought them the culprits? I couldn't help but laugh.

Maybe if he was a hobbit hater…

It was hump day. Bean had followed me to each of my classes, and he right then stood in the lunch line, whispering about our next move. "I've been thinking all night about Coach's car," he whispered, "but nothing is popping into my head yet."

I looked at Bean, surprised *anything* ever popped in his head. His hair had been severely parted on the left side, matted down with so much gel I could see the air bubbles on his head. He'd dressed in all gray. Gray oxford buttoned to his chin, gray cotton drawstring pants. Gray canvas Keds.

God love him, he got weirder and weirder.

I wasn't particularly hungry, and my gut told me—short of churros on the menu—to save the calories. Why? Mystery meat was on the menu. I could tell by the smell. The key to survival was looking the other way. Or pizza.

As Bean and I merged into the pizza line, I halfway carried on a conversation with Rudi and Justice Becker in front of me. Justice was my jock soulmate. Like me, she had broad shoulders, a gift for putting her foot in her mouth, and big lips. She was biracial, about six feet tall with auburn-colored hair, and dark chocolate eyes. Also like me, she defined the quintessential wallflower. Regarding Justice, it frankly would take an overly confident guy to win her anyway. She had a black belt in karate. Most guys lost a testicle when they found out she could kill them with her knee.

She suffered from a red-green color deficiency, and in light of her color-blindness had a tendency to dress like fruit. She wore a kiwi-green, cable knit sweater and matching leggings with dusty brown riding boots. I sported Levi's boyfriend jeans with metallic slip-on Vans and an over-sized black "Army" hoodie. Hoodies could cover a multitude of bodily sins.

"Girlfriend," Justice whispered, "I've been looking for you all day. Did you hear?"

Um, yeah, I had. I knew what Justice was going to say, and it might've been worse than the fact I had the crap beaten out of me the day before. Apparently, someone hacked into my Twitter account and sent my entire following a mass email that called Mr. Himmel a "dog-humping troll."

Problem was, it sounded like something I'd do if I'd thought of it.

Sad thing is, I'm mad I didn't.

"Yeah," I mumbled. "Finn told me this morning on the way to school. He's going to set up a new password and make me impenetrable. Does Mr. Himmel know?"

"I don't think so," she muttered. "He didn't say anything in class. Watch your back though. Somebody's out to get you."

But who would be gunning for me? Nico Drake? The Ghost, perhaps? God knew I'd turned over a lot of rocks at VHS, even recruiting others—via Bean—to contact me if they ran across anything useful. But those people, as far as I knew, only thought I had reward money to dispense.

I picked up a tray and napkin as Justice acknowledged Bean. "How's Mister Pongo?"

It was widely accepted Bean carried a stuffed gerbil named Mr. Pongo in his backpack. Mr. Pongo was a blue-gray rodent with a green bowtie around his neck—complements of Bean's taxidermist-by-night father. That probably accounted for one year of counseling all in itself. Thing was, right then Mr. Pongo peeked out of the pocket of his oxford shirt.

Some people couldn't help they were born nerdy. I figured Bean fell headlong into that category and shoved everyone else out of his way. But he *could* help his reputation if he quit parading Mr. Pongo around in broad daylight for everyone to gape at.

"He's a little under the weather," he told Justice, "but thanks for asking."

Mr. Pongo looked the same as he always did.

Dead.

Giving Bean an extra napkin, I motioned for him to cover Mr. Pongo. "Put Mister Pongo to bed, Bean," I whispered. "Someone will say something mean to you."

Bean held his head high, defiant. "My therapist said I need to embrace who I am."

Well, that was definitely one of our therapist's famed lines, but she did tend to get hit regularly with the stupid stick. "Suit yourself," I muttered.

Sure enough, some stranger crowded into line and pulled Mr. Pongo out of Bean's pocket. Bean squeezed my hand until it bruised. I pointed my plastic spork in whoever-the-guy-was's face. "Give him back his gerbil, or I'm going to get real nasty. Mister Pongo has a right to eat lunch like the rest of us."

That statement alone made me want to giggle...somehow I didn't.

The guy, so average I'd never remember him tomorrow, got flirty-faced. "Please tell me what you have planned includes pains of pleasure."

Heck, if I knew, but I assumed it involved a spork.

We were near to the front of the line—the warm, cheesy pizza smell promising to clog my arteries. Bean's breathing grew shallow. I could hear it.

Justice pushed me out of the way before I could find a retort, eye-to-eye with Mean Boy. "Give it back," she threatened, "or my round-house kick will kick your ass." The guy actually took a moment to ponder. When Justice laughed darkly, his Adam's apple bobbed with nerves, and he shakily placed Mr. Pongo in Bean's hand, returning to line a few students back. Bean shoved Mr. Pongo in his pocket...then turned and hugged me so tightly my lungs collapsed. It was one of those hugs where someone tried to step inside the other person. It wasn't about the shama lama, ding-dong. You know, boy likes girl, I'm-trying-to-steal-your-V-card or whatever.

I think Bean simply tried to be someone else.

Justice turned to Bean, pointing, "If he bothers you again, let me know. I'll rip him from limb to limb and drag his body through the streets...something poetic."

Bean looked at Justice, stars twinkling brightly in his eyes. Cupid's arrow must've hit him in the butt. "Poetic justice," he said, grinning like he'd found his soulmate.

"That's right," she said with a smirk. "Poetic Justice."

Poetic justice is a just punishment or virtue finally rewarded. In other words, people get what was coming to them. I'd like to think poetic justice was something that only visited the bad, but that didn't always seem to be the case.

Case in Point: Ivy Morrison and Clementine Miriam Rabinowitz passed by on their way out of the lunch line. Both girls' trays were piled high with calorie-packed pizzas, chips, Twinkies, and ice cream cups. Both were double zeros. Where was the fair in that? Poured into tight jeans, up top they wore white sweaters with a big black VHS stitched in the middle.

Their cheerleading outfits...how charming.

As of second period, Ivy was footloose and fancy-free. Emphasis on the "free" part. She and Jagger had called it quits. Translation? I'm going after Dylan with my peroxided hair and push-up bra.

"Hello, Darcy," she sneered, sounding as usual like she'd gargled with helium.

"Hello poison," I slipped. "I mean, Ivy."

She rolled her eyes, unaffected. "Listen, about the parking lot a few days ago with Jagger. I don't need you to fight my battles for me. Honestly, the thought of you on my side is another insult. You're such a nobody. And BTW," she said with a laugh "I heard about your little Twitter problem and made sure to tell Doctor Himmel."

Ivy, as usual, scheduled my next date with self-loathing.

I blanked my face, not wanting to give her the pleasure of seeing my panic. Ivy had recently pierced the right side of her nose and was wearing a diamond-dust earring. On some, the look was total Skankville, but dang it, the teeny-tiny size was all kinds of rad. "Did you hear the latest about Dylan and Brynn?" she continued.

Fear started at my toes and slowly worked its way up my body, like it knew something and afforded me the luxury to get used to the feeling. A lost cause because whenever I thought of Dylan with someone else, it was a direct shot to the kidneys. Did she insinuate they were an item? There was a possibility, I guess. Brynn Hathaway and her boyfriend were dunzo (locker gossip of the morning). And he was like lick-your-lips cute in an aristocratic kind of way. Collin Lockhart was his name. Collin was student council president and so silver-tongued he'd either be President one day or convicted for insider trading.

"Everyone knows they've both had a thing for each other for some time," she explained. "It's just that Dylan is a slow mover but you know Brynn she'll make it happen sooner rather than later she's sort of running scared she knows she only has a limited amount of time to land him."

Ivy's speech was one big run-on sentence—no periods or commas in sight.

Brynn was a senior, and senior girls were notorious for going after what they wanted. And why not? It was her last year, and she might as well go out with a bang. Brynn, my guess, wanted to go out with a sonic boom.

She concluded, "But I shouldn't sell myself short I mean it has to be either her or me that's what makes sense."

Ivy was a stupid, needy, attention whore.

Yup, I thought it. Thought it, and it was allllllllll truuuuuue.

I blew out some air, wringing my hands even though it made me look desperate. "I already know, Ivy, and the date was actually in August."

I wasn't sure who said that. I looked around and saw no one but me and concluded some part of my ego must've found the nerve.

She made a shocked "o" with her lips, covering her mouth with her blood-red fingernails. "Your news might be a little dated," she whispered.

I know, I know, it was Ivy—but wouldn't a sequel have been plastered all over the bathroom wall? I was actually someone who read the gossip immortalized in Sharpie, and I sure as heck hadn't heard nor read of it.

She grinned evilly. "You might want to ask him," she said.

Wow.

Huh.

How interesting.

"There's no need to throw shade," Justice grumbled for me. "I think you're blowing smoke."

Ivy cocked her head to one side, and the rhinestone Hello Kitty choker around her neck caught the fluorescent light. Justice noticed because she laughed and said, "Nice necklace, Blackbeard. I'm sure you reduced someone's Christmas inventory with your sticky, little fingers."

It was an open secret Ivy stole Hello Kitty jewelry from the mall. Seriously, she was loaded, but she was also dumb enough to confess some of her purchases came complements of the five-finger discount. Ignoring Justice, she focused on me. "Why, Darcy, the look on your face is priceless you almost act like he's cheating on you seriously get a clue."

"Trust me, there's no hanky-panky going on between us," I dumbly confessed, and why exactly did that bother me?

"Amazing," she said, laughing snarkily. And even more amazing that my foot hadn't made it inside her mouth. "Listen," she sneered, "Brynn is exponentially way more beautiful than you, and so am I."

All three were part of the beautiful crowd.

My ovaries hurt with the thought.

"Shut up," Justice warned, flooring Ivy with her eyes.

I shuffled toward the pizza (still in debate), and sure enough, Ivy and Clementine followed. I knew Grumpy had a crush on Clementine, and unarguably she was cute. A few inches shorter than me, she had tiny bones, dark skin, black hair and eyes. Her face was sort of serene. Like she was eternally happy and didn't possess a single, bad thought. But the fact she hung with Ivy alarmed me. Heck, it probably alarmed God. She was either stupid-slash-naïve or had a mean streak no one knew about.

Bean edged up into my ear. "I don't believe anything she says about Dylan." Bean had a tone to his voice like he was used to wading through lies. "Just keep moving," he whispered.

I did.

God love her...Rudi didn't...actually speaking out loud. Something she hated to do because the resulting sound was like she floated underwater. "Leave her alone," she voiced, hitching her head high. "You're an evil witch."

Wouldn't you know, Ivy pivoted around and attacked a deaf girl, laughing sarcastically. "Your voice is the most irritating thing I've ever heard," she said.

Ummm, Earth to humanity...that's offensive.

Reading her lips, Rudi cringed as if she'd been struck. Justice dropped four curse words on the spot. Right then was where the tough girl in me demanded I tell her to kiss my you-know-what. In fact, it was where I should hunker down and fight. I think the incident the day before proved I had zero fighting skills. So I did what any girl would do—imagine I beat her to a pulp and get upset when I failed to execute.

Do it, I heard in my ear.

The best way to describe my thought process was that one shoulder had an angel living on it, the other a devil. The devil ordered again, *Do it, Darcy! Do it, do it, do it.* The angel whined, *But good girls don't get in fights.*

I could look at things one of two ways. Number one, I could beat the s-h-i-t out of Ivy. I got the feeling I'd never like her, and I pretty much liked everybody. Number two, well, I could beat the s-h-i-t out of Ivy. First thing I wanted to do was knee her between the legs, but then I reminded myself she was a girl. The hair...I'd go for the hair. Nope, that'd make me look too girlie. I set my tray down, knowing that was the only way I'd respect myself in the morning. I curled my fingers into a fist and...

Someone grabbed my hand mid-punch, murmuring, "Hold on, tiger."

I didn't want to hold on. I'd been plotting that punch for years, and the person blew my opportunity to be a badass chick who punched the arrogance out of Ivy. Or should I say *Dylan* blew it because I'd recognize the warm feel of his hand anywhere.

"You almost hit me!" Ivy screamed, tears pooling under her lashes. "I'm reporting you to the office!"

Dylan calmly put his arm around my waist, tucking me into his side. "I'd think twice about that if I were you, Ivy."

She gave him a hair flip. "You only say that because you're so stupidly infatuated with her I mean really."

Something dark flashed in his eyes. "What I feel for Darcy is far from infatuation, but the moment you breathe a word of this incident, Darcy will go down in urban legend as the girl who almost hit Ivy Morrison and still made her cry. You, however, will be known as the girl who made fun of a deaf girl. Your small group of friends may have your back, but the rest of the school, I assure you, will not. Show's over, folks," he growled to those gawking at us. "Have a seat."

I stopped paying attention. I couldn't track the conversation overtop Ivy's chomping gum. I shakily picked up the salad tongs and dumped iceberg lettuce, croutons, tomatoes, garbanzo beans, and cheddar cheese on my plate in separate piles. I smothered them in ranch dressing. Even though it all went to the same place, when I couldn't control something, I strategically placed food so it wouldn't touch, eating in a clockwise pattern.

Weird, but at least it wasn't a dead gerbil.

Dylan snuggled into my side and kissed me on the cheek, smiling in a way that was heart wrenchingly beautiful. Lord, I was pathetic. Even though there was suspicion he rekindled something with Brynn, I still let him have his way with me. "Are you cool, sweetheart?"

"No," I mumbled. "We just OD'd on Ivy's barbs. Someone needs to put methadone on the menu."

Dylan chuckled and told me to join him.

The conversation between Ivy and whoever would listen to her soon collapsed, and she then hung all over Jagger who was paying the cashier. They weren't slobbering all over one another, but they did look like they'd rekindled the dysfunction.

Clementine didn't follow. She simply stood there, mirroring my every step. Maybe it was a resurrection of a little bit of pride, but I blurted out, "I long for the day I don't take the moral high ground, Clementine. What do you want?"

She looked at her feet, suddenly self-conscious. "Nnn-nothing," she stuttered.

She pivoted and walked away, a little bit of exaggerated hip action on her part. Bean's eyes bugged out of his head, so preoccupied he ran into my back with his tray. "She's so pretty," he gasped when she was out of earshot. A look at Bean's tray—which I felt positive was half on my back—showed a duplicate of mine. He even left adequate space between his salad ingredients so none of the items touched.

"You have a crush on her?" Justice said, sort of laughing from behind.

He tried to play it down, but his face gave it away. "My therapist said Clementine is like seasonal fruit. I can only like her for one season, and that's it."

I was sure there was a story there of restraining-order proportions, but I'd tackle that another day. Picking out a grease-dripping slice of pepperoni pizza, I balanced it on the edge of my plate and looked over my shoulder for Dylan. He'd returned to his seat by the windows with Finn and Grumpy. At that second, Brynn brought her tray over and squeezed into the chair that should've been mine between him and Finn. My heart peeled back like a tuna can. She placed her hand on Dylan's.

He moved it away, but still...

I wanted to break her fingers. I swear, I wanted to break her fingers and make her eat them. I shoved a bendy straw in the milk carton, downing my chocolate milk, wiping my mouth on my sleeve.

Finn caught my gaze, his eyes swearing it meant nothing. I was pretty sure my quivering chin said otherwise. I walked up to the cashier, fished around in my pocket, and realized I'd forgotten my meal card. Each semester I lost something different. Last year was my glasses. Right then was my smartcard. Figures. The keyword there was "smart." The only things in my possession were blue-foiled chocolate gelt coins from Rookie. A frown from the cashier told me she wouldn't accept the candy currency.

Racist, I almost laughed.

Our school had a strict rule about smartcard usage. Friends couldn't purchase grub for a fellow student on their cards, so unless you had cash, you pretty much were SOL. I stole a glance over to Dylan who'd pulled away from his conversation with Brynn. He was deliciously grinning, already waving a bill in the air.

I loved him, (sniff, sniff.) I hated it, but I still went all mushy when he gazed at me. And he looked yummy. He wore an oatmeal-colored sweater that hugged his muscled chest and served as a nice contrast to his coal-black hair. When I parted my lips to say, "No thanks, sugar daddy," someone came from left field and placed a ten-dollar bill in my palm.

What the...?

"We need to talk," the person said. Holy-freaking-moly, it was Slapstick Wilson. I knew Slapstick was big, but standing beside him made me feel like Tom Thumb.

When I tried to talk, nothing came out but shock. I didn't know if shock had a sound, but I sure did hear something strange in my brain. Slapstick didn't stick around. He merely slipped the money in my hand and exited the cafeteria.

Hold on. Hold on. HOLD! ON! I thought. But still I didn't manage a sound.

I threw the money at the cashier and ran after him.

Problem was, I was one slip-slide away from a school-wide embarrassment because my feet had different plans than my brain. I went down on my knees with a clonking thwack, and my tray slid like it had rocket boosters up its butt. When an accident happened, the first thing someone did was grab for safety. Secondly, the person tried to figure out what or who in the heck caused the problem. Since there was no one around, I grabbed at the air, and when a quick perusal showed nothing, the only thing I could figure was the Lord was taking me out. *Mmm-hmm, I looked like an idiot.* Then I realized I couldn't feel my legs. I'd either paralyzed myself or my legs were in on the conspiracy. I lay flat on my face with a garbanzo bean from my salad smashed to my upper lip.

Poetic justice. I laughed.

A bean.

My iPhone belted in song where it had popped out of my jeans, laying face-up at my side. Once again, I felt it fitting. I shouldn't have made fun of Grandma all month long. As I flicked the bean away, I propped myself up on my elbows, glancing at the unknown digits. "Hullo?" I mumbled into the receiver.

I heard a moan. "How's the hottest hood ornament ever to grace a car?"

I knew that voice. Slight British accent. On a really hot, copper-headed, silver-eyed guy my gut screamed was trouble. "Oh, God," I said. "Ben Ryan."

"I don't have time to talk, but I must say you've been extremely difficult to track down."

I confessed (sorta) I gave him the wrong number off the bat. "I was hoping you could take a hint," I mumbled.

Ben chuckled, and I almost felt naked. "Actually, I liked the challenge but knew there was no way in the world to mess up the *meant to be*."

I could've sworn he licked his lips.

Bean, Rudi, and Justice crouched at my side. "Are you okay?" they all three gasped.

Nothing that two extra strength Tylenols and a thousand calories of saturated fat wouldn't cure.

Dylan hovered overtop me, pulling me to my feet. "What in the," *bleep profanity*, "happened?" God only knew how, but my mind successfully censored most profanity. When I didn't answer, he repeated the question—profanity doubled.

Gasping, I whispered, "D, you're gonna make Jesus mad."

After Dylan helped me up and dusted off my pride, he murmured, "And how's that?"

I gave him a shrug like he was an idiot. "You've made it a three F-word conversation, D, not me. I was just trying to keep you from going up in smoke."

Rolling his eyes, he took my iPhone out of my hands. "Ben Ryan," I told him before he could even ask.

He narrowed his eyes. "Ben Ryan. The Ben Ryan that hit you with his car?"

"Aye," I muttered.

That was juuuuuust enough to morph Dylan into the Tasmanian devil. "Well, hello, Ben Ryan," he seethed into the receiver. "Dylan

Taylor here. Learn to fricking drive, and stay away from my best friend." When he angrily smashed his thumb on the "end" button, I bit the side of my cheek to keep from crying. The last thing I needed was angry words—even if they weren't directed at me. My hands reached back and pulled my black hoodie up over my head to hide, well...everything.

Wow, I needed a TO.

A time-out and a Coke—and I knew Coach had a well-stocked supply. "You'll have to excuse me," I told him. "I'm going to go bang my head up against the wall until I pass out or die prematurely."

Dylan grabbed my wrists, his amber eyes tenderly searching mine for answers. "Not so fast, sweetheart. Where are you going?"

The silence was deafening. A reluctant glance had me meeting eyes with just about everyone. I'd cued the gossip. Heaven help me, what was I supposed to do? Pick up my food and eat it?

"Places to go, people to see." I sniffled.

Tears to cry. Brynn Hathaway to ink-in on my hit list.

————

I file-thirteen'd my tray and left. I wasn't entirely thrilled with my acting performance, but it got the job done. After I gave Dylan a rather long, suggestive hug, he reluctantly sat back down, and I was hot on the heels of Slapstick Wilson. He'd been hovering outside, but once our eyeballs clashed, he turned and proverbially hit the pavement. I chased him down the hall, following the swagger of his old, gray hoodie, beat-up jeans, and stained sneakers. After the third yell, I gave up and simply jogged after him to a darkened part of the building in the sophomore hallway. Sort of spooky, but no way in the world would it eclipse what went down in the cafeteria.

I finally stopped, cupping my hands over my mouth, yelling, "I know you hear me, Slapstick!"

Slapstick scratched the back of his neck, slowly turning. He smiled one of those teeth-gleaming grins your dentist would love. I wasn't sure his smile held a lot of sanity, but I'd never know until we got a little more cozy. I walked twenty feet, careful step after careful step, my fear breeding like naughty rabbits. Slapstick was tons bigger than me, but I guess if things went south, I could always yell.

Once we were within inches of one another, I extended my hand, "I'm Darcy."

"Yeah," he acknowledged in a chuckle. "I've never seen someone so gaffe-prone in my life."

Talk about adding insult to injury. "Mind-blowing, isn't it?" I mumbled.

"I'd say. Are you all right?"

Eh, over it. I wasn't sure how I could ever live down an incident like that, but it wasn't my first go around with the cafeteria floor. Thing was, I didn't have time to get all woe-is-me. Besides, getting my dignity back would take more than one single act or a hug from a stranger. Public humiliation was sort of my theme song.

He clutched a copy of *A Christmas Carol* in his left hand. One couldn't escape the irony. In Charles Dickens's work, the main character, Scrooge, changed from a cold, penny-pinching recluse to the embodiment of the Christmas Spirit after a visit from the ghost of his dead partner. My ghost, however, didn't have goodwill toward men on his mind. He stole the cold, hard-earned cash of his victims.

"You're a Dickens lover," I said, nodding toward the book.

"I'm learning to read," he said, shyly shrugging.

Learning to read? I thought. Shouldn't that have happened in first or second grade? I found it interesting he said it so nonchalantly. Most would take that secret to the grave, but I figured if he could carry the brunt, then I'd be big enough to bury the shock. "You claim we needed to talk," I said. "Start moving your lips."

He cocked his head to one side. "That's actually my line. I understand you put out word you're looking for me."

Apparently, he didn't have time for games. Good, my style too.

I exaggeratedly pecked my index finger on my watch, sticking with the Veronica Mars routine. "Time is tick-tocking away here, so I'm going to show you my cards. I hear someone from our school, in Valley's backyard, is an identity thief. I know you have a record of stealing credit cards. Are you involved, or do you know who is?"

Not one of my better openers because he looked like I'd just smacked him. Eh, my interrogation techniques could use some work. I'd offended him and sounded like a narrow-minded monster all at the same time.

Lo and behold, he burst into laughter. "Dang," he said chuckling. "You truly are the gutsiest chick I've ever met."

I mentally smacked myself, still hammering away at the point. "I'm sorry that didn't come out right," I apologized, "but answer, Slapstick. I don't have all day, and if I don't put some gas in my tank, I'm going to die of starvation."

He held his chin up a fraction of an inch, his hazel eyes cutting into me like a sharp knife. Slapstick, regardless of his outward appearance, was a darn good-looking guy. His muscles had just the right amount of definition, and I could see the bulk of his legs through his old jeans. Some lucky girl would one day land him and beautify her gene pool. "Why do you care?" he asked suspiciously.

"I was offered a reward," I answered honestly.

Both his eyes furrowed, looking like a buzzard's on a rotting opossum. "If there's a reward, then that makes you a snitch."

Kinda. Sorta. Maybe. "I'm not a snitch. I'm simply a good American. We were built on the principle it's okay to love your money," I said. We were also built on the principle it was okay to rebel. But if truth be known, I was bored and had only a few weeks to make myself feel like a superhero.

"Once you get it, you owe me ten bucks anyway," he said with a smile.

"I can do that," I said, smiling back. "So are you involved or not?"

A brim of sadness marked his eyes, like he was tired of people thinking the worst of him. "Whenever I've stolen, there was a reason," he said quietly.

"You didn't answer the question."

"Yes, I did. You weren't listening."

I tipped my head in concession. Shoot, I wasn't getting anywhere, and I had a feeling Dylan had already issued a BOLO to anyone who would listen. "What about a guy named Damon Whitehead?"

His face grew colder than the Tundra. "I know him enough," he said, "and to answer the question you haven't asked, I don't know what he does in his spare time." I wasn't sure I believed him. They had the same foster parents for two years. He was merely loyal or that home had simply been a place to lay his head.

I blurted out, "Are either of you associated with someone known as The Ghost?"

Slapstick looked at me like my head was a doomsday clock. "You need to watch yourself, Walker. You're skating on thin ice.'

"So I'm onto something?"

"How long do you want to live?"

"As long as you, I suppose."

"I tend to value my life. You seem oblivious or overly reckless."

Once upon a time, that might've offended me. Right then, it was something I'd heard so often it went in one ear and out the other.

I regurgitated everything I knew about Tito's identity being stolen as Slapstick watched, astonished. I also threw in my desire to find out who vandalized Coach's car. His face said he didn't have feelings about Coach Wallace one way or the other. I then shared the names who Coach thought might have possible motives. Slapstick snorted and chuckled. "No way," he said. Add that to Bean's assessment, and I mentally crossed them off the list permanently.

A teacher stepped outside into the hall, giving us a look like we were required elsewhere—you know, SOP for the normal students.

Slapstick followed me to Coach's office where I entered the room whistling the school's fight song. I immediately opened the refrigerator.

Breathe in. Breathe out. Open Coke. Drink can.

After I did my just-get-calm ritual, I offered Slapstick a drink, but he declined. While I explained the Nico Drake situation landed me in detention, I knocked back another can and wolfed down a stale piece of Wonder Bread that hopefully was mold-free.

Dwarfed by his towering frame, I was drawn in even deeper when Slapstick talked about the book he was reading. Slapstick had a soft spot. God only knew why he always wound up on the wrong side of the law, but if he'd get his head out of his rear end, he could actually land a girl and turn into something.

"You're not what I expected," I admitted, downing my second can as we made our way to the junior wing.

Slapstick paused for a moment, debating something in his mind. "You're exactly what I expected, but I don't work for free, Walker," he muttered.

"I wasn't aware I'd offered you a job."

"Yes, you were," he countered.

Ugh, I guess I was, but it was *my* gig. I wasn't being selfish. Half the buzz was realizing I could figure things out on my own. But a flip of the calendar in my brain reminded me time was my enemy. I added him to the list with Bean, wondering if I'd invited the Devil over to play.

Chapter Eleven

SCIENCE EXPERIMENTS

"That thing in your purse...with the apple on it...you pick it up when it broadcasts that grandma got murdered," Dylan murmured.

"Uhh..."

"Let's just go with the thought that your phone is broken."

"Yeah, that's a good thought," I mumbled. Dylan stalked through the door, proving once and for all if he wanted to talk, he wasn't above driving over in the dark to speak his piece. It was Friday night, and he'd just played in VHS's basketball game (he scored a career high forty-nine points) but acted as if his dog had died. I'd bragged all over social media to anyone who'd talk to me. Evidently, Dylan didn't see his success quite as extraordinarily as I did.

Murphy couldn't make it to the game. Apparently, some lowlife scum hacked into his bank account and bought a used four-wheeler in Hyannis Port. I didn't know Massachusetts had hillbillies, but Murphy burned up the phone all evening, cancelling credit cards and cursing his luck.

First my Twitter was hacked. Next was Murphy's bank account.

A little too close for comfort.

Murphy mandated I stay home because he feared there'd be a repeat of the Nico Drake incident, and he wouldn't be there to settle the score. I was bummed because it was the official end to being grounded, so my only recourse was to cheer on the team via the school's website's live-feed. And down Coke...lots and lots of Coke.

It was a little past ten, and my hands shook from too much caffeine. Murphy and Marjorie had fallen asleep in his bed an hour earlier, and I'd been doing the usual...channel surfing the adult channels Murphy didn't know were free that month. I considered it research since he still hadn't dispensed the standard birds-and-bees conversation. Plus, I felt a little unloved—and even raunchy love sounded good.

Dylan seemed tense when one would think he'd be on cloud nine. As he sauntered to the couch, his back was extra straight and stiffer than normal. Not the normal ease in which he carried himself. I traveled behind him, tiptoed up, and helped him shrug out of his school jacket. I gently pitched it on the recliner as he fell into the couch. I stood in front of him with my hands crossed defensively at my waist, realizing I didn't look like anyone's dream girl. Ready for bed, I sported a Victoria's Secret mint and white leopard pajama set. The hem had frayed on the shirt and the bottoms had Coke stains dotting one leg where a can exploded. Add a lop-sided messy bun, smudgy glasses, and hotwired nerves, and I looked like a hobo who'd fallen off the train.

"You're quiet, D. Would you like something to eat? Drink?"

He inhaled and expelled a deep breath. "I'm good, sweetheart. But I'm beat. Lie down with me. One of my favorite things in the world is lying next to you and doing absolutely nothing."

Could. He. Be. More. Perfect.

———

Well after midnight, a scary movie on TNT hummed low in the background, and Dylan and I laid cocooned under a fake fur blanket. He looked amazeballs in dark jeans and a navy Henley. All I knew was by the way it hugged his muscles, it screamed money, stud, and fertile ovaries I needed to keep in check. Earlier, we'd had popcorn, and I'd pulled off his shoes—doing all of those coupley things that showed you loved someone. When I relaxed back onto his chest, I'd nodded off twice. When I woke the last time (okay, when I snored myself awake), Dylan was sleeping, and I knew we were moments from his mother's please-don't-be-dead call.

I crawled on top of him, my hand stroking the planes of his chest as I continued to tell him how proud he'd made me. "You're such a stud, D, and you smell wonderful. Normally, you smell like dirt," I joked, "but tonight you smell so good...I love you."

I couldn't swear to it, but I think he growled.

Dylan slowly ran both hands up and down my back, murmuring, "Always," which was the standard response when the other uttered the L-word phrase. It was one of those classic Dylan and Darcy moments where the love felt bigger than words. Our hugs could go on for five seconds or five minutes, but he always left the duration up to my discretion. But something suddenly short-circuited the mood. He stiffened, his shoulders tightening, his arms quickly squeezing and falling to his sides.

For once, he broke the hug first.

Out of the blue, he grabbed my hand, holding it to his heart. "You do realize it's not normal the way you're touching me, yeah?" he murmured.

It was a scientific fact once someone said something like that, a person immediately got defensive. My hand instantly stilled. I attempted to jerk it away—heck, I wanted to cut the dang thing off —but Dylan tightened his grip, holding my fingers in place. I couldn't look at him. *No, no, for freak's sake, noooooooooo.* "I didn't mean to embarrass you, sweetheart. Give me your face," he murmured hastily, putting a gentle hand to my chin.

Couldn't do it. So I buried myself deeper inside his neck.

Dylan did an ab curl, attempting to capture my eyes. "Darc, look at me."

Slooooowly. Slowly, I met his amber gaze. Dylan acted as though something dark and painful lived in his head. Some demons I didn't even know he battled. "Does this make me like a slut or something?" I whispered.

Sweet Lord. I didn't know whether to be mortified...*or proud.*

His temper took off at warp speed. "For God's sake, no, Darcy. You've only been with me. Let alone do anything else that qualifies in the slut territory. Don't say that." No matter his words, I still shot up, pushing myself away. Far, far away from the heat I didn't understand. "We've got some things to talk about, Darc," he said exhaling.

Dylan sat us both up, our thighs barely touching, careful not to get too close. I got the feeling he protected himself. Still wrapped snug and tight in the fur throw, Dylan wrapped it tighter around me, like he tried to make sure I stayed warm before he left for the evening. "Here lately, I feel like I'm hanging onto you with bloody fingernails," he murmured. "You mean everything to me, Darc. So much that it—"

"...hurts," I completed softly.

"Yeah," he agreed. "So what had you so busy you couldn't pick up a phone call from your best friend?"

So Broody Dylan made an appearance because he thought I'd been blowing him off?

Well, let me give a synopsis of what I'd been doing. And let me just say it'd distract the President of the Freaking U.S. of Unholy A. When Dylan called, Vinnie and I were on the phone—plotting our next adventure. I'd given him the information Finn had provided—the addresses and photographs of the people in the detention rotation for the past two years, plus a list and photo ID of those tardy on the day Coach's car had been vandalized. Vinnie said he'd be home tomorrow for a short trip to see his grandmother, and we'd stake each of them out. Our plan was to see if any of the teenagers living in those homes resembled Motor Oil Hair and Coffee Blot Boy. It was a major long shot, but Vinnie was my good luck charm. If anything, it'd be a starting place and a way to widen the net. If I widened the net, God only knew what I'd reel in.

Dylan blew out a sigh, all but convinced I'd ignored him because of some deep-seated reason I refused to address.

I dropped the blanket and took his hands, leaning forward as though I was about to hear a secret. "What are we talking about here, D?"

The subject matter gnawed at him. He gazed to the ceiling, blinked twice, got up, and immediately sat back down. Rubbing the back of his neck, he inhaled and exhaled like he was in the middle of an asthma attack and couldn't find air. Honestly, I'd never seen him so rattled, and his lack of control made me almost jump on the crazy train with him.

"Say it," I coaxed softly.

Big breath. "I intend on finishing a conversation tonight we should've had four months ago. And before you make a joke out of it, I'm begging you to take me seriously. This is my heart, Darc. Please, respect that."

Sweet God Almighty.

Wasn't that an H-bomb?

And no wonder he thought I'd joke because I'd done that before and predictably clammed up when my internal dialogue (my own fears) went haywire.

"Let me get this straight. If I understand correctly, you want something more from me than best friends?" I clarified.

"Yes."

"You want to make me Mrs. Hottie."

"Yes." Not even a blink.

"Am I allowed to laugh?" I said, half giggling. Because let me tell you, folks. That was the most ridiculous thing I'd heard in a while.

Still no blink. "You said you wouldn't, Darcy...*please*."

He said my name like a prayer—a whisper so soft and powerful it was like a breath from the gods. I had a momentary flair of panic. I'd held hands with the Devil, manufactured lies, told lies, and confessed lies all in the name of my warped sense of justice. And Dylan wanted *me? Me?* Dang, that was so freaking romantic I might write a song about it.

"I'm sorry," I said softly, "and I agree. It's about time."

My word, there might be hope for me in the communications department yet. He glued his eyes shut as if in physical pain. "Dammit," he cursed.

"I'm not sure how to interpret that," I whispered.

"This conversation is scaring me to death," he whispered back.

I punted those words back at him. "Like Brynn Hathaway scares *me?*"

The fairies of transparency just kicked me in the tail. It wasn't normal for me to be on the up-and-up with something so darn raw. Me, Darcy Walker, Queen of Rationalization and All Things Procrastinatory asked, "*Should* I be scared of something?"

Once again, I wasn't sure where that girl came from, but I was über stoked she'd made an appearance.

Dylan kept his eyes closed and looked like he drowned in an emotion he couldn't pull himself out of. When he spoke, although quiet, his words were impassioned. "I am the *one thing*," he whispered, "you should *never* fear, sweetheart. I love you as you are. You can trust me. That comes from the purest place imaginable in my heart."

My mouth went bone-dry.

Dylan had "All of Me" by John Legend screaming out of his pores.

And that was why Dylan was my best friend...

There were many things to love about Dylan. First off, the way he was loyal to his friends—no questions asked. There's the way he said my name in his sweet voice or the way he called me Darcy when he was mad. Then there's the fact he forgave my little, white lies and never held a grudge. Or poured all that hot-blooded charm on me and spoke alpha when someone messed with my heart. I loved the way he reached for my hand before I even knew I needed it. *Helllloooooo*, the way he filled out his jeans. I couldn't forget the dimples and teeth or the fact he grilled a burger like Bobby Freaking Flay. Or maybe it was all about the eye contact and the little things that made my heart melt. Like him bringing me UDF coffee when Starbucks was closer to his house. Or the way he hugged my little sister when he didn't even know I'd been watching.

But perhaps the biggest thing I loved was he always knew when my thoughts were on my mother.

Realization hit me hard.

My crush had evolved. Evolved into something that worried me. There was a brief moment where I pictured us happily ever after. Trouble was, I didn't fit the prototype of the girl a guy brought home to Mom...Brynn did.

But instead of shouting the evolution from the rooftops or declaring my undying like (or love), I blurted out, "I want to date around first. Like a science experiment or something."

I think he held his breath. I know I hadn't breathed. In fact, if my legs were long enough I would've kicked my own tail. Can someone tell me why the heck I said that? That just ensured I was one hundred percent mental. It was Dylan-OMG-Taylor we were talking about. I'd practically just turned him down.

A dark gleam flashed in his eyes, and he inched toward me and took my face in his hands. A glint of humor marked his gaze, and I swear to God in Heaven, the dang room started to sway. "You want to date around first," he said lowly.

"Yeah," I sheepishly answered.

"Yeah," he repeated even lower.

"And the rule goes for you too," I insanely added.

A slight pause. "It goes for me too," he echoed.

Wow, so much for a heart-to-heart. We weren't getting anywhere—complements mainly of me. "Kill your mockingbird, Dylan. I hate it when you do that." He had a dreadful habit of mocking whatever I'd say when he felt it was stupid. Believe me, it was highly effective because it threw me off of my game. But a little part of my brain told me I needed to be worried about what I'd just encouraged him to do. I'd die if he paraded someone around in front of me, and I wouldn't give up my seat in the Beemer without one heck of a dogfight. "I want to date around," I attempted to say firmer.

Dylan narrowed his eyes and laughed darkly. "You're joking."

"No," I said.

His eyes locked on mine, and my throat went tight with a lump of emotion that felt quite a bit like regret. "Oh, do tell. Who threatens to take you away from me in this little science experiment?"

"I don't know, but maybe he's out there."

Dylan was undeterred. Imagine that. He took my hands, gave them both a tender kiss, and replaced them back over his heart. We both watched as my fingers (again) stroked the planes of his chest. Let me tell you something. That thing between us? It had gone from friction...to heat...to straight up gosh-darned combustible. Drat! As usual, my mouth said one thing, and my body said another.

"Do you really want to date around?" he asked softly.

"No" was in my mind, but "maybe" came out of my mouth. "I don't even like you," I lied as I *still* rubbed his chest. "In fact, I hope you rot in the Land Down Under. And I don't mean where baby kangaroos frolic happily."

Dylan gave me the full weight of his gaze. Deep emotions resided there along with truths he longed to utter. Not even a sigh on his part. "You more than like me, sweetheart. Therein lies your problem."

"I would agree that you're a problem."

A teeny-tiny grin. "Then explore it, Darcy. Date me too."

I had to take a moment. We both did because he appeared to have unleashed something that'd finally set him free. Dylan had never considered himself a pinch hitter, so that was completely out of character and bizarre on a level that had no name. But a date with him would be tantamount to holy matrimony. It would mean forever—but the inevitable divorce would come, and then who would there be to pick up the pieces?

"I've had other dates, Darc," he said. "I've told you as much, but as I've lain here with you—*anytime* I'm with you—I feel more intimate than I ever have with anyone else. I know our relationship has always crossed the normal boundaries of best friends, but give me a chance. Give me a chance to show you it can be something more. Something that's getting harder and harder for me to deny."

The moron in me asked, "Is that allowed?" Dylan had stuck by me when a lesser man would've run: through puking, PMS, crying so fierce I either needed a sedative or shot of whiskey. For some reason, he kept coming back. But come on—was it wise to navigate the choppy waters of friends dating friends? We were polar opposites. He was a morning person...I was a night owl. He ate healthy...I didn't give a crap. He knew important people...I knew the gutter trash. And even bigger than the differences, I had the overwhelming fear he'd rip my heart out of my chest, shove it in a blender, and hit shred.

And if he did? Would the best friendship end as fallout?

Let me play Devil's advocate here—um, yeah.

Dylan's face was as pure and honest as I'd ever seen. "It's our lives," was his answer. "Anything is allowed we agree upon."

"You'd do that?" I said in awe.

"Darcy, I want to give you what you want, but I won't let you leave my life altogether."

My chin trembled. I scrunched up my eyes...ears...heart. Dylan's words usually cut through the noise, but my chest tightened up in a panic attack.

He leaned his forehead into mine, angling his lips to my ear.

"Shh," he murmured, "I feel your panic. If this is the only way for us to end up together, then I want you to do what you have to do in order to get to that place."

Unfortunately—or rather, *fortunately* for my libido—Dylan didn't stop there. He slowly trailed his mouth down my throat, making the circuit under my chin until his lips hovered at my other ear. "Can you do that?" he asked.

I pulled on my feline and purred. *Purred, for Pete's sake!*

Time dragged at a snail's pace before I crawled out of the Dylan lovin' and found my voice. "I must admit you have nice...jeans," I said, meaning his rear. "And a nice...shirt," I added, hinting of his muscled torso. "But I don't think that's enough to pull me away from this glorious life of a wallflower." He met my eyes with a deep grin. "This is not the competitive Dylan I know," I whispered, wondering where my best friend had gone.

"I asked for this, Darc, so I'm down with your decision, but that doesn't mean I have to like it."

Dylan's straight talk was sometimes hard to stomach. Here was the crux of the problem. If I followed through and dated someone else, I'd hurt him. If I didn't and jumped right into a relationship with my best friend, then that meant I'd be opening my heart up for a hurt too big to handle. I'd loved and lost before and barely made it out alive. I needed to call things off...but oddly a veto didn't materialize from my mouth.

I sighed deeply. "All right," I said.

Dylan grasped me by the shoulders, his fingernails digging deep into my flesh. The amber in his eyes lit up to glowing, a gaze full of triumph and swagger. "Yeah?" he said grinning.

"Yeah," I answered, grinning back.

Sweet God on the Great White Throne. My head nodded enthusiastically in agreement. We were going to date—well, as soon as I got said hypothetical boys out of my system—but I couldn't shake the feeling we were finito before anything even started.

Dylan remained undeterred. "Okay, if we do this, I have one rule. It's complete honesty. At all times."

"Even where Brynn is concerned?" I surprisingly asked.

His brows furrowed, almost as if he'd been shocked Brynn even popped in my mind. "Absolutely," he reiterated. "The rules between us don't change. I pray they never change."

Dylan switched gears, something else on his mind. "That being said, I'm gonna slip on my best friend hat. You go on this date, and if you ever feel uncomfortable—even in the slightest—you call me, and I'll come to get you? Yeah?"

It felt like someone parked the Smoky Mountains on my chest.

It was one thing to say I'd date other people. It was something else to talk about it so openly with Dylan, let alone execute. Dylan acted as if our "future relationship" was a fait accompli. Right then, I wasn't sure what to do with that, so I did the usual...nothing.

His hand slid under my head, tunneling his fingers in the hair at the base of my neck. When he parted his lips to speak, I cut him off. "I'm trouble," I whispered.

"I know," he said, grinning cockily.

"I might hurt you."

"You won't." The voltage between us piped up a notch, and his smug grin grew wider. Wicked. Dylan knew the effect he had on me, and as much as I tried to act nonchalant, my heart beat out of my chest. A fact I was pretty sure he felt against his. "I've never lost anything, sweetheart, and I don't intend on starting now." I knew that to be true. "So you can go on these experimental dates. You can even have a soul baring and enriching conversation for all I care, but in the end...*I win*. But the moment I hear anyone lays a hand on you, we've got a problem."

I hitched my chin up a notch, suddenly wanting to push his buttons. "What if I want them to lay a hand on me?"

His voice turned low, lethal. And what hair he'd captured in his hand was then held firmly in his fist. "Surely to God you aren't that stupid." With that statement, he kissed the top of my head and pushed off the couch, stalking right out the door. Not even a GTG face.

And dang, if his butt didn't look good strutting away.

Chapter Twelve

THE ISLAND OF MISFIT TOYS

*D*etention came quicker than a forest fire in the dead of a California summer. Detention usually held a shroud of secrecy if one was on the outside looking in. But since Coach Wallace was close to Grumpy and me, he gave us a heads up that our punishment—or rehabilitation—was to do homework and paint a section of the cafeteria that needed a face-lift. Can I get a what-what?! If anyone would gripe about how the VHS painting job wasn't as fun as his or her last gig (translation: Coach's car) my guess was I'd found the proper venue.

Murphy referred to detention as The Island of Misfit Toys. How fitting that one of my brothers was stranded with me.

Where I had been stoked for the entire detention experience, Grumpy seemed petrified of the possibilities. Even though his fate wasn't technically at my hands, I'd searched all week for an act of atonement. I eventually told him I'd help him land Clementine as a date for our winter formal. That at least produced a smile, and on some weird plane I think he believed detention would make him look like a bad boy.

Maybe Clementine was the bad-boy type.

At seven forty, he puttered up the driveway in his clunker Ford pick-up truck. It was at least two decades old and at one time had been navy. The passenger side door had been T-boned—the silver bumper hung by not enough bolts. Both of us dressed in old sweatshirts—mine white, his gray—with ratty jeans that looked like a werewolf had slashed into shreds. I'd added a baby blue crocheted beanie, going for a hipster look. Grumpy added—heck, nothing.

"This feels like a date, Grumpy," I told him as I sat down. Coupledom wasn't a category I'd ever place him in. Out of all my brothers, he was the closest one to blood...as dysfunctional as that sounded.

He shot over a dark look. "Shut up, Walker. This will be the *last time* I wind up on the wrong side of the law with you." Funny, I had a feeling we'd be dodging the wrong side of the law for the rest of our lives.

My iPhone rang, and a peek at the number showed my best friend's gorgeous smile. "Crap," I muttered, shoving the screen in Grumpy's face. He shook his head, calling Dylan an enabler.

"I'm cuffed and in the back of the squad car," was my greeting.

Silence for a beat. "Darcy," he started, and then I registered he was scarily formal.

"Yes, Master?"

"Do exactly as you're told, sweetheart. Don't make waves, and do *not*," he repeated sternly, "crack an off-color joke. The guys running the show might not have a sense of humor. Just shut up and take the punishment. Yeah?"

Dylan acted as though he'd be leaving a nuclear bunker unsecure. Seriously, that felt about right. "I'll try," I answered, "but when I'm nervous I say stupid things."

There was a moment when Dylan probably debated how to keep that from happening. But it was a given, like death and taxes. "Darcy," he pleaded again. "I'm here to talk to if there's something that's bothering you. Let me share some of the burden."

Sheesh, that was like a please-let-me-have-your-baby chat. What sixteen-year-old guy said 'share the burden?' I'll tell you who: the guy who was headlining every girl's naughty dreams at night, that's who.

"There's nothing to share," I muttered.

"Then please conform. Just this once."

Dylan had a great morning voice: husky, raspy, and sex hopped up on sex. If I could bottle it and sell it to the terrorists, it just might be the answer to world peace. I could do without his running commentary on my life though. In fact, I woke in a total mind squeeze when I remembered what we'd spoken of earlier. The we're-dating-once-you-conduct-a-science-experiment convo. Dylan had stripped his soul bare, and it wasn't a hey-let's-hook-up conversation. He said I meant more to him than anyone *ever* had and honestly wasn't intimidated by the prospect of other guys. In fact, his cocky self appeared humored when he claimed he'd already won. And even though I knew he genuinely cared—and we'd danced around the issue in the past—being direct had been so intense...

I seriously peed my pants a little.

I sighed. "I'll take that under advisement."

"One more thing. Swear to me you don't have an ulterior motive here. I know you didn't ask to be ambushed, but something smells wrong. You're unusually quiet—at least with me. Swear to me you aren't working one of your little schemes because nothing makes sense...except *that*. Pinky swear," he growled.

All my ventures were filtered through the how-not-to-get-caught paradigm. Dylan was the main obstacle. Problem was, I'd rather chew a kill-pill than deal with broody Dylan, but I wouldn't lie and pinky swear. I didn't have many standards, but that one I'd never manipulate.

"Call you later," I whispered, hurrying up and cutting the call.

"How was the conversation with Taylor?" Grumpy asked.

I gnawed on my pinky nail. "Rainbows and roses," I joked.

"I gathered that. Talk," he demanded. "Sounds to me like you're up to something, and he's already figured it out."

I gave him my if-I-tell-you-I'm-going-to-have-to-kill-you face. He wasn't buying it. I spit my decimated pinky nail in his direction. He tried to dodge, but it stuck to his right arm. Yeah, take that, ponkey. "Okay," I mumbled, "but what I tell you is under the brotherhood clause."

"Right," he muttered, rolling his eyes, flicking off the nail. "Blah, blah, blah, chicken dance stupid stuff...yada, yada, yada, I'm a damn idiot."

I held back nothing...

Just went from A to Z and let it all hang out.

Grumpy muttered, "You're not joking."

"No," I confirmed and explained I was after the reward Tito

swore was coming. Unfortunately, Grumpy had an entrepreneurial side I wasn't aware of. He narrowed his eyes, countering, "If I help find this ghost guy, I want twenty-five percent."

Probably fair, and my nervously beating heart said I may need some muscle in my corner anyway. Grumpy turned off Valley Lane and slowly drove into the school parking lot, pulling his clunker into a spot close to the entrance. The warm front we'd been hearing about moved in the night before, and by all predictions, the high temp would be low-to-mid 40s, practically a heat wave. Snow still covered the ground, but it wouldn't last for long. As a result, the air smelled like a big fishbowl. We held hands across the melting slush, neither of us uncomfortable by the unnatural show of affection. It was like we wanted to hang onto something familiar.

And let's face it. We'd been marked.

———

A big, white placard had been posted at the front of the building that said "Detention" with a black arrow underneath. It brought to mind one of those fancy dinners where a prominent sign, seen upon arrival, pointed patrons to the desired destination.

You know, detention...an A-list affair for a D-list crowd.

We'd been banished to one of the classrooms teaching sophomore geometry. Chairs were arranged in four lines, five seats to a row. The room had a sterile, antiseptic feeling, with a sickening Lysol smell wafting in the air. Then again, that could've been a flashback to failure. I didn't have one good memory regarding geometry. I'd been sick in there the whole dang year.

"Hola, amigos," I said, laughing while I strode through the door.

AP Unger and Coach Wallace were onsite. Both stared daggers sharp enough to nick skin and didn't find the greeting creative or remotely funny.

"Hello, sirs," I amended grinning.

"Walker, this is where you're supposed to act offended to be here," Coach Wallace muttered frowning.

Now it was my turn to stare. "Why should I act offended?" I asked. "Principal Ward is the screwup, not me."

Down, mouth, down.

Coach Wallace opened his jaw...shut it.

AP Unger did the same.

AP Unger stood a little taller than me. His gray, wiry hair reminded me of an Irish Wolfhound, especially beside his black, piercing eyes. His nose and cheekbones were sharp, like they'd been chiseled from flint. And as usual, he was in a navy suit. Why he insisted on a navy suit was beyond me, but half the time he looked like he should be on the President's security detail or a pallbearer at a funeral.

"Let's start over," I said mannerly. "You're absolutely right. I'm offended to be here."

Once again, nothing.

Tough crowd.

Coach Wallace finally found a small chuckle as he slid behind the silver metal desk with a thick manila folder in his right hand. "What's with the respectful greeting, dollface?"

"Murphy said it was required," I said, adding a shrug, "but I always thought the whole concept was demeaning to a child's rights."

Someone needed to shut me up.

Once again, Coach Wallace came in short pants, a black Valley hoodie, messy hair he'd teased too high, and glasses at least a decade out of style. He and AP Unger exchanged a few words as Coach explained the procedure. Prisoners were to pick a seat, but the chair directly across was to remain vacant. Vacant because another student would occupy the chair and tutor us if need be. Sounded great in theory, but honestly all it did was point out that others had the success thing down.

Principal Ward attended a conference where the new educational theory of the month was to put the bad, on-the-edge kids with the moguls of tomorrow and hope the smartness rubbed off. A social experiment, so to speak. So in detention, students were tutored by the brainiacs. Trouble was, their goodness didn't always rub off. Some of the badness wormed its way in. How did I know that?

Word on the street said that happened to Bean.

I grabbed a seat. The chair across from me immediately became occupied with whom I recognized as Collin Lockhart.

Brynn Hathaway's ex.

Merry Freakin' Christmas.

Collin had my coloring with medium blond, gorgeous hair and tormented sky-blue eyes. Collin dressed Ivy League in worn khakis, old dock-siders without socks, and a navy polo with an upturned collar. Other than the obvious, I didn't know much about him, only that his mother worked in the post office and was one of the few who didn't look like she wanted to gun visitors down. She always smiled and asked about your family.

"Long time no see," he greeted. "I forgot how beautiful you were up close."

Cue the blush. Collin, in all his smarminess, made my cheeks pink against my better thoughts. He offered me one of two takeout coffees from Starbucks. After a quick sip of their holiday blend, I unzipped my backpack with fingers that barely worked. The temperature hovered at icebox, but maybe I'd died and hadn't figured out I lay in the morgue's deep freeze.

"Ah, Collin," I said, shaking my head and laughing. "You like to shovel the shiz, don't you?"

Collin winked a piercing blue eye. "I hear you're trying to find out who painted Coach's car. Any luck?"

A strange feeling niggled at my spine. "Who told you that?"

"You asked the whole school, Darcy," he murmured laughing. "Believe me, what you do gets around."

"It does?" I asked in shock.

His eyes were on me like tacky glue—I fail to comprehend why. "You truly have no idea," he mumbled to himself, grinning. "So how's it going?"

"So-so," I said shrugging.

"What's the motivation?"

"Good ole, American greed," I said giggling.

"So there's a reward," he said with a grin. "Need some Christmas cash? I'm working nights with my mother at the post office, sorting through holiday mail. I can get you a shift if you'd like."

"Thanks, but I prefer to be an independent contractor."

As student council president, Collin was always in the know. He parlayed complaints, negotiated with the staff, launched his ideas for a better school, things that sounded important in Teenagerland.

Equipped with a college-prep schedule around municipal government, he also starred in several of the school's theater productions. Decent singer, better actor. He appeared to be one of the few who knew what he wanted as soon as he came out of the womb.

Pretty sure I screamed for a Coke and a cookie.

Collin leaned forward, too close into my personal space, trying his best to work that hypnotic spell. "Should we commiserate together?" he murmured.

I cocked my head to one side, taking a second sip of my Starbucks. "Huh?"

"You know, Dylan and Brynn. She likes him."

Thank you, Captain Obvious.

Dylan and Brynn starred in my dreams the night before. In fact, I hanged them both from a cherry tree with Xs for eyes. Placing my cup on the desk, I pulled out a thin, purple spiral notebook—the one used for math assignments. Even though I knew what he alluded to, I didn't want to hear it hit the airwaves. Slowly zipping my backpack shut, I debated if I should delay the inevitable or get the deets straight from the horse's mouth.

I reluctantly prodded, "Exactly what *is* going on?"

He tilted his head toward the door, biting the top of his cup so hard I heard the lid crinkle. "I'm not sure," he muttered behind it. "I know she won't leave him alone, and when Brynn wants something, she most usually gets it."

A lump the size of a boulder caught in my throat. Ain't that the truth. "So this...*thing*," I paused, struggling to find the correct word, "is it legit?"

Collin looked thoughtful, like he wasn't only debating Dylan and Brynn, but his own comeuppance in the world. No matter what success would undoubtedly come his way, Collin reminded me of a bird with a broken wing. Something deep inside seemed beyond repair. "I can't speak on his part, but on hers, most definitely."

Dylan and I never had that boys-or-girls-have-cooties ickiness between us. We'd always been on the same proverbial page, but not these days. These days we were stuck in limbo purgatory. Changes were occurring, and neither of us were comfortable with the change. Well, maybe *he* was comfortable. I couldn't quite wrap my head around it yet.

I lied, "I try not to dwell on rumors."

"You should dwell on this, Darcy. Brynn's everyone's golden ticket. There's no way he's immune."

Unfortunately, I had to agree...

Bean bounced in, grinning from ear-to-ear, thankfully putting the quietus on our exchange. Wearing a white painter's jump suit, Mr. Pongo had been safety-pinned to his lapel. I bit my cheek to keep from laughing. Holy-moly, did he spear him in the brain? Slapstick followed, sporting the same clothes as the last time we'd spoken. He gave a quick chin jerk in acknowledgment, both settling in behind Grumpy.

Slapstick texted the night before and said he and Damon Whitehead had been doomed to detention on the weekend. He said he'd have my back if anything bad went down. I didn't press for what that might entail, but after my run-in with Nico Drake, I assumed it meant a punching bag was highly possible. Slapstick's particular offense—as was Damon's—was arguing with authority. If Principal Ward was the presiding judge, it wasn't even close to being innocent until proven guilty. Besides, Slapstick didn't seem like the arguing type. Perhaps he merely took up for himself, and Principal Ward dropped the hammer unfairly.

It was five minutes until eight, and Damon had gone AWOL. I made out a grocery list, ripped my thumbnail down to the quick, and as the minute hand hit twelve, Damon strolled in, takeout coffee in hand. He wore a nice black T-shirt and new jeans, acting so used to the gig there was no room for embarrassment anymore. I had both he and Slapstick right where I wanted them—nothing could ruin the day—until Brynn Hathaway, flanked by three other students, glided in.

A collective gasp filled the room, quickly eclipsed by a male, hormonal moan.

Bean whispered, "Oh, Lordy."

Gut check. The girl looked like a Da Vinci angel. In the movies, when the girl everyone loves shows up on film, she gets extra lighting, extra makeup, and extra magic. Brynn brought in a ray of sunshine that lit up her heart-shaped face like the gosh-danged sun.

Her trademark chocolate-brown waves had been pulled back in a tight ponytail, but it wasn't tighter than her skinny jeans and pink turtleneck. We met eyes, not really smiling or frowning. She knew who I was to Dylan, and I sure as heck knew who she wanted to be to him. After a forced smile toward Collin—who returned one just as forced—she picked the space directly across from Slapstick, scooting her chair beside him. The two other females plopped down alongside Grumpy and Bean. The guy took on Damon.

Coach took a quick headcount, checked a sheet of paper, and closed the door.

"Start working, kids. Then we're going to paint."

Monday's math assignment laid in front of me, but I couldn't relax. I think I sighed.

"What's wrong, Walker?" Coach grumbled. "For heaven's sake, don't start already."

It was a shame I had a reputation. Unfortunately, I deserved every frigging insult hurled my way. My leg bounced like a basketball. "You're setting me up for failure."

"And how's that?"

"I can't relax. This whole experience could've been better if you would've turned up the heat. I guess I'm cold."

Bean's voice was small, careful. Like he feared he'd make a bad situation worse with the wrong words. "Maybe she needs her gloves."

Grumpy kicked my seat so hard it skidded and screeched. "Conform, Walker," he grunted, using Dylan's words. "For the love of God, conform."

Collin unloaded a smile your momma told you to run from. "I think that's justifiable, Coach," he said. "If that's what Darcy needs for success, then we need to make sure she gets it."

Spoken like a guy trying to make his ex-girlfriend jealous. He'd done it, too, because I felt Brynn's anger like boiling water pitched in my face.

Coach stared at Collin, then at me. "You'll come straight back?" he grumbled.

I dashed back to my locker and grabbed my coat and gloves, for once returning right away. While the others worked, I kicked off my shoes and drew my feet underneath me, noshing red Twizzlers when no one was looking.

Collin scooted his desk over, appraising my work. I asked one question simply to appease him but then put my nose to the grind-stone. I breezed through thirty-five problems with ease.

Slapstick was the first to leave his seat and slide a sheet of paper in front of Coach. Shock of all shockers, Brynn slid out of her seat, lifted a proud chin, and dutifully strode up next to him. Like *right* next to him, as though she tried to shield him from something that might be hurtful. My word, there totally went my theory that she was a vapid bubble-head who boiled baby kittens. I didn't want to think she actually cared about him, but she whispered to Coach—by the feel of things—on Slapstick's behalf. I did make out, "Seth is trying really hard, Coach."

Wow, she first-named him. Slapstick hung his head, embar-rassed, and then gave her a quick side squeeze that in no way what-soever left her uncomfortable. Coach stared intently at the exchange, at the paper, and finally touched Slapstick's forearm.

"Yes, sir," Slapstick responded to whatever he said.

Coach muttered something else and Slapstick did the, "Yes, sir," thing again, shyly dipping his head with a minor hillbilly twang. I got the distinct impression Coach wished he could change things in Slapstick's world but knew there'd be a better chance at getting the world to spin backward.

Coach ended with a grunt, pointing toward the door.

Once Slapstick and Brynn left, I slipped my feet in my shoes and skipped to the front, slamming my paper down on the desk in sweet satisfaction. Coach scanned my answers, paused to look at me, and perused them again a little more seriously. He slowly laid the paper back down, tenting his fingertips together in front of him.

He had a droll look about him. "Walker, I'm no math teacher, but these all look correct."

"Mind-boggling, isn't it?" I said with a giggle.

"Listen, dollface," he whispered, leaning toward me. "I know how smart you are, and kids like you scare the average teacher. Think what you could do if you applied yourself."

Oh, boy, here we go. The old if-you-applied-yourself speech, then you could cure cancer or something. If you applied yourself, you could be a millionaire by the time you turned twenty-five (Dylan's father's favorite). If you applied yourself, you could be anything or do anything your brilliant mind dreamed.

Soooooooo wasn't true.

The thing I longed to do most went beyond the laws of metaphysics.

Call me when you could fix that.

I dispensed a truthful answer. "I have to be in the right frame of mind, Coach. Teachers don't let me take my shoes off or wear my coat and gloves regularly. And by the time I figure out what works, the test is half over. I've made peace with it."

Soon after, Damon dragged himself to the front. I couldn't miss the cloying resentment. Damon had a short fuse from what I'd gathered—maybe the shortest I'd ever encountered—because standing near him felt twenty degrees hotter. Shoot, I found that interesting, but I needed to get to Slapstick pronto. Why call and give me the heads up on him and Damon anyway? He obviously had something to say—point for me.

Damon hadn't uttered a word, yet Coach still called him out. "Can the attitude, son," he barked. "What's eating you today?"

"What did I miss?" I asked, my eyes darting back and forth between the two.

By the look Damon leveled me with, I would've sworn he'd marched off Darth Vader's Death Star. I unleashed an equally rancid stare right as Collin pushed his way between us, hooking an arm over my shoulder. "Everything okay here?" he murmured, chewing on his Starbucks cup.

Damon gazed at Coach, to Collin, and then upward as if the answer lay in the ceiling.

I let out a big heavy sigh, glancing at my watch. My dream for reward money was on life support. I excused myself and headed straight for the door.

———

AP Unger had Christmas carols piping through the school's intercom system. In spite of his normal stiffness, he was one of those administrators who wanted everyone to be happy, every religious and ethnic group represented. He was Jewish, but on Fridays he played Christmas carols during lunch. They spun again during detention. The particular selection was "I Want a Hippopotamus for Christmas." One of my all-time favorites.

My first topic of conversation began with the winter formal. You know, a night where all the lovahs went out together and hoped they got lucky—or close to it. Since prom and homecoming were held offsite, it was the inaugural dance to basically see if students didn't somehow blow the place up. Rumor claimed fake snow, pine trees, and an eggnog fountain, and pictures in a horse-drawn sleigh would be taken. Sounded like fun, but amidst all the excitement came the usual teenage angst of *will I be a wallflower?*

Guys and girls both liked to talk about the opposite sex—even if it was unrequited. I wasn't sure what it was about me. Maybe they didn't see me as a threat, or maybe they saw my equal desperation in the wallflower world. Whatever it was, people usually opened their mouths and regurgitated their screwed-up lives even if I didn't ask.

"And I love her fuchsia weave," Bean said sighing. "I want to touch it." Dear God, he referred to Justice. He didn't have a snowball's chance in Hell of landing her. Heck, she could probably kill him with his own eyelash, but far be it from me to rain on his hormonal, delusional parade.

"She *is* pretty," I said smiling. Then that little thing that killed the cat got ahold of me. "What do people say about *me*?"

I dipped my roller inside the tray of paint and slapped a white streak on the wall. I had a theory why we painted the cafeteria. Chances were, we covered years and years of animal fat that wouldn't go away with a wet cloth.

Bean answered, "That you're taken."

Dylan. I sighed. We definitely were something, but taken wasn't it.

I said, "Would they want to date me if they *didn't* think I was taken?"

Bean glanced at the ceiling, Grumpy at his feet. It was one of those times both hoped if they ignored me long enough, I'd forget they owed me an answer.

"Don't answer that," I muttered.

Before shame could take root, I spun on my heels and hit a soapy puddle of water. My legs went out from underneath me, and the paint flew through the air, landing on the tan tile in long wavy streaks. I tried to recover but overcompensated and Fosbury flopped, landing so hard my butt felt like a popped balloon. I looked like an idiot, and the immediate laughter of the group sealed the deal.

Lovely.

As I snatched the towel a laughing Grumpy tossed over, Slapstick moseyed to my side with a mop and rolling bucket.

Well, well, well, here comes the silver freaking lining.

I dabbed at my face as he lifted the mop from the bucket and swished it across the floor. "Thanks," I mumbled. "A thirty-six inch inseam trips you up from time to time."

"Don't I know it," he said, laughing back.

I placed the rag on the table to my side, needing to spur the dialogue.

He squeezed out the mop, handing me a roller as he flanked himself to my left side. Damon lugged over his gear, parking himself to my right. He whapped an overly wet roller on the wall, paint drippings splattering his LeBron sneakers. Wow, I'd be guarding those with my life, but Damon didn't seem to have a lot of regard for anything.

"I hear you've been looking for me," he muttered, his brown eyes anything but warm.

"Yup," I answered, and I didn't get a chance to ask who'd delivered the message before he spoke again.

"Lying is not usually a good foundation to a lasting friendship, Walker," he said and smirked.

"I wasn't aware I'd just lied," I told him.

"But I hear that's what you do," Damon protested.

Okay...hated Damon.

First up, I asked about Coach's car, and maybe it was wrong, but the delivery was with more than a hint of accusation. "Everyone's heard about that," he said, chuckling with no sympathy. "I didn't do it, but why would you think I'd know?"

"Do you?"

I'd outed myself as someone who thought bad people always knew other people who did bad things. I attempted an answer, but his voice came out like thunder, growing loud and testy with each confrontational look. "You thought I was the type, right?" he accused. "The type that didn't care what the crime was, you're just always involved?"

Huh, he had a point.

But let's be real...profiling existed for a reason.

He crowded up into my personal space, eyes as cold and hard as a dead body on ice. I fought to stand my ground, but I'll be honest —it was hard. Damon had some seriously loose screws. "Tsk. Tsk, Walker. You're reputation isn't exactly stellar. Look at where you are now."

I shrugged, saying, "I plan on being a one-timer."

When I woke that morning, the last thing I considered was my reputation. But if I took the time to think about my methods of operation—which I sorrily never did—maybe the whole shebang was a tad embarrassing. Granted, I didn't do anything to land me in detention on purpose, but I needed to work on being appropriately embarrassed.

Damon gave me a time-will-tell look as I made a snowflake on the wall.

"Then answer this, Darcy. Did you think Slapstick knew anything?" Slapstick obviously hadn't mentioned our conversation. I could tell by the feel in the room. Damon kept pushing my buttons when I never answered. "I'm thinking I don't like you. It's a shame it wasn't my finger on that gun last spring. I wouldn't have missed, and your big mouth put my friend in jail."

I pulled in a breath...that wasn't exactly what I'd term welcome material.

But I was determined not to let Damon see the effect his words had on me. The shooter (who chased me with a gun, murdered three people, and shot AP Unger)—had sent me several letters over the summer—trying to be my jailhouse pen pal. To know I spoke with someone who considered that maniac a friend left me on high alert. I was stuck with the cold, stark fear that only a true sociopath could conjure. Damon Whitehead was one evil sonovagun, and I needed one eye on my back.

Swiping the wall with the roller, I made a big W and watched paint drip to the drop cloth beneath me. Damon had an opinion of me he wasn't going to change one way or another. Well, good. That made two of us. I painted on a psychopathic smile, trying to beat him at his own game.

I said, "A friend of mine had his checking account hacked, Damon. In fact, he didn't only lose a few bucks, the thief stole his personal credit information and used it to try and buy a house. I've heard that someone in Valley does this stuff for sport. Have you heard who that might be?"

Slapstick continued to paint...still not giving up we'd spoken earlier.

Once again, Damon gave me his told-you-so face. Translation, I was a bigot.

His paranoia ignited instantly. He wasn't much bigger than me, but his attitude was of a tribe of people who'd seen more hard than good. "You're just like everyone else," he bellowed. "Who says I'm into that?" Well, I could admit I'd seen his juvie record, but I got the feeling I shouldn't put my hand in his cage.

Crud.

"You're not even going to try and deny it, are you?" he barked. Damon's voice went raspy—he was either on the verge of a cold or smoked one too many cigarettes.

I stupidly suggested, "Maybe you shouldn't smoke, Damon." I didn't mean it as an insult. I, honest to God, thought he might not see thirty.

He expelled a bitter laugh—harsh, stinging, like tiny bugs biting into my skin. The sensation was so powerful I had the overwhelming urge to roll on the ground to remove it. Slapstick, on the other hand, actually looked nervous. He tripped over his own feet, sliding into his bucket, making the water slosh in a swirl. Tiny flumes of water streamed between our feet, soaking the bottoms of my shoes.

"Everything's cool, *D-D-Damon*," he stammered. "Darcy's a *n-nice* girl."

"No, she's not," Damon seethed. "She's like all of 'em. Thinking she's somethin' she's not. Girls like that should only be dealt with in one way."

Damon proved he just might be the supreme ponkey of the cosmos.

Knowing I had a lot of ground to cover, I decided to go for

broke. I'd already made him angrier than a hornet, so I decided to maximize my time—even if it meant I'd be under fire myself. I quickly pulled Motor Oil Hair and Coffee Blot Boy out of my backpack, thrusting the photos in his face.

"Do you know these guys?" I asked. "I've got a hunch one of them knocked off Nowacki's Videos and stole the owner's identity. And they also did the same to Tito Westbrook, crime reporter for *The Cincinnati Enquirer*."

Slapstick carefully took both photographs and pulled them up to his eyes, perusing them as someone would a drop of water under a microscope. Damon, however, looked like his head would blow right off his shoulders. He slammed me back up against the wall, my head banging against the cinder block in an instant headache.

Heaven must've felt sorry for me because Grumpy muscled his way over and crowded into the group. "You're barking up the wrong tree, Whitehead," he hissed, jamming a stiff finger in his direction. "Do you know who her best friend is? In case you don't, it's Dylan Taylor. After I beat the shit out of you, he'll be next...and my guess is your family will be lucky if there's a body for a viewing."

A hush filled the room.

Yeah, Dylan's name held that much weight.

"Why are you doing this?" Slapstick gasped at me.

The obvious? Tito Westbrook deserved justice, and Coach Wallace deserved a new paint job. Couple that with no life, no boyfriend, no discernible path for the future, and the motivation was simple: I was bored.

Damon took two thundering steps, chest-bumping Grumpy. "I'm afraid of no one."

Bring it on was in my mind, but absolutely nothing came out of my mouth. I tried again to speak, but Grumpy spoke overtop me, pulling me by the elbow to where he'd shoved me completely behind him. "I was hoping you'd say that," he said, laughing darkly. "Taylor delights in showing people the error of their ways."

Grumpy may be a lot of things, but he always had the gonads when it counted. Other than Vinnie, he and I spoke the closest language. It was called weathering years and years of hard times, but in our favor, it bred a very astute mistrust. He could sniff out a fake as quickly as I could.

Damon parked himself within a breath of Grumpy's face, a sick sadistic grin lining his lips. He had a gold tooth I'd never noticed, even while he'd been speaking. The more his grin tipped up to his ears, the more the gleam of gold prism'd in the light. One minute I thought he'd pummel Grumpy into sawdust. The next he backed down like a whipped dog. The mood grew crazier and crazier by the minute. Couple that with "Oh Holy Night" crooning in the background, and it was some seriously messed up shinola.

Chapter Thirteen

SKELETONS IN THE CLOSET

I'd always heard Death sometimes came just to visit. Right then, I was pretty sure I looked at the Puerto Rican version.

Claudia's sister, Ana Rosalina, blew into town along with the Devil's spawn—er, Choncho—her son. I wasn't a fan of Choncho. He had something about him that didn't jive with me. At only eight, the eyes on his pudgy, thirty-pound overweight body had a maturity to them of adults. Not ripe with wisdom, but ripe with a worldly knowledge of the bad crap that could happen. No childhood innocence was detectable anywhere, assuming it had been inside in the first place.

Claudia only had one bedroom in her apartment, and Ana Rosalina planned to stay in the states until Christmas. Murphy said Claudia could bunk at our home if she needed an escape, but so far they'd been cohabitating without killing the other.

Like Claudia, Ana Rosalina had an ample hourglass figure and was born in full makeup—her blush painted as thick and opaque as a stop sign. Both in green muumuus, they huddled over the kitchen sink, dumping herbs and what looked like indigenous Puerto Rican bugs into a pot.

For most, you'd ask, *Why?*

For us, it barely garnered a second thought.

Murphy was upstairs on speakerphone, working on a Saturday.

Word spread through the camp quickly there'd been a catastrophe in his "Dumbass Kansas Account," and Claudia and Ana Rosalina had been trying to fix things via their magic. Evidently, a cyclone decimated an entire town, and Murphy's division had underwritten two manufacturing plants. The biggie of all biggies, a VP's dead body was found buried underneath the rubble.

I bit my tongue. Claudia was right...death had come to Murphy's life.

I didn't know if the herbs and dead bugs were to raise the vice president or put a financial windfall back into Murphy's company. Heck, maybe it was to spare all of our lives from my father who right then screamed, "Eat poop and die," to someone who worked for him. All I knew was I had free time on my hands...free time to, eh, stakeout the school's losers.

Provoking them was dumb—heavy emphasis on the "dumb" part. But sometimes my crazy demanded I sic it on people. What did I learn? Slapstick Wilson was friendly, mannerly, occasionally nervous, and definitely a people pleaser. And he honestly struck me as a flower waiting to bloom if it hit the right light. Whatever mess he got into in life, my guess was he fell into it unawares, had a good reason, or went along for the ride. That being said, he claimed he didn't work for free. That insinuated he thought he'd contribute something of value. But did I actually want to hire him?

Damon Whitehead was a trash-talking, hotheaded ponkey. If he perpetrated anything, my feelings were he wouldn't be able to keep it to himself. And by his blanked-out reaction to my questions, I'd swear Slapstick hadn't tipped him off to anything. That meant he'd heard through the grapevine like Collin had.

Just the practice of dissecting these two made the truth ring true...neither was The Ghost. The Ghost was supposed to be of superior intelligence, deadly to the point of making one's skin crawl, and liked to remain hidden. Damon longed to be seen *and* heard. Slapstick was too much go-with-the-flow to be a consideration.

Crashed on the floor in the den, I snatched up my iPhone and punched in Slapstick's number. When the testosterone cleared after Damon and Grumpy's peeing match, I made sure to program his digits into my cell. After six rings on four separate attempts, I got the feeling he didn't want to speak with me. I'd cry if I had the energy, but it'd been expended playing hillbilly Barbies with Marjorie, along with the realization my best friend had changed the confines of our relationship. Instead, I developed a case of hiccups and promised Barbie everything would be okay.

It was a little past five o'clock. The sky was blue, cloud-free, with a tiny ray of sunshine trying its best to survive. Ana Rosalina had left her cell phone on the countertop. As their attention stayed riveted to the sink, I snatched it up, stole upstairs to my room, and closed the door. I thumbed in Tito's number. I had no idea if he was married, divorced, dating, or in a custody war with his baby mama. But Vinnie and I needed to point our compass somewhere tomorrow, and Tito was the best bet.

As luck would have it, he answered. "It's Jester," I said into the phone.

Tito was probably shocked I'd used yet another number, but he could trace away, and all he'd get would be a Colombian drug lord. That was some other news Ana Rosalina brought during Christmastime. She was a kept woman, engaged to a reformed drug lord who still resided in Colombia.

Suuuuuurrrreeee...pretty sure that rehab worked just fine.

"Jester," he said, sort of chuckling, "you must be a workaholic like I am."

Workaholic, I didn't know, but I might be the biggest dolt ever created. "Two things are on my mind, Tito. Number one, I want to know if you received the two Visa cards and the social security card I mailed you. Visa cards were for Lindsee Maroni and Kelley Lowder. Social security card was for an infant boy named Lucas Carlton." I then reiterated their stories, down to the last detail, and swore on a stack of Bibles I wasn't the thief.

Crickets chirping for a beat.

"That package was from you?" he finally asked with disbelief.

"No, they were from the Tooth Fairy. Of course, they were from me."

"Where'd you get them, Jester? When I wrote my article, all three of those families called to share their stories. I never printed particulars, and I never printed names."

"Well, I didn't steal them if that's what you're insinuating. I'm simply showing you how far my reach goes in case you ever have the need to doubt me or sever ties."

More crickets. "Jester, you scare me."

That might be the biggest compliment anyone had ever given me. "Thanks," I said, dumbly following up with a giggle.

Tito chuckled...I think. "You said you had another reason to call?"

Right. "Number two, I have a lead on The Ghost," I lied. "But I need to catch up with him one last time. What location did your source last see him?"

Please say it's within driving distance, I prayed. Then I looked to the ceiling hoping my many lies didn't keep me from Heaven's Gates permanently. But how could I remain lie-free when I pumped people for information? Creativity was a necessity.

"Big Moby's Cheeseburger Shack," he rattled off.

After some small talk, we disconnected.

A spoonful of peanut butter later (my cure for hiccups), Dylan sauntered through the door to a silent house. Claudia and Ana Rosalina went shopping and took Marjorie and Choncho along. Suddenly, I felt the need for allies because Dylan didn't seem as lovey-dovey as the night before. In fact, he looked like he'd opened a can of whoopass.

I choked on my tongue and coughed it back up.

The whoopass thing actually sounded intriguing.

Murphy thundered down the stairs, and by the look on his face, more bodies must've been pulled from the rubble, or he was mad about something else...*I gulped.*

When I glanced at Dylan, he lowered his voice, "Powwow, sweetheart."

Oh, God, no. Powwows were worse than walkie-talkies. Powwows included Murphy or worse yet, Murphy and Red...or God forbid, Grandpa Winston. Powwows were my family's equivalent of a come-to-Jesus meeting—underscoring the death and eternal damnation if I didn't see the error of my ways.

Now we knew why Dylan remained silent on entry. One of them was the mastermind here, and Dylan was stuck between tag teaming with my father or cluing me in.

I put my hands on my hips, wanting to kiss him and spit on him at the same time. He gave me a look that meant everything...and nothing. The usual. "What in the heck did you do, Dylan?" I said in a rare moment of anger. "Call and whine to Murphy about what big, bad Darcy was doing?"

He never admitted, denied, or even acknowledged the statement. He carefully removed his jacket, standing stoically in a white golf shirt, faded-out jeans, and Adidas sneakers. Opening the hall closet, he even more carefully hung up his coat. Once he closed the door, he lowly and slowly repeated again, "Powwow."

Like he was afraid I wouldn't understand the term.

Believe me, I got it. "I'm not in the mood for Native American culture," I mumbled, sort of giggled. The joke fell flat. When no one laughed, I decided to act dumb and blonde. "What's wrong?"

When Murphy made it to the last stair, the house suddenly took on the tenor of a den of angry rattlesnakes. He grabbed me by the elbow and shoved me into the kitchen. We tripped overtop one another, his jeans swiping my sweats, until he stopped on a dime by the kitchen table. "I understand you didn't ask to be thrown into detention," he grunted, "but did you have plans to make the best of it while you were there? In Darcy's world, poll the dang crowd for whatever stink you're currently stirring?"

It wasn't like I got up one day and said, *Hey, how about I get myself thrown into detention.* The idea presented itself with Nico Drake, and once there I decided to execute. That made me a mover and shaker. He should be proud.

"I didn't *plan* anything, Murphy."

"Bible it, kid," he demanded. Once again, Murphy was doing the talking.

I looked at Dylan and let out an imaginary eek. Before we fell asleep (and talked about our relationship afterward), Dylan had asked the same thing over and over. I'd successfully held him at bay. I got the distinct feeling my free pass was used up.

"Umm," I stammered. "We don't need to bring God into this, Murphy. He's probably busy handing out angel wings."

Murphy muttered to himself about going to church more. "That's what I thought," he grumbled. "You might be dumb in all the other areas of your life, but thank God you know you can't swear on the Good Book and lie. Your life, under current management, isn't working. That means I need to manage you. You're in the ditch, kid. Either look up and find your salvation or continue down into the pit of Hell."

God help me, Hell might be a possibility. I glanced at Dylan. He leaned up against the countertop, idly fingering the clasp on the black TAG Heuer hugging his right wrist. He was nervous. No, I take that back. He was p-i-s-s-e-d off.

"Answer the question, Darcy," he demanded, "or I'm not picking you up for school ever again."

I was reeling, my head swirling in a sickening circle. "That's Beemer blackmail," I gasped.

Dylan remained stone-faced. "Try me," he warned. "And by the way, when did you start editing our conversations?"

Oh, about five minutes ago...

Murphy hissed, "For God's sake, kid. He didn't rat you out. I *made* him tell me, and FYI, he didn't enjoy doing it. But regardless, I need an explanation. Did this Nico Drake really attack you because you defended some girl's honor? Is that all, or is there something else?"

I ignored Dylan because I suddenly couldn't look him in the face. "Some situations are beyond explanations, Murphy."

Murphy's attitude went arctic, immediately talking in terms of electronics because he thought I needed a rewiring. "Shut up, kid," he said in a huff. "Your motherboard is so screwed up. This has to be another one of your lowlife, cockamamie, screwball routines that's going to wind up with someone getting hurt. You're always rubbing shoulders with some shyster, Darcy, and God only knows who you hooked up with on The Island of Misfit Toys."

One look at Dylan showed him stifling a chuckle. Good, maybe I could salvage the evening despite the bad vibe that'd invaded the room. "Answer your father," he murmured. "He's just...*we're* just," he amended softly, "worried. Let me explain myself, yeah? I saw you go through a windshield on the first day of school. Then Bradshaw quickly follows. Besides being scared out of my mind, I was afraid I'd run over you. Then I passed out, and when I woke up, I didn't know if you'd died from hitting the pavement or if I'd killed you myself. I'm antsy. I can't let it go. That memory makes me do crazy things."

I guess that was his way of apologizing since he ratted me out to Murphy.

When I didn't answer, Murphy literally took my arm and twisted it high behind my back. "Man up," he barked.

"I can't," I said, stupidly laughing. "I have ovaries."

A moment sprung to life where they both debated laughing, but they didn't give into it.

"For the sake of clarity," Murphy growled, "I'm going to dumb this down as much as my intelligence will *allow* and your *lack of* will understand. Are you doing something that would've landed you in detention even if you wouldn't have been attacked?"

"I don't understand what you're saying," I said, giggling like a moron.

Murphy threw both arms up in the air, like defeat faced him with a six-shooter, and he had no choice but to surrender. "Oh, Good God," he fumed. "You add a whole new dimension to the term dysfunction."

"I like to think I'm resourceful."

Murphy's grumble sounded like a PO'd bear. "You're being resourceful. Well, let me tell you what *I'm* going to be." He turned to Dylan with a frown. "I'm *out,* son, because this conversation didn't take. I'll say a prayer for you upstairs, but right now, I need to take two Tylenols and crawl into bed. I'm being deposed tomorrow. On the Lord's Day, dang it, about a claim we denied because some idiot didn't understand what I told him. I don't understand why God continually puts stupid people in my life, and then I have to un-stupid their mistakes."

"Stupid is a bad word," I said, still laughing.

He gave me his standard answer. "Stupid is a frame of mind, kid. It has nothing to do with intelligence."

He shot a sarcastic wave over his shoulder and disappeared upstairs.

Once out of earshot, Dylan yanked me to the couch so hard my elbow throbbed like a heartbeat. His eyes knit together in frustration. "Cough it up, Darcy, before I beat it out of you." *Impressive threat—one I don't mind having thrown at me actually*. I laughed to myself. Those words were ultimately a fabrication. Besides, Dylan did that hocus-pocus stuff with his voice where I wound up doing what he said anyway.

I enjoyed the way he looked at me, even when angry. I fell headlong into his eyes, scorched in the amber gaze that'd kept me up almost every night for months. I shook my head so violently to clear it I probably lost IQ points. "What's wrong, D? You act like something else is bothering you."

Dylan was molten-hot and unnaturally strong. But he had a weight upon his shoulders—making him move so slowly it was like he'd wrestled with a lion...*and lost*. "I'm frigging exhausted. Dad sleepwalked out to the lake last night thinking he was crossing the Delaware fricking River. At two o'clock, I had to talk a grown man down from attacking the Redcoats in his underwear with a pool stick. Do you know what it's like to stare into the half-mast eyes of someone who's incoherent, unstable, and devoid of rational thought?"

Every day when I look in the mirror.

"I'm sorry," I said, smiling innocently. "Would you like a massage?"

He frowned when I batted my lashes twice. "Maybe later," he said. "Right now, we're talking about you, Darcy."

I picked up the remote. "Since you want to be formal...*Dylan*," I emphasized snidely, "it's sort of a long story."

"Shorten it."

I took a major gamble, but I blurted out, "As you know, I didn't ask to be assaulted by Nico Drake. That being said, I've been working on finding out who painted Coach's car. To gather information, I stole a file from his office and did some profiling. The guys who caught my interest have juvie records and do the occasional neighborhood graffiti, normally pulling time in detention. So when the situation presented itself, I introduced myself Saturday morning. To me, this is business. I did not ask to be there. I did not ask to have my favorite bra ripped. But I'd be a fool to let the situation pass me by without getting something that benefitted me. In one conversation, I'd swear Slapstick Wilson and Damon Whitehead had nothing to do with spray painting Coach's car. Now I just need everyone to leave me alone so I can figure out what to do next."

I omitted The Ghost.

I was stupid but not suicidal.

"Please, say this is a lie," he muttered.

"It's truth. Pinky swear."

When he didn't respond, I soldiered on with the bombast account and overdramatics, offering a slew of excuses why it'd been a godsend to be banished to detention. It was a contained environment, chances of random violence were slim (sorta), I could observe while I performed worthwhile community service, and so on. He still said nada. In fact, he swallowed three times and took the remote from my hands.

"D?" I said.

He scrolled through the channel guide with his left hand, holding the other palm to my face in a back-off motion. "I'm processing."

I actually felt pretty darn good. Confession's good for the soul. I crawled onto his lap, snuggling my nose into the curve under his chin. "Would it help if I said *I loved you?*"

Dang, he smelled good.

You heard it here first, folks. I literally jumped on top of him, touching anything I could get my greedy little hands on. The hair, the face, the chest—anything that said pregame activity, if you know what I mean. Dylan tensed as if it'd hurt. Here he'd led me to believe he wanted a relationship, and when I'd offered a PG hookup —let's just say he wasn't so gung-ho about getting up close and personal. Mortified, I pulled a complete-180 and pushed away, wondering where I could hide. I blamed my behavior on the three cookies I'd eaten beforehand—they weakened my brain. And if they hadn't weakened my brain, then that just proved Dylan was one step closer to stealing my soul.

Hello, migraine. Good night, libido.

"Are you going to drop this?" I asked, rubbing my temples.

"No," he murmured, and then he tenderly kissed the top of my head, his voice going rough. "Soon," he whispered almost to himself. "Soon."

———

Vinnie's pink Volkswagen Bug sounded like a dying pigeon.

"What's wrong with the Bug?"

"She's sick."

There you have it, friends—the extent of Vinnie's mechanical abilities. The calendar said Sunday morning. Vinnie and I had decimated, and I mean *decimated*, Finn Lively's list. We cruised along Mack County Road, ending our surveillance for the day before I headed into work and Vinnie back to Ohio State.

Vinnie's job was primarily to get me into places. It was my job to find out the needed information once inside. When we started our unorthodox relationship last year, I discovered he had many aliases (once again, not my place to cast judgment). The two I'd encountered then were a maintenance worker named Guido Galucci and an attorney called Carlo Corleone (yeah, The Godfather...so much for creativity). Carlo helped me gain access to my friend Oscar Small when he'd been unjustly detained in the Valley Juvenile Detention Center for the murder of a mobster named Alfonso Juarez. In both cases, Vinnie played the part and dressed appropriately, getting me out of a heated situation in an Evidence Room (as Guido) and into Oscar's presence as Carlo Corleone.

Right then, he came dressed as (wait for it...wait for it) an encyclopedia salesman. Suit, tie, and shiny black shoes a little too tight. Alias of Herb Ferrari. I nearly choked on my caramel latte because I wasn't sure encyclopedia salesman existed anymore with the Internet. That being said, Vinnie (excuse me, I mean *Herb*), successfully granted us entrance into the abodes of all five people who'd been tardy. Did I smell anything nefarious on any of them? Not a doggone, stinking thing. One was a band geek. The other smelled like a tweaker too brain-dead to construct a sentence. The third was in the honors program and a goody-goody and the final two actually dated one another (tardy because they'd been caught in the early stages of the horizontal mambo in the parking lot).

Yes, I pulled that detail out of the girl by shooting the breeze as Vinnie presented encyclopedias to her parents. Then she told me what constituted the mambo, and I honest to God, didn't understand it.

Anyway, that left us cramming in the last of the detention list before I went into work. We'd already hit four residences because they were close—none were home—and immediately took off for the address listed for Brantley McCoy.

On the drive there, I told Vinnie about Nico Drake—evidently, the story didn't end with him being expelled. Nico left me a voicemail the night before. He never apologized (red flag) but claimed he knew what I'd been doing and might have information I'd find useful (red flag, number two). First off, I was doing two things: Coach's car and The Ghost. I replayed the message multiple times, looking for clues, but any way I turned the Rubik's cube, the situation remained a jumble. Nico Drake, point blank, ambushed me from behind.

Buuuuuuut...

If he had something beneficial, then I'd be a fool to not listen.

Vinnie volunteered to visit him personally to gather the intel—he didn't have a good look on his face when he offered—but it was either Vinnie or Dylan. Vinnie was hardcore. Dylan was straight up horror show.

Um, I'd take Vinnie.

Vinnie swung a right into a new neighborhood called Calypso Cove. Calypso Cove was in the BFE section of Valley and only a year old. Still under construction, homes in the suburb were one of five modern styles with a single tree in front, landscaping along the front edge of your home, and two bushes in the backyard.

Brantley McCoy lived at 9139 Calypso Cove Drive. My mind swirled with frustration at the mere mention of his name. Who was he? And why wasn't he on Valley's radar? He hadn't appeared in the yearbook, and when I randomly polled Valley's grapevine, no one even recognized the name.

Vinnie pulled into the driveway and switched off the engine, downing a Red Bull and crumpling the silver can. Tossing it in the backseat, he whipped a moon pie out of his blazer and ripped off a big bite. Vinnie needed to be careful of the extra calories because although football season had ended, if he continued to eat his way through snack cakes, he'd never make the weigh-in for next year.

As per all the other stops, he made me endure a quick sound bite regarding his girlfriend, Donatella Ricci. I'd never heard of nor met Donatella, but Vinnie remained convinced she was the love of his life. Only time would tell because he was a notorious skirt chaser. When he finished talking about her "rockin' bod and nice rack," (Gah! No matter how you spun it, that never sounded respectful), I exited the car behind him, straightening the only dress I owned. It was a two-year-old long-sleeved black jersey—so short it rode up to the hoochie zone when I took a step. Couple that with black tights and leather spiky boots, and I looked like the bimbo of the encyclopedia world.

"You're going to get fatter, Vinnie."

"I overeat as therapy," he answered.

"Therapy," I repeated laughing.

"It helps me suppress a past too painful to acknowledge."

Here-here to that.

Vinnie's pink Bug came equipped with black plastic eye lashes on the headlights. When I exited my side, one of its lashes fluttered in the wind. Up and down. Up and down. I pushed it back into place, briefly wondering if I'd poked it in the eye.

A leather satchel in one hand, Vinnie strode out of the car, his beefy hand palming the half eaten moon pie in the other. I ripped the pie from his grasp, throwing it to the ground with a stomp. My foot twisted into the plastic and white marshmallow oozed out the sides.

"Tell me you just didn't do that!" he roared, his eyes gone wide.

I found it a waste of breath to verify what he knew to be true.

Vinnie dropped to his knees—a miraculous feat, considering I would've guessed it anatomically impossible—and talked to it like someone would a dying man. His plumber's crack greeted me with about three inches. I giggled and said, "I see London, I see France."

"Shut up, Dolce," he grunted. "Donatella can't keep her hands off my glutes."

Let's hope Donatella used hand sanitizer.

Standing up toting a smashed pie with no hopes of resuscitation, he threw his hands up in the air, frustrated. "I'm eating because I've got good news. *100 Proof Stud* was picked up for distribution, and there's a spin-off. The spin-off is called *Fat Men from Venus*," he said proudly. "I'm eating because I'm a method actor. I get into my characters by actually becoming them."

I burst out laughing, bending over to grab some oxygen. They'd need one heckuva CGI department to morph Vinnie's body into stud material. Mid-laugh, a troubling thought hit the smart part of my brain. I grabbed his forearm. "Is this like, um...er—adult entertainment, V?" Oh, God, please tell me Vinnie was smart enough to not become a...how do I phrase it?

I couldn't even say the words in my mind.

Vinnie shoved the smashed pie in his pocket. "Sure it is, Dolce. Everybody loves a good love story." I wasn't sure what he'd admitted but put the thought on the backburner.

"How's our boy?" Vinnie asked me as he rang the doorbell. My sigh could've been heard in Timbuktu. I desperately needed a friend's advice regarding Dylan, but the friend I'd normally go to was the person asking me to date him. Vinnie would be the perfect candidate for an unbiased opinion, but it made me feel disloyal to Dylan. See, that wasn't good all the way around. I'd be flying solo, screwing up unencumbered, with no sounding board anywhere.

"He's good." I shoved my pinky nail in my mouth and ripped off the tip.

"You're lying."

"No, I'm not."

"You always chew your pinky nail when things aren't right between the two of you." I didn't give him jack. "Do you want to talk about it?"

Yes! No! Maybe? "I dunno," I said, sort of shrugging. Heck, I didn't know how to answer anyway.

Vinnie punched the rectangular doorbell again.

Then again.

And again.

The black front door was ajar by about an inch. Vinnie yelled, "Hello!" then creaked the door wide with his foot. Just went right in —not even waiting for an invitation. That qualified as a maverick move—and felt freaking nuts—but I didn't care, and God knew Vinnie's conscience was harder to find than mine.

———

The front room looked like your normal home: modest blue fabric sofa, two chairs, flatscreen TV, a bookshelf on the back wall behind the TV, and a multi-colored oriental rug in the middle of a scratched hardwood floor. Beside one of the end tables was a bowl of uneaten popcorn in a gold plastic bowl. Vinnie plunged his hand inside and ate the crap out of their popcorn, flipping through his texts while I snooped down the hall.

Two bedrooms were adjacent to the restroom. I popped inside the first one and knew instantly I'd hit the nerve center. Half a dozen laptops and desktop computers were fired up, all idling on Google. A white box sat on top of the desk containing several Visas and MasterCards, social security cards, and even King's Island season passes. Thing was, no name had been assigned to any of them. They simply waited there for someone to stamp a name on the front and hand out to their new owners.

I sucked in a breath.

Brantley McCoy had some major secrets that needed to remain underground.

I squeaked open the door to the adjacent bedroom and was met with an empty twin bed. A rumpled white sheet draped the bed, no comforter. Pivoting around, I did a quick scan of the gray carpet, found nothing overly suspicious or weird, so moved onto the closet.

By that time, Vinnie nipped at my heels. "I'm getting a funny feeling, Dolce. We need to roll."

My thoughts exactly. But when I stepped inside the walk-in closet, no way in the world would I ever have been prepared for what I'd find. There was an idiom about skeletons in your closet. Trouble was, the skeleton I'd discovered still had meat on it.

"Vinnie," I whispered, "there's a skeleton in the closet."

Vinnie munched on the smashed moon pie behind me. I heard the crinkle of the wrapper. "Ha-ha, Dolce. Is this some metaphorical test I'm supposed to decipher?"

"No, like a *real* skeleton that I think is a man."

Vinnie took one step inside and dropped the F-bomb. Then added mommy-effer.

"Do you smell that?" I asked.

Vinnie's inhale was audible. "Yeah, smells like O-positive to me." Loosely rolled in a faded navy comforter were the remains of a man. He lay facedown with a small patch of flesh and short black hair still clinging to his head. That wasn't the only dead body I'd encountered, and neither was the body of a man I'd found in a dumpster last spring. I, eh, well...I found a head...buried in the sand on vacation in Orlando. I had a habit of stumbling upon dead bodies and/or body parts. Something the majority of people could go a lifetime and not have happen once, I'd experienced one too many times to count.

The smell wasn't as bad as bodies that'd recently expired, but it smelled like death, nonetheless. Death has a peculiar smell one never forgot. Covering my nose with my hand, I lifted the tip of my boot and kicked the blanket back, starting at the naked feet. Black boxers framed femurs that barely had any flesh left, and a plain white T-shirt adorned the crumpled torso. A vintage concert T-shirt from The Minstrel Cramps, a local all-girl band popular back in the day, lay beside the corpse's head.

A memory played in the back of my mind I immediately tried to erase.

A memory that'd haunted me since I was nine years old.

I couldn't do it...not again...*noooooo*...that particular scene was too raw and familiar. If I didn't get out of the place soon, I'd flip the freak out, and I wasn't sure Vinnie could screw my head back on.

I quickly turned, braced both hands on my knees, and dry-heaved three times. Bile scorched my throat, and I struggled unsuccessfully to swallow it back down. Spitting into a handkerchief Vinnie shoved over my mouth, I sucked air through my nose, trying to find calm.

Vinnie laid a gentle hand on my back. "Breathe, Dolce, breathe," he coaxed. Stumbling to the bathroom, I worshiped at the porcelain throne and still couldn't rid myself of the nausea. I ultimately gave into biology and used the commode in a half-stand, half-sit position. Did you know how hard it was to pee that way, praying I didn't leave any fingerprints or DNA behind?

Inhaling deeply, I found my calm, realizing Vinnie and I needed to leave ASAP and phone the authorities. Those plans hit an iceberg because once I joined Vinnie in the front room, I heard a *Pffft*. Then another. I was a little slow on the uptake but soon concluded the *Pffft* was the sound of something striking the couch. Yellowed batting exploded out of a bullet hole in a puff of white smoke.

Call me a genius, but I didn't consider that good.

"Down!" Vinnie roared, launching himself toward me.

Unfortunately, my legs went moron and glued to the floor. For a moment, I had a flashback of running from a shooter last spring. They say lightning doesn't strike twice in the same place...evidently, it does. My legs felt like rubber, and the room went to a dizzying whirl. Tears welled in my eyes, but I commanded them to dry up. People couldn't think rationally when they cried. Emotions ruled. I didn't make the rule. Someone else did. Problem was, my tear ducts didn't comply. I boo-hoo'd like a little girl.

Vinnie heaved us both off the floor, pitching me his keys I caught in one hand.

"Oh, God, Vinnie," I breathed, adrenaline nearly slicing me in two. It was like a *Scarface* shootout, only we didn't have a gun.

Vinnie's eyes glowed black and angry, but he took time to tenderly touch my cheek in an order. "Snap out of it, Dolce. Go. Out the back. I'll follow."

I still couldn't move.

When Vinnie whipped off his jacket to do God-knew-what, voices boomed outside as three more gunshots landed on the hardwood floor. The wood splintered into pieces, sawdust pooling like an ant mound. When a sixth shot hit near my feet, I lost my balance and cartwheeled across the floor, landing on my knees.

Vinnie snatched me up and shoved me in front of him, clutching my back to his front, acting as a human shield. Praying vehemently he didn't get struck in the mayhem of gunfire, I still was worthless while he kicked out the window and tossed me onto the ground. I landed on all fours, my hands hitting the gravelly dirt of a backyard in need of upkeep. My tights split at the knees, and the air left my body on a hiss. I crawled in an uncoordinated manner like a baby intent on learning a new method of transportation. My eyes blinded with tears, and when I made it around the air conditioning unit, my hands hit something thick and mucousy.

Pulling my shaking hand to my eyes, I recognized the red, viscous fluid immediately...blood. Blood that'd partly dried and led me to the body of...oh, God help me...help me...Nico Drake.

My stomach churned, and I felt like I'd scarfed a bag of jalapeño poppers. Nico Drake's stare was glazed over and wide-eyed, and his body so covered in blood I didn't know from where the mortal wound originated. His hands were bloody, his white shirt soaked to the skin, and his tongue hung out to the side like someone struck him from the back, and it was a reflex reaction. I have to admit I'd imagined him dead, but the reality was a whole lot scarier than what I'd pictured in my head. It was like he'd totally bled out because the ground was soggy underneath him.

I'd like to say I was surprised, but Nico Drake was mongoose-mean. Apparently, he had enemies who didn't mind to take a beef to the next level. Still, my heart broke a little with the discovery. Not even the bad should die young. Everyone should have time to live, make mistakes, make them twice, fall in love, get married, have kids, feel like their life had been a waste, make peace, and only *then* should they be allowed to die.

Whatever Nico thought would be useful to me followed him to the land of worms.

But why? Why was he *here*...and *dead?*

A shrill laugh escaped my trembling lips, followed by a cry so bizarre it felt like the earth took pause. Stick a fork in me...*I'm done.* I couldn't do it. People were falling dead all around me, and no amount of money in the world was worth Vinnie and me getting shot at. Well, getting shot at and potentially finding success.

I tried to get up and fell.

I tried again, that time even shakier.

When I finally scrambled to my feet...I realized Vinnie hadn't followed.

And that was when I heard it...

Chaos everywhere.

Furniture moved. There was a shout...more gunfire...a man's scream...the sounds of rolling and thrashing fists...the cracking of heads, grunts, a loud thud...Vinnie's muffled cry and then...

Nothing.

For God's sake...nothing.

I attempted a scream but instead whispered a strangled prayer. "God, *please*," I whispered. "*Pleeeeease...*"

I couldn't imagine a world without a Vinnie—especially when it was my fault he'd been placed in the situation. Vinnie had a life, a mom, a girlfriend named Donatella, and maybe a budding acting career. I crawled to the Bug, opened the driver's side door, and crumbled inside. "Be calm, be calm," I said, sniffling to myself. As my conscience prickled with guilt, I bumbled my iPhone out of my purse when the door was thrown wide with Vinnie tossing me to the passenger side. His gray suit had been splattered with blood, but I knew innately it wasn't his. A rip. He had a rip in his left knee. A simple rip.

I cried nerd tears. I cried happy tears.

I launched myself at Vinnie, sniffling, "Vinnie, I love you. I love you..."

Vinnie gazed at me cockily, like it was a given he would've walked away unscathed. Amidst all my blubbering, he did the indescribable. He placed The Minstrel Cramps vintage T-shirt in my lap, tenderly squeezing my knee. The dueling emotions of love and hate immediately boiled up inside me. Vinnie was one of a handful who knew what that band meant to me. What that *memory* meant. Nerd tears resurfaced. Desperate tears won out. Stabbing his keys into the ignition, he rocketed out of the driveway on a squeal. We'd raised the bar on crazy, and I bawled like a baby. At that juncture, I didn't care that I looked like a wuss...I *was* a wuss...but Vinnie was alive, and that was all that mattered.

Vinnie slid worried eyes over. "Whatever or whoever you were looking for...I saw it in his eyes. He's the right guy, Dolce, but we gotta split. I might've killed him."

Chapter Fourteen

BIG MOBY

I f my life was a bowling alley, I was the gutter ball.

Mr. B felt that was where my life was headed...*in the gutter*. When I punched the clock that afternoon, he spat nails that I hadn't worked at all the day before. A situation due to the fact I'd been banished to detention. I considered telling him I'd been abducted by the government, but one look at the Christmas tree by the checkout counter and I couldn't lie.

So I gave him a partial truth, which in turn launched Detention Lecture 2.0...yeah, call me an idiot.

"So this Nico Drake," he said with a gruffy voice. "Do I need to go rough him up?"

Um, he's already dead, I said in my mind. "No, but thanks for the offer," was my official response.

Another grunt. "I'd better not be pulling you off of skid row some day, Walker," he told me. "I love a charity case as much as any other employer, but I don't invest in idiots."

He needed to invest in a heart monitor because he was leaned over the counter, sucking the calories out of his fourth ham sandwich. I watched a greasy bite enter his mouth, knowing full well he'd taken another sixty seconds off his life.

He wasn't through yet...unfortunately. "Were you drunk?"

"I wish," I muttered.

He threw out a JC, and he wasn't praying. "You need to straighten up, Walker. God has plans for you. He's watching."

That coming from a man who should have AA on his speed dial. "He's watching?" I mumbled.

"Yeah, an eye for a porkin' eye."

That statement didn't even fit within the context of the conversation.

Mr. B had been up in my business for the past hour and a half, his jean suspenders hanging from one fat shoulder. He'd splashed eggnog—schnapps was my guess—all over my shirt. I wore my normal uniform of black yoga pants, Chuck Taylor sneakers, and bookstore T-shirt that bragged "Belinski's is the Bomb" on the front. Right then, the bomb smelled like hard liquor.

It was nine o'clock, and I closed out the cash register, waiting for Dylan to pick me up so we could eat a late dinner at Big Moby's. Somehow I'd made it through the day without raiding the liquor in the back, and that was a miracle in itself. Vinnie and I immediately went to his home and ditched our clothing. He took the bag with him back to Ohio State with the promise, "I'll take care of it."

To that, I had no doubt.

Vinnie's will to survive might be greater than mine.

We didn't know what to do about Nico Drake but assumed his parents would issue a missing person's report sometime soon.

Even so, I still had my eyes on the prize despite the fact that: (A) Vinnie and I'd been shot at that morning; (B) we found human remains in a closet; (C) Nico Drake's dead body was mysteriously present; and (D) a large possibility existed Vinnie might've killed someone. I'd had the local news rolling since arriving at one o'clock, but not one single thing went over the airwaves about gunfire at 9139 Calypso Cove Drive—what I referred to as The Bates Motel. That being said, it was paramount I inform Tito about the things and bodies I'd discovered. Trouble was, I hadn't quite figured out how to open that can of worms. If, in fact, Vinnie accidentally killed Brantley McCoy, a chance existed he could be arrested. Heck, they might even say he knocked off Nico Drake too out of vengeance for me.

How, you say, would authorities know to look for Vinnie? Let's not forget Vinnie drives a pink VW Bug...complete with eyelashes. If they went CSI on the scene, they'd discover the Bug was a one-of-a-kind in the Cincinnati area, and although I could swear no one saw us, I couldn't say for sure.

My brain was spent. Getting shot at sort of ruined anything. I ugly-cried the whole way home, my eyes so red they looked like a newborn vampire's. Plus, Dylan's and my discussion weighed on my mind. He'd accused me of editing our conversations, as if it was as devastating as finding out his spouse cheated on him. No, what was freaking devastating was getting freaking shot at.

Ugh...

"Have you learned your lesson?" Mr. B grunted.

I punched the register door shut, dusting the breadcrumbs into my hand that'd fallen from his sandwich. I didn't think we had rats, but random breadcrumbs were one surefire way to attract vermin. I dropped them into the waste can and removed the clear plastic trash bag, tying it at the top.

I reiterated exactly what I'd told Murphy. "I'm extremely remorseful, and I will never embarrass you or my family again. I plan on being a productive citizen of society, and you have my word you won't be reading about me in the prison round-up."

Because I don't plan on getting caught.

Apparently, that was all he needed to hear. He ran his greasy hand through my ponytail and lumbered back toward the break room where Chichi, real name Conchita Diaz, was preparing to read his palm.

From Ecuador, Chichi stood about five foot five with shiny, black hair and eyes that were burgundy. Her claim to fame was reading palms and tealeaves. She saw your future and those who'd make the biggest dent in your life. To the best of my knowledge, she operated on one hundred percent prophetic status. Pretty impressive for a seventeen-year-old. Although, it smelled of BS.

She planned to dispatch a communiqué from the spirit world on Mr. B's immediate future. To rephrase, could he get by with killing the "porkin' scum of the earth who porked up his place" after closing the night before? No windows had been broken, but the outside door had been spray painted with words I didn't understand nor cared to repeat. Thing was, that made two acts of vandalism in a week: Nowacki's Videos and The Double-B. As a precaution, he closed his bank and credit card accounts, but that wouldn't do any good if the thief had somehow secured his social security number. The best identity thieves only needed one set of identification for you, and they could uncover the rest.

I made my way to the rear of the store, straightening along the way.

The break room had a lime, faux leather couch made of a washable plastic. Mr. B laid on it like a beached whale while Chichi knelt beside him, closed her eyes, and did a quick meditation to herself.

I flopped down beside them when Chichi took his palm, tracing its deep lines. The moment I was certifiably bored out of my mind, Chichi dropped his hand like it had burned, darting her burgundy eyes over to me in a fit of hysteria. "A bad man will bring harm to Darcy."

Stand in line, I thought.

Mr. B looked at her grunting, "What are you talking about?"

Chichi's gaze held a weight. Like she dealt with something so heavy she couldn't quite carry it. She explained, "Darcy's and your destinies are intersecting, and it isn't good."

When Mr. B still had that dumber-than-rocks thing going on, I realized Chichi spoke in Spanish—which she only did when she was truly, out-of-her-mind scared.

Rudi, standing in the doorway, frantically signed, *What's wrong?*

When I debated an answer, Rudi actually grabbed my hand and squeezed so hard the blood flow cut off. She verbally asked, "What's happened?"

Chichi's words would give anyone the urge to pause, but right then headlights shone brightly through the front door, and Mr. Do-The-Right-Thing was moments from busting up the party. The fortune stuff would make Dylan as uneasy as it made Murphy. And it would be déjà vu all over again—someone trying to hurt Darcy—when down deep he couldn't admit I caused most of my...er, problems.

I bolted off the floor, leaving Chichi and Mr. B with mouths agape. Yelling over my shoulder, I grabbed Rudi's eyes so she could read my lips. "She said Mr. B's and my destinies are intersecting, and someone bad might try to cause me harm."

I didn't stick around for a play-by-play. I jogged to the front, grabbed my coat and purse, and cut through the door to an arctic blast. Only the day before we had what was considered a winter heat wave. Right then, I might as well have bathed in liquid nitrogen. The sky sparkled like diamonds under a cloud of white smoke. Snow skies. I knew it deep in my bones, like arthritis that ached and reminded someone it wasn't going anywhere.

"Well, aren't we in a hurry?" Dylan laughed as I settled inside. I leaned forward in the heated leather seat, trying to wriggle inside my coat with darn little success. Dylan placed the Beemer in park, helping me fish my arms through.

My normal greeting wasn't, "What's up, bro?" It was a full-bodied hug. I'd never thought that to be weird, but since we'd had a let's-swap-spit-on-a-regular-basis conversation, it felt weird *beyond* weird.

"Come here, and let me love on you," he murmured.

His charm and impossibly seductive smile was all it took for me to cave. I crawled over the console and buried my face in his neck. Dylan wrapped my ponytail in a fist, and I returned the sentiment, sliding my fingers through his dark locks. His hair was modern-messy and nothing short of mouthwatering. My dimpled best friend sported a brown turtleneck sweater, a fact I found irritating.

I needed flesh-to-flesh contact.

He pulled back with a strange look on his almost-too-perfect face. "Darc, you reek of alcohol."

I laughed outright. "A little eggnog spilled on me. No big deal."

As I tugged my gloves on, he pulled onto Tylersville Road and made his way to Big Moby's Cheeseburger Shack, leaning over to play with my new silver earrings.

"New," he said with a grin, "and extremely expensive."

"Hanukkah gift number eight," I explained. Dylan gently touched the two-inch silver, open-heart earrings. All I knew was the box said Tiffany's, and Red's grin was bigger than a Cheshire cat when I slid them on. Hanukkah was extremely good to a non-Jew like me too: UGGs, a Coach tote bag, jeggings, gelt, fuzzy black sweater, texting gloves, gift card to Bath & Body Works, & silver dangly earrings.

Hopefully, Big Moby would be spreading the love around too.

———

Big Moby could kiss my Cincinnati-born, probably Kentucky inbred you-know-what.

All I tried to do was tweak his nose, and he waved his seltzer bottle at me like I was fair game. *Ponkey*, I thought. Mother-trucking ponkey.

Big Moby was Big Moby's Cheeseburger Shack's mascot...a clown. Sometimes Big Moby was nice. Sometimes Big Moby should be put down like a rabid dog. I considered myself a brave person except for my irrational fear of clowns. It went back to watching *Poltergeist* before I could process that clowns didn't really pull someone underneath a bed. Big Moby didn't act like he'd offer any alternative warm and fuzzy memories.

He dressed like your standard clown: red wig, checkered pants, white painted face, but instead of having big black clown shoes, his feet were bananas. In Mobyland, that made sense. In Darcyville, I thought it looked stupid. In his hand, he carried a seltzer bottle, chasing kids around the play area until their food arrived. Two words? Nightmare city. Descriptive sentence? What kind of person wanted to chase around kids?

Big Moby's Cheeseburger Shack was a place the locals went to eat. Problem was, the roaches didn't care if it was day or night. When I did the usual—check for roaches on the floor—Big Moby and I had a series of awkward moments where we both juked left then right until I finally stopped cold and let him pass.

Eating fast food was a science. If patrons dined during peak time, lines were long, but food was at least hot. If patrons ate during the off-hours, chances were the meal had wrinkled under a heat lamp. The key was to special order since special orders were made real time. The evening's shift consisted of four people: one person working the drive-thru, one cooking, one taking orders, and of course, Big Moby.

All wore red shirts, black pants, and a logo over their heart of a smiling clown. Red Shirt Number One took the order. Red Shirt Number Two fired up the grill, and Red Shirt Number Three dispensed a brown Moby bag out the drive-thru window. All had the work ethic of a lump of lard. They moved slowly and constantly dropped things—just enough health code violations to make a person squirm. Big Moby gave them the death stare, and after a moment where profanity was the only language on Earth, they settled and went back to the burger routine.

After we placed our order, we were given a black plastic number so the staff could keep orders straight. Sort of pointless since the joint was deader than Murphy's love life. Anyway, Dylan took the number twenty-eight and set it on the bright yellow table as we slid inside the black, padded corner booth. I must've groaned because he stroked my hand, murmuring, "Sweetheart, don't give up quite yet. You're worried about the deal you made with Coach, yeah?"

Well, there was that, plus I worried Vinnie could be a murderer and if my DNA had splattered all over Nico Drake. You know, things every sixteen-year-old worried about.

"I need something to write on," I told him. Dylan patted himself down, but all he found was an ink pen in his jacket and a pile of napkins on the counter. He slid them over with a wink and gazed up to watch a University of Cincinnati basketball game on the TV mounted from the ceiling.

My efforts quickly run out of gas, so I decided to get visual and attempt to puzzle the stuff together. I drew a big oval building representing VHS. Next were rectangles for parking entrances and a big X where Coach's car had been parked in space 270. To the left, I drew a space for a red Mustang and silver Chevy Colorado truck, respectively in spaces 271 and 272.

Dylan leaned over and absentmindedly massaged my neck. If an intimate dinner for two had been on his mind, it was shot up like swiss cheese when a gust of wind brought Bean Anatoly through the door. He strolled in with a white, fur-hooded parka zipped up to his nose.

"Darcy," he mumbled through the fur.

I half waved, half tried to dissolve into the seat. I think Dylan chuckled. Bean trekked up to the counter, wearing boots one would see on a polar icecap. They were white and laced up to his knees with fur sticking out the top, sort of how a snowman would look if he ever became Frosty.

God help him, he needed another stylist.

Thirty seconds later, he parked himself in our booth, unzipping his coat.

Dylan spoke first even though etiquette deemed Bean probably should.

"Hello, Bean," he said, smiling genuinely. "How are you?"

Bean couldn't find his vocal chords. I'd only been around Bean in large groups. In a trio, he was nervous and fidgety—uncertain at best and disastrous at worst. He glanced to all four corners, mumbling to himself which fire exit he'd take if the grill blew the place to kingdom come. Then he promised Mr. Pongo he'd figure it out as he unclipped him from his jacket and propped him against the pepper shaker.

Bean, I'd discovered, had some major OCD tendencies. How else could I explain the fact he couldn't go anywhere without his dead gerbil?

Dylan pointed to the door closest to us, murmuring, "That's the one we're going to take if anything happens, Bean."

Bean's shoulders dropped, relaxing a little. "Y-yeah," he stammered, "me too."

After five minutes, Big Moby klutzed over to our table like one of his shoes was a size too small. I wasn't a hardhearted person. I knew fast food work was hard. Heck, maybe clown work was even harder, but if someone had a job, my feelings were it should performed to the person's highest potential. Strange coming from someone who hated schoolwork.

That particular Big Moby acted like he wanted off the clown shift.

He muttered, "Here's your food," and slammed the tray on our table.

I flinched. Heck, I think Dylan flinched. Bean just sat there, inconsequential.

Running into Bean was weird. Eating with Bean was weirder. But the real weirdness was Big Moby was never, ever, *ever* supposed to speak. I didn't care if the place was lighting up in a ball of fire. He was supposed to point to the darn door and smile.

Moby offered a gloved hand. If speaking wasn't enough, in all the years I'd been patronizing the place, Moby had never been interested in a handshake. Thing was, he touched me like we were familiar, slowly stroking my wrist like we knew one another intimately—or worse yet, he intended us to.

I came for one reason—to unmask The Ghost since Tito's source claimed it had been the last place he'd been seen. The way I looked at it, there were several ways to accomplish the goal. I could outright ask, which in my opinion was stupid. I could hint around, which felt even stupider, or I could flirt and see what developed. I'd discovered flirting to be an effective investigational tool when I ran down the particulars on a gang at school last spring. Give a temptress smile, and the floodgates of gossip would spill all over the place.

I tried my best to act like a siren, fluttering my eyes and exhaling a soft sigh. "So how's the clown business, Moby?"

"Boring."

"It seemed pretty exciting a few minutes ago."

Big Moby was in the talking mood. A sideways glance to Dylan told me he'd let the conversation play. Dylan carefully arranged our food in front of us, even pausing to take a sip of his large Coke. His hair had been on end since Big Moby dressed down the workers, and my guess was he'd already polled the crowd. If a fight broke out, it basically was him and a girl. Bean didn't count. He just didn't. How could he? Mr. Pongo was eating a french fry.

"My crew isn't always on their toes," he explained.

Odd. I'd always thought Big Moby had been employed for entertainment purposes only. Instead, he acted like management.

He pointed the tip of his seltzer bottle at the diagram I'd made of the parking lot. "What's with the drawing?"

"I'm actually on a case," I explained. "The coach at our school had his car vandalized, and I told him I'd help him figure out who did it...for a price," I added laughing.

"And you feel confident you can do that?" Big Moby asked.

"That's like asking a surgeon which are the kidneys and the liver," I bragged.

After I shoved a bite of burger in my mouth, I continued to draw characters. One stick person stood next to the red Mustang while I placed another beside the silver Chevy Colorado. Next, I included the white van that had blocked my view. Bean leaned over and drew a stick person wearing a superhero cape on the roof, trying to complete the drawing with me flying high like an idiot.

"Surely you don't think you'll be successful," Big Moby said, chuckling sarcastically.

"That's sort of harsh, Moby," I said snorting. "Because once I tackle this, I'm going to take on organized crime right here in Valley. Identity theft, vandalism, illegal guns—you name it." Shoot, I didn't know if there were illegal guns, probably wasn't, but it sure as heck was fun watching the look of shock on Moby's face.

"You're kidding," he muttered.

Bean piped up happily, "Darcy doesn't kid. She's smart."

Moby scratched his red rubber nose like it itched. "Darcy, you say."

I shoved two more fries in my mouth. "Yup, you've gotta have faith, right?"

Big Moby acted as if he'd fixated on my face. Like he tried to memorize every line and curve. Laughing, he reached out to touch my earrings. At least, that was what I thought he'd gone for. His white glove hovered awfully close to my jugular.

I attempted to pull away, but Moby grabbed a handful of my hair. Dylan wiped his mouth, murmuring, "Darcy."

First of all, he addressed me with formalities. And secondly, he said it with too much emotion. A telltale sign he'd either talked himself down or geared himself up.

I wasn't sure how it happened, but it was like one of those blackout episodes where the people in front of someone were all arranged differently when the lights switched back on. Dylan then stood with his hand wound tightly around Big Moby's wrist. Bean hovered under the table.

Dylan threatened, "I highly suggest you keep your hands to yourself if you anticipate using them in the near future."

Big Moby grunted a little. "You wouldn't hit a clown now, would-ja?" he asked.

"I triple-dog dare him," Bean said sheepishly.

My lungs froze. It was some serious shiz when someone went

Christmas Story on somebody else. Problem was, Big Moby bordered stupid if he thought Dylan wouldn't take the challenge.

Big Moby suddenly dropped my hair and earring, saying, "Cheerio," and turned on his banana soles and shuffled toward the counter. What a scumbag. My guess was Big Moby suffered from pugilistic dementia. He not only squirted people with a seltzer bottle but also ran his head into the wall to get a laugh. But I think that was last summer's Big Moby. The new guy? He took shiz-bag to a brand new level.

Chapter Fifteen

PLAN B

....

I popped open a can of Vienna sausages and lined them up end-to-end on a hot dog bun. I was a nervous eater, and I'd been attacking everything that hadn't moved for the last sixty minutes. Glancing at the kitchen clock, I groaned at the witching hour. It was too late to contact Tito, and I'd been itching to speak with him since my feet entered command central. Munching as I strode upstairs, I waited outside Murphy's room until I heard him snoring. Snore...stop breathing...snore...stop breathing. When I figured I was home free, I tiptoed into Marjorie's room and burglarized her burner phone.

Before I burrowed down, I removed my contacts and slathered voodoo cream on my chest. Claudia and Ana Rosalina concocted a paste made of island plant life that promised to boost my Barely-B into C-range if I rubbed it on during the crescent moon. I'd nicknamed it voodoo cream since it obviously couldn't be found over the counter.

Afterward, I changed into red and white striped leggings and a matching top. Padding over to the corner, I opened the cage door and threw birdseed at Churro and Chimichanga. They both blinked twice with a dead-eyed stare before I covered their cage with a black satin blanket. Then I waved at the red Siamese fighting fish Dylan surprised me with earlier named after Herbert Hoover.

I crawled into bed and turned off the light, attempting a prayer.

I found even the hardest of persons threw up a prayer frivolously, but I didn't want to fall into that group. I took a deep breath. "God," I whispered, "I'm in a mess. Odds are against me, but if you could float some juicy stuff my way tomorrow, I'll turn from my sinful ways and be a good..."

I immediately stopped, realizing I'd entered the hypocrite zone. Before common sense could knock on my brain, I dialed Tito's number despite the hour. On ring number three, I whispered, "Jester here," when he answered.

He exhaled. "Jester, you've heard."

Oh crap. Suddenly, it wasn't a good idea to eat Vienna sausages. I swallowed down a burp that burned like bleach. "Yes," I lied, "how tragic."

"My source said the crime scene was horrific."

"Who *is* your source, Tito?"

"Now, Jester," he drawled in his southern way. "I protect them as much as I protect you. But if you're longing to be transparent, who's yours?"

I laughed loudly. "Anonymous."

He laughed even louder. "Ah, you can get away with a lot of things under the cloak of anonymity."

What the shinola were we talking about? Obviously, Tito felt I was in the loop, but as usual, I was flying blind. Slapstick and Damon I'd all but crossed off the list. By all intents and purposes, I'd gone back to the drafting board.

"The Ghost is clearly causing more problems, Tito," I guessed.

"I'd say, but who in the world is the skeleton in the closet?"

I launched into a full-on panic attack. Couldn't breathe. Swallowed my tongue. Shook uncontrollably from head to foot. I ripped off my shirt and sat there in a sports bra from the waist up, trying to cool my overly agitated body. I debated going straight, but that'd chance my aunt and uncle discovering I didn't sit nicely at home like the normal chicks. That'd be dumb, dumber than what I was doing.

"Yes, Tito," I reluctantly confessed, "I know. In fact, I've seen the layout of the home, and it looked like an organized operation to me. Without any proof, I'd say there was a problem within the operation because one of them is dead. One of the players, my guess, is the skeleton rolled up in the navy comforter."

"You even know the color of the comforter," he said quietly.

"I was there, okay? I didn't do it, but there was another guy present who got beaten up. Was he found in the same situation? As in dead?"

"Jester," he said tightly.

"Answer, Tito. This is important." I'd inadvertently thrown Vinnie under the bus—crap, there was no going back after that.

A pause. "I need a moment."

Dead air.

More dead air.

"I need you to answer if another man was found," I pushed.

"No one was found," he answered.

"Do you swear? Like he didn't crawl off in the yard and die in the dirt or something? Like, uh," I paused, "like next to...*another* body?" Nico Drake.

"No one other than the skeleton was found, Jester, but a pool of blood big enough to swim in was."

Holy. Shizzers. A part of me had hoped I'd imagined the whole Nico Drake dead body thing. But I knew I didn't. So where in the heck did he go because he sure as heck wasn't whistling Dixie when I left him. And while we're on the subject, what kind of sick messed up ponkey killed someone, rolled them in a blanket, and stuffed them in a closet? There were clothes in that closet, for crying out loud. What did the guy do? Step over the body when he reached for a T-shirt? Good thing was, Vinnie was in the clear. Thank. You. Jesus.

"Listen, Tito. 9139 Calypso Cove Drive was full of material that would keep an identity thief in business for years. If that's truly where The Ghost resides, then you need to find out who owns that house."

Tito inhaled deep. Forced an exhale. "My source informed me that a black and white was called to Calypso Cove when a UPS driver dropped off a box. The door was wide open, along with a bloody mess and the skeletal remains in the closet. From what we can tell, the remains in the closet are the real owner, Bishop Fowler. He wore a watch monogrammed with his initials a neighbor identified as his. Apparently, he was single and a hermit because it wasn't abnormal for him to not be regularly seen. It bothers me, Jester, that you have extensive knowledge of the crime scene. A scene where you were concerned that there might be two more dead bodies. Don't put me in a situation where I have to give you up to the authorities, and murder is one I won't cover up."

"I already swore to you I didn't kill anyone, Tito. I'm guilty of leaving the scene of a crime. That's it."

Tito wouldn't give me anything more when I'd given him everything except the name of Brantley McCoy. And why hadn't I? I wasn't exactly sure. That would help unmuddy the waters to a degree because the question would then be, *Why would a teenager be living with a hermit, with a different last name, who more than likely wasn't his parent?*

"So are we going to play or not, Tito? I feel like I'm in a one-handed game of poker."

"Just who *are* you that you can piece all of this together?" he asked.

Someone who reads the paper, someone who watches television with mature subject matter, someone with an overactive imagination, and someone whose father...was standing in the doorway growling like a freaking bear.

"*Shiiiit*," I actually cursed. I dropped the phone and prayed it disconnected.

———

Hoover was dead...

That morning he floated belly-side up, staring wide-eyed at the Pearly Gates. It felt like I took a double-barrel to the chest. When would it end? My mind needed a recess—if only for five minutes— but Dylan showed up bright and early, all crazy-eyed like he wanted to eat me alive.

Believe me, my mood nuked his hormones in a mushroom cloud.

And that wasn't the only thing that started the day wrong.

Nico Drake, bless his rat fastard heart, was found dead in his driveway. Knife attack. To the chest. Blunt force trauma to the head. Assailant still at large. Sweet Lord in Heaven, someone had moved the boy's body from Calypso Cove because by God he wasn't in the talking or walking mood the day before. The morning DJ on

700 WLW had all the grisly, gory details. Dylan actually pulled his car over just so we could stare into space and process. Then we both looked at one another and rehashed our yesterdays in case the cops came knocking. Dylan was with his father all day except for when he was with me. I was at The Double-B and burning rubber all over Valley with Vinnie. Vinnie would take our secrets to the grave. Our only hope of not seeing handcuffs was that no one saw us at Calypso Cove.

My sanity was frayed around the edges. I was in deep, so deep Nico might've wanted to warn me or kill me. I could either buckle under the pressure or go with the lie of it being an A-Okay day. I chose to put my head in the sand—and lie until the cows came home.

I'd just crawled out of career development. One of those gimme classes students like me took who weren't busting their chops in college-prep courses. *Stupid overachievers*, I grumbled. Anyway, in the middle of class, I received a Snapchat of Vinnie's foot...what the H? I took that as opportunity to update him about Nico to which Vinnie responded, *No shiz*. I pecked back, *Yes, shiz*. I also informed him Herb Ferrari was more than likely not a murderer, and Brantley McCoy probably killed Bishop Fowler, the man rolled up in the navy quilt. Cause of death (or COD) was said to be gunshot and knife wounds, and according to the news, the coroner merely waited for positive DNA identification. So unless the skeleton came back as a zombie, more than likely we were good.

Vinnie's response? A one-worded, *Cool*.

I needed a hit of what he'd been smoking.

The hallway seemed extra congested, and unfortunately I needed to motor to the front of the building fast. I decided to cut through the gym. Its second floor ran parallel with the hallway, so people literally could go in one door and right out the other in a shortcut. Big mistake. Coach Wallace was headed for his office, and although I normally welcomed his conversations, it was a huge reminder I had bupkis.

"How's life treating you, Walker?" he asked.

He'd dressed in head to toe Under Armour: a black hoodie, athletic shorts, and black sneakers. Me, I sported the goth gear: a black polyester tracksuit, black Nike Cortez sneakers, texting gloves, a T-shirt that said "Meh" in the center with a black and gray striped toboggan on my head. It had a twelve-inch tip and a pompom on the end I'd used to clean my glasses.

I fake-smiled. "Just cozy."

He frowned. "No, you're not. You hear about Drake?"

"Yeah," I mumbled.

Both of us let that part of the conversation die a natural death—which happened to be about twenty something seconds. He then muttered, "God help us," to which I muttered back, "I've already asked Him."

"So how's the investigation going?" he asked, breaking another ten second pause.

Personally, I'd pretty much term it a bust. Professionally, I decided to answer, "I've got some leads." *Liar, liar, pants on fire*, the angel gasped in my ear.

He chuckled. "Time's running out, dollface."

No kidding, but I didn't see it as a laughing matter. I muttered, "It's only Monday morning, and in fact I'll be asking for a bonus if I have the culprits delivered in cuffs before break begins."

He laughed so loudly the rafters shifted. "You're unbelievable."

She's genius, the devil countered in the other ear. "I will deliver as promised."

"I swear, Walker," he said and chuckled. "If you weren't so sweet, I'd be tempted to say you had no conscience."

That was certainly one way to term supernatural disillusionment. I sincerely prayed for Divine Intervention, namely some juicy information, and what did I get? Nico Drake dead and two more years of psychotherapy if I cared to pay for it.

We did some sort of awkward teacher-student side hug thing while I jumped into oncoming traffic. Walking the halls was usually so mundane I normally didn't think about it. Right then, I couldn't help but ponder two points. Actually three. Number one, did any of the students know The Ghost and/or Brantley McCoy; and number two, did any of them knife the life away of Nico Drake? My guess was number one had endless possibilities. Number two was the normal crap that happened to Darcy Walker. I attracted death—it was bizarre. The third point—and bane of my existence—how would I occupy myself during science next period?

Mr. Himmel hadn't changed or softened his opinion toward me. All he'd allowed me to do was walk into class, copy the assignment, and then find whatever little corner of the school I could to complete it.

My refuge would be the Media Center, but my plan was to cry, write down the songs I'd put on Dylan's iPod playlist (if I ever got the cash to buy one), and imagine him naked underneath my tree Christmas morning (a girl's gotta have a dream).

Suddenly, my stomach was in my mouth, and dread crawled over me like another death. Brynn Hathaway was leaned against the door of my locker...*like it was hers.*

Freakin' A.

Even though every inch of my body trembled, I cranked up the wattage on my smile. "Hello," I greeted. The smell of voodoo cream bombarded me like the Japanese took Pearl Harbor. I practically OD'd on it that morning, wanting to look as good as Brynn Hathaway's...um, hooters.

Eh, it didn't work, but it did birth a chest hair.

I held my notebook tight to my body. Being within close proximity of her was gut wrenching. Her hair had been pulled away from her heart-shaped face with a tortoise shell headband. She wore a V-neck black sweater a size too small to be comfortable, skinny jeans, and black boots. Her own version of goth, I suppose, but hers worked within the laws of fashion.

Mine looked like...well, like an idiot threw it together.

She smiled back, pitching her french-manicured thumb to Dylan's locker. "Is Dylan around?"

Gag...

"He's due," I told her stonily.

She flashed her perfect white teeth, and my pits instantly drenched. "I'll wait."

She said she'd wait. OHHHH. BIG. FREAKING. SURPRISE. Sigh.

"We got separated," she beamed, "and I wanted to finish our conversation." Awww. "Did you know Willow is coming into town? She's going to work with me on my runway walk."

I metaphorically twiddled my thumbs so much I got carpal tunnel syndrome in the process. Willow was Dylan's aunt—on the cover of *Vogue* magazine at only sixteen. And to answer her question, no I didn't know, but wasn't Brynn too short for runway work anyway? I pegged her to be around five foot five. Willow was six one. I could rock the shiz out of a runway. All you had to do was act hungry and PO'd.

Brynn wouldn't shut up. "I wanted to see if he was free for the winter formal. I mean, I think he is, and I'm pretty sure he's going to ask me to go with him." She paused for effect, her insanely white smile getting bigger. "Has he told you about our relationship?"

I let that fear worm its way into my soul until it was an inoperable tumor. What in the heck had they been talking about? Or better yet *doing*? I could ask since God knew she wanted me to, but I could do without the will-he-or-won't-he theatrics. Placing my textbook on the top shelf, I took the time to alphabetize it amongst the others. Then I removed my science book and imagined she was gone (or at least wart-covered) when I turned around.

She wasn't.

Seriously?!

I desperately tried to locate a smile, but she gave me a face like she believed in addition by subtraction. "You like math, don't you?" I mumbled.

She twirled the end of her hair, pulling it to her eyes to inspect for split ends. "I'm actually very good in math. I don't even have to study. I should've taken that advanced placement class last year, but now I'm glad I didn't. Dylan's so smart," she gushed, "he barely lifts his pencil."

"Yeah, well, he's a lot of things, Brynn. And I have firsthand experience with all the intimate parts."

Ho. Ly. Cow.

Darcy Walker pulled out the big guns.

Was that illegal in the laws of God what I'd just said? It sounded like we'd done the shama lama, ding-dong. Brynn's mouth parted in shock, quickly replaced with a you're-lying look. Her nostrils flared, and I could tell I'd hit a nerve. We stared at one another, both of us knowing we were the indisputable competition for Dylan's attention. I thought about telling her to back down. Heck, I thought about decking her button nose, but right when I just about did both, Bean bounded up to my side. "I looked for you on the roof today," he belted out, "but you weren't there. Does that mean you've found out anything?"

I resisted a face palm that was begging to live.

Bean was dressed like a monk. He sported a brown wool, oversized hoodie hitting him at the knees. A frayed rope draped around his waist, dangling to the floor. I didn't dare to look if he wore tights or leggings. I didn't want to know. His hair had been styled in its usual bowl cut, but his bald spot seemed more noticeable. The shape was a perfect sphere around his crown. It dawned on me he'd shaved it on purpose because it resembled a Roman tonsure—one of those religious rites men underwent to show their subservience to God. I didn't waste the energy trying to figure out what any of it meant.

I snuggled in close so Brynn wouldn't hear. But before I said anything, I spotted Dylan effortlessly maneuvering in and around the crowd. He met eyes with me first and then smiled to Brynn, leaving his gaze locked on Bean and me until he reached the three of us. He touched me on the small of my back in greeting, leaned down, and said a breathy, "Missed you," in my ear. Cue some animalistic desire. Like monkeys screeching and guppies getting their naughty on. When I sucked in a sharp breath, he chuckled and said, "Yeah."

"Yeah, what?" Brynn interrupted with a snap.

Dylan winked at me and turned to her. "Hi, Brynn," he said, opening his locker. "Did you need something?"

My ears bled when he said her name. And it probably wasn't a good idea to ask that specific question. She probably had a lengthy list including fornication, tattoos on private body parts, and naked selfies.

Bean tugged on my sleeve. "I think she likes him."

Um, yeah. Unfortunately. Brynn had a come-hither thing going on in her eyes. Well, you know what? My come-hither was *waaaay* better than hers.

While Dylan nodded during her story time, I asked Bean, "What makes you think so?"

Bean sort of giggled. "Watch the way she looks at his lips."

Whether Dylan was aware or not, Brynn was devouring his mouth with her eyes. An X-rated picture of them together flashed into my mind, and as much as I tried, I couldn't erase the skin. Brynn was the Cadillac of girlfriends. Instinct told me it was a matter of time before nature took over, and I became a distant memory. A snarl worked its way to my lips. I felt too much pressure in my head—like I rode in an airplane and my ears wouldn't pop.

My iPhone cranked out "Grandma Got Run Over by a Reindeer," and when Dylan gazed over with his girlie giggle, Brynn went into brat mode and rolled her eyes.

Some people had zero sense of humor.

I fished my phone out of my right back pocket, glancing at the unknown number. "Hullo?"

"It's me."

"Me?" I repeated.

"Me," he said again.

Nothing but two people breathing. I'd recently given my digits to a lot of people—the students I sat beside in the hall when we had the emergency *thingamabob*, that is. I'd planned to track down the ones I hadn't heard from and beg, borrow, or steal for their assistance. How could they assist? I didn't know yet but would figure it out once I opened my mouth.

Then it hit me. Hit me like a brand spanking new Audi.

Dylan dropped Brynn like a hot plate, grabbing my arm in a steely vice. He lifted his chin arrogantly, eyes cutting through whatever bull I'd considered shoveling up. Then, as per usual, we morphed into one of our silent conversations when the words were going to get a little hairy.

Who? he demanded.

I lifted my chin even higher, *Ben Ryan,* I answered.

You've got to be freaking kidding me, he sneered.

Dylan occasionally led with his eyes, circling like a wolf before it attacked.

"You hypocrite," I said aloud.

"Is that right?" he said, snorting loudly. "Well, getting you to admit to anything might throw the Earth off its axis, so I'm going to quit while I'm ahead."

I stared at him. He glared harder.

With one long stride, he backed me up against his locker. A flare of pure jealousy ignited his eyes to boiling. Good. We were finally getting somewhere because I'd take anger over standing beside one another, acting like not a dang thing was going on. And let me tell you, that was a first. Finally, he muttered, "For God's sake, you're making this so frigging hard on me. What are you doing, Darcy?"

Holding back my puke.

My chest heaved up and down. "I was expecting his call," I lied. "Science experiment stuff."

Dylan's jaw clicked a few times, and I was pretty sure if he was a vampire his fangs would be descended. I wriggled out from underneath him and grabbed Bean's arm, continuing down the hall before Dylan could say anything else, or I could buckle.

"Hello, Ben," I said sighing. Bean and I got stuck in traffic. We didn't do anything for a bit except hover in front of the Spirit Shop, the place students bought Valley paraphernalia.

"Hello, angel," Ben murmured. "I was just making sure you hadn't changed your number." When I didn't say anything, he said softly, "What's wrong? You seem tense."

He didn't know me well enough to term me tense.

I explained, "I'm on a rollercoaster of emotions today, and everyone should approach with caution."

"So you're preoccupied."

"That'd be a safe assumption."

"I'd like to see you."

"If you had aspirations of me being under the wheels of your car, then I hate to disappoint you, but I'm not interested."

He chuckled, and it warmed me from head to toe. Gah, I didn't like it that I *liked* Ben Ryan. And I *really* didn't like that he got under my skin. "I'll have to go to Plan B," he concluded oddly. "What's the preoccupation?"

I told him about Coach's car.

Yep, it was weird to confess that too.

That was all it took for Bean to insert himself in the dialogue. He snuggled his cheek up beside mine, interjecting into the receiver, "That's right. And we only work for a price."

"It *is* the American way," I agreed.

I assumed Ben would laugh again, disconnect, or blow me off as a misguided neophyte, but he didn't. Instead, he asked, "So what's the problem?"

Oh, where to begin. "The guys I would've sworn were involved... aren't."

From what little I knew about Ben, he struck me as the organized type. Things were simple, yada, yada, yada. I mean, my word, he wore penny loafers. That was a level of distinction you didn't encounter often in high school. "Then go back to the scene of the crime," he suggested.

"Which one? Because I'm dealing with two dead bodies too."

"...*What?*"

I sighed and clarified, "So stakeout the place where it happened?"

"It couldn't hurt. Have there been any copycat occurrences?"

"Nope." *Although there'd been a lot of vandalism around town*, I thought. Nowacki's Videos and The Double-B to be precise.

"Then return to the scene and see if anything seems out of the ordinary."

Placing Ben on speaker, I veered left at the cafeteria, making my way up the stairs. Bean predictably followed, and I wasn't sure his next class was even on the second floor.

"I already took pictures," I explained, "but they're a grainy mess of the wrong rows. Besides, it would do no good to take them again. We have designated spaces."

He dramatically sighed. "Angel, I'm disappointed. If you already knew where you could find the drivers in question, then why haven't you interviewed the owners personally?" He paused, and I could feel the beginnings of a flirty vibe. "Unless you're afraid to be that brazen? Surely, you're more than a pretty face, or maybe you're simply a dumb blonde. That is, considering you're a real one."

If my foot could make it through the phone, Ben's mouth would be full of Nike. The boy had no couth. Still, I found myself genuinely laughing.

"Ben, Ben, Ben," I teased while he quickly said he was only joking. "I'm blatantly talking on my iPhone which is against the rules as I'm walking past the assistant principal. And yes, I'm a real blonde. A dirty one," I said, giggling naughtily, "but a blonde, nonetheless."

Shoot, that was slutty-girl suggestive, but I honestly didn't care.

"Miss Walker," AP Unger scolded. "Must you always buck the system?"

I waved him off, giggling to Ben, "He says hi, by the way."

AP Unger gave an exaggerated eye roll, but instead of apprehending my phone, his eyes went wide as ping-pong balls as he lunged for Jagger and Ivy. They were plastered up against a locker, putting a whole new spin on the term PDA. Hands were everywhere, and feet were...well, off the ground.

Aww. Happy. Endings.

Jagger broke free with a shaky breath when AP Unger yanked him by the ear. "She's my backup," he said, laughing in my direction. If Ivy had a samurai sword, my entrails would be decorating the ceiling.

Ben murmured, "Tell me more about this guy."

"Jagger?" I clarified.

"Is he the guy who had his car vandalized?"

That truly would be a capital offense. Jagger drove a Mercedes SUV like Rookie's—this week, that is.

"No," I answered. "It's our basketball coach's. He's divorced, and it was far from amicable." And his wife's involvement had crossed my mind, but as far as I knew she could be turning tricks on Mars.

"Give me her name," he said.

"Why?"

He chuckled deeply, like I had no clue what he was capable of. "Trust me."

I thought back to the caption on the backside of Coach's photograph and told him, "Jacinda Olivia Jemima Opal Wallace."

Ben continued with the chuckle thing. "Who in the world has five names?"

"My guess is a whole lot of woman."

He was quiet for a beat, as though he scribbled down notes. "So who's this Jagger?"

I looked back toward Jagger who futilely tried to explain his actions to AP Unger. I didn't know if I'd term him misunderstood, understood, or lost cause.

"School playboy," Bean answered for me.

"I'm assuming you're his Plan A," Ben said.

I shivered at the thought. "He's a fastard...pardon my language.

And he likes anyone he can't have, but once you fall under the spell, he jettisons you."

"Spoken from experience?" he murmured.

"Spoken from observation."

"And the guy you're with?" Ben pushed.

Bean threw his arm around my neck as we stopped in front of Mr. Himmel's door. Bean smelled like mothballs. A fact my nose was having trouble negotiating with. "I'm her best friend," Bean beamed.

Shoot, it struck me like an arrow to the heart that position might become vacant real darn soon.

"That means it's only a matter of time, angel."

Disconnect. Proverbial dial tone. Cue the confusion.

As stupid as it sounded, I found myself attracted to the guy who'd mowed me over with his car and insulted me at least three times in our five-minute conversation. But I barely knew him—I didn't know if he was a jock, member of the chess club, band geek, student council representative, or fugitive from the law.

I sighed. I sighed so loudly Bean jumped.

I needed those unconditional conversations from Dylan. You know, where I talked and he never went ape poopoo when he found out how freaking bizarre I really lived my life. Dylan would never understand in a million years that Vinnie and I'd broken into a guy's house just so we could prove he was a bad person. Dylan was too protective and sometimes too practical. Ben strangely goaded me into action, and he didn't even know it.

Chapter Sixteen

ANSWERED PRAYERS

I'd always lived my life one way: go big, or go home. I was pretty sure I was about to go crazy.

During the fifty-two minutes I was supposed to be reading my science book, I tracked down the students I spoke with in the hallway via text. The answers were one, they'd forgotten; two, they didn't remember me (blow to my ego); or three, they wanted to talk about the winter formal. So what little hope I'd had earlier had been sucked dry by idiots.

It was fifth period, government. I'd already had lunch, and the menu was bean burritos with cheesy rice. In essence, I could legitimately walk up to my teacher's desk, paint on a face of nausea, and beg to hit the restroom. Thankfully, Mr. Barton seemed distracted. When I asked, he simply replied, "Sure, Walker," and that was all it took.

So I roamed the second floor hall toward the west end of the building, facing the parking lot. The great thing about our building was the front was almost total glass. My plan was simple: look out the windows and see if anything weird was going on. Since AP Unger normally traveled that route, I ducked into the janitor's closet and immediately checked to see if I was alone. I didn't see any pairs of feet but decided to yell an, "Is anyone home?" anyway. When no one answered, I swatted away a spider's web and realized the best view to the parking lot was from the corner window, several feet from the ground.

I got my ninja on, crawled up to the windowsill, and waited...and waited...and waited. I picked at my nails, pulled lint off my texting gloves, glanced at my watch, and concluded I'd been gone for close to fifteen minutes.

Not good, not good at all.

After I played with the pompom on my toboggan, I slid my iPhone out of my jacket, attempting to snag a signal. I'd missed a text:

Jojo Wallace works at Dingo 31 at Voice of America Plaza.

Ben Ryan. I laughed. He'd spelled out and punctuated everything in his text perfectly...figures, the managerial type. Jojo was apparently an acronym for Jacinda Olivia Jemima Opal. I think I'd make an acronym, too, but who was I to debate the etymology of someone's name? My name's Darcy Walker—a dark walker. Whether it was a stroke of genius or stroke of stupid, my parents hit the bull's-eye.

Here's the thing. When Ben said to trust him, he really meant to *trust him*. But how in the world could he sniff out the lady's name, plus where she worked? I put that thought on ice and thumbed in, *Thnx.*

I then heard that still, small voice Murphy claimed was the voice of God. I didn't hear it much. Maybe it was because I didn't take the time to listen, or maybe it was because the language was so foreign it'd take years more of practice. Either scenario, I heard, "Welcome to the land of the all-knowing, kid. Here's your juicy stuff you requested. Don't question me again."

I took the time to pause. I didn't know what to do or if I should even comment that God kind of sounded like a smarty pants. Before I damned myself to burning fire, I noticed movement. Several students slowly filed out to their cars. Two guys in dark down coats huddled together, like they stole one another's warmth or perhaps talked about something private. And if my eyes hadn't fooled me, they were corralled around a red Mustang and silver Chevy Colorado. To pile on the wonder, a dirty white van pulled up alongside them, its exhaust sputtering and smoking in the frigid air.

It was darn Ground Hog's Day.

Problem was, the group appeared to be leaving. It was only fifth period, so that meant they were seniors. No one else would be allowed to take that light of a schedule except those with the required classes under their belts. I could do one of two things: chalk it up as answered prayer number two or go one step further and interview them as Ben suggested. My instincts took over, and I blood-hounded my way out of the closet like my next meal depended on it. Taking the stairs three at a time, I one-handed the door and pushed outside.

The air exploded in my face. I didn't have a coat, and the air was so blistering cold I saw my own breath. Unfolding my texting gloves, I quickly snapped them over fingers as stiff as a corpse. Then I walked—*no, skipped*—thought that looked stupid so compromised and strode really fast. I felt like a Catholic schoolgirl off the leash. It was my big break. I had no idea how to broach the subject, but I'd introduce myself and pray the rest came naturally.

Uh, a face-to-face seemed like a better idea when it was merely in my mind. All three looked at me like I was a first class idiot. Probably because the chill had reached my bones, and I was doing jumping jacks.

I produced an awkward, breathy, "Hi."

The guy from the white van opened a rusty, rickety sounding door and stumbled out. He wore a mustard-colored jumpsuit like those on construction sites do. On his head was dark blond, curly hair and black horn-rimmed glasses. A white ballcap shaded his eyes and the upper portion of his face. I couldn't get a read on him. The other two seemed like your average Joes: jeans, white sneakers, a pimple here, and a pimple there. Where most tried to avoid eye contact with seedy characters, I was the type that stared until it became uncomfortable. All three eyeballed me as though they considered strangling me or shoving me into the van.

Cue the stomach cramps.

"I'm sorry," I apologized, trying to break the ice. "I thought I knew you."

"I'd like to get to know *you*," White Van muttered.

If that was innuendo for an illicit invitation, I decided to play dumb and blonde. Stumbling three steps over, I hit a bumper and blurted out, "Did you happen to see who painted Coach Wallace's car last week? It was parked beside yours. If you didn't, maybe you've heard about it? Not much happens here that doesn't hit the grapevine."

"Or that *you* miss," White Van interjected. I cocked my head to the side, confused. Even though I couldn't place the face, my mind went crazy trying to identify the voice. Something about him seemed familiar, and my guess was it was a familiar that wasn't pleasant. If memory served me correctly, he'd left the van idling and got out long enough to high-five the others. He'd either enjoyed it the most or was the type that delighted in others' misfortunes.

My mouth did the usual—got more stupid. "If I remember correctly, *you*," I clarified, pointing to him, "thought it was the funniest. You high-fived the others like it meant something personal to you."

I think someone gasped. Shoot, it might've been me.

"We're innocent," White Van grunted. "Besides, wouldn't it be stupid to make a spectacle out of something you'd just done?"

True, but his answer about being innocent was bogus. God only knew what he was capable of because my trust radar beeped like a sonova-you-know-what simply being within inches of him.

"Listen, Coach seems like a nice guy," Red Mustang added, opening the door of his ride, "but you can't fault someone for finding the humor. If truth be known, I bet you laughed too."

He had me there.

Colorado got jumpy. He either needed a cup of coffee or was colder than me. "I just thought it was funny," he said with a shrug.

White Van stalked forward slowly, his head dipped low, like he didn't want me out of his frame of sight. "Let's continue this discussion elsewhere," he ordered.

He snagged my wrist, twisting it counterclockwise, pulling me toward that crappy white van. I wasn't a fool. Triple-coverage was a no-way-out situation. I knew enough to scream but forced a sigh, feigning boredom instead. When he twisted harder, I concluded the scared-girlie routine should've been my first route. Should I faint? Throw-up? Make a diversion?

"Shoot, fudge, and sonovabiscuit eater" fell out of my mouth in one long breath.

Chevy Colorado grabbed White Van's arm. If he seemed jumpy

before, he then acted like he was pregnant with an elephant, mid-contraction.

"Let her go, man," he pleaded.

Instead of heeding Colorado's words, White Van tightened his grip. My fear grew larger than a sci-fi monster, my eyes darting to Red Mustang for an assist. He nervously shook his head, like he wanted to help, but preferred not rocking the boat. He collapsed in the seat, leaving his door ajar. After a few beats, he turned the key over, slammed the door shut, and backed away.

I was in it alone.

God help me.

Alone.

I'd been in a situation before where things started to unravel, and I tried to stop the bleeding anyway I could. A "please" didn't get me anything more than a grunt, and an "I know important people" got me nothing more than a raised brow. Unfortunately, I ignored my basic survival instincts and kept right on jawing.

"You're guilty of something," I whispered. "Did you paint his car or kill Nico Drake? How about the skeleton? Did you feast on the remains, or are you The Ghost himself?"

Talk about going for broke.

I received another heated gaze. Chevy Colorado suddenly grimaced like someone strung him up by the family jewels. He doubled over, coughed, and then shuddered. "Holy crap, here comes trouble," he said.

He and White Van glanced over my shoulder around the same time a bellowing voice broke the tension like a foghorn.

"Darcy!" it roared. *Thank you, hot boy gods*. I sighed in relief. Dylan barreled toward us like we were insurgents, and he alone was the hit squad. His black hair blew in the wind, reminding me of a gothic wartime hero riding home in a blazing storm. Dylan Taylor and angry were two words that didn't match up perfectly together. My guess was these guys had witnessed the boom or heard of the legendary explosions.

"Darcy," White Van repeated, dropping my arm with a crazed grin.

"And you are?" I somehow managed.

When he didn't answer, I conjured up an equally twisted smile.

White Van muttered, "Toodles," quickly jumping back in his ride. I zenned out for all of two seconds when my blood pressure dropped to woozy. Through his window, he painted his lips in one of those perverted, ruthless grins, made his fingers in the shape of a gun, and mouthed, "Bang-bang."

I mumbled, "Okay," to the spluttering trail of smoke he left behind. I didn't know if that meant I'd accepted his challenge or accepted my fate. When Chevy Colorado peeled out on a screech, I slowly and reluctantly turned. Like I knew it'd be a mistake, but if the day was already bad...eh, I might as well take it to the lowest level of crap. Dylan wasn't walking. Heck, he wasn't running. It was like he levitated through the air by some unknown force.

My legs struggled as though they'd frozen solid, which was odd because I'd been so afraid I'd sweated bullets big enough to down a dinosaur. While the wind whipped through Dylan's black hair, as bizarre as the last few minutes had been, I still had the desire to run my fingers through it.

Darcy, Darcy, Darcy, I told myself. *You really ought to find some self-esteem.*

Dylan reached me first, saying, "What the" *bleep* "are you doing out here? I felt you leave the building."

If I'd doubted beforehand our cosmic connection had severed, it was times like these that erased any misgivings. I felt him, and he felt me. Sometimes it was a trying experience. Others, it came in handy. When he saw my knees knocking, he took off his coat and draped it around my shoulders, wrapping his arm around my waist for extra warmth.

"I-uh," I said. "Umm," I started again. "Well, it's like this," I said exhaling.

I felt a little light on my feet and fell into him. I swear, right when I'd planned to 'fess up and ask him to beat the big, bad uglies to a pulp, he stopped, holding up his palm. "Did anyone hurt you?" he asked tenderly.

"No," I said truthfully. "We were just talking," I half-lied.

In a rare out-of-character moment, Dylan accepted my answer and didn't push for particulars, which told me he hadn't seen what White Van had attempted to do. "Then let me start again," he murmured. "Sweetheart, we're out of sync. I know you've had some bad luck lately, but maybe we can do something to cheer you up. Guess who just got a text from your aunt?"

Oh, God, no. That meant one of two things. Red wanted him to rat me out on something, or worse yet, she wanted him to take me...someone help me...shopping.

Ugh, ugh, ugh.

Shopping was okay when I was in control.

Not when someone was trying to morph me into someone else.

When I winced, he grinned. "The occasion is Rookie's party," he explained. "You're an honored guest and have an unlimited shopping spree under my fine eye. Come on, Darc," he murmured and winked. "Let's get these last two classes in. I'll blow through practice, and then we'll go stimulate the economy."

My uncle hosted a holiday bash each year for all his hoity-toity friends who helped him get elected. For some insane reason, he felt it was a good idea I was on the invite-list. There was no real good reason to protest. They'd already made a unilateral decision I would go. I didn't have the energy anyway.

Dylan led us back up the steps in a run, not even broaching the subject why I'd been standing outdoors, barely clothed, talking to total strangers. That seemed Grade A stupid to me, but Dylan occasionally operated under the auspices I'd been behaving.

God love him. Sometimes he was an idiot.

After one class (our sixth periods weren't together), we met up going to seventh period English. While we navigated our way through the crowd, Dylan got sidetracked talking to Grumpy and Finn. Grumpy had his cell phone half hanging out of his back pocket...so I picked it while we were walking. When he spun around with a huff, I basically barfed up my entire day, starting with Brantley McCoy and Nico Drake's dead body, ending with my run-in with the three guys in the parking lot.

"Does Taylor know this?"

"No. Does that make me a bad person?"

"It doesn't exactly make you humanitarian of the year. He's like the nicest person I know, Walker." I pulled my books closer to my chest, trying to dematerialize. "You're honestly taking this reward seriously?" he continued in surprise. I gave him a sullen nod. "Red

Mustang, huh?" Another nod. "I know him. I'll talk to him tomorrow about Coach's car."

"Throw out Nico Drake's name too."

Grumpy's gaze went hard as granite. "And why would I do that?"

"Do you remember me asking Slapstick and Damon about The Ghost?" Another granite gaze. "Well, just do it. And ask them about the creepo guy in the white van. I don't like those guys, and I don't know why."

At least, that'd be something. I attempted to explain the word patience to my brain as Grumpy scratched his brown mop-head. Looking over his shoulder for privacy, he whispered, "Listen, Walker," while we dodged in and out of the crowd. "I'm getting desperate here, and the dance is knocking at my door. At this point I'd take the closest air-breathing mammal who looks halfway monogamous."

Shoot, I'd forgotten about Clementine. Well, not totally, but I hadn't given her high priority. I told him, "I'll work on it."

"But it has to be *her* idea, Walker. A guy has to keep his reputation."

Once again, I muttered, "I've got you covered."

"And if not her, then I'll take Ivy...if she's still single, that is."

Gross. Grumpy needed his head examined.

I didn't want to be an intergalactic killjoy—that was his shtick—but we needed to have a heart-to-heart about his choices in women. Trouble was, he'd probably want a heart-to-heart about my choices of recreation. As a whole, he was a well-adjusted guy, but around the holidays he was like everyone else—no one was immune to that feeling of desperation. The feeling you'd be all alone and that peace on earth stuff would choke the life out of you.

Chapter Seventeen

SOCIAL MORES

asketball practice dismissed early when the cops busted up the party. Dylan, Finn, and Grumpy evidently were on the menu regarding Nico Drake. Can you say, *Instant PR problem?* Evidently, Dylan's father had gotten a heads up they'd like to question the three, and since he was in Europe, his superstar attorney dropped everything and met them in AP Unger's office.

It was a short meeting, but when the cops discovered I was on-site (seriously, I'm not sure why I wasn't on the invite-list initially), after a quick call to Murphy, I opened the floodgates and told them what I thought: Nico was a douchebag, threatened girls, felt them up, didn't know that no meant no, and given that his actions were deplorable and probably deserved death, I'd come to the conclusion I wasn't sad he was dead—even though I had been initially.

I then confessed I felt better for getting that off my chest...

Superstar Attorney dove across the table and slammed a palm over my flapping gums. Dylan dropped an F-bomb, immediately demanding I shut up. AP Unger said, "Ditto." I didn't look at Grumpy and Finn. I chose to believe they were silently laughing rather than paralyzed with shock. Thankfully, the four of us had alibis, but it was a good guess the cops left with me on their radar. That was what happened when a person was unstable. The trained could sniff the crazy out.

But a funny little thing happened in that meeting. Everyone wanted to know the name of the girl Nico had accosted. Uh, yeah... me too. AP Unger divulged her name as freshman art enthusiast, Madison Flannery. Well, guess who was Madison Flannery's new best friend? I raised my hand in my own demented mind.

Dylan and I had just picked four dresses off the rack at Nordstrom's Department Store, on the quest to find the holiday dress my aunt insisted I buy. I'd already test-driven three and stared at myself in a long-sleeved, siren-red mini. It fit me like a glove with textured fringe on the bottom. Falling mid-thigh, the fringe added an extra illusion of length.

I giggled over the changing room door. "Come and feast your eyes on the goods, Big Man."

Dylan chuckled. "Darc, when are you going to realize we're not six years old anymore? I can't see you in your underwear."

"You see me in a bikini every summer."

Pause. "True, but we can't. Come out, and let me see it."

"I can't get it zipped."

"Aw, Darc, I can't do that either. The females near you won't appreciate the intrusion." Debatable.

I frowned, throwing both arms over my back, attempting to grab the little hook and pull north. "Do you zip Sydney's dresses?"

He didn't answer right away. I took that as confirmation enough. "That's different. She's my sister."

I played with the fringe and wondered what Murphy would think...I knew. He'd wonder where the rest of the dress was. "You don't love me like you love her."

A smile was in his voice. "I love you differently than anyone, sweetheart."

Before I could talk myself out of it, I blurted out six words that proved I had no pride whatsoever. "Would you zip Brynn Hathaway's dress?"

There was an undertow of shock in Dylan, him sounding offended without even voicing a peep. He shifted around, mumbling things I couldn't unravel. "Why in the world would you say that, Darcy? You know what I've asked of you, and those feelings haven't changed." I stared in the mirror, realizing I'd broached a subject I wished I could immediately take back. Guys didn't like desperate girls. I didn't know much about relationships, but everything I saw on TV showed them running for cover when the girl became clingy.

Thank God Dylan granted me the gift of silence.

After some self-loathing, I mumbled, "I apologize. That sounded whiny and desperate. And every bit of research I've conducted claims whiny and desperate are major turnoffs."

He chuckled deeply. "Come here, Darc, and let me get my hands on you. You're the only crazy blonde I want in my life."

I stole one last glance in the mirror. It'd been a long day. Not only did I have raccoon eyes but hair that looked like it belonged on a chinchilla's butt. I looked inebriated, and the strongest thing I'd ever consumed was cough medicine with codeine. Holding the back of my dress together, I unlatched the door and took a step. There was no sexy way to walk with socks rumpled at my ankles plus an unzipped dress I tried to hold together. I just hoped my butt and naked skin scored some points. Trying to walk like a sexpot, I tiny-stepped it to Dylan who sat on a red leather sofa, scrolling through his cell phone.

He'd cleaned up well. He still wore the same clothes as that morning, but his "Ranger" hat covered his modern-messy hair. The swallow in his throat alerted me he struggled with the assignment. That brought on a deep feeling of sadness. We'd definitely crossed the barrier into male versus female, appropriate and inappropriate, no turning back.

Great if things evolved into something everlasting.

If it didn't? That would plain suck.

I lifted my hair off my neck and turned my back to him. Dylan stood up, placing his right hand on the small of my back, pulling my zipper up with the other. His hands were hot on my skin. I shakily pivoted to face him, trying my best to act unaffected.

"What do you think?"

He ran both hands down the sides of my dress—leaving them on my hips a little longer than warranted—then held his index finger up over my head, twirling it like a merry-go-round. I gave a slow 360-degree turn.

"We're done," he murmured resolutely.

"Does it make my chest look bigger?" I asked, still not convinced. Dylan rearranged his hat, nervously looking over his shoulder like he dodged a spear. "It doesn't," I whispered when his eyes grew wide.

"I do not concur," he murmured, grinning obviously out of sheer obligation. Dylan was dumb. Grabbing my face in his left hand, he tilted my face upward. "I think you're the most beautiful thing I've ever seen. There's not one thing about your body I'd change."

I turned, crashed on the couch, and burst into tears. I looked like an idiot, and Dylan was the biggest liar who ever walked the face of the third planet. My athletic socks hung at the ankles, and my glasses were coated in a misty fog. I not only looked like an idiot, I looked like a depressed idiot.

"I'm a freak," I sniveled.

"You're too cute to be a freak."

I looked down at my chest and knew my own personal endowments weren't anything to jump for joy over. "Maybe I would be less freakish with a push-up bra."

Dylan gave me his TMI face. "Oh, God," he whispered, rearranging his hat again. "I shouldn't have taken this job."

I blubbered like the fat on a whale. "Best friends are supposed to talk about these things, but you won't talk anymore. Then you want to...*date me*. What would that do to us, D? Don't you see a pattern here?"

Surely to God, he saw the signs...right? My God, did he not watch talk shows? "Please, don't cry. Dating would only make our relationship better."

No, dating me would be like an eventual death sentence, but he seemed determined to shake hands with the Grim Reaper. ""Then answer about the bra," I said sniffling.

He swallowed. "I think I feel nauseous."

God help me. That crying jag was worse than the first. Dylan scrubbed his forehead so hard he left a red mark. "D, I don't like change. And you'll barely talk as it is."

"We're talking."

"I'm *making* you talk. There's a difference."

He pushed my hair off my face, sliding into the seat beside me. "Okay, ask me anything."

"Everything is overwhelming. Push-up bras are overwhelming.

School is overwhelming. The things you make me feel are over-whelming."

Dylan stared hard—a brief moment of triumph in his eyes—but it quickly dissolved, and he rekindled the staring. He eventually found his way back to the subject at hand.

"What's Murphy say?" he asked.

"About three years ago, Murphy gave me a book about the changes a girl goes through. A *book*," I whispered, "that's all." I shook my head and waved my arms in exasperation like I'd been robbed in the parental-guidance department. "Who gives their kid a book?"

Dylan ran his hand down his jaw, crossed and recrossed his legs. He sometimes got fidgety when conversations made him uncomfortable. That didn't happen often, but he looked like he'd rather play *Twister* with a python. "Was it a good book?"

"It was a book of Grandma Marjorie's from the turn of the century." Dylan burst into rumbling laughter, throwing his head back. "Haven't there been medical break-throughs in the meantime?"

He laughed even louder, covering his mouth. "The body still works the same," he said. "The wording in today's books might be more user-friendly, but anatomy is anatomy. Have you talked to Red?"

Listen, my problems ran deeper than Puberty 101. It stemmed from having a father who was *afraid* I'd turn into a 'ho with too much information and an aunt who was *convinced* I'd turn into a 'ho out of curiosity. "Red is happy I finally got a chest," was my answer. "I think she hopes I'll get the rest on the bus."

I felt like an idiot. Add Claudia and her malfunctioning voodoo cream and my closest girlfriend being a boy, there was no wonder my grasp of the birds and the bees—let alone the flowers and the trees—was severely stunted. "Can't you see why it would never work? I'm asking you to explain the birds and the bees when you're asking me to experience the birds and the bees *with* you."

"Oh, God," he whispered. "The conversations we have keep me up at night." He looked me straight in the eyes. "Seriously?"

I nodded, wiping away my pathetic tears. "The adult channels really aren't informative."

With that statement, Dylan dove in like a health teacher—oblivious to anyone who came near. I pivoted toward him as we talked about the birds and bees, pollination, and the mating habits of the rabbit. Then he analyzed, dissected, and basically gave an oral report on the human version as my heart was thump-thump-thumping against my rib cage. Beads of perspiration formed over my lips, and I coughed a few times in disbelief.

When he finished, he murmured, "You can close your mouth now, Darc." I couldn't. "Well, at least breathe." I couldn't seem to do that either.

"Are you s-sure?" I sputtered.

"Happened the same way for centuries."

Murphy left out quite a few details, and Grandma Marjorie's book didn't explain the gymnastics of the process. "It sounds sort of scary," I said and shivered.

I felt like I needed a shower.

Dylan's eyes softened. My guess was he hadn't expected my reaction, but really, how did guys think we felt?

"I promise you," he murmured, "with the right guy it will *not* be scary." He threw in the word marriage. One prerequisite Murphy *did* drill into my head.

Funny thing was, I'd prefer living with Dylan as my roomie than marrying someone I'd known for only a few years. He was the one who picked my head up and twisted it on in the morning. How could someone replace that?

"If my science experiment or you and I don't work out, can we live together?" I asked sheepishly. I sounded like a skanky 'ho-bag, but oh well.

"Darc, you have to be the most naïve person I've ever met, but if it makes you feel better, then yes. I'll make sure you're not alone." I was giddy with the possibilities. I wouldn't have to cook, and if the urge didn't strike, I wouldn't have to clean. Dylan lost most, if not his entire smile. "Why is it you make everything so frigging hard?" he muttered to himself.

I stood up and moved toward the mirror, literally lifting my boobs with both hands. Okay, it wasn't my boobs. It was more like my ribs.

He massaged both temples. "Please," he whispered, "don't do that around me."

Apparently, he thought it was futile. Dylan and I defied social mores even having those conversations, but those were things girls confessed to one another while they lie in their sleeping bags, talking about the hottest guy on campus. It stunk when your best friend was a boy. There was no squeezing into a single stall to give a thumbs up or down. There was no running to get another size while the girl safely stayed tucked away. No, I had to walk outside, hold my zipper together, and beg Mr. Too-Mouthwatering-For-His-Own-Good to zip up the body fate screwed me with.

I rang Murphy, checking in before leaving Nordstrom's. "You'd better hit the road, kid," he grumbled. "This storm system rolled into the area in record time, and I'm afraid you're not going to make it home before the accumulation hits."

"It's snowing?" I said shocked.

"That's one way to term an avalanche," Murphy grunted. "Get home. Now."

Dylan pulled his wallet out of his inside pocket, handing the sales associate an American Express Centurion Card. That was just wrong. No teenager should have unlimited funds—which is what that black card promised—and by the look on the sales associate's face, she could not disagree more. She'd pulled two pairs of shoes earlier—a black ankle boot with a three-inch heel and flesh-colored gladiator-like sandals with a four-inch stiletto. Jimmy Choos. My God, they cost more than Murphy's 401(k) monthly contributions. When she saw Dylan hadn't been swayed by the price, she dumped several earrings and bangly bracelets on the countertop, declaring they were the next big thing.

After a quick phone call to Red, my aunt ordered we purchase them all. Where the two thought I'd wear them on a regular basis was beyond me, but my guess was I'd look mighty fine lying at home on the couch.

———

Snow shaped like sparkly soap flakes fell gracefully to the ground. Those living in a wintry climate knew that type of precipitation was bad. It piled up fast, producing whiteouts and conditions so treacherous only the natives or those with a strong constitution were qualified to drive.

Just my humble opinion...

It was after eight. Cars moved at a slow crawl, and my stomach growled like a motorboat. My sense of humor had long died, but when I was copilot in what appeared to be the worst snowstorm of the season, my job was to keep it together.

For once, Dylan had both hands on the steering wheel, textbook ten and two position. Even though I wasn't driving, I could feel the tension in the car's engine. A misty rain fell earlier, and with the dropping temperature, the pavement had frozen like an igloo. Snow accumulated on ice, making traction hit-or-miss.

We listened to the weather report on 700 WLW, and it pretty much reiterated the obvious, "Get home. You're stupid if you're driving in this hellacious crap!"

A direct quote from the DJ.

We pulled left onto Montgomery Road, full intentions of traveling northbound on I-71 back to Valley. We'd barely traveled one hundred yards when the Beemer skidded sideways. The anti-lock brakes strained and gripped, promising an eventual stop, but problem was we didn't know what would happen in the interim.

Dylan barked, "Hold on," as he twisted and turned with the steering wheel. I threw a two-handed grip on the dash while we fishtailed into the opposite lane. Thankfully, no car moved in our path, just another driver several feet back who maneuvered his car so methodically it seemed to have stopped moving altogether.

Snow fell so fast the windshield wipers barely kept up. Dylan flashed his blinkers, asking permission from the automobile behind to enter the exit lane again. Once he put us back on course, the car to our rear hit the same patch of ice, repeating the fishtail we'd come out of. He or she wasn't so lucky. The car behind tapped their rear.

"*Ay, caramba*," I whispered.

Holy heck, we hadn't even made it onto the interstate without a minor incident. A look across the overpass showed conditions more deadly. Multi-vehicle pileups decorated two lanes, and that didn't count the areas I couldn't see beyond the horizon. We'd be stranded for hours.

Dylan pointed to the mass of red taillights in the bumper-to-bumper traffic. "Ah, Darc," he groaned. "We aren't going anywhere."

It wouldn't be so bad if we had food. The gas tank was full, so we could burn it until we hit "E." And for that matter, the company was (sigh) Dylan. But dang it, the last thing I'd eaten was a Slim-Jim and Hershey kiss I'd found in my locker at three o'clock. I digested stomach lining at that point.

Dylan rhythmically rapped his left thumb on the steering wheel as traffic completely stopped. I felt bad he was in the situation. My guess was Red felt worse. Not to mention what our parents were thinking. Dylan rarely got rattled, but he seemed pensive, wondering what move to make next. Leaning over, I braced my right hand on his knee, the other around the nape of his neck, planting a chaste kiss on his cheek.

I'd never initiated a kiss of any kind before...as in ever...as in never, ever, *ever*.

"I love you," I whispered in his ear, "and don't worry about us. I trust you. More than anyone."

When I pulled back, he quickly reached up and cradled my face with his palm, forcing the physical contact to not end quite yet. A single look from Dylan could communicate something fierce, something probably best he didn't put to words. My instinct was to crawl back to my seat, folding my hands together like a good, little girl. He'd gone sugar daddy in the mall and bought me a Burberry wool newsboy cap—to my protest. I pulled the three-figured hat down over my eyes, trying to hide. His gaze slid over me like hot, molten lava. He also recognized the never, ever, *ever* occurrence. I mean, it was only because I wanted to comfort him...*right?* Before I attempted an explanation, both our cell phones rang within seconds of one another.

I reached inside my pocket, glad for the interruption. For me, it was Murphy. "Hey, Murphy," I greeted. "We wrecked, and I'm lying in the middle of 71 North with a severed femoral artery. My shoes and pants are missing, and my guess is it's going to end me within twenty minutes. Bury me with my fish in the backyard."

Dylan answered his phone. "Hey, Mom," he murmured with a

giggle. Then a short pause appeared where he briefly touched his heart. "Aw," he soothed tenderly, pulling my fingers to his lips, "don't worry. We're going to be okay."

All I heard through my receiver was "Gosh-danged idiots... stupid dress...family meeting when you get home...say your prayers...be a lady," followed by a "Good Lord in Heaven, help me." Next was his standard Kentuckyized profanity, "I will spit on their graves, kid. I swear it. I will spit on those meteorologists' graves."

Finally came a resigned and soothing calm as Murphy exorcised himself of the worry. "Kid," he grumbled, "Red's going to be waiting on you. I've talked to Susan Taylor, and she agrees that's where you should head. Be careful," he whispered, "you're all I've got."

Dylan mouthed, "Red," as I nodded. I had to agree. Four exits south was her house. Five exits north was traffic hell.

————

After Red phoned that she and Rookie were snowbound about an hour away, I quickly nuked the leftover Naked Pizza in her refrigerator, trying my best to ignore the name of the establishment and its connotation. Let me tell you, Dylan and I made love to that pizza, relishing each mouthwatering bite until halfway through when poof the electricity went sayonara.

Using the flashlight app on my iPhone, I sifted through Red's dresser trying to find us both something comfortable to sleep in. From the looks of things, she and Rookie might as well have still been married. Her clothes were crammed into her side, no organization at all. Underwear in with her jeans, socks in with her shorts, just crap that made sense in her own mind. Rookie's side of the dresser, however, looked immaculate. Underwear on top, socks below, with sweats and T-shirts rounding out the bottom.

"Does Rookie still live here?" I whispered to Dylan.

He chuckled devilishly. "He still wears a wedding band. Don't you find that strange?" Not really, Red and Rookie flew far outside the realm of your normal fly zone.

Closing the drawers with a tap, I snagged a pair of lavender fleece pajama bottoms and matching top, giving Dylan a pair of gray checked flannel pants and a white sweatshirt. While I quickly changed in the restroom, Dylan had just finished pulling the sweat-shirt on when I rejoined him. Um, wow. Too bad we were in the dark...would've been awesome.

Our plan was to crash on the couch in the living room. While we felt our way down the hall, I continued the conversation. "I just assumed Rookie couldn't let go."

Heck, I think I had the can't-let-go gene too because I had a death grip on Dylan's sweatshirt. As I crept behind him, I wondered why things felt natural. I whispered, "Don't you think it's weird that we're here together, in the dark, and it's not all *weird* between us? Shouldn't this be *weird?*"

I had no compunction whatsoever about being alone with Dylan. What would be weird was if I suddenly developed a hesitation.

Dylan actually took the time to let my words sink in. Just us breathing. His shadow appeared softer in the dark, masculine still, but perhaps more vulnerable. "I don't think anything will *ever* be weird between us, Darc," he answered. "I love and respect you, and you love and respect me. Most people wait their entire lives for that sort of commitment."

Oh. You. Silver-tongued. Devil.

I plastered myself to his back in a bear hug. God knew I was a compulsive person, and the biggest compulsion I had was to get as close as possible to Dylan Taylor. He chuckled one of those totally masculine, barbaric sounds. "Watch yourself, sweetheart. You're standing on top of me. Believe me, I like it, but you're making me want to kiss you."

Cue the swelling music. "Kiss me," I whispered.

Dylan halted his steps altogether, his voice dropping an octave as I slammed my nose into his shoulder blade. "I must say," he murmured, "I've been wondering if you still taste the same." I swal-lowed, coughing on my own saliva. "Yeah, you remember, don't you?" he flirted. "We've kissed before."

How could I forget? That kiss was killer. Freaking fantastic actually.

"My mouth was full of cookies," I whispered.

"Chocolate chip. I've tasted you for four fricking months."

Dylan whipped me around and roughly slammed me back up

against the wall. A painting beside us rattled in its glass. Something in the nearby bathroom tumbled to the tile and shattered. My chest heaved with the surprise, and I gasped. Oh, goody...that right there was long overdue. Problem was, I felt like I'd die before the good stuff got started. I needed a will, mourners, and time to make a video doing things Murphy would be proud of (there weren't any).

I finally decided not to think and let my hormones go straight to the equator.

Dylan hadn't moved, only kept me tucked tight up against him. Out of sheer necessity, I lied to myself. I vehemently denied his body was rock-hard. And I vehemently denied I wanted his mouth *anywhere* on me. But then I heard that little devil on my shoulder taunting, *But girrrrrrl, we like hard bodies.*

For a split second, I thought I'd get my first legitimate kiss. In fact, I *wanted* it. I wanted a dizzying kiss that made me forget how to spell my own darn name. Instead, at the last minute he whispered, "God, you make me crazy," in my ear.

I knew that...

Problem was, I wanted to *feeeeeeeel it.*

I tried to count up all the reasons why it was a bad idea but couldn't remember how to count. Add the burning feel of Dylan's body, and I knew he didn't want to bury it either.

Then I think...I think...I think I whispered, "Go for it."

I could feel Dylan looking at my lips. The heat grew hotter the closer he eased toward them. He'd moved both his hands up by my face, caging me in. A little secret? I didn't plan on going anywhere. "Don't play with me, Darcy," he growled.

Those five words took every bit of energy I had to not throw him down to the ground and roll on him. The night alone, snow-storm aside, was so close to perfect I didn't want to chance ruining it with acting too soon.

I swear to God, I spoke anyway, discarding my vow to conduct a science experiment before riding off into the sunset with my best friend. "I'm not playing with you," I whispered confidently. "It's a law of nature that I'm always going to find you attractive."

His left hand came to the back of my neck, pulling me closer. "About fricking time," he growled again. He breathed that right into my lips. Right. Smack. Into. Them. Dylan had been doing that a lot lately. Touching my lips with his, but not actually kissing. I found it to be deadly hormonal and alarmingly lethal. My mouth instantly went dry...I licked my lips...problem was, I licked his in the process.

A groan emanated from the back of his throat and vibrated into my mouth. My insides melted, my legs turned to jelly, and my dark, forbidden nether region started singing pornographic operas. In fact, it was freaking rejoicing. When I collapsed into him, Dylan took his right arm and held my weight. Almost blasé. Like he knew things would happen, and he merely performed the steps. I didn't know where we'd gone, but by goodness, I had no interest in returning to the land of wallflower.

Imagine the disappointment when Farrah Aaronson, Red's housekeeper, unlocked the door, shining a high-beamed flashlight. Yeah. You heard right. Busted.

Red took on a housekeeper about seven years earlier. She stood a little over five feet tall with graying blonde hair and sapphire-blue eyes. She seemed delicate, like a china doll. Her hair was pulled back in a tight bun, but she hid her beauty behind wire-rimmed glasses. Farrah lived in a modest apartment up the street No children, no man in her life, just the few homes she took care of for other people. She wore black galoshes up to her knees and an old, gray wool coat buttoned to her chin with a gray crocheted toboggan and gloves, circa ten years earlier.

"Hi," she said quietly, carrying a loaded brown bag in each arm.

Now I liked Farrah. Or at least I *used* to. She seemed like a nice lady, but at that point I wanted her to spontaneously combust. Talk about bad timing. Dylan went rod straight and propped me up to a standing position, his hand left at the small of my back because I teetered like a baby tree in a storm. I looked at him...he looked at me...and we both knew the evening we'd both hoped for was just that—a hope.

"God sent you, didn't he?" I gasped and giggled.

Farrah explained quietly, "Tabitha phoned. She's stranded in the outskirts of the city and was adamant I come over. She was afraid you wouldn't have any food."

I took that as solid indication Heaven thought it should bust things up.

Dylan—trying to connect with his inner-altar boy—was no help whatsoever. In fact, he acted as though someone shoved a frog down his throat, and its legs were kicking his uvula. I rolled my eyes in my brain...men. Still, a smile crept up my face. For once in my life, I realized I had power over him. Lots. Of. Power. Skipping over to Farrah, I kissed her on the cheek and smacked Dylan on the rear who stood silently beside me.

"No premarital sex tonight, Big Man," I said, winking up at him. "Erase those naughty thoughts from your mind."

Chapter Eighteen

NETWORKING

*P*eople come in all shapes and sizes. Big, small, short, fat, beautiful, ugly, and so on. On that last category if someone's heart was in the right place, those other characteristics didn't matter. That's right. If a person was friendly, by God, the Hunchback of Notre Dame could land Miss freaking America. Just put love out in the universe, and that divine wheel of fortune would bring it back.

Sometimes, a girl could run across a person who seemed to deserve the maximum amount of hate she could give though. Madison Flannery could die in an acid bath, and I'd never bat an eye.

Yeah, Madison wasn't as innocent as my heart had led me to believe.

"And why did you call me?" she barked.

First off, I saved her sorry butt from a sex crime by Nico Drake. One would think she'd be singing my praises. Nope, Madison acted like I was the thorn in her paw she couldn't remove. While on Twitter earlier, I noticed her account was public, and she was even dumb enough to have her cell phone listed. So what did I do? I phoned her.

"Honestly, I only called to check on you. I'm sure you heard about what happened to Nico?"

"Nico probably deserved it."

"It doesn't make you feel bad? I thought the guy was a douche, but no one should ever be murdered."

"Like I said. He probably deserved it."

There's a reason Madison was in Coach's office. I believed she had been blowing time. Getting a taste of her attitude, my guess was little Miss Madison had in-school detention the day I saved her sorry-mouthed butt.

"I'm thinking you might not be so nice, Madison."

"Why, Darcy. What gave you that clue? The fact I've been rude or the fact I'm a little disappointed your friend—what's his name, Vinnie?—didn't get killed along with Nico when you broke into the house on Calypso Cove."

Let me take a minute here.

I needed to breathe. Pray. Smack my own dang face. I needed something because I felt like she'd shoved me in the electric chair.

"Were you there?" I whispered. "Did you and that other guy kill Nico?"

Hysterical, in-your-face laughter. "I didn't kill him, but I'd sure buy the knife that did."

By the way, Madison wouldn't tell me what she was mixed up in, but I could assume she was onboard with whatever else the identity thief had planned. Because as soon as I mentioned those two words, the girl cursed and hung up.

After I pulled myself together, I called Finn and begged him to find out what he could on the victim named Bishop Fowler. Within six hours, he phoned back with a, "Crikey, Sheila. Bishop Fowler was a computer programmer working from home. Thing was, he pumped gas at Kroger earlier and bought a packet of cotton candy Bubblicious."

File that under *News That Will Blow Your Mind*.

That meant The Ghost might've committed the ultimate identity theft scheme. Kill someone and then steal his or her identity altogether.

Glancing at the digital clock on the microwave, the time glowed at ten fourteen when Finn and I'd ended the call. Murphy and Marjorie had fallen asleep, and I needed caffeine to erase the memory of Madison and relax me into oblivion. After I nuked some Chinese takeout, I slid a black *World's Worst Dad* mug under the

Keurig (my gift, of course) and selected a K-cup called Donut Shop, extra bold. Shoving the little pod into the Keurig, I clicked it shut, pushed a button, and within sixty seconds had piping hot coffee.

Just the thought of everything was overwhelming. I juggled so many balls one was doomed to fall.

And let us not forget Dylan.

Dylan, Dylan, Dylan.

Monday night obviously didn't end as I'd hoped—the two of us snuggling on the couch, solving the world's problems—with a kissing marathon. No, Monday night concluded with Farrah snoring like a diesel truck in a sleeping bag beside me.

A fact that could've been remedied by a pillow if I was a murderer.

After Dylan's and my "almost" kiss, I was so geeked up I could've run the Boston Marathon at a record pace. Dylan, however, was able to shut that stuff down. My eagle eyes stalker-watched him and his megawatt abs all night. I found he slept in one of two positions: on his back with his arms thread behind his head or on his stomach hugging the pillow. Then there was his smell. My God, the cosmos hated me. It was sensual, masculine, and naughty things on the beach, all wrapped up in the biggest freaking mind buzz I'd ever encountered.

One word: yum.

Descriptive sentence: my V-card was in danger.

Thumbing off the TV, I took my coffee and pork fried rice upstairs and group texted Justice and Rudi. Rudi and Justice would appreciate the specifics because the three of us had been on a quest to find the perfect setting for the perfect kiss since we started wearing bras. Their experiences mirrored mine. Neither had kissed a boy let alone went on a date. Our conversations didn't revolve around our sordid affairs. They revolved around reviews of the Hallmark Channel marathons where plain-girl-gets-hot-guy and goes to work with him on the family farm. We kept our dreams small in the romance department.

It was a coping skill.

Problem was, when we got down to it, I felt like I'd be disloyal to Dylan if I uttered a word. Instead, we shot the breeze about whom we liked and didn't like in school. That was when Rudi unloaded the knowledge she thought Jagger Cane was beyond cute —uh, she'd drank what I called the Jagger Juice. I'd cover that later. She also said Slapstick told her in study hall he needed to speak with me. We talked a little about Nico Drake, and even though I wanted to tell them about Madison, I wasn't sure how Justice would handle the news. To paraphrase? She might kill her.

I ended the chat, still overwhelmed, and right when I'd decided to curl into a ball and fall into the land of delusion, my iPhone pinged with a nightly invitation to SKYPE.

Dylan was one shrewd businessman.

He hadn't said a single word during our morning-after conversation, wasn't any *more* or *less* touchy-feely than normal when he drove us home, and in fact was back to status quo. I didn't know how to interpret that—regret, indifference, or stalemate.

"Speak," I said.

Honest to God, he was so deliciously disheveled it made my chest ache. His eyes were heavy-lidded, like he fought sleep. His lips gave a lazy smile, and his hair might've been in worse shape than my hot mess, but on him...well, it almost looked *edible*.

"Hey, gorgeous," he said and grinned. "You talk in your sleep."

I shook my head, refocusing. Crappity, crap, crap, crap. I'd begun to grow fond of stalemate, and Dylan's grin said he planned to get in touch with his pushy side.

"Noooooooo," I said, nervously laughing.

"Yeeeessssss," he mocked. "You mentioned the school parking lot and Coach Wallace. Wow, sweetheart, I must say, I admire your work ethic. You're on the case even in your dreams."

Thank my lucky stars I hadn't spoken of his boom boom, hoohah. My name for his otherworldly butt. The subject of Coach, however, reminded me Dylan didn't look so shocked when I found out about his not-so-secret marriage. He'd hidden details, and it seemed as good a time as any to yank them out of his gorgeous mouth.

"Why didn't you tell me Coach was married and divorced, D? Why didn't something like that ever come up?"

Dylan frowned a little, guiltily. "He was so upset I guess I kept it private for him."

Of course, that was what he'd do—because he was almost gosh-danged perfect. "So she honestly bashed up his stuff?"

"So he says."

"Any proof?"

"He found her standing overtop his car with a baseball bat. I assume he thought that corroboration enough. I don't know any other details. I simply overheard him talking to my father. Darc. He didn't confide in a teenager." I must've been frowning. "Would you like me to tell you things like that in the future?"

Let me see if I heard things right. He asked if I honestly wanted to know the gossip? I decided to blame his idiocy on the late hour. Touching the screen, I ran my index finger around the collar of his dark sweatshirt. "It's just that I thought we told one another everything," I said sighing.

The angel on my shoulders gasped, *You're a liar.* The devil laughed and said, *So what?*

"We do," he said as an apology.

"We do," I repeated like a dishonest cockatoo.

Dylan held up three fingers, as if he recited the Boy Scout's oath. "Scout's honor, we will have no secrets."

"Scout's honor," I echoed.

My cheeks burned with embarrassment, guilt, or something. Dylan's eyes sparkled with unreleased laughter. He knew, dang him. He knew I'd have trouble holding up my end of the bargain. I hadn't failed to notice he hadn't pinky swore—our failsafe of always telling the truth. Could mean nothing or could mean everything—like he had many (or, God forbid, *more*) secrets than me.

Scanning the sound bites in my brain, I weeded through the things I could tell him, separating them from things that seemed downright dumb. For the next ten minutes, I confessed everything—or close to everything—I'd uncovered about Coach Wallace's car. Since Dylan had already deduced I had a mission once inside detention, I told him what I'd learned about Slapstick Wilson and Damon Whitehead: Slapstick was a follower who couldn't read, and Damon was a raging hothead.

After Dylan ruminated the fact Damon had a screw loose (believe me, I didn't tell him Damon went bat-poop crazy on me), he then asked if I thought they were guilty. I took a deep breath and explained, "Slapstick doesn't smell of guilt, but Damon smells like twenty-to-life."

I was unexpectedly thrilled when he murmured, "I can appreciate that."

Feeling it'd be a behemoth mistake, I omitted Slapstick wanted to speak with me. I had no inklings to what that conversation would regard, but I didn't want Dylan to run interference and spook him away. Believe it or not, I also divulged I'd run reconnaissance in the parking lot the afternoon before, trying to judge whether the guys in the red Mustang, white van, or Chevy Colorado knew anything. That part of the conversation I watered down—as in almost drowning it altogether. The one detail I'd disclosed, however, was that all three morons claimed their innocence.

Of course they would.

Cruella De Vil said the same thing when she stole those puppies —and we all know how that played out.

I didn't tell him about Vinnie's and my trip to Calypso Cove Drive, nor the fact Slapstick was almost scared impotent at the mention of The Ghost, period. It felt good to semi-confess, even if that was all it amounted to. And wasn't that me in a nutshell? Halfway doing everything? Halfway confessing, halfway making-out, halfway answering anything Dylan had ever asked? The duplicity had to be killing him.

"D?" I whispered. "I need to circle back around with you about last night. I know I did some things totally out of character. I basically attacked your mouth like I'd spent the last six months in nun school and wanted to shank the Mother Superior. I need to…" I paused, "I'm bipolar in the commitment department," I spit out, "and that's not fair—"

Dylan's voice went gentle and affectionate, demonstrating the indisputable reason why I cared so much for him. "We'll talk when you're ready to talk, yeah? I'm patient, sweetheart. I'm going nowhere. Tell me one thing," he paused softly. "Am I getting closer?"

My chest seized, and I thought, *Oh, shiz, you're perfect.* And my crush just shot from peacetime to military alert. I could've sworn Dylan read my mind because his eyes briefly softened, going straight to boiling butter before I answered in a nod.

The accompanying grin was like none I'd ever seen. Smaller than normal, it held a hint of teeth, but something else that scared the living daylights out of me. It wasn't only predator. It was king of the freaking jungle and then some—so intense I think it bruised my eyeballs.

Immediately, I took a screenshot of his face, deciding to use it as my latest and greatest wallpaper on my phone. That grin would be the death of me or give me something beyond my wildest dreams.

Chapter Nineteen

'BEN'GE AND PURGE

*W*ednesday night at Belinski's Bookstore was like any other night...a mausoleum. The only upside was a Mexican feast was spread out in front of me with a Coke chaser. Afraid Mr. B would undress her under the mistletoe (a possibility, he was a letch), Claudia packed my dinner and allowed me to drive her conversion van to work—something I normally would've jumped for joy over, but it was a conversion van, for God's sake. It had draperies in the windows.

Licking the fork of the last bite of cheesecake (yes, it was my first course), I popped the lid on the plastic container holding pork sofrito and watched Chichi speak with evil spirits. Let me correct myself. She said spirits. I was the one that added evil. In the break room, she sat Indian style with a white piece of linen cloth covering her head, the fingertips of both hands resting lightly on the little ivory pointer. The Ouija board was a two or more person game. Technically, it wasn't supposed to move with one person's energy. Chichi, evidently, was wired differently. She could get it to fly across the room if the inclination so hit her.

Personally, I hated Ouija boards. When I was ten years old, I watched my neighbors play and it set off a series of events: I crushed my cheekbone. Murphy had a tree limb fall on him, and Dylan broke four of his fingers.

Was I superstitious? Only a moron would walk away thinking it was a party.

Shoveling a few bites in my mouth, my mind took a little vacay and rehashed what Grumpy reported earlier after speaking with the driver of the red Mustang. His quote was, "He doesn't know," *bleep* "about" *bleep*. Although the news was disappointing, I vowed to try and work profanity into my everyday language. It might make me a more interesting person.

After the Ouija distinctly spelled the words gun, knife, and sale, the timer on my iPhone beeped, reminding me my fifteen-minute break was a thing of the past. Just as well. My heart beat so fast when the board spelled "Darcy dead," I prayed someone knew CPR. Pushing back from the table, I wet a paper towel and cleaned away crumbs, throwing the disposable containers in the trashcan. Still hungry, I snagged a package of cream-filled chocolate Ho Hos Mr. B had left on the countertop. I'd been binging on sweets since breakfast and had the beginnings of two pimples the size of the Grand Tetons. My sugar benders were sometimes hard to stop. The end of this one would take my blood sugar spiking or someone telling me I was fat.

Taking a tug on a Coke, I ripped the package with my teeth and removed one Ho Ho, stealing a look outside. The sky was a mousy gray with a small splatter of stars, and the snowy slosh on the ground resembled dirty bathwater. At half past seven, only a handful of people congregated in the store. I hadn't been scheduled to work but picked up an extra shift since my only other option was to sell my body. I fought a sigh. I didn't know if it was boredom, frustration, or both. After I shot a few baskets in the Nerf hoop over the trashcan, I rode my RipStik around the store and thought about my situation. There were several reasons I needed cash. Other than the obvious, I had to feed my coffee addiction, fund a weird fascination with one-of-a-kind vintage T-shirts, keep my sister stocked in slutty Barbie dolls, plus...well, I wanted to buy my own car.

Drive myself to school.

Beemers could crash and burn for all I cared.

The day had a decent start. I'd actually warmed up to the thought of being Dylan's love slave until sixth period when Collin Lockhart peed on my parade. Brynn's ex-boyfriend or soon-to-be ex (who knew with them), texted me during Spanish IV about some "concerns" he noticed during their AP math class. When I pushed for particulars, he gladly imparted the juicy, gory details. Apparently, Dylan and Brynn sat beside one another, like right on top of one another, and were math partners—whatever that entailed—all year long. Dylan had never mentioned the partnership, and God knows he'd had ample opportunity.

Here was a rewind:

Brynn knows how to flirt without really flirting, he'd texted. *You can get caught up in her spin before you know what's going on.*

My dumb response? *Paint a picture, Collin.*

Brynn and I'd just broken up, he'd said, *and as usual, she immediately moved in on Dylan. I was right there, front and center. She said some joke and leaned her entire body into his—like right into his grill, if you know what I mean—hugging his waist and subliminally begging to get closer.*

I bleached that picture from my mind with little success. I tried not to focus on Dylan's package—like ever. I thought that'd take a step into slutty I couldn't easily back out of. But put Brynn in the picture, and that was all I'd thought about all day—science and testicles...not a good mix.

What did Dylan do? I stupidly wanted clarified.

He grinned so big my stomach turned.

Jeez, he'd given her The Dimples. *Soooo...*I texted back.

So it was like watching something private, Collin explained. *It made everyone uncomfortable, and then Brynn did the usual.*

Which is? I typed.

She rolled out her sob story of the week. Whatever it was, he pulled on his knight-in-shining-armor.

Ugh, that sounded like Dylan. It was widely known he had a hero complex. I didn't begrudge him the trait. Rookie made a career of it. Murphy only went hero if he liked a person. Otherwise, you could drop dead and rot.

Exactly what was the sob story? I'd pushed.

Collin might be smart and good-looking, but he was a tool. He left me hanging, and there I was several hours later, still with no answers. Whether it was all smoke or if there was fire, I began to build a tiny wall where Dylan was concerned. I tried not to, but the bricks kept going up regardless.

I evaluated my situation. I could ignore Collin or go back to the original plan of performing a science experiment with a member of the opposite sex. Did I want to stick it to Dylan? Heck to the freaking yeah...

Right then, Justice buzzed. "Speak," I mumbled, picking up the call.

"Hello to you too, Grouchy Pants," she said and laughed.

One thing about Justice, she always had her ear to the ground. If something was to be known about Dylan and Brynn, she'd have every detail this side of the North Pole. "Did you hear Brynn was all up in Dylan's business today?"

"Uhhhhh," she stumbled.

"Come on, Justice," I begged.

She groaned like a crappy lawnmower trying to start. "My information comes from Collin, whining to Ivy and Trudi. They were talking right beside my locker. When Brynn busted up their little huddle, all three asked for details of her love life, and Brynn was like a toothpaste commercial...one big sickening white smile. I actually phoned to see if you'd heard anything. Promise."

Interesting recap. Totally unsubstantiated, but not totally ludicrous.

While relaying the story, Justice swore she didn't trust Brynn, and that she really didn't trust Collin. But what would Collin gain from lying, pray tell? Nothing to the best of my knowledge. After we ended the call, I opened a cardboard box of new books, piled five large stacks on a metal cart, and placed my second Coke on top. I wheeled them back to the science and religion section. No slam against the science and religion writers, but people rarely visited that section unless there was a report due or they wanted to nap.

Unless it was me...I had two reasons.

Dylan gave me a great idea on a legitimate science experiment on the drive home. I'd videotape how to drop an egg two stories and not have it break. Evidently, it was a pretty common experiment, but no one would rock the project like me. I decided to name my eggs after some of the worst villains of all time. Egg One would be Adolf Hitler. Egg Two would be Count Dracula. I'd call Egg Three The Joker. Egg Four would impersonate Principal Ward (I expected backlash here), and Egg Five would be Mr. Himmel. I hadn't decided whether to call him Mister or

Doctor yet. I'd probably compromise and write Mister first and then cross it out and add Doctor. To gain brownie points, I'd allow Mr. Himmel's egg to live. How would I accomplish that? I'd bury him in a jar of peanut butter, drop the plastic jar, and resurrect him in one piece.

After I snagged a book to use as reference, I stared at the land-line phone mounted to the wall. Scanning for Mr. B, I lifted the phone off the receiver, squatting down on the green carpet to call Slapstick. I thumbed in the digits Rudi had given me. I wasn't sure why I remembered phone numbers when I could barely tell someone what I had for dinner the day before. Funny, how that recall never transpired into schoolwork. Made me think my learning curve was more psychological than skill-driven.

One ring...two rings...three rings...

I almost cut the call but heard a "Hullo?" on the fourth ring.

"Slapstick?" I said.

"Yeah?"

"Darcy Walker."

I heard rustling of papers and what sounded like a door closing. "Hey, I'm assuming Rudi told you I needed to speak with you, so here it goes," he said quickly. "Damon knows more than what he's giving you about this guy called The Ghost. Like *a lot* more."

When I asked Slapstick if he cared to expound, he stuttered, "*I-II*'ve already said enough. *Bb*-e careful."

He delivered that blow and ditched me. Seriously, that'd been a total waste of time. Thumbing in Tito's number, I didn't even care if The Double-B showed up on his caller ID. My guess was I could explain it away.

I shoved two books on the middle shelf and lined up their spines when he answered, "Tito."

"Jester," was my greeting. A bone-chilling, knee-knocking awkwardness followed. The kind you get when you find out you're not really welcome or as smooth as you thought you were.

"Jester," he finally repeated.

I cleared my throat. "Is this a bad time?" No answer, so I took a drag on my Coke and dove right in with what Finn had discovered. "Listen, I get the feeling you're busy, so I'll make this quick. Like you said, the victim is Bishop Fowler. Problem was, Bishop pumped gas at Kroger earlier and bought a pack of cotton candy Bubblicious while he was there. Do you know what that insinuates?" Still nothing. "If The Ghost was his roommate, then that implies he committed the ultimate scam on him too. Actually, it's rather ingenious. Kill your roommate, hide the body, use his credit cards, and rack up debt on someone who's too dead to complain. Do you feel me? He literally assumed his identity, Tito. Like he was trying to do to you."

He blew out a breath of frustration. "Yeah, I feel you I'm just trying to figure out who you are, Jester. I haven't heard of this, and I'm gonna brag, darlin'...I'm good."

I lifted another book from the cart, placing it on the shelf above the previous two. "I'll take that as a compliment," I said, munching a bite of Ho Ho.

"You're calling me from Belinski's Bookstore, Jester. That's in the Valley Galleria. From what I'm hearin', y'all are havin' a lot of trouble up there. Wasn't that strip mall vandalized twice in the past week? Are you the cause?"

I laughed so loudly I snorted.

"That laugh," he said, reluctantly chuckling. "The sound is familiar, but I can't place it."

Shoot, I sounded like Red. But his reference to vandalism got me to thinking. Perhaps he could find out if Jojo Wallace had any records in her past. And as they say, two heads were a heckuva lot better than one.

"My nose is clean, Tito. Usually, I'm as dirty as they come, but on that offense, I'm as innocent as a newborn baby. Can I ask you a question? There's something..." I stopped, searching for the right word, "something...*else* I'm working on."

Another phone rang in my ear, and by its rock-and-roll ringtone, I knew it had to be another cell. Did the man actually carry two? "Hold on," he muttered, hitting mute on his phone.

I stuffed the remaining Ho Ho in my mouth and grumbled into dead air. "I'm giving you everything, Tito, and you're giving me nothing. I haven't given you Brantley McCoy as The Ghost, and by God, I'm not going to. That would mean my claim to reward money would go up in smoke if you deliver his name to Cookie Harper

Stark before me. And by the way, what self-respecting woman allows herself to have a nickname of Cookie?"

A voice murmured overtop me, "Ask if the authorities have any new leads on The Ghost, angel. That'll wake him up. And by the way, *that's* a project you didn't share with *me*. And here I thought we didn't have any secrets between us. We need to go to couple's therapy before this becomes a bad habit."

A figure loomed above me with a grin that spelled sin in any language.

My mouth. Gaped. Wide.

Shoot. Did I say, *Shoot??!!*

Even though I fought it, invisible strands of rope pulled me toward his cocky grin. Swallowing too much Ho Ho at once, I lifted my eyes to view him dressed as usual—brown leather bomber, white oxford peeking out the top, and although I couldn't see his legs, my guess was starched khaki pants and penny loafers rounded out the ensemble. The eyes were like liquid silver, and his copper hair had recently been cut, barely brushing the top of his shirt. I preferred the longer length. Right then, he looked as refined and proper as the rest of him...except for that cocky smile. It quirked up at one corner and suggested he wasn't proper at all. In fact, the grin in his voice suggested he might be a fastard.

"Ben Ryan," I sort of coughed, sort of cursed.

"I prefer the father of our lovechild. So what do you say?"

I go to the opera, but I don't sing. In other words, I might fantasize about guys, but I was too chicken to participate in the things that'd make a baby—and I didn't want to be a 'ho-bag either. "Why are you here?" I groaned.

Ben leaned into my personal space and traced a strong finger down the profile of my jaw. "Isn't it obvious?"

Oh, shoot. Shoot, shoot, shoot.

Ben had channeled Dylan. His touch was different, but considering I wasn't sure what Dylan had done with Brynn's girl parts, maybe I could get used to the change. When I dragged my face away, he nodded toward the phone still balanced under my chin. "What are you planning, angel?"

"My exit strategy," I mumbled.

Ben threw his head back and laughed. "Get him to share, angel.

By the sound of your conversation, you're doing an awful lot of sharing. Make it a two-way street or back out of it altogether."

Excellent point.

To make matters worse, the next thing I heard was a beep-beep-beeeeeeeep. Tito either accidentally hung up or cut the call on purpose. I belted out, "Dang it!" and then sighed and said, "Dial tone," to Ben.

Licking Ho Ho off my lips, I recalled I'd left the other up front by my purse. Ben unwound the fingers of his right hand, slowly sliding the Ho Ho across the shelf. "I saw this when I walked through the door and figured it was yours. But you're sweet enough, even without the chocolate."

More overt flirting. I didn't know how to respond.

Standing up, I recradled the telephone, half grinning and half frowning. It annoyed me he'd figured me out so easily, but I wanted that Ho Ho more. "Um, thanks," I said giggling.

Ben brushed his fingertips across the Burberry cap on my head. I had a serious case of wardrobe malfunction going on. The hat didn't match my ensemble, but I couldn't seem to remove Dylan from my life. Shoving half the Ho Ho in my mouth, chocolate particles dribbled down my chin onto the front of my black T-shirt.

Ben gazed at its design, chuckling. "The bomb, huh?"

Glancing south, I shrugged at the red, sparkling grenade. He had the bomb part right. The Double-B could be a ticking time bomb, and everyone working at the place was willing for his or her guts to be spilled onto the ceiling.

"I guess it depends on who you ask," I said, lifting my shoulders in a shrug. Ben moved around to squat directly beside me. He cracked his knuckles and picked up the remaining six books, quickly shelving them and reaching to the bottom of the cart to do the same with the dozen or so there.

He stood back up as I swallowed the last bite of Ho Ho. "I'm surprised you didn't try to find me, Darcy. Most can't resist my charm."

When my mouth stayed on mute, he leaned up against the bookshelf, looking me up and down as though he memorized each tiny detail. It left me uncomfortable, especially when he murmured, "I wouldn't change one thing about you."

He must not have seen the two pimples my sweat glands had been working on. I said, "What brings you to Belinski's, Ben?"

Ben had a crooked smile—what I referred to as the rocker snarl. He quirked the left side up higher, and I knew immediately what he claimed about most girls not being able to stay away was true—there was no denying he was cute.

"I'm here because I'd love to go out with you this weekend," he said.

I gave him my sober face. "I've come down with necrotizing fasciitis. Unless there's a particular body part you're not fond of, it's not safe to be around me." God help me, I looked right at his crotch to deliver the message.

Ben chuckled even deeper. "I suppose I deserve that."

"Yeah, you do. Besides I'm a virgin."

Just. Kill. Me. Now. My mouth has no filter.

Ben didn't cower, his grin still trying to snake charm me into accepting the proposal. My first instinct was to scram away from the embarrassment. I wheeled the empty cart toward the front of the store, tripping over my feet and praying Ben didn't see it happen. Rudi and Chichi straightened displays, both their mouths dropped wide and short of dragging the floor. Both wore cheesy smiles. No one needed to point out the cute guy. It just sort of happened.

"Ben Ryan," I said to both as we padded by. Neither gave their names. I opted not to speak for them.

"Tell me about yourself, angel."

I didn't want to give him anything. In fact, other than having an affair with sugar I was pretty sure I was cosmically insignificant. "Where exactly are you from, Ben? And how in the world did you figure out Jojo Wallace's name and workplace so quickly?"

"Tell me about yourself first, and I'll give you anything you ask."

That statement made me sweat. "No," I said firmly. "Answer about Jojo."

"No," he argued. "If I do that, then I may walk away not knowing anything more about Darcy Walker."

He had a point. I rattled off, "I'm Valley born and bred and fall in the jock camp, I suppose."

My hair lay in a messy ponytail tucked up under my cap. A few tendrils had fallen out, and Ben felt the need to retuck them. "You're a jock but yet you might be the most accident prone person I've ever met."

I should be offended, but sometimes the truth was too hard to avoid. I could shoot a basket like I was in the NBA, water-ski like my feet were made of boards, shoot pool and swing a club like I'd mastered the art of physics, yet couldn't walk across the floor without eating the carpet. Odd thing was, I had no desire to participate in organized high school sports. I'd burned out as a kid.

I parked the cart behind the counter, motioning to the trashcan. "Watch this," I bragged, picking up the Nerf ball I'd played with earlier.

He gave me a grinning wink as I broad-jumped onto a bookshelf a little over four feet high. I glanced over my shoulder to ensure Mr. B was still MIA and then threw a high-arcing shot in the air. After a twenty-foot flight, it landed easily in the middle of the can.

"Nice," he said laughing. "Do it left-handed, one row back, and I promise to kiss you."

I had no interest in kissing him, but throw me a challenge and I'd bury the guy's mouth. Once again, I stole a look to the break room, hopped down, jumped to another shelf, and fired off an ambidextrous rainbow shot.

It swooshed in perfectly. If only school were that easy. My body was tomboy coordinated. My brainpower left a lot to be desired.

He offered me his hand while I jumped down. Then homed in on my mouth. "Okay. When and where?"

I went speechless...he was serious. I got so nervous my hand went haywire, hitting the shelf I'd been standing on. Two books dominoed down an entire row of classics.

"Aw, angel," he said chuckling. "Don't be afraid. I promise to forget the fact you smell like a Ho Ho." I flexed the fingers on both hands ready to smack or punch. I hadn't made up my mind which. "Are you serious?" he said, chuckling deeper, eyeing my fists.

"As a heart attack."

"It'd be totally unfair for me to engage in combat with you, not to mention unethical and probably illegal."

I snorted. "Is that right? Your khaki pants and loafers don't depict the picture of masculinity, bud. The odds are stacked in my favor."

Ben took a swipe at my head with a roundhouse kick and landed in a different fighting stance, chucking a punch under my chin with his left elbow. His chest was square and straight, legs long and flexed, ready to spring into action. "Five-time world champion, mixed martial arts. Undefeated," he said, grinning cockily. "Press releases are on the web. Of course, it's not evenly matched. I'm a stud."

That answered why his body was Greek-statue hard. "Show off," I muttered.

The cocky grin returned. "I don't show off. I win."

I grabbed the books I'd knocked over, looking for someone to get me out of the mess. Mr. B had probably crashed in his food, and Rudi and Chichi remained suspiciously absent. And didn't that just pile on the discomfort? "I don't think I've ever hated anyone so intensely," I almost screamed. "And if you haven't noticed, this isn't a good time. I'm sad. All day long I've been contemplating my cosmic insignificance, and I feel like a big fat phony. I probably put on five pounds in the last half hour. I don't have any money. I don't have the name of the spray painter. And although I think I have the name of The Ghost, I can't prove it. Plus," I sputtered, beginning to cry, "I actually want to binge on another Ho Ho when I should find a healthier way to purge."

And I think, I said to myself, *I think Dylan's messing with me*. Down deep, he might be a fastard. It didn't get much worse than thinking my best friend might be playing kissy-face with the world's most nauseatingly perfect teenager.

Ben gently grabbed me by the elbow, turning me toward him as my eyes flooded with tears. I tried to speak, but all that came out was some distorted, embarrassing sounds that reminded me of sick mice.

"I'm sorry," he gasped, searching my eyes. "Sometimes, I come on too strong."

The contours of Ben's face cut me to the core. What was hard and confident a few seconds earlier, then showed a vulnerability that'd be easy to give into. Yeah, he had some serious mojo power that needed to worry me. "It's not you," I sniveled.

"Then what is it?" he murmured. "I'm a good listener."

"I don't feel comfortable confiding in you."

He wasn't offended. "Well, can you at least talk to your mom?"

And that was all it took for the floodgates to open...

Ugh, just...*ugh.*

A lonely, desperate tear fell. I blurted out, "I'm raised by a single dad, and the reason for that *was* and *still is* an unimaginable pain. Plus, I'm a girl. You can't talk about everything with your dad, you know? I have so many things I need help with, and I don't know what to do."

If either of us was going to run for the hills, Heaven knew it was the appropriate time. But neither of us moved. When the subject of my mother came up, I usually pushed that information into a mental box, slammed it shut, and addressed it to *Counseling Session Number Three.* Yet, Ben Ryan had a bewitching spell on me. He'd hit me with his Audi, insulted me numerous times, and I'd already told him the deepest, darkest secrets of my soul. I had the overwhelming urge to wrap myself around him like the first time we'd met...*but why?* Because there were no past disappointments between us?

I gazed into his silver eyes, whispering, "You're not going to say anything?"

Ben's eyes tendered. "I wasn't sure you'd finished." I hadn't finished. I simply couldn't find the words almost seven years later. My life was splashed with humor and heartache. Most days the humor won out. Right then, the heartache weighed heavily.

"*Sh*-she," I stammered. "*Sh*-she's just..."

A sigh punctuated my words as he tenderly brushed both thumbs across my cheeks, removing the tears. "Why don't you make it your goal to give me two sentences before the school year's out?" Trust me, that was one sleeping dog it was best to let lie. I nodded anyway. "That's a start. Please, don't cry."

Ben pulled me into a familiar hug. Like a magnet drawing us upward, both our eyes super-glued to the mistletoe overhead. The sound system took that moment to gently pipe in a slow tune that screamed baby-making music.

"That's a sign from Heaven if I ever heard one," he murmured lowly. With heavy-lidded eyes, he left one hand at my waist, the other wrapped loosely around my shoulders. Slowly, slowly he inched toward my lips. My hands braced against his chest, but they couldn't decide whether to push him off or pull him closer. The indecisiveness made my heart pound, but all of a sudden the indecision flipped into a smoldering desire.

I glanced up to the mistletoe and closed my eyes.

Oh, yeah...yeah...that was what I needed.

I heard a throat clear. Heck, the man in Bumfudge, Egypt heard a throat clear. It belonged to someone extremely unhappy who'd already devised a way to remove the source of his unhappiness.

I braced.

Getting up on my tiptoes, a tentative look over Ben's right shoulder showed none other than—you guessed it—Dylan-possible fastard-Taylor.

Dylan stared at us with eyes showing more white than amber. He wore his favorite jeans, gray and black Nike sneakers, and a black down North Face ski jacket. Black gloves hugged his hands and a toboggan topped his head. In his left hand was a T-shirt that said "No Coffee, No Workee" on it. He'd bought it for me. I sighed. I'd seen it when we bolted out of the mall because of the unexpected snowstorm. Of course, he'd remember.

My vocal chords went AWOL.

He murmured, "Are you sure you want to be under that mistletoe, sweetheart?" I was pretty sure I shook my head no, but my lips might've been saying yes. I squirmed against Ben and then slid down his body.

Ben tightened his arms, whispering into my face, "Boyfriend?" he said, in no way intimidated.

"*Best friend,*" I whispered.

"*Possessive* best friend," Dylan bellowed. "Come over here, Darcy, unless you want a kiss to be on someone else's terms and not your own." I straightened my rumpled clothes, obediently scuffling over. It was a conditioned response. Call me Pavlov's dog. He said fetch. I went for the bone.

Ben folded his arms over his chest, that cocky grin growing by leaps and bounds. "I'm fairly confident Darcy and I were on the same page. Plus, Darcy's sort of fascinatingly bizarre. For someone as picky as me, she's definitely a keeper."

Dylan placed the T-shirt on a nearby table and slowly slid out of his jacket, the wheels in his brain cranking like a steam engine. Laying his jacket next to the shirt, he slowly removed his gloves and toboggan. He seemed casual, laid-back. The moment his eyes met Ben's, however, he sucked the energy out of the room, replacing it with heat and I'm-going-to-have-your-head.

He extended a hand to Ben. "Dylan Taylor," he said all formally.

Ben stood up straighter. "Ben Ryan," he said, shaking just as ceremoniously. "The new kid in town who's in love with your *best*," he emphasized, "*friend*. Darcy and I've gotten rather close, and I'm disappointed to say you interrupted something that's been coming for quite some time."

Dylan was a hair-trigger away from going gonzo. Ben? He just might be stupid.

Dylan bent his arm back, shoving me behind his body. I knew Dylan. His attempt at being mannerly went out the door when Ben pulled on his ponkey. "You're the guy who hit Darcy with his car," he said accusingly. A muscle ticced in Ben's jaw, but he didn't comment. "Let me make something clear here, Ryan. I'm not a fan of yours for various reasons, but if you ever try to force something on Darcy she clearly isn't ready for, then you'll have to answer to me. And when I say *answer to me*," he said snidely, "it won't necessarily be with words."

Translation? Get out of my lane, fastard.

Ben laughed with a loud sarcasm. "Well, guess what? There's a new sheriff in town."

"You don't say," Dylan said slowly. "I thought *I* was the sheriff."

"Let me see your badge," Ben taunted.

A dramatic, smirky pause...and then Dylan said naughtily, "Not in front of Darcy."

Ben looked pensive and perplexed at the same time, and then Dylan's innuendo slowly bled into his eyes. Fire ignited the silver, and I could tell he bit the shiz out of his tongue. My guess was he wasn't used to the subject of a guy's manhood being an opener. Heck, who was? But that was vintage Dylan—insinuating he was blessed with more below the belt than Ben. Dylan liked to have the last word, occasionally at someone else's expense. Cocky, but in all fairness, Ben might be just as cocky...or cockier.

The air crackled with testosterone as they stood stoically, sizing one another up. Dylan had two inches and about forty pounds on Ben, but Ben's personality was so big it didn't seem to matter. They were total opposites: jet-black hair versus a coppery brown...bulging muscles versus long and lean. Dylan's face was classically handsome in its symmetry—the type sculptors mimicked when they thought of the gods. Ben's was more angular and rugged—the kind in cologne commercials where a girl thought about shacking up in the woods. What they both had in common were egos the size of the hole in the ozone and a ridiculous fascination with me.

Ben spoke first. "Let me start again," he said. "I really like Darcy, and we were having a private conversation where she confided she needed to purge some things from her life. I actually have some ideas on what she could start with."

It was settled...Ben was definitely stupid.

Dylan cut him off, laughing arrogantly. "Private conversation?" he mocked. "Well, I'm always going to know a little bit more than you do, Ryan, and by the way, why don't you leave, or I'll purge *you* out of existence."

I put my hands on Dylan's waist. "Play nice, D." He wouldn't budge. "D," I whispered, tugging his white sweatshirt, "he's a five-time, MMA world champion. Maybe you shouldn't provoke him."

Dylan totally ignored me, like his ego said it was a moot point.

"You look like a one trick pony to me," Ben taunted.

Dylan's voice dropped to a growl. "My one trick will drop you to the mat so fast you won't even have a chance to tap out. Then I'll get up and have dinner while you're crying for your mommy."

Ben egged him on, either overly confident or overly dumb. I gave him a mean look because the way he provoked Dylan had begun to bother me. "No beating around the bush with you, eh?" Ben said, taunting with a grin.

"I'm not big on diplomacy," Dylan replied.

"A lot of senseless wars start that way."

"Sometimes people just need their asses kicked."

"You don't like having your power usurped?"

Dylan shrugged. "I'm still waiting for it to happen, and you haven't made a move yet."

If the theory of body language is true, then Dylan's message was loud and clear. No poaching allowed. I'd seen many a movie where love triangles like that left someone hurt—why did I think that someone would ultimately be *me*? But I knew Dylan, and I sort of knew Ben. Dylan wouldn't quit until the threat was neutralized. I had a feeling the competitive persona of Ben behaved the same way. Heck, he claimed he had the trophies to prove it.

Colliding thoughts consumed my brain. Dylan would always be my best friend. No question. But he claimed he wanted to be a couple, and I couldn't deny the physical attraction any more than I needed air to breathe. Ben likewise had asked me out for a legitimate date. You know, where the girl dressed up nice, the boy picked her up, and then they went somewhere in public declaring they were a couple—at least for the night. Ben pursued me. *Me*, I emphasized in my head, when I knew he could pretty much have whomever he wanted. Enter Brynn Hathaway. Enter Collin Lockhart's words. And something came over me. Something daring, brave, or utterly out-of-my-mind mad.

I grabbed Dylan's gaze and lyingly declared, "Ben is my science experiment, Dylan. We're going on a date this weekend."

It took awhile for those words to register and for Dylan to call up the conversation that hopefully didn't forever ruin our friendship. His chin raised a fraction, and he ran his hand tenderly down my jaw. His eyes softened. He was going to cry. I knew it, and then I'd be a blubbering fool. Instead, he looked Ben square in the face, threw his head back, and burst into laughter.

A life is not important except in the impact it has on other lives.

—*Jackie Robinson*

Chapter Twenty

ROAD RAGE

*D*ylan was smooth, polished, and seductively alluring. Ben was brusque, edgy, and had no couth whatsoever. That was too many adjectives to think about at the moment. Besides, Dylan acted as if a dirty bomb had been strapped to his privates, and I needed to steer clear. I found it confusing Ben had gotten so close to me, but he wasn't the person I thought about when I tracked on the mistletoe. No, my mind had shifted to Dylan...then I thought of Brynn...then I thought of Dylan and Brynn and a set of twins.

I deserved a happily-ever-after, right?

So why had Dylan even graced The Double-B with a visit? Claudia flexed her matchmaking skills and had a neighbor drop her over to pick up her van, phoning Dylan I'd need a ride.

Sneaky woman. Could she be more obvious?

But let me tell you. That ride home had been the car ride from futher-mudging Hell.

Dylan's car felt like a sauna. I wasn't sure if that was the heat rolling off him or the fact I was a little warm and fuzzy inside myself. Mr. B had lumbered up to the front desk and broke up the nonverbal posturing between Dylan and Ben. Ben dispensed a cocky smile and stupidly ran his knuckles down my cheek, promising, "Later."

Something snapped behind him, and I realized it was the pencil

Dylan had been twirling. I tried not to smile but couldn't help it. The look on Dylan's face was priceless. *Whatever*, I told myself. I'd probably never see Ben again, but it was nice to know Dylan could lose his cool and Ben had found me desirable.

We'd driven a few miles and a stubborn line painted on his jaw while his mouth clamped shut. I wished he'd scream, curse, or throw things upside my head. His lack of words was my cue to spur the conversation, and surprisingly I felt a transparency that lately I'd kept hidden.

"What's wrong with you?" I asked.

"Seriously?" he laughed sarcastically.

"Yes, seriously," I said quietly.

"I've had a bad day, Darcy." Well, his day sounded pretty darn good from what Collin claimed. Brynn was all up in his umm... personal effects...and he didn't seem to mind the intrusion.

I ignored him and soldiered on. "He asked me out, D. Should I go?"

Dylan glanced up in the rearview mirror, and a deafening silence cut through the air. I'd always admired the way Dylan drove. Confident, skilled, and sexy as heck—just like the rest of him. Right then, however, he seemed jumpy. I heard a muttered F-word and the angel on my shoulder told me I blackened up not only my soul, but his.

Grrrrrrrreaaat.

I repeated the question. Dylan's resulting sigh made me immediately regret it. "No," he answered. "You don't know him."

"I kind of know him."

"First I've heard of that," he added.

"Yeah, a lot of firsts are going around," I countered.

"*...what?*"

I circled back to the original subject while Dylan's eyes remained riveted to the rearview mirror. "Isn't dating when you're supposed to *get* to know someone?"

After about fifteen seconds, he answered. "It is, but I didn't actually think you'd follow through with it. Do you *want* to date him?" Dylan's voice went tight. Like something caught in his throat he tried to swallow down. *No*, I told myself. I didn't want to do anything except spend time with him, but somehow we'd wound up where we were with that stupid science experiment looming over my head. I simply didn't know how to go back.

"I don't know," I said and exhaled. "You have more experience than me. I hear you and Brynn have gotten close. She *is* your math partner, right?"

Dylan's eyes flashed angrily. "You're trying to find any excuse in the world to start a fight. I swear, Darcy, you're like a fricking moving target. Every time I make headway, you shoot up another diversion, and I'm back to kickoff. Do you know what makes me angrier than this so called science experiment?" Well, no, but I thought it'd be dumb to ask. "It makes me angry you think I'd even come at you if it didn't mean something. You've been my best friend for years. I'd never screw with your heart unless I believed it could be the best thing that ever happened to us." His face went blank for a moment, and I couldn't read him. "Are you sure about your feelings for *me*?" he finished.

My answer came fast. "Always," I said sheepishly. "That's the only thing I'm sure of in my life."

Instead of fostering one of those heart-pounding reunions, all it did was fan the flames on his anger. "Then that means you aren't sure about *me*," he barked. "And that irritates the hell out of me. But to make myself clear, if you aren't willing to give us a chance, then you should never date someone who treated you disrespectfully. Ben Ryan is an ass. You saw that in the way he treated me. And I'd *like* to think that maybe you've got my back as much as I still have *yours*."

Direct hit.

Straight to the heart.

My voice was small, embarrassed. He was right on all counts. "Of course, I have your back, D." Silence on his end. "I didn't like what Ben said, but you don't always leave room to insert dialogue. I'm sorry if it looked like I didn't care when he was goading you."

"Seriously, I didn't need the assist," he said, snorting and rolling his eyes.

Now I was confused. "But you just said—"

He cut me off. "I know what I said, Darcy, but actions are an indication of how someone feels. Sometimes I feel so unbelievably close to you, and others, I feel like you have a gun trained on my heart, and you've pulled the trigger."

"I'd never hurt you," I said quickly.

"Not intentionally," he amended, "but we're off, Darc. How do I get back in there, honey? Tell me."

I dumbly said, "I don't know." Dylan didn't say anything, just kept up with the quiet church mouse routine. "Why are you being so quiet?"

He closed his eyes. Opened them. "I'm wondering how patient I am."

For those of you who are idiots, allow me to translate...

Dylan had grown tired of the gig. Once again, he shot his gaze through the rearview mirror. That time with an accompanying frown. It was an emotionally charged conversation, and it grated on my last nerve he only halfway listened. "You're not even paying attention to me!" I snapped.

He gave me a split second of his amber eyes. "I *am* paying attention, Darcy. I'm just trying to figure out why this guy has been tailing us for the last three miles."

"Maybe he's just going in the same direction."

"Perhaps, but that car was parked outside of Belinski's when I arrived and also when we left. A guy was sitting in the passenger seat, texting on his phone. I didn't pay much attention at the time. When leaving, the car was empty."

"Do you make it a habit of casing the place?" I mockingly laughed.

He gave me his eyes for another beat and glanced back up into the mirror. "When I'm with you, yeah. I hate to break it to you, sweetheart, but you don't exactly behave like your average girl. And frankly, I'm getting a bad vibe."

Pivoting in my seat, I tried to get a bead on the automobile behind us. The silhouette of a male illuminated its cab, but mix its headlights with the Beemer's taillights, and I couldn't make out anything more. Others might have been in the car, and the reason I assume that is because Dylan had witnessed someone sitting in the passenger side beforehand. That meant the passenger merely waited for the driver to return. Let's theorize they *did* mean us harm. More bodies meant Dylan could be double or triple-teamed. I didn't like those odds. My eyes snagged a partial license plate number—CBH4 something-something-something.

While I committed it to memory, Dylan swung a left onto a side street, speeding up and taking a sharp right onto another road. The car behind us...*followed*. My stomach suddenly jumped to my mouth. If Dylan's gut was right, a good possibility existed it was Brantley McCoy. He didn't know me as Darcy Walker, but if the theory of crooks was true...that they all knew one another...then he'd be aware Vinnie Vecchione was the one who'd almost killed him. It was plausible he saw us driving away from his home, and it was common knowledge Vinnie and I were BFFs. Thing was, Vinnie was just Vinnie. A guy who grew up hard, but his heart was always in the right place even if his actions were questionable. Brantley was different. According to Vinnie, he was only one breath away from insane.

"Did you get a good look at him?" I whispered.

"Not good enough."

Okay, Dylan was borrowing trouble. We were good. Nothing was wrong. We needed to rebound back to the conversation. Ben Ryan. Me. Science project. "D—"

He uncharacteristically interrupted when he stopped at a red light, his eyes still riveted behind us. "Listen, sweetheart," he said tenderly but with a mulish determination. "I *know* how this is going to go down between us in the end. Do I like what happens in the meantime? No. But I agreed to it. What I'm saying to you doesn't come from jealousy, although a little bit admittedly does. It comes from me worrying about you. I will worry about you until the last breath leaves my body."

M'kay. That statement burned all kinds of HOT.

I fought the overwhelming desire to launch myself across the seat and have my wicked way with him. Rip his clothes off. Maybe some hair. Anything I could get my stinking hands on sounded good. Holy cow, I didn't have the chance because next thing I knew, the car behind us tapped the bumper. That's right...tapped it. I gasped and shakily swiveled around. Yup. Still one guy. When I settled back in my seat, Dylan's face and body hadn't changed. He merely leaned forward on the steering wheel, not tearing his eyes from the mirror.

"D, just drive," I begged, grabbing his leg.

Those words were futile. Dylan never backed down. He was

born a fighter, whether right or wrong. His lips parted, but his words were drowned out by another, harder double tap on the bumper. All I kept thinking was his car was a Beemer. *The Beemer*, I emphasized in my brain. That was like breaking one of the cardinal laws of the universe: never mar a German-made car...*ever*.

After one more tap, Dylan leveled me with a seriously deadly stare, leaned over, and cupped my chin in his hand. Tugging me across the console, his head slanted across mine, and he pressed a hard kiss on my lips. Stunned. Seriously stunned. Add speechless to the mix too. It wasn't the kind of passion I would've considered ideal, but the emotions in his car would no doubt paralyze a monk. I wasn't sure I liked that type of kiss, but I sure as heck didn't *not* like it either. It was angry and challenging, and he proved it when he pulled back and ordered, "No matter what, you *do not* get out of this car. You hear me? Call 911 and stay put, yeah?"

The tone of his voice was soft yet downright scary, but I still wondered if we were in *The Twilight Zone*. That stuff didn't happen in Valley, but the file clerk in my brain reminded me I'd found a partially decomposed skeleton over the weekend. And I could add that Nico Drake got killed and then walked home. But you know what? That was *my* life. I wasn't normal. Stuff like that happened to *me*...it wasn't supposed to happen to Dylan. Before I could answer, he grabbed a baseball bat from the back seat and jumped out of the car, ready to beat the holy shiz out of the driver.

What the ever-lovin' minion of Hell...

He thought I'd stay put?

I was a verb, for God's sake—not some whiny, teenage girl too stunned to move. I was his wingman, and I'd never leave him unguarded, even if it meant I might get my lights punched out while covering him. Not to mention he was in possession of a deadly weapon. Even if he'd been unprovoked, the law wouldn't look too kindly on someone swinging a wooden bat.

I got my verb on and pushed the passenger side door wide. "No, Dylan!" I screamed.

Dylan had no sooner made it to the driver's side window than the car backed up in a squeal, peeled out, and tore through the intersection.

———

After a few strained I'll-see-you-in-the-mornings, I made my grand exit, blew out a sigh, and shuffled inside the house. Dylan wasn't so fond of my newfound badassery. In fact, I got a glare that nearly melted the skin from my bones. To give him credit, he stopped at a glare. Believe me...I got it. Guys were bigger and stronger than girls, but I wasn't the type to sit idly by and watch a fight happen in front of my eyes. He knew that...or at least, he used to know that.

Pretty freakin' sad.

Earlier, when the cops came to the scene, we did the I-saw-this, they-did-that gig. Then I gave them the partial license plate, and we phoned our parents. It went better on Dylan's end than mine. I might as well have called Baby Jesus a homegrown terrorist, but really...there were no words.

Murphy was sprawled out in the leather recliner, watching television. A can of Coke in one hand, a cloud of cigar smoke over his head with a bag of chips balanced on his gut. He didn't acknowledge me when I walked inside.

Call me Albert Einstein, but that wasn't good.

Throwing my purse and jacket on the couch, even though I was freaked way the heck out, I decided to forgo rehashing the we-were-attacked conversation and dive straight into Ben Ryan. I needed Dylan as far away from me as possible. Preferably in Alaska or another place surrounded by water. Until Brantley McCoy was found and brought to justice, Dylan could feasibly be carrying a baseball bat around.

I'd been categorically insane for considering us as a boyfriend/girlfriend unit—even though he conjured up conflicting emotions. At one point, he'd been in full snarl. I didn't know whether to cry or ask him to strip me bare. Lately, I'd been embracing that passion. Yup, Darcy Walker had become an embracer. Problem was, his soul was good. In fact, he went to Confession each week and confessed whatever little sin he *did* have. A priest would need notebook paper or the memory of an elephant to record all of mine.

I flopped onto the couch across from Murphy. "Other than the fact some moron hit the Beemer, I almost got kissed under the mistletoe tonight," I said. "Don't worry about any lip action. Dylan broke it up after he said he'd leave the guy crying for his mommy."

Murphy crossed his legs at the ankles and shoveled another chip in his mouth. "And that's why I can sleep at night," he said, chomping another bite. "Remind me to upgrade his Christmas present tomorrow morning, kid." Murphy's temper was like a mile-wide hurricane. I expected more of a reaction. Heck, I thought he'd be screaming bloody murder after the night's events, but the UK Wildcats were playing, and Murphy pretended he was the sixth man.

"Thing is, I'd like to have a date with him, Murphy. It's Ben Ryan."

Murphy's head swiveled around like Linda Blair's in *The Exorcist* when the demon was inside her. "The kid who hit you with his car?"

"I walked out in front of *him*, Murphy."

"Well, yeah, but don't you have any higher standards? I'd think number one on the list would be, *Don't date someone who hit me with his car*."

Put that way, it kind of made sense. "So can I?" I asked.

Another munch of chips. "And Dylan was okay with this?"

"He wasn't exactly off his holy rocker, if that's what you mean. In fact, he said...he said..."

I buried my face in my hands. "Aww, for the love of Pete," Murphy grunted. "Spit it out, kid."

"He said he'd wait on me."

Murphy furrowed his brows, took a deep breath, and then barked out the laughter of a seal. He laughed so loudly he bent over and wheezed, the cosmos reminding him he needed to cut back on the cigars.

"Bless him, Lord," he said with a chuckle, referring to Dylan. "Listen to me, kid. I suggest you put this thinking thing of yours into high gear and just make a decision. But you're a fool if you mess with that boy's heart. He's good. He's patient, but every man has his limits," he finished as an aside.

After I kissed Marjorie goodnight, I creamed off my mascara and did a minimal amount of maintenance in the bathroom. Once I removed my contacts, I changed into blue Cookie Monster fleece bottoms, a black sweatshirt, and knee socks. Crawling into bed, I switched my sound machine to Ocean Waves and pondered how I'd gaslight Damon into giving up information about The Ghost. I also needed Tito back on the phone to see if he could find the owner of the white van at school. It might help with Coach's case, which surprisingly had turned out rather difficult to crack in a school that loved to gossip. Oh yeah, and I hadn't forgotten that Coach Wallace's ex-wife might be guiltier of something other than being an ex.

My God, let us not forget I had a real science project due in days. Days, people, and it knocked at my door like the Big Bad Wolf.

When I was depressed, I drew things. I sketched the lines, shadows, and contours the way I saw them. I could make everything the way I *wanted* it to be—to where the picture came alive from whatever angle I looked at it. I grabbed a scrap piece of paper and drew a picture of a rotting skeleton. Weird, but oh well. As I drew, it became clear the answer was simple: if I wanted information, I had to go after it myself. Or better yet, draw out The Ghost and make him angry enough to mess up.

I made a few phone calls and waited...

Right when I counted thirty-eight sheep, my iPhone's buzz startled me awake. Fumbling around on the nightstand, I squinted at the number and practically did a cartwheel midair. "So you'll go?!" I almost screamed.

"I'll be there bright and early, Dolce," he murmured. "I finished up classes today."

―――――

I'd risen early, searching for the perfect excuse. I ran my tongue up and down the escalator and caught a stomach virus. Or someone sneezed in my face and I came down with tuberculosis. Perhaps I contracted an incurable disease by exchanging money. Or something more practical like my resistance was down because I never got a full night's sleep. My mind played through the lies with each nervous gait to Murphy's room. All I had to do was stumble to his pillow, cough "I'm dying," fake-sneeze a few times, and he grumbled, "Dang it, kid, cover your mouth."

Simple.

That morning I beat Dylan to the punch. I texted him at half past five, telling him I had yellow fever, mosquitoes were everywhere, and to look for me in the morgue. I didn't even receive a reply, and thankfully he never showed at his usual time.

The house was completely abandoned by eight o'clock. Murphy departed at his usual seven, and Claudia and Marjorie left early to hit Walmart before first grade started. Once I heard the front door close, I showered and pulled my hair back in a wet ponytail. I applied blush, mascara, and pink lip gloss. Standing in my underwear, I stared at my clothes and decided all black was the best route. On went a black turtleneck, skinny jeans with my new black leather ankle boots. Once I was satisfied with the look, I placed my lucky hat on my head. It was a menswear houndstooth bucket hat I'd bought last summer at The Gap. It made me look brainy with glasses.

The moment I stuffed a cherry Pop-Tart in my mouth, the door-bell rang. Looking through the peephole, I was convinced it was the dumbest decision I'd ever made. With my hand around the doorknob, I opened it up with a semi-fake smile.

Visitor number one...

"Nice place," Bean said with a sheepish grin. It was safe to say if his goal was to accentuate his nerdiness, he'd hit the darn mark. He wore a three-piece, navy pin-stripe suit with a white tie on a navy shirt and white patent leather shoes. They squeaked like they'd been filled with water when he walked through the door. On his head was a white cowboy hat with a red feather tucked inside the bill. In his pocket (of course) was Mr. Pongo dressed as a twinsie.

Enter visitor number two...

Vinnie was dressed in jock-boy chic. Sneakers, gray sweats, and a new gray hoodie with Ohio State written across the chest. He stole one look at Bean and his body shook with laughter.

Bean did an effeminate twirl. "Like my outfit?" he said, grinning proudly.

"Yeah, it lets everyone know you're single," Vinnie said, cackling louder.

While he and Bean introduced themselves, I secretly grabbed Murphy's GLOCK pistol and shoved it in the waistband of my pants—no bullets, but no one needed to know what I considered a minor detail.

Bean had brought in the morning paper. Tito Westbrook penned the lead story about the ten thousand dollar reward Cookie Harper-Stark was offering for info about The Ghost. My heart went aflutter.

"So that's what we're after?" Vinnie murmured grinning.

"Yeah, and we're going to get it," I said, grinning back and telling them the layout for the day.

Vinnie clarified, "So we're going to find out why Jojo dumped Coach, who painted his car, and if The Ghost is Brantley McCoy—the guy you think bumped you and Taylor?"

I nodded. Vinnie gazed at me intently. "Totally doable," he encouraged. "Now do you want to tell me why that skeleton freaked you out like it did? You've seen worse, Dolce. You've touched worse."

True dat...

No one appreciated a looky-loo more than me, but I had no inkling Vinnie'd found my reaction odd. Sure, I'd seen a dead body, detached hand, and severed head. My God, I'd tripped over Nico Drake. Things much worse than the man in the closet, but that particular scene was like a moth to a flame. The closer I got, the more I'd get burned. The Minstrel Cramps T-shirt delivered the final blow. My mother founded that band and sang lead vocals, but the band broke up when she became pregnant with me. I only spoke of her with Dylan because he could draw me back from the psychosis. I couldn't chance a conversation with Vinnie, although he'd given me the T-shirt because he remembered that Gemma Walker, at one time, was "THE SHIZ." That's right...my mother, point blank, was the hottest thing the town had ever seen. Until some psycho stalker SOB did the unspeakable...he killed her.

During the reunion tour I talked her into.

After all these years, I still couldn't place that on a shelf in my mind that explained why something like that was okay to happen. God was supposed to be good—and want good things for a person. I believed that most days, but what happened didn't make me a better person. It didn't make me a worse person. It just made me... sad.

But life was like a vapor—here one minute, the next vanished into the wind.

Burying the pain, I switched on the part of my brain that helped me survive and piled into the Bug with Vinnie—armed in nothing more than enthusiasm, bonded by our idiocy. Ten minutes later, we stood in the middle of Dingo 31 at nine-thirty, opening time. Dingo 31 is a new store to the area specializing in designer brands for less. In any other situation, I'd be excited to scope the place out, but traveling with Bean and Vinnie was like herding cats. I tried to give instruction, but Bean headed straight to housewares. Vinnie headed for the ladies' underwear.

Throwing my shoulders back and attempting to look professional, I passed the handbags on the left, stole a glance at the size eight rack of shoes, and strolled to the rear of the store to the first associate I made eye contact with. He was a male not much older than me. I'd found in all of my excursions I garnered more information from males than females. Throw in a flirty smile and a girl could unbooby a booby trap.

We met up as he parked a buggy full of merchandise in front of a bathroom display.

I extended a hand. "Hi. I'm uh...Jester, and I'm looking for Jojo Wallace."

He shook my hand, half asleep, half awake. His red hair was a stiff mess of styling gel, and his energy level resembled a slug trying to make it up a concrete wall. "Who?" he asked.

I tried again. "Jojo?"

"Oh," he shivered. "She's in the back." The shudder made me curious, and what better way to gain information than from someone who already had strong emotions.

Picking up five or six towels, he slid them onto an endcap, lining them up by color. "What's she like?" I said, offering a smile.

Squinting his eyes, he tried to gauge my reaction and called her the B-word.

"Oh," I said. "Always?"

"Born that way." He gazed over his shoulder toward the swinging doors of the stock room. Rolling the buggy up four aisles to the shoes, he pulled out five pairs of size six leather boots, positioning them on the top shelf.

"What does she do here?" I asked.

The instant he opened his mouth, the swinging doors flew wide with who I could only assume was security, a manager, or someone who'd gotten their cereal peed in and needed to vent. A look at the nametag on her overly buxom bosom said, *Jojo*. Underneath in block letters were the words *Store Manager*.

Fudge...

Jojo looked like she'd slept in a tanning booth. She wore too much base makeup with two stripes of orange blush on both cheekbones. Her eyes were shadowed in light blue with mascara that'd been applied overtop an earlier batch. Her eyebrows were crayoned in, and her forehead was devoid of personality—Botox, the culprit.

Jojo donned a navy Ralph Lauren double-knit jersey sheath that had a leather gun patch at the right shoulder. Black Label league. I nearly dropped dead. No wonder Coach Wallace was broke. That dress was close to four figures. I knew that because Red had a duplicate. When Jojo turned sideways, I got an eyeful of her profile. Her stomach was protruding and round—not overweight—like she had a bun in the oven.

Umm...*wow*.

I didn't profess to know a lot about pregnancy, but I *did* know to never ask women their due date. There was always the remote chance they weren't really pregnant, they were fat, or God forbid, they'd never lost their previous baby weight and gave up on the dream.

Striding toward her, I told myself, *Above all, say nothing stupid or risqué*. Consequently, I blurted out, "Please tell me that's just a gas bubble."

Vinnie appeared out of nowhere, chuckling. "It's going to be a great Christmas."

Jojo wanted my head on a platter. Registering her death wish, Vinnie gripped the hand at her side, murmuring, "Hello, I'm BJ Monaco. Life coach and personal trainer."

Of course he was.

"We're screwed," I said out loud.

Jojo lifted a chubby hand to cover her laugh. "And you think I need a personal trainer? Honey, I'm pregnant."

Normally, I could talk myself out of any situation. Heck, I talked a mobster out of killing a kidnapper and me last summer while a commode overflowed at our feet. But right then had absolutely stymied me.

A customer had left a chocolate bar on a nearby endcap. Jojo snatched it up, gave the wrapper a jagged rip, and took an unladylike bite. Vinnie gazed at the candy bar like a succubus looked at a fresh neck. Licking his lower lip, he still remained in character. "Well, let me just say, you wear it well, Jojo." He produced a white business card, placing it in her palm. "Here's my number for after the blessed event takes place. Does your partner want to join us? I've got a family deal going on until the end of January."

"That would be a capital NO," she said, frowning deeply. "My husband and I are divorced. I didn't want a divorce, but he's too soft. You raise your voice, and he thinks it's a fight. My God, the situation I'm in, does he expect me to always be in a good mood?"

"Men," Vinnie said, snorting and touching her shoulder.

"You've got that right," she agreed, voice rising. "And I didn't do that to his car. Those stupid kids at school did. I might've dented it a few times before, but that's it."

I tried to keep my voice emotionless, nonjudgmental. 'Oh, wow. So your husband's car has been vandalized?"

Closing her eyes, she actually appeared to be in some sort of pain. Taking in one big breath she expelled it slowly as though anything faster would produce more agony.

Verrrrrrrrrrrrry interesting.

"Yes, I'm the first person he called."

———

Vinnie drove us downtown, chasing a solid lead on The Ghost. In an alley behind Sixth Street, his cousin appeared, produced two white silk cloths, removed my glasses, and blindfolded Bean and me. My heart stopped, or at least stutter-stepped. I knew Vinnie had a cousin but had no idea he was Italian good-looking with big brown eyes and full, rosy lips. A normal-looking businessman. He was a runner in a law firm and was dressed in a dark gray three-piece suit as if he'd just ended a day in court. As soon as my mouth opened, Vinnie angrily shooshed me and unceremoniously forced me into the backseat of the Bug, settling in beside me. Bean, I assumed, was in the front seat. His cousin was then at the wheel, driving what I'd estimate to be two miles. When the ignition switched off, Vinnie placed my hand in his and led us into what I knew immediately was an abandoned building. Well, abandoned of a lawful business, I should clarify.

"Remember whose side you're on, Vinnie," I seethed into his back. "You could've given me a heads up on the blindfold."

"Shut up, Darcy. You've now entered the big leagues." He was rude, plus he called me Darcy—something he rarely did, even more rarely than Dylan. Navigating through three right turns and then a left, he abruptly stopped and roughly thrust me into a metal chair. That wasn't the Vinnie I knew. Vinnie loved me. Vinnie had my back. My brain was so stunned it didn't even try to dissect the shock. Vinnie then gave me the OMG moment of all OMG moments. He squeezed my shoulder and lower back at the same time—alerting me he'd already noticed I came packing heat. Problem was, Murphy's GLOCK was unloaded. U-n-l-o-a-d-e-d for those who needed it spelled out. I should've put a bullet in the mag.

Oh, crap.

Crap, crap, crap.

While the minutes ticked away, I tried to get a feel for my surroundings. The smell of Italian food hit my nose, and my taste-buds shot straight to drool. Where was I? I'd never been in that situation before—waiting for a criminal—and since I didn't know protocol, I found myself whistling. I'd slaughtered the second verse of "High Hopes" when a deep bass voice finished out the last stanza.

The world came to a crashing halt.

Diabolical laughter pierced straight through my bones, and that deep voice stroked a large tender hand down my jaw. I nearly bit it out of sheer anger. My God, Vinnie had delivered me up to someone my thumping heart told me was even bigger trouble than me. Vinnie had delivered me to...*Jaws*. Who is Jaws, you say? Jaws was the SOB who'd had my back when I chased a murderer last spring—actually giving me the name, albeit too late—but had eluded me for months when I tried to track him down. I should probably be thanking him. Instead, I longed to smack him because—well, because he might be smarter than me.

"Jaws," I said sultrily. "How's it going, big guy? I'm assuming house arrest is a thing of the past."

Laughter rang from the walls as his hand again traveled to touch my face, lingering in the dimple of my chin. "Jester," he said, chuckling deeply, "you never fail to impress."

I squirmed like a dying worm. Jaws didn't give me the impression I wasn't safe, but call me a wimp because I'd feel more in control if I could see him. "I'd impress you more if you'd remove my blindfold."

My hair was styled in a low ponytail, peeking out from my lucky hat. Jaws twined his fingers in the baby hairs at the base of my neck, and I knew immediately Vinnie wasn't present anymore. Vinnie wouldn't allow him to touch me in any way, shape, or form. That meant Bean must be somewhere else too. Which also meant neither was allowed in Jaws's presence. Vinnie had obviously set up the meeting with the caveat I'd come alone. I'd been under the impression Vinnie knew what Jaws looked like. At the time, I wasn't so sure. Knowing how difficult it'd been to track him down, I believed Jaws had people masquerading as him all over the city. In fact, someone I assumed was Jaws crashed Dylan's sister's party last spring in order to warn me about the murderer I had been chasing. That guy couldn't have been Jaws. No way. If he were, once again Vinnie would've been allowed to stay.

"I'm going to make a guess here, Jaws, that you don't allow anyone to see your face."

"Like Jester doesn't allow anyone to know her real name. You're definitely a study in psychology...Darcy Walker."

That secret ranked up there with where the government kept aliens.

I'd kill Vinnie if he gave me up, but I knew deep down in my fiendish bones he hadn't. I thought silence was my best option.

Reaching back, I let my right hand rest on the cold stainless steel of Murphy's GLOCK, just in case I needed to threaten him. "I'm not much on games, Jaws, so I'm going to get straight to the point. I need to know who The Ghost is."

A chair screeched across the floor, and Jaws slid into it—directly across from me. Our knees touched. Too intimate. Familiar. And after the run-in I'd had with Nico Drake, I bit back the urge to panic.

"Ah, yes, the identity thief," Jaws said. "He's a chameleon from what I hear. Acts one way in public. Someone totally different in private."

Even blindfolded, my face had to be clueless. "A chameleon," I repeated dumbfounded. "I was thinking more along the lines of greasy."

"No, he's a chameleon, Jester, and I hear he likes good-looking girls."

I mean, derr...what guy didn't. "So someone has seen him? They know what he looks like?" I asked.

"The someone I asked doesn't always walk away with details, babe. I wish he did, but I keep him around for other things."

I didn't push for clarification. "Well, does The Ghost have a record?"

"Not to my knowledge."

"Doesn't it make sense that he would?"

"Not necessarily."

My theory of Motor Oil Hair and Coffee Blot Boy was shot to mother-trucking heck. "Can you at least tell me if his name is Brantley McCoy?"

Jaws paused for a second as though he committed something to memory. "I don't have a name, but I *have* heard of Brantley McCoy. Didn't he knock off his roommate and steal his identity?"

Somebody needed to kill me or sedate me. I'd been right, and the fact Jaws had that knowledge didn't set too well on an empty stomach—especially since the news and authorities had no idea of my suspicions about McCoy. I got the distinct impression Jaws might own Cincinnati—at least in the capacity that mattered to organized crime.

"Does The Ghost live in Valley?" I asked, not acknowledging I'd come to the same conclusion.

"Yes, my source says he's in Valley."

"Which part of Valley? Mack County isn't the biggest, but it's still big enough."

Amusement was in his voice. "Jester, I don't know. Do you make it a practice to question authority?"

"Only when it's stupid."

Jaws's chair shook with his laughter. "He's the whole package, babe. Good-looking guy. Preppy. A real dresser. And a genius with a great future but is so greedy he's bound to blow it. Apparently, he's into some weird shit too. His date had on a nice white jacket. Leather and skin tight. When she wasn't looking, he'd run his lips over her shoulder, smelling it...then licking it."

"That's not so weird," I lied.

His deep voice went husky. "It's weird, babe. You know it, and I know it."

Noooo, pretty sure what I was doing was the weirdest.

In that moment, I got a peek into Jaws's psyche. Although, he could feasibly play on the wrong team, it was a choice for him. He could hang on any side if he chose because his brain and moral compass hadn't totally been fried. Still, the predator smell was like a stink on a skunk.

"Did you have anything to do with my best friend and me being the victims of road rage last night?"

His energy went ice-cold. "Qualify."

"We were followed from my job for close to three miles. When we stopped at a red light, our bumper was tapped several times, trying to invoke a fight."

His energy went even colder. "This I didn't know," he continued. "Did the cops reel him in?"

"I'm thinking they went straight to Dunkin' Donuts. We haven't heard anything."

"You probably won't," he said. "The longer it goes, the less likelihood of finding the perpetrator. Do you think it's McCoy?"

"He's a good guess."

"And why would he even know of you, Jester?"

"Because Vinnie almost killed him."

"Backtrack, babe, you're losing me."

I sighed. "We broke into a house where McCoy was supposed to be living, and while we were there, we discovered evidence that points to him being the identity thief. Plus, you can tack on the extra bonus of a decomposing skeleton in the closet. The skeleton turned out to be the real owner of the house, Bishop Fowler...the guy you were just referring to. Vinnie and I were set to leave, but gunfire rang out, and when I went out the back, I fell over another dead body named Nico Drake."

"Same place?" he asked. I nodded. "I remember reading about this Drake kid's death."

"Yeah, but he was found dead at his own home. Let me assure you, I saw him dead as a doornail in Fowler's backyard. Somebody moved him. I have all the dirty goods on McCoy, although I haven't snitched. And there's this girl named Madison Flannery who knows everything. She told me she wished Vinnie would've died when he fought McCoy."

More thinking on his part, and then a tired sigh. "Jester, babe, you have one foot on a skateboard, the other on a banana peel. You need me." I didn't respond. "If you're intent on continuing the cloak and dagger, then I'll ask around. But you need to watch the game you're playing. I almost didn't make it in time before, and I hear you were shoved in the trunk of a car at the end of that day."

Noooooo.

No. No. Noooooo.

It felt like I'd been forced into a bottle that'd been corked.

Jaws wasn't the man from the yellow Dodge Charger...*was he?* That man's voice had been burned into the neurons of my brain. It was deeper than Jaws's and sounded regal and poised—even though his demeanor was dark and ruthless. Jaws, I feared, had some Hannibal Lecter in him. And here I was, playing patty-cake...

I kept my voice even keel, not one bit of emotion found anywhere. "Was that you?"

"If it were me, I'd show you my face."

I wasn't sure I bought into that. "Tell me what you know about the man in the yellow Dodge Charger, Jaws. He has information about my mother. I know you know something. It's leaking out of your pores."

"The time hasn't come for you to know yet."

The air went still.

My pulse quickened...yeesssss, I knew it!

I balled my fists, needing to hit something. I'd been chasing the truth about my mother since she'd been abruptly and wrongly taken away from Marjorie and me. That truth churned in my gut, and I wanted those answers more than anything. More than making Murphy proud. More than a relationship with Dylan. More than living on this godforsaken earth. Murphy and Red had more information than I did, but I gave up asking long ago. The mention of her name nearly disabled them, and as much as they loved me, I knew they'd lie to keep some secret they felt I couldn't handle. Thing was, when I was shoved into the trunk of the yellow Dodge Charger, the man stared in my face like I reminded him of someone. I knew deep in my bones he conjured up memories of my mother.

Jaws gasped...I heard it.

Steeling my face, I didn't chance a move because he was key to getting the answers I'd craved. Just when I thought I couldn't be shocked more, he knocked me for a loop with the following statement. "It took some cast iron balls coming here, Jester, and I'd like to offer you my protection. But that's going to take a relationship with me you have to make sure you're ready for."

The fiddle of "The Devil Went Down to Georgia" started plucking between my ears.

I didn't need eyesight to know his eyes were hooded, and his smile was wide and anticipatory. Anticipatory of what, I didn't know, but I had a feeling he meant relationship-relationship. God help me, I was drowning in the deep end of the pool.

People have voluntary and involuntary reactions. The part of me begging for answers—for me, an involuntary need—pulled Murphy's GLOCK out from my waistband, sticking the barrel in his face. "I don't like getting played with, Jaws. And being your friend is a little too Stockholm Syndrome for me to consider comfortable. Show me your freaking face, or I'll put a bullet in your brain."

Jaws chuckled low in his throat, but nothing about his demeanor changed. So if I'd gone for the shock value, I failed with a crappy delivery. "Babe, you're not the type to bring a loaded gun."

Tears stung my eyes, and my chin trembled with anger. "You don't know that, but listen to me now. There's nothing I won't do... *nothing*...to get to the bottom of what happened with my mother."

Jaws removed the shaking gun from my hand, allowing it to clink on the floor beneath us. Placing both my hands in his, his thumbs slid over the tops of my knuckles in comfort. I latched onto his grip and yanked. Yanked with a silent demand that he'd comply. I felt a deep scar on his left hand, but when he realized what I'd done, he withdrew with a soft squeeze. And with that, I knew he symbolically withdrew information too.

I screamed and cried like I'd gone off my meds. After a few failed attempts to swallow the tears, I abandoned the effort and let them flow, my shoulders quaking in years of defeat. I clawed through pain, desperation, and guilt, knowing someone couldn't possibly take it away—but hoping they'd just...ease it. *Ease it*, I cry. *I just wanted it eased.* Jaws had quit talking. After half a minute, I'd had enough. Ripping the blindfold from my eyes, I stared at an empty chair.

Chapter Twenty-One

THE SILENT TREATMENT

*V*innie made me swear on his Grandma Mimi's Bible that Jaws hadn't touched me. Bean appeared to not even understand what that statement implied. In fact, undercover work seemed to sit well with Bean because all he did was talk about wanting to take Justice to the winter formal...get her a wrist corsage..."go big" and buy a Shirley Temple. Not the reaction I would've expected considering he and Vinnie had been held hostage in another room—heavily guarded (with guns) by Jaws's people. Vinnie wouldn't tell me what chip he'd cashed in to score me an in-person meeting, but I knew it had to be something big.

Yes, Vinnie had been acting—and I must admit, he had some chops. In fact, he was so distraught over his behavior that he held my hand the whole ride home. I didn't need an apology. I needed to know what Jaws knew.

Rudi pulled my shift Thursday night in my stead. Murphy said if I couldn't carry my sorry body into school, then by God, I couldn't carry it into work. I understood his reasoning. Thing was, Rudi said Tito phoned The Double-B trying to reconnect with someone named Jester. If Tito decided it warranted an in-person visit, my days of anonymity would go the way of the dodo bird.

Switching off the lamp, I snuggled under the down comforter, begging for REM. For some reason, I felt extra jumpy—a feeling that oftentimes alerted me to danger. Other times it was my conscience giving a lecture it knew I wouldn't heed. Other than Jaws—which honestly didn't spook me—I needed to lay the smack-down on Mean Girl, Madison Flannery, and tell her to kiss my you-know-what. I couldn't allow her to have the last word, especially when Dylan had apparently been targeted along with me. In fact, she might be the key to everything. Why did I think that? She'd texted me four times, and as of yet, I hadn't answered. Messages where she said: *You're dead. You're stupid. Watch your back.* And my personal favorite, *I'm going to take your boyfriend away from you.*

I'd just finished my nightly SKYPE with said boyfriend (he was suspicious why I'd missed school), and decided to round out the evening requesting a play-by-play of the day from Grumpy. Grumpy had surprisingly visited Red Mustang again, that time in the presence of Chevy Colorado.

"What's wrong with you, Walker? You've barely listened to anything I've said. You've appropriately commented, but you just seem...holy crap...I'm afraid if I say *sad*...you might keep me up all night with the details."

I was as nervous as a groom on his wedding night. But it wasn't Jaws. It wasn't Madison. It wasn't The Ghost. My God, that left my totally FUBAR'd personal life.

I exhaled, channeling my inner-Eeyore. "Don't pay any attention to me. No one else does. Speak."

"Like I said, I tried another tactic. Perhaps I'm scary because this time both guys squealed like pigs. The guy in the Red Mustang crumbled first. It probably helped when I backed him up against the bumper of my truck and told him castration was next. When the Chevy dude witnessed his balls shrinking, he caved almost as quickly. Both swore they didn't do anything to Coach's car, and I believe them."

I didn't particularly want to talk about happies, but when my BFFs were guys, I had to embrace my inner-bro and let the locker room stuff slide. "Did you mention Nico again?"

"Yeah, both were dumber than donkeys."

Figures. "Did you get their names?"

"John Brown and John Smith," he muttered. "Could you get more average American than that?"

Come the freak on. He had to be kidding. I'd memorized the list of tardy students backward and forward. No John Smith or John Brown had been listed. During interrogation, Grumpy also unearthed the name of the creepo guy in the van. I almost broke into "Jesus Christ Superstar" but was afraid Jesus would think I sucked.

"They know him as Young, Walker, and they said he's kind of seedy. He's the type that's always trying to sell you crap." I was zero for three and struck out. Plus, I found out White Van was a weirdo who didn't even go to our school. "Remember you owe me a date with Clementine."

God. Save. Me. From. My. Stupid. Promise.

"I'm all over it," I lied.

———

Three days later, I was still as lost as an Easter egg. Meh.

Finn and I ran into a little snag. Seems the school detected a breach in security—Finn swore he'd protected himself—but as a result of Valley's new firewall, he couldn't hack into the school's computer system as easily. He promised he'd eventually get back in, but with basketball season and finals, he said it'd be a few weeks at best. I didn't have a few weeks, folks. My wallet was in a slow bleed as it was.

That left Tito.

"It's an old white van," I told him. "Probably ten years old. Looked like a Ford. The driver's last name is Young, and he doesn't go to Valley although he lurks around. If he doesn't own the van, then let's hope he at least lives with the person who holds the title. Can you get his name? Possibly his digits?"

Tito never confirmed nor denied anything. Instead, something told me I needed to play the waiting game until my face went blue.

He buckled first. "I'm going to ask again. Tell me your real name, Jester. And does this white van have anything to do with the guy who robbed me blind? When I've redialed your numbers, to date I've talked to two Mexican women I could barely understand," *Claudia and Ana Rosalina*, "a little girl who wanted to know if I'd like to play Barbies," *Marjorie*, "and an extremely disgruntled book-seller," *Mr. Belinski*. Not to mention you masqueraded as Tabitha

Arthur on Shepard Johnson's cell phone. Who on Earth are you, and in what circles do you travel?"

Like I'd answer that...

My chest started to wheeze, and it sounded like I'd coughed up a lung. Heck, maybe it was my conscience trying to free itself. "A busy girl," I answered, clearing my throat.

Tito groaned sympathetically when the cough pitched its proverbial tent and decided to stay. "You're sick," he said. "Let me help you, darlin'. Do you live on the streets or somethin'?"

I might be if Murphy discovered what I considered recreational. "No, it's just cold and flu season. Listen, I don't have time. The white van more than likely has nothing to do with what happened to you, but it will be a big story for you nonetheless. Are you going to work with me, or do I have to take other measures?"

He sighed...and grunted. Then I think he voiced some sort of show tune.

Whatever, I thought, *if singing show tunes helps us get to the journey's end quicker, then bring on Broadway.*

"Okay, Jester," he finally muttered. "This *is* the weekend, so I promise the information by Monday morning. Once you speak with this person, you call me immediately. If you *don't* call immediately, then our relationship is over, capeesh?"

"Capeesh," I repeated in the best Italian accent I could muster. But I couldn't help but throw in cockily, "Remember who's buttered your bread here lately, Tito. Remember it was little ole Jester who told you Bishop Fowler bought gum and pumped gas long after his heart quit beating. And I'm working on something else," *Brantley McCoy,* "and when I get that to you, I'll accept the apology you already owe me."

"Sweet Lord," he prayed and laughed. "I'm going to show you how good I am because I'm going to put that info in your hands by the end of the night. Have a good evening, darlin'. I never renege on a deal. You keep your end and produce whatever this other big story is, and we'll still be chatting years from now."

Disconnecting, all I wanted to do was make it through the week...$10 Gs richer.

———

I made that phone call four hours earlier.

The time rolled at sevenish on Sunday night when I realized I hadn't seen my best friend in over forty-eight hours. When he took me home Friday, the plan was to join him at Valley's basketball game that evening. Unfortunately, I got another coughing spell and collapsed as soon as my feet crossed the threshold of my room, sprawled out on the carpet like a dead cockroach. I cracked open an eye long enough to send him a text that said: *I might've infected you. I'm sorry. And please don't let it end our relationship.* I think he texted back: *I love you. Don't worry. I'm indestructible.* But when I went to my phone the next morning, no evidence existed of our exchange. Did I delete it, or did I imagine the whole flipping thing?

Home for Christmas break from OSU, his sister, Sydney, hosted her annual *July in Christmas* party Saturday night. Convinced I was on the speedy road to recovery, Dylan phoned, requesting I be his date. I wasn't so sure I'd been healed, but my codependent self buckled when he murmured, *Please.* When I stumbled up to get dressed, I coughed so much I ralphed phlegm all over the wall. Talk about embarrassment. I told him what'd happened, and when Murphy walked by as I sponged it up, he looked at me with a gag and grunted, "Politely decline, kid. I swear, you gave him the plague through the phone."

We ended with some small talk, but the operative word there was "small." I wasn't positive he believed me, and why should he? There'd been too many negative emotions between us lately—most of them my fault.

Murphy had dropped me off at The Double-B at noon where Rudi and I literally and figuratively watched the paint peel. It was Rudi's cell I'd used to call Tito. A pretty dastardly, crappy deed if I cared to think about it. She used her cell to text only, and I knew if Tito called, she: (A) wouldn't hear it or (B) would be so uncomfortable she'd hang up.

I told myself it was for a good cause, but the sharp pain in my chest said I might want to reacquaint myself with good person behavior.

That wasn't the only thing alarming.

Ben called Murphy.

Murphy liked him.

I'd dove headfirst into Bizarro World. The only upside from being sick was I had an excuse to not go out with him.

As I added a stack of one-dollar bills to the register, Collin Lockhart strolled in. Just looking at him was discomforting enough. He'd dressed in expensive jeans, an expensive green sweater, and an expensive black pea coat that hugged his shoulders like a sports car hugged the road. He was too pretty, successful, and (make me want to gag) enamored with Brynn Hathaway. I'd rather open Hell's gates and dive in headfirst than listen to him snivel how the rumor mill had already begun to churn about Sydney's party.

"You didn't know?" he asked as I counted and recounted the ones.

"No," I tried to say emotionlessly. "I didn't."

"I hear they were surgically joined at the hip, and she bent his ear all night long. Apparently, it was nauseating, like Italian-men-serenading-you-with-a-Stradivari nauseating."

Actually, being serenaded with a violin was pretty darn romantic, if you asked me. I took a whiff of Collin, wondering if he fired on all neurons. Last spring, he crashed another of Sydney's parties and left drunker than a monkey even though no alcohol was officially served. Funny, he and Brynn were estranged then and even more estranged at the moment. I saw a pattern occurring.

I picked up the Abe Lincolns and nervously continued to add.

"To be honest, Collin, your relationship has been stuck in the breakup/makeup status for years. You'll be back together before morning."

Here's to crossing my fingers.

"Well, this one is for good. She did the worst possible thing you can do to a person."

"Being?"

"She unfollowed me on Twitter."

Oh, God...that WAS serious.

He leaned across the counter, instantly causing me to recoil. "They're at dinner tonight. Did you know that?"

Actually, I didn't.

Dylan texted me a good morning and later called that he wouldn't be able to pick me up after work because of a corporate Christmas party his father was throwing for all his cosmetic minions. There'd been no mention of Brynn. Although, it was plausible she would be in attendance. Her father was a Go Glam! executive too.

"Doesn't that worry you?!" Collin roared when I ignored him. Just the thought gave me a bad case of indigestion. Putting my fingers in the compartment of twenties, I lifted them out and counted, recounted, and counted again. When Collin didn't move, I slid one eye over not really knowing how to answer. Of course it bothered me, but I wanted to protect my feelings more than commiserate with someone who wasn't really a friend. When I gave him what I hoped was a disinterested shrug, Collin grabbed his blond head with both hands, like the ambiguity caused him mental pain.

Next thing I knew, he started talking to himself. "You're Collin Lockhart," he muttered. "You can accomplish anything. You're student council president, good-looking, and you will own this town one day and everybody in it."

Yup, Collin was still ate-up with himself...

When I nearly suggested the psychiatry aisle, he mumbled, "Bathroom," and strode to the back of the store. He left his wallet, car keys, and cell phone on the countertop. Picking them up to place behind the counter, I quickly recognized the opportunity Providence had placed in my palm...*a phone.*

I looked to the ceiling with a smile.

A little over four hours had passed since Tito and I'd spoken—let's see how good he really was. Punching in his number, I repeated Collin's mantra. "You're Darcy Walker. You can accomplish anything. You're...*not* student council president," I amended. "You're *not* good-looking, and this town will eat you alive if you don't burn it down first."

When he answered, "Jester?" I said, "*Soooo?*"

"*Soooooo,*" he drawled out even more.

We remained silent—him, relaxed...me, breathing like I had one foot in quicksand.

Tito eventually said, "There are a few details we need to go over again, Jester." I sighed, feeling as though it was a waste of time. After he swore *he* was confidential and that *I* needed to be confidential, he said, "The guy you're looking for is Eric Young. The van, however, belongs to Evelyn Seacrest. No known relation but my contact says he does work around the house for her."

He rattled off Evelyn's digits. I repeated them back three times, forever planting them in my brain. When I got nothing but what sounded like a slurp of pizza, I asked, "Anything else?"

"I was waiting for a thank you, darlin'. But maybe I'm just old-school."

When Collin materialized with a more sedate face, I dispensed a heartfelt, "Thank you," disconnected, and lied that I'd answered his phone for him.

Collin's face bled into a blank slate when I placed all his things back in his hand. "This is what we should do," he said confidently. "We need to date merely to rub it in their faces. Fair is foul, and foul is fair."

Tempting, I thought, in a *Macbeth* sort of way, but overall it felt skeevy. When I uhh'd and well'd, and I-don't-know'd, he released a sad nod and slowly turned and walked out the door.

Guess he got the picture.

The next two hours might've been the longest of my life. By the time my shift ended, my fingernails were down to nubs, and I feared I'd acquired a permanent eye tic. But the night didn't end in bore-dom. Far from it. Evidently, in one of my unhygienic moves, I'd either sneezed in Marjorie's face or left snot on the doorknob because she had "a smoker's cough with a side order of black lung."

Murphy's words, of course.

He grumbled, "I'd give her some cough syrup with codeine, but I'm afraid she won't wake up, kid. I need you to run to Kroger on the way home and pick up some cough medicine. I don't want to leave her alone. Can Dylan pick you up?"

"I fear he's fornicating with Brynn Hathaway."

"Come again?"

"Brynn Hathaway," I repeated as if it was anathema. "I'll call Justice." *Or Ben*, I thought. I didn't know where he lived, but dang it, turnabout was fair play.

"Murphy, would you be upset if Ben Ryan brought me home? That is, if he's somewhere close?"

I got the impression Murphy would eat him alive if he had a fork. Oh, boy, then came the conduct-unbecoming-of-a-lady speech.

Here was a replay...

"If you get a drink, don't put your Coke down," Murphy grunted. "If you go to the bathroom, get a new Coke when you come back. Don't kiss him. Don't let him touch you anywhere. Don't even smile if you don't feel like it, and there's this date-rape drug called a roofie that's really bad news."

I giggled. "You've just traumatized me."

"I feel like if I don't traumatize my kids, then I haven't done a good job. Besides, you can get pregnant by spit, kid. I'm from Appalachia. I know these things. And I also need to find out if he has any STDs."

"STDs are only communicable during the shama lama, ding-dong, Murphy."

"That's what textbooks say, but it might be a conspiracy by the government to knock off certain branches of people." His following statement was so low I almost didn't hear him. "Is this to get back at Dylan?"

"Probably," I said just as lowly.

No words on his end. "Listen, kid. I've played the game you're playing. One too many times to be proud of. I'm not sure what's going on between the two of you, but don't do something you can't undo." Murphy was a notorious cheat until he met my mother. God knew he didn't get a happily-ever-after. "That being said, I talked to Ben, and surprisingly I like him. Normally, I prefer a face-to-face before you get in the car with him, but if he's close, then I'm good with him being your ride. But you know to be a lady, right?"

"I'm sure it's buried somewhere in my gene map, Murphy. Hope-fully, I can conjure it up when he's molesting me."

"Good God," he swore and hung up.

———

Ben rolled into The Double-B in thirty minutes...perfect timing, considering I needed to lock up, wait for Rudi's father to show, and put Mr. B to sleep on his side in case apnea struck. He arrived in the same Audi he'd hit me with, dressed the same, only his hair was slightly damp. He smelled of a body wash that left my nose doing a striptease. I'd never been alone with anyone in an automobile other than Dylan (well anyone who counted)...but smelling a similar scent was like his territorial self was marking our date.

I was starving. Dylan normally took me through a drive-thru, so when I requested Ben swing by for a Moby burger, the issue of how bad fast food was joined the conversation. Ben had some Svengali tendencies—unfortunately, they weren't much different than Dylan's alpha male macho crap.

"My mother and I are vegan," he murmured after he insisted on paying for my meal.

"Oh yeah," I said. "Did you want to be vegan?"

He gave a small shrug. "I think I just wanted to do the opposite of my father at the time."

"Rebellious phase?"

"An *always* phase. My father wants what my father wants, and he drags you along with him."

So here was Ben's story. His father's in the Air Force and recently took a new post at Wright Patterson Air Force Base in Dayton. Ben was sixteen and born in Great Britain (ergo, the British accent). His parents had been looking at houses in Mack County and were spending a few weeks at the Marriott Hotel in Union Center, about twenty minutes away from my home. Convenient.

And even more convenient when Ben admitted he used the resources at his father's disposal to do a little detective work on his own—mainly, Jojo's name and workplace and how he'd figured out my real cell phone number.

I licked mayo off my lower lip. Ben leaned over with a grin and placed a napkin in my hand. "The two of you aren't close?" I said.

Ben sort of frowned. "We're extremely close. Just sometimes I remember what it's like to leave your best friends behind. On those days, I don't particularly like my father."

The ride was silent for a few beats. Ben came complete with deep emotions. I liked that in a guy, and I realized how surprisingly easy it was to have a conversation with him. He was a feeler, when most guys his age only felt with one body part. "Sorry," I apologized. "Do you need a hug?"

Ben didn't get a chance to say yay or nay. I crawled over the console, arms outstretched, and knocked my Coke from its holder.

The low quality plastic of the Big Moby's lid collapsed, and it geysered up and hit Ben in the lap.

He jumped like he'd collided with an electric fence. "Whoa!" he half screamed, half laughed.

Word of advice? Save a hug in the future.

I was mortified.

Ben ripped his shirt up out of his khakis, and I handed him one of my low quality Big Moby napkins to wipe off with. That sucker disintegrated as soon as it hit the liquid. While he dabbed at his stomach, I gazed at his abs and counted six reasons why I should jump out of a moving car.

Ben saw where my eyes had fixated and subsequently dropped his silver gaze to my mouth. "We can save that for later, angel."

My face blushed. I felt the burn. For five point five seconds, I considered murder...something slow and heavy on pain. Ripping a chunk out of my Moby burger instead, I moved on to the greasy fries and ignored his dirty, dirty mind.

Ben leaned across the console and stroked the bill of my Burberry cap. I immediately wondered what Dylan was doing and what he'd think of Ben, me, and Ben's abs. "I was only joking," he said softly. When I slid over a frown, Ben gently snagged my hand, lifting my fingers to his eyes. "God, you're cute. And the fact that you bite your nails might be the cutest thing I've ever seen."

Please. Tell. Me.

He. Did. Not.

Just.

Say. That.

I wanted to punch him, yanking my hand away. "Darcy," he murmured and chuckled, "that's just rude. I wanted to hold your hand."

Ben's spiritual gift was sarcasm...

"Who's calling *who* rude? I didn't even start it!" I yelled indignantly.

His cocky grin quirked up at one corner. "That's *whom*." he said chuckling, "but I'm willing to overlook your lack of grammar skills if I get a kiss."

Is that right?! Well, a goodnight kiss was sadly not in the playbook.

Ben set my teeth on edge, and that wasn't exactly a guy I'd choose to lock lips with. I stuffed the Moby wrappers in the takeout bag and angrily collapsed it with a big pop. "Our relationship is like a verbal car crash. Why in the world do you provoke me?"

He briskly shook his head, as though he fought through shock. "I'm not actually sure, but you're already in my blood. Listen, Darcy. I always come on too strong—even with a joke—and I didn't mean to hurt your feelings. I like you. I like you more than I want to. God," he swore, briefly wincing, "that didn't come out right either. I've never been so nervous around the opposite sex in my entire life."

Right hand to God, I was elated when he pulled into Kroger. Leaving the car idling by the door, with little grace and a whole lot of stupid, I fell out of the car and walked crooked—like the ground crumbled beneath me. Maybe Hell needed a new citizen. Finally, I found my pride and jogged straight to the cough medicine aisle as Murphy called, figuring I'd need hand holding on the assignment. Deciding to pick up a multi-symptom syrup, I headed for the self-checkout aisle.

"How's it going?" he asked.

"I'm still a virgin, and I turned down the crack he offered, if that's what you mean."

"Good God, kid. Watch your mouth." A pause. "Your friend Chichi phoned."

Another pause. Oh, boy, Chichi must've had a bad read on the Ouija. To paraphrase, I must still be dead-before-her-time. Picking up a cheese cube from a sample tray by the meat section, I plopped it in my mouth. "Yeah?" I said, sort of giggling.

Murphy grumbled, "Yeah, she wanted you to know she had another vision about you and someone with a limp...she said you'd understand."

Eh, normal Chichi behavior. On occasion, she modified her visions, but as far as I knew, the modifications were usually spot-on. First thing to pop in my mind was when I perched myself on top of the school building, scoping out the parking lot for clues. Other than multiple frostbitten appendages, what I took away from that excursion was a gimpy guy in a white van. Speaking personally with him a second time, I concluded he might possess more of a creep factor than normal. Could mean everything or could leave me with a big, heaping helping of sorry-about-your-luck.

But I knew him to be Eric Young, though, and I had his digits.

Murphy requested I snag a gallon of milk and frozen waffles. As I made my way to the middle of the store, no sooner had we disconnected than someone brushed by me, knocking me in the hip with the brown plastic basket he carried. The guy should've gotten a cart because his basket was piled high with oranges, frozen vegetables, a six pack of beer, and bread on the bottom. When the majority tumbled to the ground, I quickly bent to pick them up, but he waved me off content to let them lie.

Thing was, the guy limped away...yes, by God, I said limped.

Dressed in khaki pants, leather boots, and a faded Sherpa jacket, he looked like any other Cincinnati male in the winter...just trying to keep warm. When he waved me away, I saw a tuft of dark blond hair stuffed under a gray toboggan.

Not knowing if it was destiny or something darker, I attempted to yell, but all that did was birth a coughing fit which made the woman nearby scramble for cover. Bending over the blood pressure machine, I realized I was in a quandary. I could calmly sit down and cuff myself in (probably the smartest choice), or I could rip the tab off the cough medicine, do the chug-a-lug, and run like the wind.

Reminding myself I was a verb, I tore the tab with my teeth, twisted the childproof plastic free, and slurped four burning gulps down.

After three steps, I coughed like a car with a bad muffler. Covering my mouth with an elbow, I carried the cough syrup in my hand, hacking my way toward a young girl—early twenties in a Kroger outfit—stocking a circular display with fruitcakes.

I asked, "Did you see where the guy with the limp went?"

The stock girl gave me her I-hate-fruitcake face. Deciding to jog straight ahead, I turned left at the International Foods aisle and spotted him. Sweet Baby Jesus, I saw the mysterious man with a limp. Hobbling at the end of the aisle, he headed for the freezer case holding frozen fish.

Stalking like a ninja with a sharp sword, I tried to be soundless— at the same time fighting the cough tickling my throat. While he talked on his phone, I hit up a sample station, advertising the guacamole of the day. Picking up a triangular blue corn chip, I glopped on guacamole, slam-dunking it in my mouth.

While he grabbed fish sticks from the bottom shelf, he barked, "It's your own fault, you fool. What do you expect *me* to do about it?"

I glanced at my watch, discovering I'd been in the store for almost twenty minutes. That was twenty minutes leaving Ben to sit idly, which if I was a guessing woman was not one of his strong suits.

When the limper muttered, "I'll be home in a few," I pumped my legs to a run and immediately regretted the decision. I seal-slipped on spilled prunes and hydroplaned about six feet on my belly. I hadn't really thought of my final demise, but I *did* know I didn't want it to be death-by-prunes. When I eventually righted myself, my situation didn't look much better. Goo was all over the bottom of my shoes, and I more or less swam in an oil slick.

Wouldn't you know it? I went down on all fours.

The noise must've been immense because the man startled like he'd seen a phantom, locked gazes with me, clicked off his phone, and hightailed it to the front for checkout. I yelled for him to stop, growling, "Ouija Board wacko," knowing that was probably un-PC in the Wiccan world. "Are you Brantley McCoy? How about Eric Young?"

Totally OTT, but in the crime business, sometimes I had to multitask.

"Angel!" I heard an angry voice roar. Blech. The British accent.

I ignored him. And I ignored him more when I realized he called me angel, even when he was angry. Weaving in and out of the glass, I crawled on all fours, ignoring the dirt and grime, trying to make it to the door. Somehow finding vertical, I juked my way in-and-out of the crowd. The more I ran, the faster he limped. One would think gym class would make me outmaneuver him, but unfortunately we'd rotated to a health segment, and I'd apparently gotten out of shape. A stitch developed in my side, and right when my peripheral vision caught a flopping white string, my other foot chose to trip over it.

My sense of humor was officially compromised...I looked stupid.

My chin bounced on the floor, and orthopedic shoes were at my head, some grandma's pink girdle blinding me at a ninety-degree angle. After five seconds of dumbstruck awe, Ben grabbed me by the scruff, picking me up with one hand. He threw me over his shoulder, his hands locked at my thighs in a fireman's hold. A fireman's hold, for Pete's sake. My butt was in the air, and if that wasn't degrading enough, one of his hands slid up to securely fasten overtop my behind. Oh, no. *No, no, no.* I was *not* his woman, and by goodness, I would *not* withstand cavemanish behavior from one more male in my life.

I struggled to move, screaming, "Let me down, Ben! Let me down!"

Ben, however, was like wrestling a rhino. His voice came out rough, angry, and maybe a little amused. "Angel," he murmured, "I'm disappointed in you. Next time invite *me*."

———

I'd yanked on two pairs of socks, long white underwear, and a black long-sleeved T-shirt with the words "And Then Satan Said, Put the Alphabet in Math." Still shivering, I'd added texting gloves. Begging Murphy to crank up the heat, all I received was a lecture about rising fuel prices and a suck-it-up face. While I waited for sleep to claim me, I got preoccupied counting Marjorie's coughs. Seven minutes apart, they sounded like a sputtering steamboat when she'd been given the maximum dosage.

The good times just kept a comin'.

My date with Ben didn't end with a goodnight kiss. Instead, I got a you guessed it...a lecture. Ugh, I attracted one type of guy. It might have been the worst mistake of my life, but I looked him right smack in those silver eyes and upchucked what I'd been doing. Coach's car (he knew that), The Ghost (he knew über little), raiding the Calypso Cove home (not a freaking clue), and discovering a skeleton while tripping over Nico Drake (he gave no reaction whatsoever...only stared). Shockingly, he found it intriguing. So if my goal was to push him away, I think I drew him closer.

I painted my toenails in OPI's Suzi Skis in the Pyrenees and watched a rerun of *Vampire Diaries*. Amidst the coughing and snoring, sleep played at my brain...but I needed to talk to Dylan. I missed his nightly SKYPE. He'd missed mine, and I felt the need to cement us back together. The thing with me, the sleepier I was, the more honest my answers became. Call me a hypocrite, but I wanted to know the deep dark secrets of his soul—I didn't necessarily want him to know mine.

Totally breaking the hard-to-get girl code, I punched in his speed dial. After four rings, he answered in a raspy voice, "Sweetheart, what time is it?"

Dylan had a sexy sleepy-voice, the kind that made you need birth control. I fanned my face. "It's thirty minutes past the time I'm supposed to turn into a pumpkin."

Dylan went with it, halfway giggling, "Sorry, Darc, I fell asleep. Are you okay?"

Not by a long shot. It was technically Monday morning, and I still hadn't garnered enough courage to ask him about his weekend-slash-probable date with Brynn-baby. Sunday dinner was a big deal to the Taylors. Even if it was business related, the fact she'd been on the invite-list was enough to make my blood boil.

Curling to my side, I blurted out, "Are we okay?"

A split second of silence. "Well, yeah, why wouldn't we be?"

Spit it out, Darcy. "I feel something is different between us, starting with Brynn Hathaway."

"...what?"

I repeated, "I want to know what's going on with you and Brynn. I've heard it from multiple sources, D, and before you get all high-and-mighty, the people were Justice and Collin himself."

Dylan rustled in the sheets, shifting positions. "Hold on, Darc. Let me wake up." A few seconds later, he murmured, "Exactly what is it I'm being accused of?"

"Here's how I feel, Dylan. You know what went down between us at Red's house. And we both know what would've happened if Farrah (dang her) wouldn't have interrupted. Imagine how I feel when I don't see you all weekend, only to find out you've spent it with Brynn two nights in a row. Then I've got that little voice in the back of my mind of Collin giving me a play-by-play of what regularly goes on between the two of you in class. A play-by-play corroborated by Brynn who Justice overheard bragging to her skank squad."

"And what exactly was *that*?" he predictably asked.

"The two of you were all over one another."

Dylan laughed sarcastically. "Sounds like something Collin would say, but to answer your question, Brynn and I were *not* all over one another."

If my condition didn't seem bad enough, hearing him say Brynn's name just shaved five years off my life. "I'm not sure I believe it," I said truthfully. "Remember, Brynn said it too. So you're asking me to believe both people are liars."

"And the flipside is that *I'm* a liar."

"The math doesn't add up," I kept saying.

"Nothing is going on," he repeated adamantly.

I heard it in his voice. He'd left chill and shot straight to PO'd.

"That's what I thought you'd say," I muttered. "So I'll be more specific. Did you hug her when she was upset?"

A sigh. "Yes."

Ouch. "Well, at least tell me what she got all teary-eyed over. I want to know the exact thing that caused you to put your arms around her and freaking squeeze."

Oh, boy, Darcy had gone straight to fifth gear. He let out a slow, sleepy, thoughtful sigh. "I wondered how long it would take before a version of this incident got back to you. And that's what it is, Darcy, a version. But other than being a story that's not *true*," he emphasized, "I find it extremely alarming you're talking to other people about our relationship other than me."

I snorted, deciding to do a full-court press. "Nice pump shot, Dylan. You still never answered. That must mean you don't trust me."

An even deeper sigh tumbled out. "I trust you more than anyone, and you know that." The little angel on my shoulder whispered in my ear I was a two-faced lying 'ho. "But to be clear," he answered, "Brynn said someone scared her with his advances."

"Collin?"

"No, although I hear he has problems of his own."

"Then who?" Another sigh. Only one person I knew could be relentless in the pursuit. "Jagger?"

"The one and only."

Heck, I didn't know where to go with the conversation, but my guess was she should've told her parents and let them handle it.

Brynn wasn't stupid, and her ulterior motive was bigger than the Cincinnati Bengals's desire to win a postseason game. But let me give you my two cents' worth. Jagger was a fastard, but he'd never force himself on anyone. At one time I believed he would, but I'd since changed my position.

"I call BS," I said, snorting again.

He didn't give his opinion one way or the other. "And that statement right there makes me wonder where my best friend went," he muttered.

"What's that mean?"

"It means we never had to wake one another in the middle of the night because we didn't trust the other. It means you used to know who Jagger Cane was and that you should be leery—"

"I judged him wrongly," I interrupted.

"Jagger," he said, snorting loudly.

"Yes. I know he's a fastard, and I'd never listen to him treat you badly, but there's good in there. I've felt it."

"Maybe you're judging Brynn wrongly too. Brynn and I've been friends for years, Darcy. It's almost inevitable that our relationship will be misunderstood."

Pretty weak argument. We'll see how that panned out. "So her modus operandi was completely innocent?" I asked, knowing the answer.

He answered too quickly for my liking. "Yes."

Excuse me while I pull on my waders. The bullcrap had piled all the way up to my butt. Laughing overly loud, I heard Murphy snort and roll to his side in the other room. "You seriously don't believe that, do you?"

He didn't answer.

The ambiguity between us dripped like water on a rock, slowly chipping away until a crevice formed that couldn't be repaired.

Dang you, Brynn Hathaway, dang you.

"This was a mistake," I whispered.

He paused and muttered, "I guess this is what it feels like for the best friend to suddenly become irrelevant."

Tears of anger choked me, closing my throat to the point of what felt like suffocation. "Irrelevant?" I sniveled. "How?"

"A conversation with your best friend should never feel like a mistake."

Dylan and I talked...about everything. Futures, the unexplainable, why bad things happened to good people. We had deep, meaningful conversations that remained between the two of us. And as teenagers, we talked about the good and bad we saw amongst our friends. Why some treated others badly and why some thought so little of themselves they allowed it—heck, why many ever appeared to enjoy the abuse. Dylan had always been my voice of reason. Who in the heck was I supposed to turn to if crap hit the fan? Especially since I feared he might be one of those guys.

I couldn't help it, but the tears came harder.

"You're that guy, D. The guy...you told me...to always...stay away from."

My tears came so fast, he must not have understood. "Darcy, I didn't hear you. Please, don't cry, honey. I can't stand to be the cause of your pain." I blew my nose and took a deep breath, wondering how in the world I could back gracefully out of the conversation. Unfortunately, Dylan wasn't through and the argument went into OT.

"Tell me why I couldn't get in touch with you tonight," he murmured.

You know what, right or wrong, I just said it. "I had a date with Ben Ryan."

Pause.

Longer pause.

Then Dylan commenced with a few, choice words, his temper rising to the danger zone. "You go out with Ben Ryan and then call *me* to ask what went down with Brynn Hathaway?"

True. I didn't have a right to call with that conversation, but sorry, folks. I wasn't always so noble.

When I didn't respond, he grunted, "Well, well, well...that might be the most sanctimonious—"

"Don't finish that sentence," I interrupted. "You're going to make me hate you."

His voice lowered. "I'm going to finish it, dammit, because I love you. And when you love someone, you step in when they're taking a wrong path. It frightens me you're even interested in him, Darcy. The guy hit you with his car and yet you can't stay away. You talk to him. I hear it in your voice. That scares *me* way more than Brynn should scare *you*."

"He didn't actually hit me, D. I stepped into traffic while I talked to you if I remember correctly."

"And already you're defending him. This is typical Darcy behavior. You want to talk, but you hold back on things you think someone doesn't want to hear or might incriminate you. You called *me*, so give it to me straight. How much does he mean to you?"

Heck, I barely knew him, and Brynn had psycho-stalked Dylan for years. "I don't know him that well, but Brynn likes you. You've even dated her. And that revelation only came after I backed you in a corner and you caved. So pardon me for being a little insecure with how you claim you feel about me."

Dylan's voice broke the sound barrier. "Well, let me reiterate what I told you regarding Brynn months ago. I care for her, but I care for you *more*. She was a stand-in, Darcy, and I'm not embarrassed to admit that to you or anyone else. You were always *there*," he suddenly whispered, "*there*...in the back of my mind. And the revelation I'd dated her would've come from me anyway. I don't like secrets with you. I never have, but don't think I didn't notice you tiptoed around the answer to Ryan as only you can do."

"What's that supposed to mean?"

"It means you called *me* yet you still won't show any of your cards. I swear to God, Darcy. I can't crack your code, and it's driving me insane."

"Then why do you put up with me?" I whispered.

"I put up with it because you're cute as hell, but you're the worst liar on the planet. And you've been lying to me a lot lately. Don't think I haven't been killing myself trying to figure out who and why someone bumped my damn car. Was it someone from my grandfather's world back after us, or was it *you*?" He paused, waiting for my reaction. Unfortunately, I gave him nothing but respirations. If I told him about Madison Flannery, it would make things worse. Trust me. I should've told earlier. "You're doing something, aren't you?" he said on an exhale. "But if I ask what you're doing, you'll lie. You'll look me straight in the face and fricking lie. You're lying about everything, so much that I know you're also hiding how you truly feel about *us*. It's all over your face, Darcy, and the other night it was all over your body. That's why I've put up with your little science experiment because I know it's going to blow up in your face...if it hasn't already."

The.

Freaking.

Nerve.

Just like that, angry Darcy was back in the driver's seat. "Did you hear that?" I seethed.

"No," he seethed just as deadly.

"That was me giving you the silent treatment."

His voice immediately went soft. Careful. As if he handled a treasured possession and feared one wrong move would make it crack. His concerns were legit, but by God, I wasn't a sure thing. Dylan was definitely gorgeous, but it was the kind of gorgeous that'd leave a girl begging at her knees. I couldn't chance breaking. I just couldn't.

"Don't hang up, sweetheart," he begged hoarsely. "My relationship with you trumps everything else. So what if the conversation took a dramatic turn? It's better to talk things out than hang up angry and not solve anything at all."

"Ah, for crying out loud, hang up the dang phone," a voice grumbled near me.

Murphy stumbled through the door, hair in Einsteinian disarray, right as I dabbed the tears from my eyes with a tissue. "Don't pick me up tomorrow," I whispered. "I've already made plans."

Dylan's voice was racked with grief. "Don't," he begged. "Don't hang up like this, *please. God, Darcy*, I'm half asleep."

I hung up anyway, wondering if we could declare our semi-relationship dead...it was close.

———

I hadn't slept with my father since I was nine. At that time, I did it for an entire embarrassing year. I made a deal with God if he'd help me make it over that hump of pain, I'd never do anything to immortally embarrass my father—i.e., things including mug shots, embarrassing press conferences, teenage pregnancies and such. The first two I'd probably negate before I saw twenty. But don't waste any breath on the last one, considering I'd just blown my relationship with Dylan all to heck and back.

I was curled into Murphy's chest, blubbering like a lovesick fool. "D-Dylan wants us to date one another, but I told him I needed to date other people first, just to be sure. Why I said that, I honestly don't know. All I know is there's a girl named B-Brynn Hathaway he's dated before, and I don't think a m-mmoose tranquilizer will slow her down."

Whooo...that felt better.

I wasn't sure it was understandable.

Murphy grew still beside me, and then after a few seconds grumbled something about young love, heart attacks, and too many hormones in today's cattle. "How do you know he's dated her before?" he asked. By the sound of grief in his voice, you'd think he was the one who just got dumped.

"He told me. And when they're together there's too much emo."

"What in the heck's an emo?"

"Emotions," I explained. "It's never good when girls look like their world is ending when their crush simply leaves the room." I sighed, feeling like an idiot I even had to spell things out. "Murphy, if you haven't noticed, Dylan is girls' locker room conversation."

"I can see that, but what I don't understand is why you're so upset if he said he'd like to date *you*."

"I'm not sure he'd be able to remain exclusive," I explained. "I've heard a few rumblings at school that something with Brynn might still be going on."

"Reliable sources?"

"I'm not sure." Ivy, no. Jagger, maybe. Collin, uh, why would he lie?

Murphy fell silent again, as though he didn't believe it. "Life is always best operated under the truth, kid. You know that."

Well, the truth and I'd had a lot of communication issues lately, so pardon me if I took a pass. "She's just so—"

"Pretty?" he interrupted softly.

"Crushing," I said and sniffled.

He snorted. "I doubt she's as crushing as you, and I think Dylan's already registered that."

I was a D-movie wannabe. My guess was Dylan hadn't registered *anything*.

My head buried in his sweatshirt, Murphy could barely understand my words amongst the tears, but he'd deciphered their meaning anyway. "I'm so sorry, kid."

I cried even harder because I expected him to issue his standard Dylan-would-never-do-that disclaimer. "He doesn't feel...safe for me...anymore," I cried.

Murphy kissed the top of my head. "You tell him that?"

"I tried, but it didn't...come out right. Why do I feel like something is ending?"

Chapter Twenty-Two

THE GREAT INQUISITION

The makeup call was an epic fail.

For the first time in modern history, I told Dylan to stick his BMW up his tail pipe, even though he phoned with the sweetest voice ever. Unfortunately, my unexpected stubborn streak banished me to the bus. My God, I hated Bus 150. It was like taking a tour through Nastyville and being asked to lick the street. I wasn't sure what my feelings were. Basically, I was numb but feared Dylan and Brynn would be Valley's new power couple by the end of the week.

Since Dylan and I were in an "off" period of our best friendship, I texted Finn, brother number two. Finn fortunately was back to driving the Kia Forte. His ex-girlfriend, Gucci Grayson, allegedly moved on with a yet-to-be-named senior and appeared to let bygones, be bygones. Anyway, he returned my text five minutes after I pressed send. We made small talk about what'd happened with Dylan, with him simply replying, "Sorry, luvie."

That was all it took for the tidal wave of tears to crash my weary body. I cried during breakfast, made-out with ice cream, battled a small heart attack, swallowed three TUMS, and cried some more. The problem with my life was too much testosterone. Needing an estrogen injection, I convinced Finn to pick up Rudi, Justice...and Bean. Bean phoned the day before, desperate to link up with Justice for the winter dance, Thursday night. A school dance was the last thing on my mind, but thinking of it made me wonder if Dylan already had plans.

Before my butt even got warm in the seat, Bean almost barfed up what went down with Jaws just to impress Justice. It was no secret I'd been trying to find out who vandalized Coach's car, but it was definitely a secret I'd been trying to unmask The Ghost. To save the day, my alter ego, Jester, grabbed the mic and maneuvered the conversation around to the photographs I stole from Coach's file—the photos I allowed them to believe I only confiscated because they held possible spray painters. I explained I needed to restore one of them (Coffee Blot Boy)—the deadline, yesterday. Finn felt confident he could do the job in his graphic arts class, chattering on how he needed a challenge.

Whatever, he'd recently been invited to join Mensa. My request seemed like small potatoes.

Bean begged for another assignment, so I commissioned him to talk-up Grumpy to Clementine Miriam Rabinowitz. I knew Grumpy said he'd go with Ivy, but it'd be a cold day in Hell before I'd sanction that union. I also gave Bean the list of people in detention for the past two years. His job was to see if they'd ever heard of Brantley McCoy, his past or present extracurricular activities. The story didn't end there with Bean though. When he figured out Finn was my brother, he pitched a hissy-fit until I "made" him and Mr. Pongo into the mob.

I'm serious. I now have a brother that's a dead gerbil.

What. The. Freak.

As for me, I'd closed the door on Damon once and for all—well, almost. Slapstick said he knew more than he'd let on, but I had no immediate direction where Damon was concerned. My guess was Damon would have to come looking for me before I knew what to do about him.

And maybe I'd inform Coach Wallace he might be Jojo's baby daddy. By no means would it be the prettiest of all reunions, but some secrets were made to get out.

"Let's get this out of the way," Justice said as soon as the business part of the conversation was over. "What's going on with Dylan?"

I would've preferred having the convo looking dead ahead, but

Rudi was seated beside her, and I'd always felt it rude to leave her out. Justice didn't always sign. Turning so Rudi could read my lips, I signed, "Our status has changed to complicated."

Justice's bass voice barked like a dog. "Yo' Darcy. You know I'm happy to ride in the sadmobile, but do not put me in the middle. I love both of you, and I'm afraid you're going to screw up something good." I found it strange Finn didn't join the great inquisition. Perhaps he thought he'd be intruding. Perhaps he didn't care.

Rudi, however, gave Justice that 'hos-over-bros look. But Justice was more male than female. She merely didn't have the gonads to prove it.

"You're the one who corroborated the story, Justice," I muttered. "A story you felt juicy enough to ruin my day with."

She twirled the end of her fuchsia weave, my heart beating double time. "This would be true," she said, "but I simply wanted you to know what was being said—even if I didn't believe it."

All I knew was if my heart didn't resume a better beat, I'd be shaking hands with Jesus (or his southern counterpart) before my time.

———

The tension between Dylan and me, whether real or manufactured in my own psyche, was doing me in. If I was a confident girl, I could brush the rumors of Brynn off (I wasn't). And if I filled out a bra the way she did, I wouldn't care (I didn't). Or if I was in AP math flexing my scholarly muscles and up in his, umm business, it wouldn't matter (eh, try again)...but I was Darcy Walker.

Darcy Walker was a psychological train wreck of Biblical proportions.

Readying to follow Rudi and Justice into the restroom, my plan was to make a mad dash to my locker and grab my things before The Dimples could slay me. Keeping my eyes glued to the floor, I sprinted in my new ankle boots (yes, I'd gone glam), opened the door, threw my things in, and grabbed my math book. When I pivoted to leave, I heard that deep baritone voice that always gave me bad-girl thoughts.

"Not so fast, sweetheart," he murmured. "My ride to school was horrible. I need you to kiss my broken heart and make it all better."

Oh, Lordy, did he have to talk that way?! Of course I wanted to kiss it—maybe even go to France—but someone needed to tell my eyes that ogling Dylan was the gateway to Hell...lined with sweaty bodies and self-regret.

I swear, I got so nervous my darn eye twitched.

Covering the twitchy fool, I reluctantly caught his grin and mentally sighed. He sported a new toffee-colored sweater that high-lighted a V-torso, revealing a nice contrast to his rich, amber eyes. His legs showcased his favorite dark jeans that hugged his too-taut behind. God. Hated. Me. No one could look at Dylan and come out sane.

He stalked forward, one muscled leg after muscled leg, stopping mere feet from me.

My.

Oh my, oh my.

He smelled like...SIN.

"Crawl on up in my personal space," he murmured, "and show me some love."

"I don't want in your personal space."

"Yeah, you do," he said and winked.

"No, I don't."

"Do."

"Don't." My God, I crawled up in his personal space while the smart part of my brain screamed I was an idiot. I then remembered I'd gone out with Ben...a date I might continue later...and realized I looked like a tease. If I genuinely would try and make a relationship outside of Dylan work, then I couldn't do that type of thing anymore. It wasn't fair, and frankly, I didn't like the way it made me feel.

My arms hung limp, just dangled at my sides like dead weight. The only muscles operating in my body were the ones in my nose. They did the chicken dance and the hoedown in between moans of pleasure and cheers of applause.

Like a moron, I played my cards. "You smell good."

I considered biting my tongue off...I honestly did.

A deep rumble originated in his chest and traveled straight through to mine. "Are you flirting with me? I'll let you in on a little secret, sweetheart. I'm a sure thing. You don't need to expend so much energy."

There he was...the incorrigible male whose flirt knew no bounds. I went inside my head to find a happy place—unfortunately, Dylan followed. "I missed you," he murmured and sighed.

"Quit flirting," I mumbled into his chest.

To make matters worse, he didn't even seem mad.

"I only flirt with you. Besides, you flirted with me first." Frankly, I couldn't comment on that with any validity or certainty. I might've been drooling. All I knew was rumor said Brynn seemed awfully happy these days. Here's to crossing my fingers she'd have an awful Christmas.

By the Grace of God, I came to myself and plucked imaginary stray hairs from my clothing. I wore a pair of tight, straight-leg jeans and a charcoal-colored turtleneck that cut off my air supply. It gave the illusion I had boobs the size of a breastfeeding mother. Okay, not really, but they looked bigger than the day before.

Dylan walked me back up against his locker and then took his left hand and casually ran it down my arm, lacing his fingers with mine. "You look gorgeous. Love the boots," he finished, slowly glancing down.

"I'm too tall," I whispered.

"All the closer to my mouth."

God. Help. Me. He leaned in and lightly brushed his lips against mine. Seriously, I was en fuego right then. He ran a warm breath across my jaw and down my neck. "How was your little science experiment? Did the date flame out?"

What? Ohhhhhh. Yeah. The science experiment. "W-w-wonderful," I stuttered in a lie.

He gave a slow blink. "Is that right?"

"R-right."

"Did you kiss him?"

My face instantly reddened. "None of your business!"

His grin widened. "Oh, it *is* my business, and I'd lay money it wasn't memorable or you wouldn't have called me."

"You're so cocky," I muttered.

The grin grew wider. "I prefer the word confident. All I know is if you would've kissed someone, you'd smell different, and you smell exactly the same."

"Maybe I don't kiss and tell," I said snorting.

"Sure you would. You don't have a private bone in your very cute, big mouth, sweetheart. And even if you *did* kiss him, which I highly doubt, it wasn't the stuff of legends." He took the time to throw his head back and laugh to himself. Jerk. Dylan could be such a jerk.

"What makes you think so?"

A small shrug. "I know you, Darcy. You're a passionate person. If you had this wonderful, nonexistent kiss," he said and grinned, "it would be written all over your face."

"And how do you know that?"

He smiled even deeper, dimples imploding. "That's what you'd be doing with me."

Dylan crawled inside my body with those words, placed his soul around my weary heart, and squeezed. I felt as naked as the day I was born. The fact he still had that effect on me ticked me off. I angrily blurted out, "Then why don't you kiss me and prove it?"

Dylan's face lost all emotion. Just poof, the flirting went bye-bye and was replaced with something so hotly erotic, I stumbled and banged my head against my open locker door. "I'm waiting until you beg," he answered.

My. Jaw. Dropped. That might've been the cockiest thing to ever come out of his mouth, and believe me, I'd heard a lot. "Don't hold your breath, Attila the Hun," I hissed.

He leaned in even further, his torso brushing up against mine. "Come on, Darc. Center your thoughts, and tell me what I want to hear," he said, complete with a wicked grin.

I was struck with the realization Dylan might not always be a good guy. Sadly, I liked it. *I'm begging!* I wanted to yell. Yet my brain wouldn't work. Heck, *nothing* worked. I think all the blood went straight to my mouth.

"This Saturday night is mine, Darcy," he murmured.

No! my pride screamed, but a silky, "Yes," oozed out of my mouth.

―――――

"Look, luvie," Finn murmured, depositing a glossy headshot of a young man in front of me. "I hope this means something because I literally used all of my extra-terrestrial skills to recreate it."

We were supposed to be quietly studying the reproductive system, but Finn, Grumpy, and I'd stolen into Coach's office—well, just because we could. Plus, I had full-intentions of replacing the file I'd stolen two weeks earlier.

Grumpy was relaxed in the black wingback, his hands thread behind his head, feet propped on the desk like he owned the place. I, however, was slumped forward, my legs spread wide, my head buried deep in my hands. I had white knuckles and the beginnings of an ulcer. That happened when I was the brains behind the operation...I carried the burden...I needed to delegate more.

"Look at it," Finn said again, crouched alongside me and gently lifting my chin. "The only thing I couldn't get was the address, but you've got a name. That's a starting place."

Pulling the restored photograph of Coffee Blot Boy to my eyes, I expected the worst—that he was yet another guy in the mix or not even in the mix at all—but was so stinking surprised it was like I'd been named *Playboy's* Playmate of the Year.

The individuals were the same, I gasped. The same as Motor Oil Hair from Rookie's and Red's photographs, and the same as Brantley McCoy's student ID photo in the detention file.

The same.

The same.

The freaking same.

I drew in a lungful of air. And another. Then coughed on both like I made out with cancer sticks every day. What in the heck should I do? I had a picture and a name, but if I told *anyone* I had a picture and a name, I'd have to admit to breaking quite a few laws. Top of them being obstructing justice, breaching school security, stealing confidential files, and probably ten more I didn't know the names for. Not to mention being the ringleader of a boatload of sin.

Licking my finger, I flipped open the file and replaced the coffee-stained original of Brantley McCoy, keeping Finn's copy for myself. Next, I spread its contents wide like a rainbow while both boys thumbed through the sheets, realizing we were looking at Valley's skid row.

Grumpy and I stared at one another processing the same things, wondering if we were in over our heads. My nervous giggle pretty much answered in the affirmative.

Finn slid into the black folding chair next to me, and after a few more beats of what the H, he finally stood up. "Am I supposed to corral Taylor for a while?" he asked. My word, Dylan would kill me, he'd kill Grumpy, and heck...he might just eat us.

Grumpy chuckled while I rocked back and forth, gnawing on my pinky nail. I briefly wondered if I was going mad. It was possible. The Walkers had some crazy people in the bloodline from what I'd been told. "We're not exactly on good terms," I whispered.

"So that'd be much appreciated," Grumpy completed for me.

Finn looked at me with one of those laughing frowns. A cornsilk colored tendril of hair had fallen from his ponytail, leaving him still overly masculine. No wonder Gucci went crazy. He was too beautiful to not look at yet masculine enough a girl would consider doing bad things. "What kind of spell did you cast on Taylor anyway, duckie? He was in a better mood, but here lately, I feel like it's a health hazard just to be near him."

Those words were all it took to spur a coughing fit. Finn pounded on my back while my nose ran like a spigot into my mouth. Afraid I'd infect him, Grumpy pulled his shirt up over his nose, shoving over a beat-up box of tissues probably from last year.

Once Finn felt comfortable I wouldn't drown in my snot, he strutted his long legs out of the office. It was Grumpy, me, and a percolating pot of hot coffee. I played waitress.

When I sat back down and blew into the Styrofoam container, it dawned on me we lounged in a man's office who rode around with "wanker" on his bumper. That was my original caper, and I'd all but abandoned it thinking ten grand was the answer to all of life's roadblocks. Not totally true, but the trail had gone cold, and the next step wasn't readily clear.

It was like Grumpy read my mind. "Listen, Walker," he said, blowing into his cup. "I remember you were after reward money for this guy called The Ghost. I'm assuming these photos have more to do with *him* than Coach's *car*. Am I correct?"

"That would be a ten-four."

"Well, do you have a plan?"

Hmmm, good question. I gave him a sheepish shrug. In another word, nope. Besides, if I had a plan, then I wouldn't be Darcy. I always performed better on an as-needed, in-demand basis.

You know...the interchanging verb.

"Just so you know, Taylor cornered me this morning and asked if you were up to anything bizarre. I held him off, Walker, but I can assure you that won't be for long."

Actions I could've predicted—but Dylan cared. Of that, I had no doubt, but a part of me still couldn't buy into his forever-after spiel. Deciding to worry about things later, I brought Grumpy up to speed regarding Mean Girl, Madison Flannery. Before school dismissed, I marched straight to the school office, trying to find out her schedule. Imagine my surprise when I discovered she withdrew from school via telephone. I mean, wow. Where did that leave me? When I told Grumpy she knew the Beemer had been hit—and I suspicioned Brantley McCoy was the driver—we both realized we needed to put our energies elsewhere.

"We need to shakedown Damon Whitehead, Grumpy."

A transistor radio sat on a bookshelf up against the wall. KISS 107 spun "Holly Jolly Christmas," which was like projectile vomiting Christmas joy in your face.

Grumpy looked like he stood in front of a stampede of wild horses. "Sure, Walker. I can shake Damon down, but that dance is Thursday night. I'm still stag."

Slumping down in his seat, his brown hair covered his eyes, and his orange sweatshirt had mostly faded to peach. The laces of his sneakers should be retired. I had my work cut out for me, but my guess was it would take a Benji to make him look presentable.

I'd run into Bean outside the bathroom, and he claimed Clementine was game for Grumpy to call (introducing Bean Anatoly, salesman of the year). I forced a grin, wanting someone to be happy. "By the way, Clementine is expecting a call."

Once in a blue moon, Grumpy broke into a smile that showed his teeth. Right then, I got the full-faced grin. He made some sort of kissy mwah sound with his lips, which I took as a thank you. "What about you?" he said, coming back down to earth.

I felt like I'd just given birth—without an epidural. Snagging the pencil on top of Coach's desk calendar, I drew a stick figure of Dylan with a donkey tail on Thursday's date. My guess was he had other plans. He said we were going out on Saturday...not Thursday.

Chapter Twenty-Three

THE REAL MCCOY

*R*ealizing I might need snakebite medicine, I punched the directions for BTCC into Jagger Cane's GPS system. I'd taken a creative route to my locker and then the parking lot, still not positive I wanted to run into Dylan. Let me rephrase, I always wanted to run into Dylan. Trouble was, I wasn't sure what I'd do when I found him. Smack him, kiss him, or burst into female tears and ruin my kickass reputation. Okay, I didn't have a kickass reputation, but Lord help me, I wanted one.

It wasn't like I'd left him high-and-dry, without a final word. I made up notes for the evening's basketball game in seventh period and stuffed them inside his locker door. The notes included average free-throw percentages, who tended to shoot twos or threes, and who had a tendency to foul out. I'd watched a video of the opposing team's last game on their school's website when I couldn't sleep. Shoot, that screamed of codependent behavior, but people like me kept shrinks in business.

When I had one leg and hip in Jagger's Mercedes SUV, Finn literally pulled me out of it by my hair, foaming at the mouth about ending Armageddon. I'd like to say we drove home silently, but Finn had diarrhea-mouth. "Are you stupid?" he bellowed. "He's such a bloody bugger, luvie. Don't you know what he's capable of?" He'd stop only to breathe and regroup, throwing in, "I'm not one to be a critic, but you're being wonky. There's no other word for it."

Remembering Dylan left my mouth en fuego hours earlier, I lightly ran my finger along my bottom lip and attempted an explanation. "To quote the immortal rants and ravings of Ivy Morrison, whatever is going on with Dylan and Brynn will definitely be getting a sequel. What's going on between them, Finn? Is it going to intensify? Is it possible to deep-six their fledgling feelings before they mature into something else? Because let me tell you something, Dylan was all over me this morning like a cheap suit, and I liked it. Me," I said, snorting in surprise, "but I didn't like it enough to become one of those girls who gets dumped on."

Wow, poetic.

My English teacher would be proud.

Finn's response was curt. "Quite flowery, luv, but I cannot answer that."

Cannot or will not?

Finn was *my* brother, but again he seemed to forget our brotherhood creed. Escorting me to the door, he shoved me inside, giving Murphy a downturned look like I deserved to be locked in a torture chamber.

Egads, my life stunk.

"You work your guardian angel overtime, kid," Murphy grumbled when I told him what Finn was angry about, "and I hope he's at least getting paid time and a half."

Still in reindeer pajamas but with a healthier glow, Marjorie laid on the floor of the study, half of her body underneath Murphy's desk, the other half outside playing with a naked Barbie.

"What if *he's* a *she*, Daddy? You can't say for sure if Darcy's guardian angel is a *he*," she said adamantly. My sister was a full-blown feminist at six years old. God only knew if she'd be burning her bra at seven.

Murphy mumbled to himself about going to church more as he dropped his weary body into his black leather chair, surrounded by a pile of bills two inches high. While he continued to lecture that he "had a good name" and to not "screw up the Walker lineage," I snagged the remote from his desk, switching on the small flatscreen TV mounted to the wall. Giving him a half-hearted, "I'm sorry," I flipped to a vintage Hong Kong Phooey cartoon. I thought of Hong Kong Phooey's superhero skills and how he was kind of like me—he never really had a plan. He sort of fell into the answer.

Straining to hear Hong Kong Phooey overtop Murphy's tirade about hidden cell phone charges, my iPhone jumped around in my jeans with a text. I downloaded a ringtone for texts the night before that sounded like gunshots. When it blasted at the highest setting with a *pop, pop, p-pop-pop-pop*, Murphy shook his head, praying, "Good Lord."

Pulling it out of my back pocket, I glanced at the number and slid into the navy leather chair in the corner. Ben Ryan's name popped up in the center of the screen.

How'd things go with Jojo? he texted.

Once again, that served as a reminder I had nothing for Coach Wallace. I fought a sigh. I'd failed him, and my investigational skills were second-rate at best.

Not guilty, I typed.

Sorry. What now? he asked.

My mind went on a walkabout. Taking a sip of Murphy's V8 Fruit Fusion, my next immediate move was Brantley McCoy. The Calypso Cove address—where I'd swear Vinnie fought him—we knew belonged to Bishop Fowler. I still had no answer why Fowler and McCoy apparently shared an address, and the man who could fill in the blank was on a slab in the morgue.

I typed, *I need whatever you can find on Brantley McCoy.*

Why?? Ben responded.

He's The Ghost.

THE IDENTITY THIEF? he returned in all-caps.

Yep.

Ben didn't respond right away. My guess was he'd changed his underwear or debated how many moral and penal codes he'd break by being associated with me. He'd helped me out with Jojo for some reason, and I never questioned it. And he'd obviously remembered that Tito and I were in partnership with The Ghost. So the big question was, why did he even care?

Maybe that was something I should worry about.

Murphy kicked my foot, jerking his chin toward my iPhone. "Who are you talking to, kid?"

"Ben Ryan," I said shrugging.

"The boy who hit you with his car," he clarified.

"The boy who hit me with his car," I echoed. "You know, the boy you said I could date."

"Well, you don't have time to think about boys. What you need to be thinking about is tomorrow, kid," he said, pointing an angry finger in my face. "You're going nowhere real fast, racking up quite a reputation for yourself. How about we make this the year where you get all As?"

Good God, he was serious.

Trying to look naïve and innocent, I gave Murphy my best I'll-give-it-a-shot face. He wasn't buying it...imagine that.

When the doorbell rang, Murphy leaned out of his chair and put two fingers through the window blinds, peering outside. "Dylan's here," he grunted and grinned. Immediately, my lips felt like an inferno. He should be dribbling all his cares away, but if he'd come back for some lip action, then maybe...

Murphy narrowed his eyes, giving me a look like he wasn't budging, so I trudged to the door and gazed through the peephole, eyeing Grumpy.

"Oh, God." I groaned, banging my head twice against the door. "I've died and gone to heck."

"Don't curse, kid," Murphy said from the study.

"I didn't. It just means Grumpy's here."

Grumpy'd sprained his ankle over the weekend and wasn't slotted to play. My guess was he'd been sent for the search and rescue. I opened the door, and when he smiled, I slammed it in his face.

He rang the bell again. "Kid, you're rude," Murphy mumbled. "Open the darn door."

Opening it again, when he smiled bigger, I slammed it even harder. "No dwarfs," I yelled.

Murphy pushed away from his desk, stepping overtop Marjorie, winding his hand around the knob, cracking the door wide. "My daughter has no manners," he murmured, chuckling deeply. "Come in, Jon."

Wearing a brace around his ankle, Grumpy lumbered across the hardwood floor, eyeballing Claudia who'd slumped onto the couch, her green and white muumuu scrunched up above her white slip.

"Si, Grumpy," she waved. Then on command, her eyes closed.

"What's wrong with Claudia?" he asked, scratching the back of his neck.

"She takes to the bed when she gets rid of a bad spirit," I said.

"Takes to the bed?" Grumpy asked.

"Kentucky talk for when she lies down, son," Murphy explained, as he went back to his chair. "Apparently, she's a little overtaxed. Must've encountered some bad ones."

Claudia occasionally cleansed the house of bad spirits. Sprinkling holy water, praying over each room, chanting Puerto Rican gibberish that made Murphy as nervous as a sinner in church. Marjorie would walk through the room, and she'd smile and say, "Angelo." I'd walk through the room, and she'd gasp, "El Diablo," and flick a dab of holy water at my forehead. No wonder the holiday season was confusing. My best friend was Catholic. My Puerto Rican nanny was a Catholic who performed exorcisms while my protestant father basically hid under the bed reciting the Ten Commandments. Then consider my aunt—whose favorite part of the Christmas story was the donkey in the "Little Drummer Boy"—the ass. Christmas was about hope and faith and goodwill toward men, but all I wanted to do was enjoy a coney hot dog with my rebellious, half-breed Jewish uncle during Hanukkah season.

That spelled stability in anyone's lexicon.

Grumpy laughed and said, "I bet she spends most of her time in your room." All on its own, my hand landed on the top of his head.

"Ouch!" he screamed, rubbing his crown. "Why did you smack me?"

"Blood is allowed to smack," I said shrugging.

Murphy raised a brow and shook his head. "You're so screwed up, kid."

"That's not all she is," Grumpy added.

Murphy took one last gander at the bills and marched to the kitchen to make dinner. He'd been hinting since morning he needed soul food. Whenever Murphy got his Kentucky on, that usually meant his world was falling apart. He'd surround himself with mashed potatoes, green beans, cornbread, and fried chicken or pork chops. Dessert would be fried apples or banana pudding with a midnight snack of cold, congealed leftovers.

I shivered at the thought of congealed anything.

Grumpy still wore the outfit he'd sported earlier at school. His hair had been combed...I think. Like Murphy's, it curled in humidity of any sort, and instead of it falling over both eyes, it only fell over his right. As he pushed it back, I was greeted with the scar in his brow from a headbutt gone awry with Finn. Clementine must see something that wasn't readily apparent to me—maybe it was his I-don't-care attitude. I knew he had a nice enough body. I'd seen him without a shirt numerous times. To only be sixteen years old, it was inflated nicely.

"Did you call her?" I asked, wondering why chests were on my mind.

Embarrassed, he glanced at Marjorie who was nothing but smiles. "I thought I'd wait until tonight," he whispered. "I didn't want to appear too desperate."

I sensed the whites of my eyes rolling automatically. Wasn't that what was wrong with relationships—the game playing? "Then why are you here, Grumpy?" I said, followed by a frown.

He groaned. "Taylor said I *had* to come and pick you up "

A nuance I'd expected...

I think I know every little nuance about Dylan at the moment, too, all the way down to the color of his socks (black, by the way). I was a stalker of the Wes Craven variety. And I may not have been a stalker in close proximity (I ditched him at lunch to sit with Bean), but I sure as heck was one from afar. To me, he bordered perfection, but in the blink of an eye, I saw Brynn...I saw Ivy...I saw the yet unnamed women over the years who'd vie to take him away from me. I didn't have the confidence to deal with that. In fact, I'd rather slit my wrists or have a sex change operation.

"Tell *Taylor*," I emphasized, "I'm spending the night at home. I've got a lot of things on my mind, and I need to rest my brain. Besides, I haven't eaten and Murphy's getting his Kentucky-on."

For a minute, Grumpy debated the Kentucky thing. He licked his lips and glanced down to Marjorie who gave him a thumbs up. Rubbing his jaw, he shook his head, finally protesting, "You can eat at the concession stand."

"I have absolutely no desire to watch the male species dribble a ball up and down the court and sweat all over the place in polyester clothing."

My word, I think I actually felt my nose grow.

Grumpy grinned...a process I would've thought anatomically impossible. "He said you'd say that, but I've been instructed to bring you anyway." I hated Dylan because he always knew beforehand what my arguments would be. "Come on, Walker," he begged. "Tip off is in an hour, and I don't want to deal with him if I'm not successful."

True. Dylan was like a pit bull on a bone when he wanted something. He'd lock on hard and not give up until he grounded you in one heck of a bloody fight.

Grumpy and I followed Murphy to the kitchen. He opened the refrigerator door and pulled out milk and eggs. "Things better between the two of you?" he said to me.

"They're better for Dylan, obviously."

Murphy chuckled. "Good to know he's not a grudge holder," he said. "Grudges are bad."

I laughed, and God love him, so did Grumpy. Everyone—and I mean the man five houses down—knew Murphy held grudges more than the people in the Middle East. Murphy shot Grumpy a frown that made his happies shrivel. "Do you drink?" he grunted.

"No," Grumpy said proudly.

"Smoke?"

"No."

"Seatbelt?" Murphy added.

"Every time."

"Insurance?"

"Yes."

"What carrier?"

"Nation's Best."

"Wrong answer," I said with a giggle. "They're a competitor."

"Sorry," Grumpy said quietly. "Not my call."

"Any tickets?" Murphy continued. Grumpy got silent. "Name the offense," Murphy demanded.

Grumpy sort of shrugged, sort of whispered, "Parking illegally." Murphy took the time to ponder as he cracked two eggs and poured them in a stainless steel bowl. He glanced to me, back to Grumpy, and then at the clock on the wall.

"I know she's ridden with you to your little vacation on The Island of Misfit Toys, so I suppose it's okay if she films a repeat. But listen, son. If something happens, I'll make you wish you died in the crash."

Okiedokie. Some welcome wagon.

Murphy took a step forward and towered overtop Grumpy's generous listing at six feet. "Five miles under the speed limit the entire way. Fathers have a way of finding out if you piss on their requests. Ask Dylan. I'm not someone you want angry."

Grumpy cleared his throat. Pretty sure he didn't need the details.

He waited the fifteen minutes it took me to change into a pair of tribal print leggings and an oversized white hoodie that had "Fighting Buffalo" in black capital letters. Our mascot was a buffalo, for God's sake. Half the time when something great happened, I didn't know whether to grunt, snort, or moo. The hoodie was Dylan's and had the number eleven embroidered over the heart. It seemed like something a girl would wear when she was in a relationship...um, we weren't a couple, but I wanted to be a face-rubber anyway (hello, Brynn Hathaway).

Whatever. Sometimes I felt like Dylan's community service project anyway.

Pulling my hair into a ponytail, I reapplied the trifecta of mascara, blush, and rolled on lipstick called Chastity Belt (no kidding). It was hot pink with shiny sparkles. It didn't particularly remind me of a celibate attitude. It reminded me of blinking lights and stripper poles. Afterward, I stepped into red and black Asics running shoes I kept on hand in case I ever became a serious runner.

My look wasn't complete until I was tatted up. Dylan's mother found a bunch of temporary tattoos she gave me for my birthday. I'd wear one on my face each game. Turning on the faucet, I ran the little white square back and forth under the water and then carefully stuck it to my cheek. After thirty seconds of pure nothing, I slowly lifted the paper and looked at a perfect number eleven.

After I slid my lucky hat on my head, I trudged downstairs

finding Vinnie (yes, I said Vinnie) playing naked Barbie's with Marjorie—in little girl voices. Marjorie's Barbie squeaked, "Love makes you desperate."

Vinnie grumbled, "Don't I know it, but the guy in *100 Proof Stud* is worth all the drama." Vinnie then produced an 8x10 glossy head-shot of himself, giving it to Marjorie with a grin.

I broke into giggles. Vinnie was a walking advertisement for his new movie, complete with a Fu Manchu mustache the spin-off must require. "Why are you here, V?"

"I'm feeling the Valley game."

Grumpy snagged a warm biscuit from the countertop, pitching another toward Vinnie's open hand. Grumpy took a big bite and gazed at my sweatshirt with a grin.

I shot him a warning glare as I pulled on my coat. "I hate him," I mumbled.

"Yeah, Taylor says he hates you too," Grumpy answered.

Piling into the Beemer, as usual the black leather interior was immaculately clean and still had that new smell going on. Grumpy immediately played with the new-fangled gadgets, as if it would increase his odds of owning a duplicate one day. Picking a country station, he warbled away about crying in his beer while I tried to still my mind. I read somewhere if you could still your mind, you'd find the answers you sought.

Dude, all I got was white noise.

Glancing at the console between the seats, unfortunately I noticed something that shattered my attempts. An ebony-colored hair clip lay nestled inside a cup holder. *My specific cup holder*, I should qualify. And the clip wasn't mine. Instantly my blood boiled, and just as fast, my anger flipped into an agonizing despair—if it wasn't mine—then whose was it?

While Grumpy continued to sing and Vinnie practiced lines for his movie, I clasped it between my fingers for a few miles. It was expensive. I could tell by its feel. My first desire was to roll down the window and toss it in Valley's gutter. But then I got hit with a better idea. In my brain, I knew my plans were the actions of an unstable girl in the throes of an unhealthy crush—but I didn't care. If it was Brynn's, how in the heck did it find its way out of her hair? *Passionate frenzy?* I gulped.

I wore one of those energy bracelets that supposedly emitted negative ions beneficial to your health. Pulling the red band from my wrist, I slid it over my fingers and dropped it in the exact spot where Brynn's probable hair clip had been. In other words, if I was a dog, I peed on her spot. When my ringing iPhone broke the mood, I fingered it out of my purse. The screen lit up for the second time that evening with Ben Ryan. Wow, Ben must be the pushy type.

When I said, "Hey," he grunted out, "Brantley McCoy," in greeting.

"Hello to you too, Ben," I said, laughing at his bad attitude.

I couldn't tell where Ben was or what he was doing. It sounded like multiple adults talking in the background of a high-energy meeting. "What are you up to, angel," he asked, "because suddenly I'm nervous. I don't get nervous often. In fact, I'm *never* nervous, and I don't like the feeling."

"Spill the beans, Ben."

"I have nothing to spill. And I tried."

Grumpy reached over and pinched my arm, twisting the flesh between two fingers. Ben Ryan, although none of them had ever met him personally, had made the naughty list of my bestie guy friends. They were overprotective and suspicious of our budding friendship—although the accident was my fault.

With that, I thumbed him off and finished the conversation via text.

I typed like a mad woman, sparing no detail. Telling him I feared Vinnie killed Brantley McCoy when we broke into Bishop Fowler's Calypso Cove address. The moment I typed my last word, Ben screamed in all caps:

BACK OUT OF THE EQUATION, CALL THE AUTHORITIES, AND TELL THEM WHAT YOU KNOW!

My word, he should know better than to use math lingo with me. After a few beats of the cat stealing my tongue, he then texted back:

I know you well enough to say you're going to do what you want to do. Be careful. I'll keep digging.

The resources at Ben's disposal began to gnaw away at me. Sure he said they came via his father, but our relationship was new. Too new for me to make a final assessment of him. I was either paranoid or maybe I needed to take a step back and figure out who and what exactly the guy was. Besides, the information he gleaned for me no doubt was a total misuse of government property, and ergo illegal.

Not that I was complaining...but why?

As fate would have it, Big Moby's Cheeseburger Shack was at the next light. Big Moby's was supposed to be the last venue Tito's source saw The Ghost. Thing was, I had no idea what I'd look for once inside. Sure, I had a face, but what would I do if I actually bumped *into* that face?

The verb in me, or idiot rather, considered that a minor issue.

"Grumpy, pull over," I asked, touching his arm. "I need to Moby up my life."

He would've dragged me behind the car if he could escape a murder indictment. He barked, "No, Walker. Taylor asked me to bring you, and this is his Beemer. I'm doing exactly as I was directed."

I laughed so loudly it was probably heard in the next town. "Dylan would pull over," I said.

"Dylan would *not* pull over."

"Dylan loves me, and he'd pull over."

"Dylan's probably wondering where we are."

"I could eat a burger," Vinnie piped up from the backseat.

I grinned with a plan percolating in my mind. "I'll make a deal with you, Grumpy. Pull over, and I promise to give you a makeover so fab that Clementine can't keep her hands off of you."

You know, there was someone for everybody, but the thought of kissing Grumpy was like sucking on a sourball...it'd have to be an acquired taste. After we stared at one another, he realized I wouldn't shut up and that he *needed* a fashion overhaul. His answer came in a grunt and a quick swerve into Big Moby's parking lot.

Slowing the engine, immediately he headed for the drive-thru. A logical choice, but the drive-thru line was as long as my list of sins. Besides, what would I see from a car anyway? It took some arm-twisting, but Grumpy agreed to pop inside for the burger I was quote-unquote "dying to have."

Finding an empty space between two dark-colored vans, he carefully maneuvered inside, saying out loud, "It better not get dinged."

Dropping my phone in my purse, I asked, "Did you speak to Damon Whitehead?"

"Damon hasn't returned my calls," he grunted, shutting off the engine. He slid his eyes over, full of questions. "I'm thinking he's scared to death."

Or guilty.

Once inside, we filed like cattle behind the only cashier line open. It was a four-person crew dressed in red shirts, black pants, with a smiling Moby over the heart. Not much older than me, the cashier was medium build, brown hair and eyed, and barely made eye contact—just a hand out for the money and a yell to the cook who appeared new to the job. He was fidgety and jumpy, and when I offered a smile, he hunkered over a beef patty and started flipping.

The same guy as last week manned the drive-thru, still appearing grossly underqualified for the task. He had fries, chicken nuggets, and burgers all lined up in a row, furrowing his brow, trying to figure out which brown bag to drop them in.

Big Moby's Cheeseburger Shack was one of those joints that if a drive-thru order wasn't straight off the assembly line, they'd ask the car to pull up to the curb where they'd deliver the special order. Big Moby was the burger express, so to speak.

As I ordered a Moby Meal, I stole a glance outside watching Moby deliver a meal to a female in a maroon Chevy Impala. Moby put his white-gloved hand into her rolled down window, and when they exchanged bills, he pulled a plastic Ziploc baggy out of his pants pocket full of what looked like dirt. On impulse, I pushed my way out of line, walked to the window, and made binoculars out of my hands, scrunching my eyes and nose up to the glass.

The female was hunched over her steering wheel in a black coat and baseball cap. Pulling the bag up to her eyes for inspection, she gave Moby a hurried nod.

It wasn't dirt, I told myself. *It was a bag of marijuana.*

Chapter Twenty-Four

CITIZEN'S ARREST

itizen's arrest, the angel cheered. *Let him be*. The little devil laughed. *He's making a living*.

I couldn't breathe. In fact, I was in danger of losing all bodily functions in my pants. Dodging a little boy carrying a tray, I hustled back to line, told Grumpy as fast as I could, to which he rolled his eyes totally unaffected. "Maybe it was spices, Walker," he grumbled, looking at his watch.

"I'm pretty sure it wasn't basil and oregano, Grumpy."

I'd seen marijuana. My grandfather lives in Kentucky. Kentucky people knew all about Mary Jane—even if they were clean—and then the knowledge was passed on through the placenta.

When Grumpy didn't give me anything more than an eye roll, Vinnie murmured, "You're so cute."

The nerve. I flipped them both off in my mind and yelled, "Big Moby's passing out drugs!"

A hush filled the room.

Those were fighting words amongst the parent crowd—especially when it was Kid's Eat Free Night. But no one made a move to apprehend, defend, or do anything. Heck, they didn't even look frustrated. They just stood there, wondering how their favorite clown had turned into a freaking felon.

It didn't take long for me to make the decision to get involved, and come hell or high water, Big Moby would go timber before sunup. Leaving Grumpy and Vinnie, I slammed my body in fifth gear, pushed the side door wide, and bounded outside under the security light. In unison, Big Moby and the young woman locked on me, mouths agape, faces shocked-out with that busted looked.

No lie, the female was Madison-I'm a beeyotch-Flannery.

The moron in me yelled self-righteously, "Citizen's arrest, citizen's arrest, I'm busting you for possession of a controlled substance."

Madison dropped the bag of weed and went from zero to sixty off the property. Big Moby snatched it up and immediately plopped it in his mouth. Then he came at me swinging all limbs like he'd lost his mind. He smacked me in the head with a Moby bag, and if that wasn't insulting enough, he squirted me in the face with his seltzer bottle.

When he took off running across the lot, at that moment I felt like a superhero. I dove at him—you heard right, dove at him—and took him out at the knees. Moby went down hard, me on top of him, and suddenly I was eating clown. Clown in my mouth, clown up my nose, clown in the beds of my fingernails. Moby and I rolled around the snow-filled pavement on old french fries, gum, and probably E. coli and the rotavirus, but the verb in me was going for the memorable.

Amidst the flailing of our arms and legs, the bag of pot plop, plop, plopped out of his mouth and bounced on the pavement. If pot came out of his mouth, I didn't dare think what'd come out of any other orifice. Big Moby was scum of the earth. I was positive he had no scruples.

"Cuff him, Grumpy!" I yelled.

Grumpy was in slow-mo at my heels, partly in shock, partly due to the fact he might just be a noun. Lord help me, I needed more verbs in my life, but I had to work with the tools I'd been given. "Cuff him?!" he screamed back. "I don't have any cuffs, Walker!"

True, but by God, improvise!

Moby wiggled out from underneath me, stumbling past a still shell-shocked Grumpy, heading straight for the drive-thru in a fit of panicked hysteria. Knocking over a red trashcan, he jumped up on the curb, placing his hand on the driver's side door of a green Jeep Cherokee. He yanked it wide, pulling a startled teenager out by the shirt. The boy went down hard, but Moby stepped over him, full intentions of taking off in his idling car.

I had a decision to make. I could call the police and give them a description of a clown, or I could dive onto the car and pray Moby pulled over. Without another thought, I dove spread eagle onto the hood, a whole lot of don't-die-a-virgin giving me flight. Big Moby cursed words so obscene I think my immediate consciousness blocked them out. I heard a B-word, a C-word, and an F-word that frankly made no sense. What I did make out was a laughing, "Ta-ta," and I knew innately he had plans for me eating the pavement. Swerving the car right then left, we'd traveled a good seventy-plus feet, neither of us giving up the fight. I glimpsed people peering out the windows, cheering me on or shaking their heads in disbelief. My right leg fell off the car when Moby hit the brakes, trying to jar me loose, but somehow I held on, staring into the face of a certifiable psychopath.

Moby and I had one of those moments. A moment where our eyes met and the bad in *him* met the trying-to-be-good in *me*. A sick, twisted smile lit up all that clown makeup, and I briefly said a prayer I'd make it to the Promised Land if things ended badly. Right then, I had a connect-the-dots moment. I recognized him—even through makeup, I recognized him as Brantley McCoy, the photo ID Finn had given me from the detention list.

"You're Brantley McCoy," I half whispered, half yelled. Moby grinned so big I didn't need him unmasked. Right when the small part of my brain told me I should've followed by car, Vinnie and Grumpy made the scene. One would think they would've arrived quicker, but all of it took place probably within thirty seconds. God help them, their reaction skills sucked. Vinnie lunged for Moby's door. He wrestled his way inside, punching and shoving as Grumpy opened the passenger side door and went for the emergency brake.

Trying my best to hang onto the windshield wipers, all at once it felt like the car ran full-force into a brick wall, six feet thick. I performed a backward roll down the hood, bounced arm and elbow first onto the front bumper, and launched about twelve feet back-ward like I had been shot out of a cannon. I landed on my left leg, hearing the knee of my leggings rip wide in protest, scuffing the skin with black, pebbled slush.

Then the inconceivable happened. Someone started snapping photographs. When Grumpy yelled, "What the h-e-double-l," Vinnie called up his thespian side. My God, he turned and offered up a red carpet smile for the camera, long enough for Big Moby to yank free and run for the hills, like a starving wolf on the scent of a bleeding squirrel.

We'd lost him...

———

"Madison Flannery, right?"

I nodded. "Yes, she recently withdrew from Valley High School, so I'm not sure where she is now."

"That's all I need for now," Officer Abbott concluded, flipping his notebook closed.

I was outraged. "But don't you want to hear my theory on the identity thief? I think this guy—"

The officer interrupted, cocking his head to one side. "You nabbed a drug dealer, kid. I didn't see evidence of identity theft anywhere. And frankly, the guy got away. I don't even have him to question."

When I belligerently pushed ahead, Vinnie stepped on my toe. As I glanced up into his dark brown eyes, his gaze went as hard as nails, giving me a nuh-uh look. That gaze said Moby was indeed the same guy he'd fought at Calypso Cove—like I'd suspicioned—who I knew in my gut to be Brantley McCoy. I'd learned to trust Vinnie. If he didn't think I needed to spill yet, then I wouldn't spill. I'd call Tito, have him work his magic, and pull the employment records for Big Moby. We'd shut that lowlife clown down before midnight.

———

Valley High School's one of the largest schools in the Greater Cincinnati Area. That could be good if someone wanted to hide, but if your aspirations were to make the school athletic teams, you'd better play like a professional or have pushy parents on the PTA.

Competition was fierce.

The place was packed like sardines in a can with dads living vicariously through their sons...others glancing at their watches, just doing time until they could get home and retire with the remote. The gymnasium had stadium seating and was fairly comfortable, but it smelled like a two-hundred-cow dairy farm and the emotions of a big rivalry.

The pep band finished "Let's Get it Started" by The Black Eyed Peas and segued to "Blow" by Ke$ha when we entered Buffalo Nation. It was halftime, the murmurings grumbled at a lower decibel, but the promise of verbal brawl tickled the air. It was like sitting in a beaker being boiled without any fluid inside. Everyone knew what would happen. It was only a matter of time before the explosion.

Athletes from both teams warmed up at their respective baskets doing layups and shooting threes readying for the next half. We'd missed the first two quarters because we were cleaning up society, and Grumpy was as nervous as a pizza boy who hadn't delivered the goods on time. Me, I still reeled from the fact I'd seen Brantley McCoy—I knew it deep in my soul—but I nursed a bad feeling he'd be coming for me.

Listening to sneakers squeak on the hardwood while I padded down the gray painted steps, my eyes landed on my best friend first...how could they not? Polyester was one of those fabrics if Nature gave someone extra bumps, bulges, or cottage cheese-like cellulite, it could be a fashion disaster. On the other hand, if the person was hard, chiseled, and mouth-wateringly perfect underneath? God bless polyester because it accentuated the positive. Dylan? He literally had the kind of body that'd make a girl walk right out of her clothes.

It was reality.

I didn't make the rules.

Dylan was also one of those players who'd always shine. Indisputably the best athlete Valley had ever seen, he dribbled effortlessly, making every attempt he threw up, rebounding others' shots, and turning and dunking the ball. More than likely he'd be a McDonald's All American again, and he could add that bullet to his résumé of Ohio's Mr. Football his sophomore and junior football seasons, plus AP and *USA Today* National Team honors as well. In the short run, that meant captain of the teams. In the long run, that said, Arrivederci, Darcyville; hello, college scholarship.

It sucked.

As Grumpy, Vinnie, and I squeezed into the student section, I put my thumb and index finger in my mouth in the shape of an "o" and blew hard. A high-pitched noise was born, loud enough to echo along the cinderblock walls. A few individuals jumped at the sound, but most chatted, ate popcorn, or tried to access free WI-FI on their cell phones.

Dylan slowed his dribble at half court, turning toward the noise.

One Mississippi...two Mississippi...

He met my grin with a knowing smirk.

Cupping my hands around my mouth, I yelled, "We performed a drug bust on the way over! Lights, sirens, the whole gig. I'm thinking the eleven o'clock news."

Dylan stopped mid-dribble, narrowing his eyes with one of those I-can't-hear-you faces. "What?!" he yelled.

I waved him off—more or less communicating I'd fill him in later—but Grumpy muscled his way down five rows, making drinks, popcorn, and some misplaced band instruments casualties of his mood. *Hey, watch out* and *What's your problem* were some of the minor phrases that followed. The others were so truck stop, I tried to think of baby bunnies.

Before anyone with half a brain could stop him, he furiously barreled out onto the floor headed straight for Dylan. I had a feeling he'd only replay the scary parts and leave out the fact we were successful, and in my world, that was all that mattered.

Grumpy may be a lot of things...but a coward wasn't one of them. When he was chest-to-chest with my slightly embarrassed best friend, he rammed his pointed finger in Dylan's face, shoving his car keys in his hand. "Don't *ever* ask me to pick Walker up, chauffeur her around, or pull her out of a ditch," I read his lips say. "I'm off-duty. Permanently. She's fricking nuts! She's cursed. She dove onto a fricking car, and Claudia took to the bed because of her!"

Dylan glanced at me, hovering outside the free-throw line, and I just shrugged. Unfortunately, Grumpy's words were a fairly accurate account of what'd happened. Placing the basketball under his left arm, Dylan crooked his finger, motioning for me to join him. All around, players took their last shots, some even venturing to the sideline to ride the bench and wait for the buzzer to go off. When I looked at the clock in the upper left hand corner, it said three minutes and thirty-nine seconds until the beep. Shaking my head no, I gestured there was no time as I tapped the watch on my wrist.

Dylan lowered his eyes, his voice nothing short of a bullhorn, yelling, "Darcy!"

What the heck, I thought. He pulled on the leash, and I usually trotted to his yard. Shuffling quietly past the broadcast desk, I met him half court. "Hello, sweetheart," was the first thing out of his mouth.

I greeted with a smiling, "I hate you."

"Naughty," he murmured, grinning with a wink. "That has potential."

A bead of sweat trickled down his temple, and suddenly my mouth was parched like the Mojave Desert. By goodness if we were alone, I might throw him down and lick it. "Darc, you and Bradshaw need to sit down," he murmured, lovingly squeezing my shoulder. "The game is about to start, and we'll begin the whole thing with a technical if you don't get off the floor." He glanced around, a deep frown marking his forehead. "We've been about to blow all night."

No kidding. I could feel the animosity. "*You* told *me* to come out here, D."

The question was, why did I do it?

He winked. "That I did, but I wanted to see you. What took you so long?"

"Drug bust," I said with a shrug.

Dylan assumed I was joking, giving me a good-one look.

"Come on, Grumpy," I said with a giggle. "Let's leave Dylan to live in his nice, little bubble world where everyone makes blankets for the homeless and obeys the law."

By that time, Vinnie had his large butt beside me, munching on a bag of popcorn I didn't remember him purchasing on the way in.

"Hey, Taylor," he murmured with a grin. "It's been an exciting night."

Dylan opened his mouth, but Grumpy drowned him out. "I'm

not going anywhere!" Grumpy barked. "Do you realize she caused Vinnie to pull someone out of a high-jacked car and tackle him to the ground? And when that happened, I dove into the passenger side and pulled the emergency brake so Vinnie wouldn't get dragged to death."

"Yeah," Vinnie agreed, tossing another popcorn in his mouth, "I forgot to thank you for that."

Dylan cleared his throat, rubbing his forehead so hard he had to have lost two layers of dermal flesh. "What happened?" he whispered.

"Nothing," I said shrugging.

"Nothing," he repeated.

Cue the mockingbird. I groaned. "We went inside to get a Moby burger, and I witnessed Moby drop a baggie full of marijuana into someone's meal. It got a little hairy, but I'll live."

Dylan didn't want any details, just ran his finger along the side of my jaw. "Are you sure you're good?"

"Peachy keen," I said, grinning like an idiot.

Grumpy groaned and actually punched Dylan in the shoulder. "Dear God, Taylor. Can't you ever see anything she does in a bad light? Ask her how she stopped the car." Grumpy gave me an I'm-telling-on-you look. The same one a kid brother gave to get the other sibling in trouble.

Dylan resumed a dribble that resembled a jackhammer, looking white as a ghost. "How?" he demanded.

I sort of coughed out, "I dove onto the hood and held on."

"While it was *moving*?" Dylan shrieked. "Sonova..." Yup, the B-word.

"Of course while it was moving," Grumpy said in a huff. "She's certifiable!"

Dylan immediately moved all of his attention to Vinnie. Vinnie was one of the few—and I mean *few*—that never flinched when Dylan was angry. In fact, it usually humored him, and he'd laugh in his face. "What exactly were you doing, Valentine, when she got into this situation?"

Vinnie's grin grew as he tossed more popcorn in his mouth. "I was signing autographs, man. The first fifteen minutes of my movie leaked online, and I've already got fans. I did my part. I hit him."

"Porno," I whispered, joking.

Dylan blinked, trying to process the "porno" part of the conversation. Grumpy screamed, "You almost killed him, Vinnie!"

Vinnie shrugged. So did I.

"So Moby's in jail?" Dylan asked, wanting immediate clarification.

All three of us wore our not-quite face. "No," I mumbled. "He got away when Vinnie smiled for the cameras."

"Cameras?" Dylan's mockingbird sang again.

"Fans," Vinnie said.

For a moment, I thought Dylan would kill all three of us. Turning to leave with a giggle, I bumped into a frazzled Coach Wallace. I'd meant to tell him about his baby daddy status, but every time I opened my mouth, I chickened out. Glancing over his shoulder, I saw a referee not far behind, thundering toward us with a whistle already in his mouth.

Uh-oh.

"Walker, sit your tail down. Make her sit down, Dylan," he fumed, turning toward him. "You need to sit down, too, because God knows this place is about to erupt."

I balled my fists. "I *tried* to sit down, but Grumpy wouldn't let me. He's mad about the drug bust when frankly I wonder about his sense of the common good."

"Drug bust?" Coach screamed. "Here?" The referee looked concerned.

"Big Moby's Cheeseburger Shack," Vinnie added.

"I ate there tonight," the referee added.

"Drive-thru?" I asked.

"Yes."

"Passing out marijuana," Grumpy grumbled.

"Scrawny-looking kid with dead eyes?" the referee said.

"No, he's just dumb. It was Big Moby," I answered.

The referee winced. "Ah, that's just wrong."

"Walker, you're the pied piper," Grumpy groaned. "You've delayed this game by five minutes. And the people who should be angry are standing here listening to you blow the stupid pipe we're all dumbly dancing to."

I embraced that as a compliment.

Still, I did my best imitation of a pied piper dance but stopped when it garnered a whistle from the visiting team. Dylan angrily turned, threatening the wolf-whistle thrower with a terrifying, heated glare. "Shut the freak up!" he seethed.

Only a moron wouldn't notice one particular guy had his eye targeted on Dylan. He'd probably been paired against him, and by the look at the twenty points we were ahead, his pride probably suffered from small gonads syndrome.

The referee patted me on the back with a smile. "Good story. My kids eat there all the time. Gosh, the world's going to pot, isn't it?"

"Literally," I mumbled, "but don't pat me on the back yet. He got away and so did the buyer. Who, by the way, was Madison Flannery."

"That doesn't surprise me," Coach Wallace muttered. "Everyone is giving the slip these days. Just like the guy who painted my car."

Dressed in a white shirt, black slacks, and tie, he ran his fingers through his overly teased hair. All that did was make it bunch up on one side like a balloon losing air. "I'm screwed here. It's Christmas, and I'm having my car repainted."

"I've got a few more days!" I eeked. "Don't give up on me yet!"

"Darc, why are your leggings ripped?" Dylan asked. Before I knew it, each dropped their gaze to my tribal leggings. Looking down, I saw a bloody blotch and sticky red substance oozing its way toward my ankle. Sure enough, a hole lay overtop one knee.

Dylan squatted down on the balls of his feet, lightly touching the area. "You're bleeding," he groaned.

"Wow, I didn't even feel it. Must've been when I fell off the car."

"Adrenaline," the referee explained.

"You mean when you bounced off the windshield and rolled off like an idiot," Grumpy clarified.

I stuck my tongue out at him. "I'm thinking bad words about you."

Dylan stood up, massaging his heart like it was a toothache.

Coach motioned frantically to the trainer. "Get over here, and see if this wound needs stitched," he said when he tromped over, "or we're going to lose Taylor from the game. Walker," he said, talking to me, "I don't even want to theorize on why you say and do the things you do. You're killing me, doll. You really are."

"Stitches would be cool," I said, adding my patented dumb grin.

The trainer pulled up my leggings and swabbed it down with a cotton ball full of a burning antiseptic. Just a nasty scrape. "Sit down, Walker," Coach requested.

"I'm sorry," I said, shrugging with a stupid grin. "My father's fundamentalist value system says I'm not allowed to leave until I've been excused."

Coach tried...no dice.

The referee tried...still no dice.

Vinnie made a weak attempt and Grumpy didn't try at all... instead threw a mental dagger at Dylan. Dylan threw his head back and let out a deep, rumbling laugh. His laugh came accompanied with that look...the buttery-eyed look that melted my heart into a sticky mass of love poems and embarrassing greeting cards. I sighed, and then I sighed even deeper, hugging his waist.

The hug was short-lived because Dylan got jumped by the opposing side.

———

Cue the Crack!

Drama.

Oh, Good God, there was nothing sweeter to watch than a fight in high school sports.

Ironically, the pep band transitioned into "Light 'em Up" by Fall Out Boy, and the two teams obliged. Both benches cleared, and while Dylan yelled for Vinnie to get me to safety, he wrestled someone off of him and took a shot to the jaw. That went on two more times, and I knew precisely what Dylan's pause was for. He'd been waiting until it was obvious to whoever reviewed the game tape he'd reacted merely in self-defense. No surprise, the ponkey who jumped him was the guy who'd given him the death stare moments earlier. By the gleam in Dylan's eye, he'd been itching for a chance at him too. Thing was, Dylan's southpaw was money. I'd never seen him hit anyone who didn't wind up having a glass jaw. After one punch, the guy landed facedown with a moan.

Fights had a rhythm to them. It was pound-pound-pound in the beginning, bystanders trying to break things up, some getting involved, and they'd either take one for the team or things would amplify to an even higher level.

While Dylan and frazzled parents separated players and d-bags from the bottom of the piles, Vinnie tucked me under his arm but caught the hook of some moron who unfortunately woke up Vinnie's beast.

He shoved me toward Grumpy.

Grumpy shoved me toward a stranger.

The stranger shoved me toward the stairs, and I glanced up to Brynn's horrified face and realized the time was right for me to get in on the action. She'd run up the stairs with the rest of the squad, but even in the brawl, her hands stayed clasped at her hips, perfect cheerleading posture for the captain, no less.

With bodies falling around me, I lifted my chin and strode over like I was the Queen of the Paris Catwalk. We met eyes and the world stood still. Confidently walking up eight steps, I took a hand from her hip and literally pried open her fingers and dropped the hair clip inside. Her eyes dropped down, gazing at the ebony barrette until she finally pieced it together like a complex puzzle. She pursed her pink lips into an angry line, and by the inflamed hue in her blue eyes, I'd been right. Oh! Snap!! She'd pulled on her beey-otch. Her eyes shot off laser beams, and she looked like she'd launched straight to atrial fib. When I opened my mouth—hoping God would fill it—I seethed in her face, "Don't pee in my spot ever again."

She gave me a la-di-fricking-daaa face.

Well, peace the heck out to you too, Brynn.

Evidently, I'd thrown the gauntlet.

———

Believe it or not, the game was finished under police guard. Totally off the hook and freaking awesome. After officials reviewed the game tape (a fifteen minute process), three players were ejected. Two from the opposing team and Jagger from ours...no shocker. Vinnie was given a warning—uh, Vinnie hadn't even jerseyed up.

Dylan had been spared, although that, in itself, nearly spurred another brawl when he resumed his position as point guard on the floor.

Talk about a nail-biting experience. Vinnie, Grumpy, and I caught the last half of play standing on the second floor balcony with Dylan's father, Colton. Vinnie was on his fourth hot dog. I was on my second, and Grumpy bit his nails like a dog attacking fleas—a habit I didn't know he possessed.

In the last few minutes, a brooding Collin Lockhart joined us— and gosh, what a Debbie Downer he was when he espoused his list of regrets with Brynn. "Would you like to go to the winter formal with me?" he flirted.

"Um, no," I responded.

"It'd be a great way to get back at everybody," he coaxed.

"Not interested in getting back at anyone," I answered. Not totally true, but Collin and I linking up merely to stick it to two other people sounded like wasted brainpower. Plus, I didn't necessarily want to see Dylan with someone else. Remember, he asked me to keep Saturday night open. There'd been no mention of Thursday or Friday.

The game was tied up until Dylan shot a three-pointer at the buzzer to win. The crowd went wild, and the band went ballistic with the ultimate face-rubbing song, Steam's "Kiss Him Goodbye." People rushed on the floor like a pack of dogs fighting over fresh meat. For a moment, Dylan disappeared into the rush, only to reappear seconds later with Brynn and man-hands, Trudi Hatchett, hanging all over him.

Both girls wore six-inch, white skirts and matching turtlenecks that could honestly fit a Polly Pocket doll. I mean, really. They were practically naked. Brynn was extra effervescent...gag. With black VHS letters bouncing on a chest that defied gravity, she jumped up, winding her legs around Dylan's waist, riding him like a carnival ride. I swear, if I had a gun, I'd shoot her in the skirt. Dylan's eyes flew wide, and his face flushed to pink. I would've thought that impossible with his dark skin, but the embarrassment washed over him like a drizzling rain. Murphy claimed there was a time in a guy's life where he enjoyed the sorts of shenanigans Brynn readily aspired to...even if they'd been raised to be above it. I hoped Dylan's time had come and gone right under my nose. With a nervous chuckle, he gently put her down, discarding her like a finicky mouse would a stale piece of bread.

Uh-oh, Brynn didn't like that.

In fact, she held her chin high and let out a big *humpf* when the rebuff was noticed by Ivy who laughed loudly and said, "Omigosh!"

I would've sworn Brynn would be embarrassed. Heck, *I* was embarrassed for her, but I think she was the type beyond mortification. She seemed merely frustrated, formulating her next plan of attack. Dylan? I couldn't tell what Dylan thought. He'd moved on to accepting congratulatory hugs from teammates and parents, but when Brynn circled again like a buzzard, he wound up giving her one of those side hugs anyway.

I actually heard myself say, "I hate him." And a part of me did.

I was content with watching the show from the second floor, but Grumpy dragged me out onto the hardwood, making a beeline for Clementine. Evidently, he subscribed to the in-person type of invitations and didn't wimp out by phone or even wimpier, by text. That was the second time Grumpy had impressed during the evening, and by Clementine's bounce into his arms, apparently she'd been impressed too.

Suddenly, I was embarrassed I had Dylan's number on my sweaty face. In fact, I think I lost a couple of inches on my stature because I felt myself shrink away to nothing. Perhaps Dylan felt my unease because overtop the masses congregating midcourt, he desperately looked for my face, winking a flirty smile when he found me. "Come here, sweetheart," he murmured.

Dylan held both arms wide, wiggling his fingers for me to crawl inside. I rolled my eyes and started backing my way out. I was desperate, but by gosh, I wasn't *that* desperate. Besides, Brynn had her claws sunk in his jersey, and I had no intentions of hugging her bouncy boobs.

"That wasn't a request, Darcy," he said, throwing his head back with a laugh.

Brynn acted like someone had stabbed her. She jerked and gave Dylan a cold, hard stare, angrily mouthing words I couldn't make out. All that was missing from the tantrum was Brynn lying face down, pounding her fists and feet into the floor. With a jaw dropped so low she could've tripped on it, she flipped her ponytail in the air and stalked off toward her parents who didn't appear a bit fazed by her behavior.

Dylan didn't seem bothered by what she'd said because next thing I knew, he bellowed out a, "Darcy!" so loudly anyone who knew me gave me a you're-in-trouble look. Letting out a resigned sigh, I crammed myself inside the crowd and tried to find my hutzpah when I wrapped my arms around his waist. My brain screamed that was girlfriend behavior from someone who was merely the best friend. I knew to stop, but my arms couldn't heed the command. I loved him. I hated him. It was a mind-bending, twisting road of psychological warfare.

Dylan's chest rumbled as he engulfed me with his entire frame, murmuring his standard, "I missed you." His shirt was soaked with a salty perspiration, yet I stood there hugging him, wondering how to reverse the hands of time to where it was only the two of us. With a quiet kiss on the top of my head, he said, "Talk to me, sweetheart. I can tell something is troubling you."

"The day didn't go as I'd planned," I answered. And Brynn-I've got a movie star's name-Hathaway just made it worse.

Chapter Twenty-Five

THE LOW ROAD

*A*nswers were nowhere to be found...and it wasn't for a lack of looking.

I'd phoned Evelyn Seacrest from Coach's office earlier, on Wednesday, the plan to straight up ask if I could speak with Eric Young. Unfortunately, the phone rang non-stop—not even an answering machine. Add the sudden disappearances of Slapstick, Damon, and Madison, and it felt like everyone placed a double order of let's-mess-with-Darcy. Bean even performed the job I'd asked him to—he'd contacted not one, but all of the people on the detention list, and none had heard of Brantley McCoy. Odd...which meant McCoy had either been sentenced to detention and never went or they were scared poopless of his memory.

So here was what I was looking at.

Big Moby was missing.

Big Moby was probably Brantley McCoy-slash-the identity thief.

And Eric Young might've spray painted Coach's car. And why did I think that? Because Heaven help me, no one else had come forward, and I would've heard already.

Justice had brought Rudi and me to school since a mandatory basketball team meeting had been called due to Monday night's brawl, called by the athletic director. It seemed we made the national news—Go Bison!—and he wasn't too happy about the exposure. Whatevvs...he should be more proud the boys didn't lie down and take it.

For once, I was glad for the emotional reprieve. Dylan had been my ride each day since Monday night's game, and Brynn had phoned both mornings on the way to school. He never answered her calls... not one of them. *I* did, however, since I took that as a stab at me. Especially when she sweetly thanked me for returning her hair barrette—the one she'd left in the Beemer. Brynn. Aboveboard. That was a new tactic. Here's the thing. Dylan had already told me he'd given her and her mother a ride when he passed them and their family Jag broken down on the side of the road. And although he volunteered before I even asked, I'd thrown the gauntlet with Brynn. I wouldn't let her one-up me. So I gritted, "Glad to help," through my teeth and gave Dylan's knee a soft I-trust-you squeeze. Seriously, it was out of character, but I decided to go for it.

Thing was, if I thought Ivy was a helium head, Brynn was like sucking nitrous oxide. Her emotional depth was as shallow as a spring mud puddle. I found myself stifling laughter from her juvenile bent on the world or nodding off to sleep as she described her new designer shoes—size six, of course. I'd always thought if I tried to figure out whether dating someone was worth the emotional investment, the first questions I'd ask were, *What's your political party? Do you like animals? How do you feel about the working woman?* And by gosh, *Do you believe in aliens?*

For me, that last one was a deal breaker.

Thing was, Brynn was like a bad cold I couldn't shake. She'd be back to drain me again tomorrow.

Once inside VHS, I opened locker twelve and shrugged out of my coat, hanging my purse and backpack on the hook in the back. Snagging my math book, I took an OCD moment to align the books on the shelf and alphabetize what I'd haphazardly left in a mess: math, health, career development, science, government, Spanish IV, and English literature. One would think I'd be basking in the land of almost-caught-criminal Euphoriaville, but I felt like a pressure cooker about to blow.

You see, I'd even phoned Tito like I'd planned (three times), left a lengthy message about what happened with Big Moby and

Madison Flannery (still three times), and even told him I'd consider getting together to talk (yup, three times).

What did I get?

Not even a returned call.

With a heavy sigh, I spun around to see Rudi in full-on cry mode, her shoulders quaking with tremors. Since I'd told her what'd happened with Big Moby on Monday night, she'd daily nipped at my heels like a dog that didn't want me to leave. "Don't worry about anything, Rudi. I know what I'm doing," I assured her. Thing was, I was a work-in-progress...in every sense of the word.

Rudi tried her best to stop the tears before they melted her mascara, finally giving up and removing her fogged glasses. *You're all I've got*, she mouthed. My word, she'd recycled Murphy's standard line.

Diving on her with a full-bodied hug, I'd always considered myself observant to those around me. I made phone calls, sent cards, and even held hands when a friend was dumped or wanted the opportunity just to get dumped. But at the moment, I felt like a self-centered schmuck. I'd been so wrapped up with trying to score a ten grand reward and five hundred big ones from Coach Wallace that I'd missed something going on in Rudi's life. As I pulled back to wipe a thumb across her cheeks, I locked my eyes on hers, speaking slowly so she could read my lips. "What's wrong?" I asked.

"I'll tell you what's wrong," someone sneered. "The both of you are blocking the hall with your disgusting display of togetherness." When I pivoted around, Rudi followed as we fell into the gaze of Ivy who opened the locker fate happened to park right across from mine. As usual, Ivy was Barbie-doll sublime, but she'd mixed it up and bypassed her standard snow-bunny white. A tiny orange sweater skimmed her navel and a black skirt hung so low and tight, sitting down would be like viewing the San Andreas Fault. Anyone behind her would get a geography lesson.

Immediately intimidated, Rudi's shoulders hunched and she mouthed a, *Sorry*.

Ivy rolled her eyes, opening her locker. She carelessly threw her things inside, not concerned her white purse alone cost in the high three figures. Why should that surprise me? She toyed with feelings the exact same way or worse. Once she pulled out her books, she turned so Rudi could read her lips.

She mockingly made an attempt at slow-mo conversation. "What-ev-er, but you might want to re-ap-ply that make-up."

My blood instantly boiled. Rudi lived in a trailer park. For all I knew, her makeup came from magazine samples. My normal MO would be to ignore her barbs and secretly cry in private—even throw in a sneer that accomplished absolutely nothing—but I felt differently when it applied to someone else's honor. I'd almost fought the girl before, but Dylan broke it up.

Well, guess what, he wasn't here, and I decided to unleash all my crazy.

For the record, I wasn't dressed for fighting. I'd actually made an effort—shocking on a million different levels. I'd parted my hair down the middle and used a curling wand with a trifecta of cosmetics. Wearing dark-washed, straight-legged Hollister jeans, I'd zipped my black spiky boots on, topping the ensemble with a skin-tight, white turtleneck sweater. If I started to lose O2, I could stomp her to death, I suppose. In my ears were the pièce de résistance—tiny pierced crosses dropped from a gold post, dangling at half an inch. Here's to hoping Jesus would lend me some butt-kicking skills or at least forgive my step into redneck.

No lie, I had an out-of-body experience. I watched myself elbow inside a scrambling crowd that had grown to frantic pace. There were roughly ten minutes before classes started, and for me, math was all the way on the opposite end of the hall. I didn't give a flying flip about pi and his little friends or the fact that being late meant a trip to AP Unger's office.

The way I saw it, that shiz was ON.

"Shut up, Ivy!" I hissed. "You remind me of one of those yappy, little dogs that bark so much they make the dog lovers want to kick them. Well, guess what? I've got my dog-kickers on, and since Rudi's too upset to fight for herself, then *I'm* going to." Jeez, that sounded so Kentuckyesque Murphy would be proud.

Ivy lowered her head. "*You're* going to," she repeated.

"That's right," I said, nodding like a fool, "and I'm going to start by telling you that orange washes you out. So you might want to skip first period and go home and change. Find some pants, too, because those look like they could fit my little sister who has a better butt than you."

Take that, Ivy Morrison. Crap, what was next? Should I slap her in the face? Punch her in the ovaries? Wait for her to smack me first?

Maybe I was thinking too much...

It was hard to hear anything above my own anger, yet the moment my finger poked her in the chest, Ivy backed me up against the wall, her hand steeling around a chunk of my hair. Her blue eyes went hard as diamonds, and the necklace dangling from her neck was...Hello Kitty. Hello Kitty, for God's sake!! No way in the world did Hello Kitty want the association.

My eyes told her, *I hope you burn in Hell.*

Ivy's eyes flashed, *Not before I send you first.*

I was more of a lover than a fighter, but I was determined to not allow it to be another bullet for my *Darcy's Such a Spineless Dweeb List.* It had been said heroes rise to the occasion when no one else will. I glanced around, and all I saw were dropped jaws, and Justice running full sprint half a hall away. I knew she came as backup, but I might be dead by then because Ivy's face went Wicked Witch of the West. Rudi tried to help, but Trudi Hatchett—who I referred to as Brynn's lapdog—pushed her out of the way, circling us with wannabe members of the skank squad. When Rudi fell to the floor on all fours, my hero gene kicked in, and I went *Call of the Wild* on Ivy.

I reared back, and...

Justice took us out in a tackle.

FOILED AGAIN...ERRRRGH.

Justice had literally run through me to get to Ivy, gearing into beeyotch smackdown mode. Collapsing into a side roll, I took out a guy and his stack of books, staggered up, and landed right on a couple of girls who played soccer. Their mouths were agape— watching Justice and Ivy roll around like pigs in fresh mud. Justice had some savagely powerful karate moves in her arsenal, but the fight here?

Alllll girrrrll.

They slapped, kicked, screamed, cursed, and before I could say, *For God's sake, fight like men,* I dove into the middle and started yanking whatever object I could get my hands on. I grabbed hair, a foot, maybe a boob, but someone ripped my ankle boot off in the scuffle, and some guy behind squealed, "Girl on girl action! Shiiiiiiii—"

Next thing I knew, cell phones went paparazzi and started snapping pics.

The three of us moved in tandem, like a snowball going downhill and gaining speed. While Ivy smacked anyone near, Justice cold-cocked Ivy's jaw. I ripped her shirt, yanked Hello Kitty from her neck, and God help us all, Justice's weave was in the palm of my hand.

Sweet Lord Jesus, how would I live that one down?

When Justice delivered one last whomping whack to Ivy's face, she pulled me up, thinking our message had been delivered. Thing was, my knee gave out, and when I stumbled to recover, I caught my heel on Justice's jeans and spilled flat on the tile, looking right up Ivy's skirt. Oh, goody. I'd gone *Star Trek*, boldly going where every man had gone before—or was that phrase where no man had gone before? Before I could correct my TV trivia, Ivy was on top of me again, Justice followed, and the three of us sprawled again on the floor like a bag of marbles.

"Darcy! What the…" someone bellowed, and when I say bellowed, I mean the whole foundation had to have crumbled.

An arm went around my waist, lifting me off the floor in one fell swoop. "Settle, *Jersey Shore*," he growled.

I literally ran in air. My options were to pull the person with me or gnaw my arm off, continuing the pursuit. But the person was so strong it was game-over for Darcy. And there was only one person I knew…

"What?!" I barked, craning to see his gorgeous face. That was said with supreme catty, righteous indignation. Now I didn't normally possess supreme catty, righteous indignation, so I was dang proud of myself. "That high road thing," I growled back. "That's the old Darcy. The new Darcy—"

"Takes the low road," he interrupted. Dylan literally had me tucked up under his left arm, me dangling like a football. When I tried to wriggle free, I was rewarded with an even deadlier, "Settle."

My eyes landed on Jagger who'd split the crowd across from us.

We got another "What the...?" from him, but like Dylan, there was too much shock and awe to add the profane ending.

"They were trying to kill me!" Ivy screeched at the top of her lungs when Jagger took her by the hand and helped her up.

I snorted. "Wow, narcissistic *and* crazy. Winning combo."

"Shut up, Darcy," Ivy yelled. "I'll make sure to get you first." I gazed at her with an evil laugh, giving her a promises-promises look. That was where I normally turned the other cheek. With Ivy, I'd run out of them.

Justice scooped her fuchsia hair over her shoulder, pausing to pick up the weave I'd smartly left on the floor. "Bring it on, beey-otch," she said, chuckling in her bass voice. "That threat is as fake as yo' boobs." All eyes glued to Ivy's chest. I'll be the first to admit I didn't make a habit of looking at Ivy's boobs, but they did look a little more boobified than normal. "And next time, I won't fight your style," Justice taunted, laughing in her face. "If you mess with my friends again, I'll go dojo on you, and you'll never speak again."

"Yeah," I added, "what she said."

Dylan's chest silently bounced up and down when I said that, like he fought a laugh. All I knew was I hit Ivy Morrison, and IT FELT GOOOOOOOD.

"Cane," Dylan murmured. "Take Ivy and handle things. Neither of us want this to go any further, yeah?"

Dressed in dark jeans and a red sweater, Jagger appeared emotionless: no flirtatious smile, no suggestive wink, no promise to impress the wow out of me if I'd let him have his way. I met his eyes, still running in the air like a moron, but he had zero time for me. His gaze shifted to Rudi with an intense and vested interest.

See, I told you...

Jagger had good in him. Question was, was it the majority clawing its way out? Or the minority choking on its last breath?

With one nod toward Dylan, Jagger placed my shoe in my hand and grabbed Ivy by the elbow, leading her sniveling, cursing butt away.

Dylan gently set me down, and I tugged on my boot. Problem was, I was so pumped up I couldn't stand still. We were in trouble. There was no way around it. Our school had a zero-tolerance policy, and even though Ivy pulled my hair first, Justice and I finished it. My victory deflated a little, but honestly, not by much.

She'd had it coming since the dawn of time.

Dylan dragged a hand through his hair. "Tell me you're okay," he murmured. "I just caught the tail end of that, but it was enough to need a portable crash-cart."

This was what my brain was thinking...

I hope you get zits. Like a dozen of them in all of the most prominent places.

Only then could I find a backbone. With his jet-black hair styled on the left side, he was wearing his black VHS letterman jacket, red and white Asics, and well-worn jeans probably outlawed in the state of Utah. Something just as delicious was hidden underneath the jacket, but when the outside looked that good, who the heck cared?

Dylan's eyes spilled unspoken emotions as Rudi and Justice smooshed us together like PB&J. Wrapping my arms around his waist, per usual, it didn't matter we were in a public place, log-jamming the hall. We were just Dylan and Darcy. I melted into him, placing my nose and lips into his neck. When his thumb brushed underneath my sweater, my breath caught, I recovered, and when he did it again, I shivered a little.

Make me a 'ho was the first thing that came to mind, but "*Mmmmm,*" actually made it out of my mouth.

He murmured in my ear, "That's right, sweetheart. There'll always be something bigger between us than a disagreement or anything we could ever explain. Now if you ask me nicely, I'll take you to the dance."

Huh, wasn't that a shift in dialogue.

We hadn't talked about the winter formal, and I didn't know whether to feel offended or relieved. To be honest, it was the first thing that popped in my mind when my feet hit the floor that morning. Well, after *I need coffee.*

"It is truly with a heavy heart I must inform you *that* will never happen," I said, giggling and sidling even closer.

Not having a clue how, suddenly I was backed flush up against my locker, the silver metal handle biting into my backbone. Dylan still had one hand around my waist...the other hand spread wide against the locker up by my head, as though he held up something that threatened to crash down around us.

"You mean everything to me," he murmured, leaning his forehead into mine.

My idiocy spoke for me. "Yeah," it said, "me too." My God, I was a moron.

"Did you miss me this morning?"

My lack of pride answered as I gripped the sides of his jacket, wondering why I wanted to unzip him and...well, explore. "Desperately," it whispered.

Dylan was a naughty boy because I swear he said, "Go with me," in my ear a little more breathily than required. My kneecaps started sweating—wasn't sure what that meant—but I knew it'd probably make Murphy and my health teacher mad.

"You're a really bad person," I told him. Dylan's chuckle vibrated low in his throat, realizing exactly what he'd done as the hand around my waist was then halfway up my shirt. "Do you realize your hand is up my shirt?" I asked.

"I'm aware of that," he murmured.

"You might give me cooties."

"Maybe I'm in the mood to share."

"Stop," I half-heartedly demanded. "I can't think when you do that. Besides, this puts the last in last minute."

Dylan pulled me tighter with an even deeper chuckle. "Why don't you try that answer again, sweetheart? You want this, and I want this. And yes, this may feel like last minute, but I honestly hoped you would've asked *me*."

A million whoas and hold-ons looped in my brain, but I couldn't seem to muster the required energy to execute the sounds. It was like a marionette began to operate my mouth. "Will you take me to the winter formal tonight?" I asked.

The jerk breathed again in my ear, that time at a temperature resembling an erupting volcano. "I'd be honored, sweetheart," he murmured, "and preface that with the caveat that if you'll be good —and cut the *Jersey Shore* routine—I'll take you to dinner."

"You always take me to dinner."

"This time will be different."

"How?"

"I'll kiss you goodnight." Yowza. I didn't do anything except stare at his mouth. "Cat got your tongue?" he said and chuckled. I think the cat ate my tongue, to be truthful. "I'll pick you up at six, take you to dinner, we can dance the night away, and do whatever... comes naturally," he whispered out on an exhale.

I swear, I wanted to crawl inside his body, walk around, and figure out his hold on me once and for all. But at the end of the day, I was Darcy Walker. The Darcy who wanted to *try* to be in control even if it was a big stinking impossibility. Gently pressing my cheek to his, I pulled back—careful not to break contact—and slowly maneuvered my lips across his mouth, breathing heavily the whole way, ending only when my lips rested above his opposite ear. "Yeah," I breathed back. "That sounds about right."

Dylan's voice caught, like he'd been deep-sea diving and his tank ran out of oxygen. "You're evil-incarnate," he struggled out in a chuckle.

Whatever headway I made, I then threw in an embarrassing and totally transparent, "My God, you smell incredible."

Why was I obsessed with the way he smelled?

Dylan giggled like a little girl—high-pitched and unexpectedly humored. "Soap, sweetheart, but I'll tell my mother you approve."

Valley had one of those warning bells to alert students when they were within minutes of reaching tardy status. It blared with an ear piercing shrill, the stuff nightmares were made of if you hated the textbook and pencil gig. Dylan peeled my hands from his jacket, propping me up against the locker and casually checking his TAG Heuer like he had nothing better to do.

"What did you do to me?" I asked, shaking my head.

"I restored the balance of power."

"More like tipping the scales if you asked me," I mumbled to myself.

Sometimes I hated Dylan, especially when he exploited my feelings to get what he wanted. But wasn't that the question? What exactly did he want from me anyway? While I tried to not pant like a dog, my stomach flippity-flopped into my spine with the realization of what we'd just done.

It sounded like a real date with real flirting that actually meant something...not just Dylan being Dylan.

Chapter Twenty-Six

WINTER WONDERLAND

"*J*ester, it's Jaws. Listen, babe. I called in quite a few favors because I was concerned about you. This ghost guy, he's sick. My contact has an address for him, but Jester, I want to go with you." Big breath. "I'm not sure what your goal is here. To put him in jail, get back what was stolen, or if you intend to cut the head off the snake. If your intent is to do the latter, then I definitely insist on going. Either scenario, do not go unless you're accompanied by me." An even deeper breath. "Listen, babe. I'll call when I can do this but just so you know, I can count on one hand the number of people who know what I look like. That's how serious this is. Don't make me deliver a postmortem lecture in the morgue—because let me make myself clear. He likes to kill."

Dead air.

I didn't know what was more disturbing. The message itself or the fact Jaws felt I was capable of cutting the head off the snake. Whatever the case, it sounded like the break I'd been hoping for.

Can you just say, *HOLLAAAAA?!*

If I would joystick the situation, then two things could be accomplished: I could nab The Ghost, and by goodness, I could paint a face to Jaws. For the time being, I decided to pull on my teenager and wait until Jaws contacted me again. Pulling on my teenager didn't exactly leave me as fired up as Jaws's message, however. In fact, I was Wednesday's child...the depressing kid full of woe.

After I woke from a power nap, I jumped into a cold shower at five o'clock. I squeezed on Bath & Body Works Dark Kiss and let the stream of soap slough down my body all the way to the drain. As though it washed away all of my self-deprecating, self-conscious, and let's be real—self-imploding tendencies.

I'd turned in my science project, all but convinced my efforts deserved a Nobel Prize. Vinnie helped film the night before, the dramatic climax having me pull Mr. Himmel's egg out of a peanut jar, totally uncracked and pristine. When I fired up my laptop to show Mr. Himmel, his face went all kinds of psycho. Wouldn't you know he'd be allergic to flipping peanuts? I swore on a stack of Bibles I had zero clue. I think he bought it, but I'd never know until grade cards went "live." Anyway, the YouTube video had gone viral, and watchers were LOLing all over the comment thread.

The day was...crap to the max.

A huge blow to the school's female population, the place was abuzz that Dylan was taking me to the winter formal. I hadn't said a word. Dylan was the big-mouthed town crier. Girls either high-fived me or brushed me off so badly one would think I had head lice. But why didn't I want to go? Was it his Good Samaritan gig to close out the year? He had a tendency to go all soldier with that "never leave a man behind" creed, and maybe he felt he'd be leaving me in his wake. Even if his heart desperately wanted something—and it would inevitably hurt me—I think he'd deny his own happiness to keep me smiling.

Perhaps that was why I had difficulty placing the two of us in a dating category. Oftentimes life with him was a tease. Flirt one day, the next best buds. But it didn't feel like a tease. The intense turmoil, unending questions, and scary desire lit him up inside the same as me, rattling our foundation and upsetting what we considered norm. The one thing I knew about Dylan was that he wasn't the type to lie—I just didn't know if I wanted or could accept his truth, no matter how small or massive the consequence.

I camped in the shower for fifteen minutes, trying to dial down my I'm-so-nervous thing. Once sufficiently pruned, I toweled off and slid into a white terrycloth robe. Next, I applied blush and a light pink lipstick, swiping my lashes twice with black waterproof mascara. Digging around in my cosmetics bag, I found eye shadow in a gray duo and lit up my eyes.

Finding some Chemical Romance on my iPhone, a quarter-sized dab of mousse went to my cowlick, and I blew my hair out straight. I pulled on black hipsters and my new Miracle Bra. I rummaged through my closet, hoping my clothes would speak to me. It amazed me once the word date was applied to an event, I automatically thought twice about what I'd normally wear. Dylan and I had been hanging out for years. Since the evening would be something different, I felt inept to make even the smallest of decisions. Should I go slutty? Sophisticated? What kind of girl did Dylan go for anyway? I ultimately decided to go regular chick and give my new leggings a whirl, along with the fuzzy black Hanukkah sweater that hit me at the hips. Once I stepped into my black leather ankle boots, I slid the open-heart dangly earrings in my ears. Sigh. Let's be honest. I wasn't *Best in Show*, but it was the best Darcy I could come up with.

Oy. Vey.

The clock said five fifty-nine when a frizzy-haired Marjorie cut through the door and jumped into Dylan's arms. One look at him and I temporarily went to Badgirlville. I felt giddy, like right-before-you-walk-down-the-aisle kind of giddy. My emotions were all over the place—from the jitters, to out-and-out fear, to the thank-you-Gods that Dylan decided to be dumb for the evening. Garbed in black slacks and a cashmere sweater, Dylan was a canvas of perfection all the way down to his Italian loafers. His long limbs moved with confidence, bringing along a well-formed chest and flat abs. His hair lay in a sophisticated side part, showcasing a strong brow and cheekbones. My hands ached to slide through each tendril and freaking pull. Seriously, the guy's body really kicked-A.

Sweat instantly beaded under my nose, and I did a quick dip of my head to wipe it on my wrist. Point blank, I wasn't supposed to dress up for my best friend, date my best friend, anything with my best friend other than whine about how much my life sucked. It was totally ridic, and I didn't know whether to punch him or kiss him.

"D, you look beautiful," I whispered when I glanced up.

Carrying Marjorie along with him, Dylan neared me in a slow-motioned strut, and I would've sworn the Earth had moved. "I think that's my line," he murmured, "but thank you. You're still," he paused with emotion, "the most beautiful thing I've ever seen."

He'd been smoking crack.

Or at least marijuana.

Dylan's face did one of those round-the-world gazes where he checked out every inch of my body, starting at the head, going to the toes, and slowly rising up my front to wink when he caught my eye. I coughed. I couldn't help it, but he gave me a coughing fit like I suffered from a fatal case of pertussis.

His face went totally wicked...in a good way.

As Dylan hauled me into their hug, I went as still as water and got the strange sensation times like these would be few and far between.

———

Murphy had given the green light to go, but that didn't mean he wouldn't go all twenty questions at the eleventh hour. "So this is a date-date," he grumbled.

"A date-date," I told him as Dylan helped me into my long black coat. "And don't act like Dylan didn't ask your permission because I know he did."

Murphy's smiled quirked up at one corner, sliding an eyeball over to Dylan. "Number eleven, kid," he then said to me. "Don't forget the eleventh commandment."

I answered, "The eleventh commandment is thou shalt do as Darcy says." My standard line I gave anyone who balked at doing my underhanded work.

Murphy grunted, "Well, then it's twelve. Number twelve is thou shalt keep thy clothes on at all times. Am I speaking a language you understand, son?" Once again, that eyeball grabbed Dylan's gaze and went straight to his groin. I swear, my eyes followed, and then both of us were staring at Dylan's happies.

Dylan didn't even blink. Only nodded his head.

I frowned. "Did you dispense this speech to Ben when he phoned?"

Dylan shifted uncomfortably to my left. Murphy narrowed his milk-chocolate eyes at his reaction, and once again leveled a lethal stare at him, instead of me. "Maybe I didn't feel there was a need."

At that, Dylan grinned.

"You might not want to think about Dylan and me alone, Murphy, if your heart's a little iffy," I joked, throwing a big bear hug around Dylan. Dylan put a fist over his mouth, choking back a cough.

"Dear God," Murphy grunted, glancing to the ceiling for help. "Let me think about this. I don't want you to be in the dark where the natural male and female urges are concerned, kid. So if we address this dating and feelings thing head on, then that means you won't be so, um..."

"—frustrated," I added.

"—when you're alone," he finished. "And you'll—"

"—keep my clothes on," I interrupted jokingly.

"—because we've had this talk and everything isn't so forbidden." Murphy scratched the back of his neck, hemming and hawing at his pancake batter. Dylan continued to cough, shifting uncomfortably, pinching my lower back so I would cry uncle.

"Gosh, I feel better," I said, giggling at his attempt at a serious talk.

"Me too. Glad we had this discussion," Murphy grunted. And once again, Murphy concluded uncomfortable conversations before they ever had any substance to them.

Murphy hunched over a stack of pancakes when we left, grumbling about the sinking economy, informing Dylan to keep me on a short leash. Murphy was a little more dark and broody than normal, dressed in pajamas earlier than decorum deemed acceptable. And he'd definitely picked up on the fact our date-date was different, telling me twice he'd have his cell phone on at all times.

A little over an hour later, Dylan and I'd finished a Mexican meal at a new place—Mexican Food Whore was my middle name. Stuffed to the gills, we pulled into the school parking lot. It didn't feel like a date. It felt normal. But then again, Dylan always paid for my meal, always opened my door, and we always held hands wherever we went.

Our norm was different than everyone else's definition.

Finn phoned around twenty minutes earlier, wondering where

we were, telling us the place was a "sweat-box and packed to the rafters with dirty-dancing fools."

Dylan's naughty response, "Sweat sounds nice."

I wasn't exactly sure the origins of his words, but his naughty grin told me it meant corruption.

The sky sparkled with blinking stars, and the cool night air was the kind that made people snuggle closer to those they loved. Dylan hooked his arm around my waist, drawing me into his warmth as we walked up the steps, going inside.

Directly in front of us was a placard broadcasting "Pictures," pointing toward the cafeteria. A long line had already formed with people dressed similar to me and others dressed like I'd be their hired-help. After Dylan checked us in at the welcome desk, he pushed the gymnasium doors wide.

The room was darker than a cave, lit only by the many disco balls hanging from the ceiling. They'd nailed the winter wonderland theme and added some major mood ambience. Powdered snow had been strewn across the floor and different types of live fir trees were scattered throughout. Hand-made wooden reindeer pulled a red metal sleigh on the second floor catwalk. In the upper right corner sat a small concession area, and if the rumor mill got it right, an eggnog fountain was the main attraction. Altogether, it felt cozy and intimate. All that was missing was a bearskin rug and raging fire.

One set of bleachers had been pushed back against the wall, making room for two floors of dancing. Finn said we'd find him on the second floor, so Dylan took my hand, meticulously cutting a path through the crowd. It struck me again how our behavior seemed date-like but still our everyday norm. We'd been holding hands since we were six, and all these years later we'd never stopped.

Ivy and Jagger stomped past us like they were putting out a fire. And the GF didn't look too happy. I glanced at her. She glared at me, and we had a rare meeting of the minds. We both acknowledged we hated the other. On my part, I'd had the last laugh. By the end of the day, a dancing GIF had circulated of her, Justice, and me rolling around on the floor, our heads superimposed with Wonder Woman (Justice), Super Girl (me), and Osama Bin Laden as Ivy. Sometimes karma got it right.

Dylan murmured in my ear, "Forget them, sweetheart. Let's dance."

Umm, good idea.

The music roared as loud as a jet plane, and the DJ spun Lady Gaga's "Applause." Coming up behind me, Dylan wrapped his left arm around my waist, swaying us back and forth to the beat. Reaching back, I clasped my hand at the base of his neck, relaxing my cheek next to his. *This feels right.* I sighed to myself. And although I'd arrived sans confidence, I was determined to remember it when insecurity chipped away at our bond.

All at once, he twirled us over to Grumpy and Clementine who danced by Finn. Clementine moved with the pep of a cheerleader. Grumpy had the rhythm of a white boy too dumb to know he sucked. In the twenty or so seconds we'd been beside them, he'd bumped her head twice and stepped on a foot.

I promised him a makeover before the party that, with my meager budget, consisted of gifting him with a pile of Murphy's skinny clothes and floating him a loan for McDonald's (you know, spare no expense). He'd left my home in a white button-down oxford, navy sweater, khaki trousers, and brown tie-ups. I gelled his hair in hopes to find a style consistent with the decade, but it ended up looking like a Chia pet. So I 86'd the idea, and finally trimmed two inches. Then I shaved his neck. I nearly threw up twice because it took two disposable razors to bush hog what belonged on a yak.

A look to my right revealed Rudi, Justice, and Bean (yes, I said Bean). Rudi looked normal, Justice danced the robot, and Bean was...well, Bean was twerking. You heard right. He'd gone Miley Cyrus. His and Justice's hands occasionally touched, like they'd come to the party together—or at least had plans to leave that way. Rudi was decked-out similar to me. Justice had dressed like a warrior-ninja princess in black parachute pants and a flowy blouse. Bean and Mr. Pongo brandished matching red velvet suits that'd make Elvis Presley proud. When Justice's back turned in a whirl, Bean caught my eye giving me a thumbs up as if he'd landed the woman of his dreams.

That was one story that would not wait until tomorrow.

A glance to my left showed Finn and Gucci. Gucci sported black leather and too much gold. She wasn't exactly Hell's Angel's material, but she definitely rocked the biker babe look. Grumpy boogied next to them, right then playing tonsil hockey with Clementine while they moved. Both his hands tangled in her dark hair, and Clementine lifted his shirt out of his belt, wadding it between her hands. Then...he devoured her mouth like Weight Watchers members did carbs on cheat day.

"Check out Grumpy," I whispered to Dylan, blushing for the both of them.

Dylan glanced over his shoulder with a little girl giggle. "Bradshaw looks like a happy man."

I wasn't positive what Grumpy looked like, but he made me feel like a creepy voyeur. Predictably, he ruined the love and togetherness moment by grunting, "Clementine, no matter what happens here tonight, I want you to know I'm disease free."

Yup. That was what he said.

Heard it myself.

My lusty truck driver laugh sprang to life. "He probably should've told her that before he took her to France," I said, laughing in Dylan's ear.

Dylan did his little girl giggle again. "I swear, Darc, your naughty laugh can be so obscene."

The music went old-school, segueing to a Marvin Gaye song. Nothin' said lovin' like Marvin Gaye. But the song choice of "Let's Get it On" left me stifling another laugh. My guess was the song was snuck onto the DJ's playlist unbeknownst to faculty.

Dylan drew me into his chest and took my right hand in his, holding it against his heart. In that moment, we reminded me of my mother and father. It didn't matter the occasion, if my father wanted to dance, he'd wrap my mother in his arms. Murphy, by nature, was uptight and edgy, but with Gemma Walker, he was as relaxed as his DNA would allow. I thought about her at dinner. I would've loved for my mother to be alive—just a simple word of advice would've been treasured. But no matter how hard I tried, I couldn't will-back the hands of time.

"I choked," I whispered. Dylan knew immediately I referred to the deal I'd made with Coach Wallace.

He kissed my hair, resting his chin on my head. "Aw, sweetheart. Darcy Walker is capable of great things. Don't ever doubt that."

Dylan could be a motivational speaker. But great things? I was one breath away from the sanitarium.

"I try and try and never get anywhere. It's so frustrating."

"Let's rehash the details. I'll call Coach and get you an extension."

"The trail dried up days ago. I just wanted to buy something nice for my family and friends. I already had your gift picked out, D. Maybe I'm greedy. The universe doesn't like greedy."

"No, you're a businesswoman. Take the pressure off yourself. Don't even think about me."

"No," I replied.

Another kiss to my head. "I don't want to offend you, but can I at least float you a loan?"

"No loan," I said, shaking my head and sighing.

I stood where every girl in the room wanted to be standing. And P.S., what precisely had I done to warrant the privilege? A lasting friendship? Dylan pulled me a little tighter, and when I glanced up to his amber eyes, they'd melted into liquid gold. Falling into their depths, my eyes grew bedroomy, and I gulped down some unexpected desire.

His voice lowered as he ground his fingertips into my lower back. "I believe in you," he murmured. "How about we get out of here in a bit. Just the two of us, some place private."

Stare. Stare harder. Then triple it up with one more for good measure.

Sweet Jesus, that was romantic. Stop my beating heart. He pirouetted me around, holding our joined hands over my head, allowing the concept to jell into place. The sadist in me would give her left lung to go some place private—I didn't need the time to jell. "Omigosh," I surprisingly whispered, "there really is a God."

Dylan chuckled low in his throat, his muscular neck begging to be touched. There was no time for return banter because several feet over, Finn was the victim of another guy's fists. After one sucker punch, Finn slid across the floor like a bowling ball taking down pins. In light gray trousers and a white silk shirt unbuttoned to his chest, he looked like he belonged in New York, not sweeping up the floor of the gym. After two headshakes, Finn came up swinging at holy heck...Damon Whitehead?

So I was guessing Damon was Gucci's formerly new and right then ex-boyfriend?

Um, that made as much sense as everything else that'd happened lately.

Dylan finally came to himself and cursed a few choice words, launching into I've-got-your-back mode. He took off running like Moses parting the Red Sea, but before he made it to them, Slapstick Wilson entered the fray. "I told you, Damon!" he roared, big fists flexed at his sides. "This is not the place!"

Let me say again...that whole scenario made zero sense.

Damon never struck me as the boyfriend type. Especially with someone as trendy and cute as Gucci. But what did I know? I was pretty sure Dylan had some stupid in him since he'd brought *me*. Slapstick quickly muscled Finn out of the way and jumped a nicely dressed Damon before he could even say boo. The noise sounded like the crack of two rams colliding in an open field. Grunts, screams, and guttural groans accompanied each of Slapstick's punches, but despite getting pounded to a pulp, Damon remained intent on having his piece of Finn. As Finn one-legged it up to stand, Damon pulled him by the other leg, and Finn collapsed back on the bottom of the pile. Finn got off a couple of shots, but by that time, Dylan—flanked by Grumpy and me—arrived and dove into the middle, pulling Finn out by his shoulders. Slapstick slugged away on Damon and then circled his neck with a strength that lifted him off the ground. After what seemed like forever, he threw him one-handed across the floor, shattering the eggnog fountain (bummer) and jumping on top again to finish what he'd started.

Sweet Jesus, it wasn't over.

Twenty feet ahead, huddled between friends, Brynn elbowed to the fracas dressed in black stockings, boots to the knee, and an über expensive-looking, long-sleeved LBD. Thing was, her little black dress looked like it'd been shrunk on high heat in the dryer. Hugging her curves like a stock car took the Daytona 500, anything meant to be bouncy was bouncy, and anything meant to be taut was taut. Suddenly, I became awkwardly aware my Miracle Bra needed to be retired. Either that or I needed to triple-up on the voodoo cream and deal with the resulting chest hair.

Brynn quickly clicked over to Dylan's side in her Louboutins and begged (yes, I said *begged*) him to corral Slapstick. You see, I *knew* Dylan. Even though he probably wanted Damon's head bashed in like a pumpkin, if he could keep Slapstick from a temporary insanity defense, he'd do his civic duty. Plus, his hero complex had probably kicked in, and he'd want the honor of silencing Damon himself.

And let me add as a side note, *Where the heck are the chaperones?*

"D," I whispered. "Do it. He's a good guy."

Dylan gave me a BRB face and ponied up and grabbed Slapstick by the shoulders, the plan to throw him to the side. When he got his hands on him, Slapstick barely conceded an inch. Dylan got a look like he'd witnessed Jesus Christ splitting the sky. He wasn't used to not dropping someone on impact, but Slapstick was like a wrecking ball. Taking out anything and anyone near him. With an annoyed frown lining his jaw, Dylan grabbed Slapstick once more and got his legs into the toss. With more determination, he lifted him up and thrust him ten feet away. Slapstick's embittered breath came out in a wheeze.

Damon crawled off into the crowd.

What did I think of Damon's fighting skills?

Snore.

Slapstick's?

What freaking planet did he come from? Krypton?

While Dylan had done his thing, I couldn't miss Brynn's reaction. If he was a new car, let's just say she contemplated the test drive. A looooooooong test drive. Maybe a naked test drive. I hated her. My. God. I actually think I hated her.

By that time, a parent chaperone joined the mix—red SOLO cup in hand—and spoke with Dylan, Finn, Grumpy, and Slapstick. Damon had disappeared...probably lamenting how badly he got his butt kicked in public. Brynn clicked back to the circle she'd been conversing with. Someone in the back came forward and placed a tender arm over her shoulder. The male was over six feet wearing dress-khakis, a light-colored sweater, and some sort of loafer...expensive stuff...possibly tailored, because everything hung on his long and lean body like a second skin. Their corner was dimly lit, making faces and hair color recognition all but impossible. Squinting to focus, as soon as I got a load of the profile, momentarily I was struck dumb. Like I'd been kicked in the head by a mule and was a vegetable. I'd recognize that square jaw anywhere.

Ben Ryan. I gulped.

I felt like I was in a tailspin and had a thousand feet before I kissed the ground. Like I needed to add another layer to the Darcy drama? *Omigosh, Ben Ryan,* I said to myself again. Heck, I might've yelled it...because there he came...strutting my way.

Ben left Brynn pouting, artfully navigating through the crowd, his coppery-colored hair and intense silver eyes extraordinarily different. Ho. Ly. You. Know. What. I'd only had two Cokes. I'd need four more and perhaps a cigar to deal with Ben.

Like Dylan had done earlier, Ben's devilish eyes slid over me, pulling one of those head-to-toe deals where he checked out the whole package. Unlike Dylan, he blatantly craned behind me to catch a view of my backside. I felt the heat in my cheeks, and if he laughed, I swear, I'd knee him in the 'nads.

I held up a hand, waving him off like a taxi I decided not to take. "Go away," I choked out.

"Darcy," he murmured. "I've been looking for you."

"I'm...*b*-busy," I stammered.

Inhale. Exhale. Inhale. Exhale. *You can do this, Darcy,* I told myself. *He's just another pretty face, nothing more.* Yanking the chain on my boy-crazy, I tried my best to remember good girls didn't have bad thoughts. Good girls didn't look at Hot Boy B when they went to the party with Hot Boy A. And above all else, good girls weren't attracted to boys they knew absolutely nada about...who'd hit them with their Audi.

With a desperate turn to find Dylan, I heard Ben chuckle from behind and circle his arm around my waist, turning me back toward him. Slowly, he drew my body into his like we were...

Shoot, I didn't know, like we were two familiar people who did more with one another than mere talking. I had goose bumps over every inch of my body, and I blushed with embarrassment because I felt Brynn's eyes on me like a sniper with a clear shot.

I tried to say, "Don't," but all that came out was a nervous giggle.

"Yeah," he said with a grin. "I'm happy to see you too. Marry me."

It struck me like a crashing car that Ben was a fastard. When I clamped my jaws shut, Ben shrugged and moved us back and forth to the slow song playing. "Okay," he amended, "one date. Then we can get married." Theoretical dates with Ben rolled on my inner hamster wheel. They chugged in a nauseating circle not gaining any ground, just making me dizzier.

Collin Lockhart danced close to us with a redhead I didn't recognize. Dressed similarly to Dylan, he did a few spins, but right when he leaned into her for close conversation, Brynn practically jerked his arm out of his socket, tearing him away. She dragged him with her—Ben and me as the destination. Collin ran a shaky hand through his thick blond hair, and his eyes blinked in flat-out confusion. But it wasn't a confusion that'd lead to publicly embarrassing a pushy Brynn—or reuniting with the redhead he'd left standing. In fact, he looked like he'd take whatever Brynn dished out.

Ugh...what kind of power did she wield over guys?

I shook my head in wonderment, turning my attention elsewhere. "Why and how are you here, Ben?"

"I've been worried about you," he said oddly. "I've crapped out with Brantley McCoy, and that insinuates big problems. You need to give me more to work with. Why are you holding out?"

"You never answered my question," I diverted.

"Just enrolled, angel." Shoot, the nervous giggle came back. That time with a panicked shrill. "I start in January and was personally invited by the principal tonight. And by the way, *you*," he emphasized, "never answered *mine*."

"I gave you everything, Ben. I swear it."

"You're not kidding," he said, his face suddenly grave.

Brynn and Collin hovered next to us, practically stealing our air. "Have you given up on the ten grand?" Ben asked, not caring they eavesdropped. Wasn't that the million-dollar question? All I did was shrug because frankly I didn't have another plan. "What about this guy with the limp?" he murmured.

I'd forgotten I'd told Ben about Chichi's prediction. As I looked at my surroundings all week, I'd pretty much come to the conclusion everyone had a limp of some kind and left that one to the Fates.

"Haven't found him," I said.

Another frown. "What about the spray painter?"

My breath caught. I negotiated with my lungs to ditch the spasms and prayed to God Almighty I didn't go female and dissolve into tears. "Deadline was today," I replied soberly, "and I failed."

Ben placed his hand at the nape of my neck, tilting my head so he could speak into my ear. "Failure is never final. It simply means you try another angle."

As he attempted to rock us back and forth, I stood rock solid, trying to convince myself failure wasn't final. But the trail was so cold it was frostbitten. Ben ventured to place my hands around his waist, but I remained uncooperative. My gut said there were things about him I needed to stay away from. Dylan was the consummate gentleman. Ben—I somehow knew—was a cad.

Dylan and I had an otherworldly connection, and all at once, a burst of adrenaline shot straight into my chest. Maybe that was our destinies realigning, or maybe it was Survival 101. Looking over Ben's shoulder, my entire body jerked and tingled at the sight of Dylan splitting the crowd. Closer. Closer. Closer. Definitely Survival 101.

Dylan pulled a double blink when he saw Ben's arms draped lazily around my waist. His eyelids then dropped low, and I swear, I think he growled in possession. "Easy there, Ryan," Dylan said darkly. "Why don't you put your tongue back in your mouth before I rip it from your jaw?"

Dylan strode over and placed his hand to rest possessively at my lower back. I moved toward him and circled my arm around his waist. My God, I looked like a tramp. I wasn't sure how I got into the situation, but I didn't want Dylan to think I'd initiated it.

"She's beautiful," Ben gushed more than necessary. "It would be a crime not to enjoy what simply is not the every day." I fought the urge to laugh—and lost. Ben was definitely the wordy type. In any other situation, I might be flattered, but I knew beyond a shadow of a doubt it would end in one way if Ben didn't shut his dumb-butt mouth. Dylan semi-fought already earlier, but that was defending someone else. If he was the main event, we'd need the fire truck and ambulance on standby.

Dylan's jaw set tightly. "On that we agree, but news flash, Ryan... I. Don't. Share."

"Me neither, but if things were so absolute between Darcy and you, then why do you seem so threatened?"

That was like muttering a dare to a nut job strapped to C4. "Stop, Ben," I whispered.

"Perhaps the only alternative I have to get you to shut up is to shove a fist in your mouth," Dylan warned.

Collin and Brynn were all ears. I mustered up my best back-off glare—just threw that sucker in their faces—and uh...they didn't even move. Ponkeys.

Ben shrugged. "Well, in that case, we could take this outside if you'd prefer."

Dylan's laugh was hollow...rude...and out-and-out cocky as heck. "Honestly, I'd rather handle this grudge match inside. I prefer public takedowns over the private."

Ben's jaw steeled. Totally shut up. In that moment, I think he realized Dylan would tango...any time...day or night. It wasn't a physical punch, but it definitely had been a jab.

In the blink of an eye, it was all Party-de-Highway-to-Hell. Dylan wanted him dead. Ben was stupid enough to drive the death-bus. Swear to God, I almost laughed again, but I knew neither would understand. If I had the time, I'd hypothesize about their true motives—was it merely to claim the fair Darcy Walker, or was it two arrogant, territorial lions seeing who had the loudest roar?

I did the only thing I could possibly do...I left Ben standing. I came with Dylan. I'd leave with Dylan. Still, I wriggled my jaw around because it felt like I'd just got clocked by both of them.

Chapter Twenty-Seven

EMOTIONAL HANGOVERS

I had an emotional hangover—best friend induced—but the way I felt, an alcohol-induced hangover might've been less miserable. My date-date with Dylan hadn't been a date-date after all, but a category-five disaster. He'd "friended" things up as the night wore on, ending the evening with your standard hug, standard *I love you*, and standard goodnight kiss on the cheek.

Same old. Same old.

He'd dropped me off at work the following morning, and he, his sister, and the Beemer—which I'd silently sat in, pretending all was well—went shopping, God knows where. Rather than having free time on the first day of Christmas break, I'd been scheduled for a full shift.

Thank you. No thank you, Mr. B.

Making the best use of my time, I decided to close up loose ends —that was the message I left on Coach Wallace's voicemail. "You might want to sit down, but Jojo's preggers. I think you're the father, sir. And here's my two cents' even though you didn't ask for it. You don't want to be a deadbeat dad. Murphy is everything to me. He stepped up when circumstances and destiny dictated otherwise, and that's a special memory I'll take to my grave. Your kid won't forget how you handle this, and even if it's not your kid, well, it seems like he or she needs a dad. I might not be perfect, but believe me when I say I have experience with crazy. Jojo might've messed up your car in the past, but this time she didn't."

I signed off, straightened a knocked-over cardboard snowman, and hand-dusted crap while I rode my RipStik. I steered back to Rudi in her regular spot behind the customer service desk. Although deaf, she didn't mind speaking to customers while she worked. Sad, but understandable. Most at school were self-centered, judgmental SOBs, and that was on a good day. While she looked up a book on the computer, I folded my arms on the counter, lay my head on top, and sighed.

"Late night, angel?"

Somebody strangle me...

Rudi jerked excitedly on my arm. I peeled open an eye with an accompanying death stare. Yep, Ben Ryan.

His smile quirked up, and those silver eyes cut straight into me like twin lasers. He duplicated my posture, leaning across the countertop to touch my hands. "You like what you see, don't you?" he flirted.

Somebody did...because either Rudi or I was hyperventilating.

I backed out of his grasp to a safer distance. "Ben, Rudi," I introduced, jerking my chin at both of them. "Rudi, Ben." After Ben explained he was "the new kid in town," he asked Rudi where he could find the latest James Patterson for his mother. He signed the question. Of course, he would. The ponkey was pretty much as perfect as his clothes. I ditched those two to roll up front when I heard the doorbell ring.

"Who are you?" I asked Ben when I felt his heat beside me. "You literally materialized in the Valley ether from nowhere. Excuse me if I'm the suspicious type, but here lately, I need to watch my back."

I opened the drawer, ensuring we had enough change. As I counted out five hundred dollars' worth of money, I expected to get more of the same...which, in Benland, was nothing but wanting to talk about me.

Ben sighed. "I'm not sure that I'm very much of anything, Darcy. I'm sort of a rolling stone. My father is Lieutenant General Vaughn Ryan. Most of my life I've been a denizen, jumping from base to base, but he promises this will be the last stop on his quest to conquer the world."

I pivoted around to peer into his eyes. Nothing but purity and truth resonated in his gaze—not one hint of sarcasm. And by the sound of that title, Ben's daddy might just run the place. "That might be the first time I've heard anything sincere come from your mouth," I gasped.

He shrugged. "Not the first time, but the statement is definitely the truth."

"So you're a citizen of nowhere, huh?"

Once again, the flirty smile quirked up at one corner. "You actually know what denizen means?"

Annnnnnnnnd just like that, Ben ruined the moment.

I swiveled back around and slammed the register shut. I swear, he hadn't been in town long and must've heard the rumors I was the dumb type. "Goodbye, Ben," I muttered.

"Did I say something wrong?" he asked, sounding panicked.

I headed back for the break room to see if Mr. B had passed out in the corner or, God forbid choked on a ham bone. Rudi, Chichi, and I hadn't seen him for the ten hours we'd been on duty. No lie. So here we were, three teenage girls, manning the store.

Not exactly safe.

Ben grabbed my arm, twirling me toward him, his eyes softening to liquid silver. "Hey," he said seriously, "let me take you out tonight. It's not like I ask you to pick out china patterns or anything, Darcy. I'd just like to get to know you better. Let me show you I can be someone who doesn't put his foot in his mouth every five seconds."

Here's the thing about Ben. Sure, his good looks and rocker snarl were tempting—but a conversation with him was like riding an unending freight train. You either hung on or got flung off into a ditch. I already had one guy like that in my life. God help me, there was no room for another.

"My shift ends at nine."

"Supper," he murmured grinning.

I. Flat. Out. Turned. Him. Down.

Ben left his number (already had it), new address (didn't want it), and the lingering scent of an evening all too tempting. Why tempting? Ben had secrets. Secrets I needed to put names to. Anything would be better than the sauna of disappointment suffocating me.

When he cockily strode out the door, Ivy and Collin blew in about a minute later. Well, well, well, wasn't there a story there all in itself. Zipped inside a white North Face coat, Ivy unloaded a scowl that shriveled my self-esteem. "Don't you look all Belinskified."

I rolled my eyes. "Ivy, Collin," I greeted. "I was hoping you'd stop by." NOT.

"So how was the dance last night?" she asked.

I ignored her but couldn't help but notice Collin seemed even more interested than her. "You missed one," he said.

"Huh?"

Collin pitched his head toward the register, eyeballing a five-dollar bill hiding behind a stack of books.

"Oh, er, thanks," I muttered.

"Need some help?" he murmured and grinned.

I stepped behind the counter, keying in my employee number to open the drawer. Once I hit "enter," the register dinged, and I tagged the Lincoln in the appropriate slot. "My math isn't *that* bad, Collin. I can handle placing a five in a drawer of five hundred."

Ivy leaned across the counter and deliberately allowed her eyes to drift to my Chuck Taylors. "Sneakers," she said, laughing in an amusingly breathy voice, "how fashionable."

"Don't hate on the Chucks," I said. "You should count yourself lucky they haven't found their way up your butt. But hey, the evening's still young."

Ivy straightened her hair and smoothed her coat down with blood-red nails, like she worked on her appearance while she conjured up more atrocities in her mind. "So where is Dylan?" she sneered. "He looked gorgeous last night at the dance, but then he always does."

"I don't have my crystal ball on me, Ivy, but he's somewhere shopping," I declared proudly, immediately wishing I hadn't even given her that.

Ivy gave me one of those shrugs to say she knew more about Dylan's private life than I did. So wasn't true, but God knew she threw enough gasoline on the fire to make me doubt it. Picking at my nails, I couldn't help but wonder what Collin's take was. He looked physically drained, as though the emotional rollercoaster of Hathawaywood had taken its toll.

Shoving his hands in a navy parka, Collin gave me a head jerk in acknowledgment, his blond hair so gelled-up it looked crispy-done. When his cell phone rang, he removed it from his jacket, answering a text with what had to be a simple yes or no command. The moment he finished, he and Ivy headed straight for the magazines while I discovered more areas that needed cleaning—wasn't that one heck of a metaphor considering the current clientele.

I slid my iPhone out of my back pocket to phone Vinnie. I found it extremely troubling Jaws still hadn't gotten back to me, and if the situation with Brantley McCoy was so dire, then why stay underground? I rapped my fingers on the countertop, pinky-to-thumb, pinky-to-thumb—waiting for Vinnie to answer. The call terminated with a voicemail.

"Vinnie, it's me...Darcy...if you're having a dumb day and don't recognize my voice. Tell Jaws I need him. I need him in a bad way. He'll know what that means."

Schomberg's Drycleaners was broken into last night, Rudi signed as I killed the call. *They emptied the register around midnight*. She gave me a look like where's-our-boss, but I shrugged it away. Both of us had a key to the front door, knew the code to deactivate the alarm, and the combination for the wall safe in the break room...and we were sixteen. That had to be against the law, and if it wasn't, it probably should be. Our boss not showing all day was minor but justifiably scary when I thought of the things that could go wrong without adult supervision.

"Schomberg's was broken into?" I repeated.

She signed, *Mister Schomberg hid in the back but said he saw them drive away in a gray van. After they spray painted his place.*

Mr. Schomberg was blinder than a one-eyed man in a cave. His version of gray could fall anywhere along the spectral colors of the rainbow. Casting a look across the street, the thought didn't escape me that Brantley McCoy-slash-Moby was still at-large. But he wouldn't come here, would he?

Chapter Twenty-Eight

FEAR CAGE

*W*e had ten minutes until closing and had already closed up shop except for counting cash and placing it in the safe. Mr. B finally went E.T. and "phoned home," claiming he'd gotten sick on too many crab cakes. Rudi, Chichi, and I hunkered on the break room floor, chowing on stale Doritos and cans of Coke and orange Fanta. Chichi argued with the Ouija that the man with a limp needed a name. The board only replied, "Limp hurt, Darcy."

Amend that: it actually spelled my name Darsee...her board was an idiot.

Since Dylan headlined my naughty girl thoughts, I asked Chichi for a read on him. The brown cursor flew around in circles, spelling out 100 Proof Stud, Dylan, and Ben.

I burst into giggles, explaining about Vinnie's movie and reminding them who Ben was. Chichi sounded frustrated, her burgundy eyes growing wide as silver dollars. "I suppose the board likes the stud reference, but regarding Dylan and Ben, both have exceptionally strong yet different auras," she said exasperated. "I don't have my K2 reader with me which measures electromagnetic fields. When there's a high EMF reading, my abilities go haywire. Something's wrong in here," she muttered, casting a look over her shoulder. "They're cancelling each other out one minute and amplifying one another the next."

Chichi scared the pants off of Rudi and me, telling us EMF fueled paranormal activity and too much EMF could make a person sick. She called it a fear cage. "The only thing I see definitively is a lasting relationship with both of them. In what capacity, I don't know."

By my last Dorito, I was convinced it'd be friends-only for both boys.

I couldn't imagine Ben Ryan being the father of little Darcy Walkers or Dylan Taylor wanting to mate with a lower species.

Frustrated, Chichi placed the Ouija back in the box like she handled the Holy Grail. My first thought was to accidentally set it afire when I could legitimize the crime. Rudi tossed our empty Doritos bags in the trash, crunched up our soft drink cans, and two-pointed them into the same bin. She pulled a paper towel from the wall rack, wetting it in the sink and cleaning off the white table.

You know how you sometimes get a dark feeling of impending doom? I was all-too familiar with that shiz in my life—more so than the average chick. All of a sudden, the fear cage grew larger than my list of worries because it felt like someone walked across my future grave. Or worse yet, I had eyes in the back of my head and saw who had plans to shove me in it.

I wheeled around so fast I gave myself whiplash.

The break room was situated in the back of the store with a straight-shot view to the parking lot. First thing I did was look outside. The night was pitch black, snowy, and horror-movie scary. To add to the suspense, the front door chimed with a customer entering the store. I stole a glance at my Citizen. It read nine o' clock on the dot, effing closing time. Who in the heck would stroll in at closing?

My gut told me to duck back inside. "What's wrong?" Rudi and Chichi asked at the same time.

I shook my head, holding my index finger to my lips in a quiet, "Shhh."

Voices broke the silence. Males, at least two, stood in the front of the store. Normally, I'd greet them with a Double-B smile, but things felt off. And when I bravely (or stupidly) jutted my head out again, I saw both sported black hoodies, one wearing a mask. The mask was pasty white with cutouts for the mouth and eyes. Curly neon-red hair was sewn on the back, bushing out like the Mad Hatter. Here was a reality check for you. A person never wears a mask to a bookstore—not ever.

That spelled at least felony and hopefully not Murder One.

The guy in the mask was relaxed, holding a Starbucks takeout cup in his right hand and collapsing the plastic lid with his thumb. He spoke so low and muffled I couldn't make out anything, but the other voice...*I knew*. With my back flush against the wall, I heard him say, "Are you sure about this? Come on, man. I like her. It's Friday night. Let's go have some fun." The voice had that aw-shucks thing going on, sort of country with a twang, but aw-shucks aside, my trouble-meter beeped at its highest alert.

My stomach bottomed out as the gleam caught what appeared to be a six-inch blade, death-gripped in his right hand. Oh, God, that wasn't good.

Not. Good. At. All.

Oh, jeez, who was the *her*? Glancing at Rudi, I saw a paralyzed confusion, even after I mouthed we were a robbery-in-progress. Focusing on Chichi, the wide-eyed stark terror said a good possibility existed she was the *her*.

A story for another day.

Both girls immediately huddled together, arms around one another's waists like they shivered in a blizzard. Again, I put my index finger to my lips, mouthing a soundless, "Shhh."

Times like these I wished I had a regular prayer life. If I had a regular prayer life, perhaps I'd approach the Throne with confidence. I threw up words of desperation in every language I knew (heck, I even tried Morse code and gangsta), hoping God would answer in one of them. Then, for Heaven's sake, my iPhone sang "Grandma Got Run"...as all three of us went for my right butt cheek to silence the noise.

Except the number belonged to the one person who always showed up when things went all to shiz. Switching off the lights and peeking through the crack in the partially closed door, I hit redial. "D?" I whispered. Rudi and Chichi likewise started the quiet-as-a-mouse routine, Chichi unplugging the percolating coffee pot, and Rudi still paralyzed, literally gnawing on two of her fingers.

I heard the smile in his voice. "Hi sweetheart, I'm back.

Remind me to not go shopping with Sydney again," he said, chuckling with no humor. "Although I did get you something that's so insanely awesome, you're going to be indebted for life. I've missed you. Are you hungry? I'm starved." Someone's voice resonated in the background. "That's Vinnie," he groaned. "God help me. We ran into him at the gas station this morning, and Syd invited him along. I deserve a medal, Darc—and a tranquilizer. My head hurts from hearing about his budding acting career and how he's the ultimate 100 Proof Stud. Seriously, I told him that was *me*," he said, giggling loudly. "But as long as *you* think I am, that's all that matters."

I was pretty sure I'd be 100 Proof Dead by morning.

Vinnie chuckled into the phone. "Evenin', Dolce. Sorry I didn't buzz you back, but I took care of it."

Took care of Jaws? I thought. "Yeah," Dylan grumbled. "Why did Valentine get a call, and I rated a couple of texts? We can cover that later—"

"D," I interrupted in a low voice, "I'm in trouble." Dylan instantly turned silent. Like someone snatched out his tongue and refused to give it back. "Did you hear me?" I whispered.

"Define trouble, Darcy."

"Rudi, Chichi, and I are in the break room and some guys are robbing the store. Mr. B's home sick. We're here all by ourselves."

"Dammit, Darcy, this had better not be a joke."

"Pinky swear," I whispered. "I can't see their faces, but one of them has on a mask, the other has a knife. At least, it looks like a knife. That's not good, is it?"

Dylan said something unintelligible. "You should've called 911!"

"But I prayed and prayed, and you called," I whispered.

The phone was full of running footsteps. "Darc, let me get my house phone." He barked an order to Vinnie to tell his father what was going on. "Stay on the line with me while I dial 911."

I couldn't.

My nose had gone down to the ground, sniffing like a bloodhound that'd been chained too long. "Dylan, I'm going to give my cell to Chichi and crawl out there. Talk to them, so they won't be so nervous. One of the voices sounds familiar, and they specifically said they were coming for a *her*. I've got a feeling someone has a mark on her head, and if I don't stop things, she's not going to pass go and collect two hundred dollars."

Dylan bellowed, "*No! No! No! Darcy Walker, stay put and no crawling!*" I shook my head and handed my phone to Chichi, which she wouldn't take. Speaking rapid Spanish, Chichi called me every profane word she could think of with a remote association to "raving lunatic" in the English language. Rudi began to cry, her glasses fogging as she grabbed the back of my yoga pants, not wanting me to go anywhere.

"Chichi," I whispered, breaking free from Rudi's grasp, "Dylan wants to talk to you."

Once again, Chichi resided in the land of Mexico. "*No, I don't!*" he growled. I then heard Dylan tell the 911 operator where we were and what'd happened, in between begging me to heel.

"I love you," I whispered.

"Aw, Darc, don't," he whispered even lower.

Rudi squeezed my hand as I placed my cell phone in hers. "Darcy, please," she mouthed.

"Don't worry," I told her. "I *know* that voice. I'll be quiet." I was an absolute moron. Why I liked to live on the edge befuddled me as much as it did my father and best friends. But I knew that voice. Question was, *Where?* Gas station? Metro stop? Mall? Christmas party? I dropped to my knees and army crawled into the aisle, took a left, pausing behind the fourth and fifth rows.

I steadied my breath and scooted forward, crouching behind the self-help books, the top of my head peeking out into the aisle. Briefly, I wondered if how-not-to-get-killed-by-vandals was covered inside, but I had a feeling it was about simplifying a person's life— not making it more complex.

The snowmen perched atop the front two shelves blocked the torso view of both of them, so all I could do was pray they kept talking. Balancing myself on my elbows, I tracked my vision to the sound of their voices. I gulped and right then saw four sets of shoes —two sneakers, one loafer, and snow boots moving back and forth as though they debated whether to pitch a tent or scram. My mind was stuck on the loafers...*penny loafers*, I qualified with a gasp. I only knew of one person to wear them: Ben Ryan. And Ben's build and the guy's build were one and the same. God help me, I'd *talked with*, *flirted with*, and *conspired with* someone who'd obviously been playing me for weeks. And the timeline fit. Ben and his brother showed up on the night I found the stolen credit cards and social security card. Ben Ryan had been present, pulling my strings from day one. If that wasn't bad enough, the fourth pair of shoes, snow boots, was limping. Like he had a bad case of gout or shoes that weren't his.

WHOAAAAAAA.

So it's game day, I thought. I'd take on Ben Ryan and meet up with the owner of the limp.

"No one's here," Black Sneakers spoke adamantly, his body turned toward Penny Loafers who wore the mask. Black Sneakers was the largest of the four, gripping the knife. Masked Penny Loafers didn't reply, took two steps backward, and flipped the *Open* sign to *Closed*.

Masked Penny Loafers had my assessment as the ringleader. Black Sneakers whispered something to him too low to decipher. Then the other pair of sneakers, custom Air Jordans, touched Black Sneakers on the shoulder and pulled out an even larger switchblade.

This is a really dumb idea, I told myself. There were a few punch-and-shoves between them, but when Black Sneakers barked, "I told you, this is not the place," it literally felt like I took a kick to the stomach.

Those words. I'd heard those exact words at the winter formal.

Slapstick Wilson...I choked.

And here I'd felt sorry for him and begged Dylan to intervene during his recent bout of I-must've-lost-my-mind. Hurt and betrayal, mixed with my own stupidity hit me all at the same time. What I'd hoped was just a gasp inside my head turned out to be the audible reality. Immediately, there was whispering and dancing around with Masked Penny Loafers motioning for Slapstick and Air Jordans to check out the noise. Masked Penny Loafers headed straight for the cash register along with Snow Boots. After Slapstick and Air Jordans checked each aisle but the back two, they noticed the slightly ajar break room door, nodded to one another, and headed straight for it.

I couldn't let them discover Rudi and Chichi. Rudi hadn't kissed a boy, and Chichi needed to live another day just so she could kick the habit of talking to evil spirits. With a deep breath, I threw up a quick prayer, slowly stood up, and stepped out into the aisle, running straight into the eye of the storm.

Slapstick.

And Damon freaking Whitehead...I should've known.

Slapstick jolted, his hazel eyes going wide with surprise, and maybe a little bit of anger. Anger I wouldn't have thought possible until I witnessed him beat the crap out of Damon the night before.

Somehow I managed, "Hello, Slapstick. Did you and Damon kiss and make up?"

Slapstick said nothing, absolutely nothing.

My face flushed, and my blood pressure skyrocketed. I already had a bad case of heartburn from the Doritos and Coke—add a rising BP and I probably needed a daily aspirin. First thought that came to mind was I was the proverbial paper trail, and their job was cleanup.

Where Slapstick remained mute, Damon was Damon. The douchebag of all douchebags. "It's now gonna get fun," he said, laughing with his dark brown eyes bloodthirsty and merciless. "And it's going to be even more fun when Taylor and his crew get wind of what I have planned for you."

"By all means, don't hold back on my account," I muttered.

Slapstick's silence was quickly jettisoned for cold, hard terror. His gaze said to cut it out, pronto. "Please," he begged to me out loud.

Huh...didn't know what to make of that.

When Damon lunged at me and twisted my arm behind my back, I fought to find a position, which wouldn't rip my arm from my socket. Even amidst the pain and threats, I wasn't as intrigued with my likely demise as I was with the two guys behind the register. Masked Penny Loafers cracked his knuckles and then got down to business, taking a long, four-inch tool out of his back pocket, ramming it into the side of the cash register, and popping open the drawer. As he expeditiously handed bill after bill to Snow Boots, Snow Boots gazed in my direction, purposefully making eye contact as he stuffed the bills into a black nylon bag.

"Hello, Darcy," he said, grinning evilly.

Ho. Ly. Mo. Ly.

I finally clued in where I'd recognized his voice. He was the guy from weeks earlier, milling around in the store, not buying a thing. It was the night of the freebie hot dogs, and a guy I referred to as Creepy Teenager accompanied him. Jeez, he'd been casing the place out. Likewise, I'd chased him in Kroger.

God help me...he was also Big Moby.

I stared into the eyes of Brantley McCoy. "Hello, Brantley," I said.

Deep from underneath the counter, Mr. B's cell phone chimed "On the Good Ship Lollipop." It was just too freaking bizarre to not laugh. When the sound bubbled up my throat, Brantley hissed, "Shut up!"

I did...

While Masked Penny Loafers continued about his work, Brantley fumbled around until he found the phone, glanced at the screen, and thrust it in my face.

Dear. Holy. God.

Tito Westbrook.

"Answer it!" Brantley barked. "And do it on speaker. That man has been gunning for us, and I need to know what we're up against. We even tried to buy a house in Brunswick to start over, but he caught on too soon."

Brunswick, Maine, I thought. Of course...Tito said The Ghost had tried to buy a house there in his name, but the bank flagged it before anyone signed on the dotted line. A chill worked its way up my spine. Murphy's bank account had been hacked where someone attempted to buy a four-wheeler in Hyannis Port. Another East Coast town.

My God, they'd been after me for a while.

Thing was, if I answered Mr. B's phone, they might track on the fact I was Jester—the last thing I wanted—but that might be my one and only opportunity to get us out of here alive.

Taking the phone in my hand, I nervously answered, "Hullo?"

A relieved exhale. "Darlin', thank God. I've called every number I've had for you in the past fifteen minutes. I'm sorry I fell off the map...long story...but listen—"

"Tito..." I interrupted.

"Let me finish, darlin'. Whatever you're doing, stop right now.

Here's what happened. I've got a friend who works at the State Police. She found some paperwork that Eric Young has a heavy foot. Evidently, he got a speeding ticket in April and showed proof of insurance. With that, I got the name of the insurance company he and Evelyn Seacrest use. When I called them, the agent I spoke with pulled the original paperwork for Evelyn and Eric. He had a photograph copy, clear as day, of Eric Young's license. Here's the thing, the accompanying social security card number is for our dead guy—Bishop Fowler. Should the BMV's computers have caught that? Absolutely, but these guys are computer geeks. My guess is they somehow overrode the system. And when I contacted Fowler's family, the photograph they faxed me is not the image of the Eric Young on the license. I know in my gut the guy was The Ghost because even though he's wearing glasses, he looks a little like a photograph I have of him. He messed up," Tito said, half laughing. "We've got him. I have a feeling you may know him with another alias. I need to know that other name. Give me the name, and I can easily put a face with him. Then we can take this to Cookie tonight."

Oh what tangled webs we weave.

Only in my world would the driver of the white van—Eric Young—have Bishop Fowler's social security card number. And if I had money, I'd bet every last, red American cent the photograph on Young's license was of Brantley McCoy. The fastards were one and the same.

"I wish I would've had this earlier," I whispered.

"Jest—"

I made the executive decision to go solo and struck the "end" button. Possibly not the right move, but I acted on impulse. If Tito and I got into a more harried conversation, then a good possibility existed I'd get stabbed immediately. If I screamed, Rudi and Chichi no doubt would start crying. Crying meant they'd be heard which meant a knife might find a way into their chests too.

And that situation was exactly why I should've given Tito the alias of Brantley McCoy initially, but my greedy self didn't. And no one knew of the Brantley connection but me (and Jaws).

Stupid, Darcy. If you make it out of here alive, you now know to always CYA, or cover your a-s-s.

My eyes landed on Masked Penny Loafers who had stopped his work to crack his knuckles. Oh, God. Red said The Ghost had the personal idiosyncrasy of cracking his knuckles non-stop. He'd done it twice since he entered The Double-B. "Why are you staring at him?" Brantley growled.

"Because he's the one in charge."

I swear, you would've thought I'd smacked Brantley because his head jerked like a heavy hand struck his cheek. Brantley wanted to usurp the power of whom I'd swear was Ben Ryan. It was written all over his demeanor.

One would think I'd be little Miss Manners, but frankly, I was tired of the whole gig. I was tired of figuring things out and not getting a monetary reward. And frankly, I was tired of the leader wearing the gosh-danged mask. In that moment, it became crystal clear Brantley wasn't The Ghost. The Ghost was the coward behind the mask. As if on cue, Masked Penny Loafers raised a hand, motioning over his head, bellowing, "Bring her here."

There were a lot of things I could do in the situation. I could kick and scream and expend valuable energy, or I could relax, hold my head high, and go out like a proud misfit when I hoped a plan would materialize.

And then I saw it...

A silent red light rhythmically blinked on the security system pad by the door. Blink, blink, and another slow blink. In about ten minutes, the lights would click off on their own if Rudi, Chichi, or I didn't do it manually. All that would be left for illumination would be the security light overtop the door and one in the rear lighting the hallways by the back entrance. In my case, darkness might be good.

If I could stay alive for the next ten minutes, perhaps I'd have a chance. But a lot could happen in ten minutes. A pot of water could boil. I could poach an egg, change my sheets, sort my bills, watch a sunset, or in my case get stabbed and be well on my way to bleeding out...tragically, a virgin no less.

Damon parked me in front of the counter as if I purchased a book, waiting patiently for someone to ring me up. Once all the bills were removed, Masked Penny Loafers shut the register drawer, turned around, and grabbed a handful of his mask's red curly hair. In one smooth motion, he ripped off his disguise, revealing one of the most attractive faces to ever grace Valley.

Model-like bone structure...unforgettable, luxurious hair...sky-blue eyes.

You could've knocked me over with a whisper.

"*Collin Lockhart*," I gasped. "I would've sworn you were Ben Ryan."

I wouldn't have predicted that turn of events in a gazillion years of reading spy novels. I'd always thought Collin to be ambitious, but right then, he reminded me of when a bull sees red. No one knew what a bull actually thought. All they knew was the color red sent them to Psychoville. Other than the mask and shoes, he looked totally different, wearing a black hoodie when he'd always been Ivy League. He'd visited The Double-B earlier with Ivy. Obviously, he'd ditched her and went home and pulled on a different persona.

I drew in a sharp gasp of breath as fear clamped down on my neck. "Hello, Darcy," Collin said dryly, and when I scrambled for the back door, he jumped across the countertop, grabbing me by the hair and yanking me to his body with a thunk. Collin trailed his lips down my neck, pausing to suck my cross earring into his mouth. Let me tell you, folks, Jesus didn't like that. I didn't even need to ask. Next thing I knew, the four-inch tool he'd used to pop open the register was poking right against my brainstem. Darcy was gone, people, but that was Darcyville, wasn't it? I didn't always choose these situations. Somehow they just happened, and I found myself wondering how it would ever turn out in my favor.

One glance back to Collin unveiled the sick, sadistic smile of Brantley McCoy. They were brothers, I gasped, and no one had to tell me otherwise. But Brantley had been living in the wind. Could Collin actually have a brother—who'd gone to our school two years earlier—that no one even knew was his? When he scraped the instrument down my neck and shoved me toward the back exit, I knew I should beg, cry, curse, or something. But for a second, I froze. Honest injun, I froze. I tried to have ethics in life. Don't lie, don't cheat, don't steal, hold the door open for the elderly, but I wasn't above emotional blackmail. After a few seconds of scrutinizing the situation, I somehow found a tear. It was beyond...and I mean *beyond*...embarrassing. Not to mention futile. Did I actually think I could make Collin Lockhart birth a conscience?

Right then, it all fell into place.

I. Mean. All. Of. It.

"You used your nice mother, Collin," I whispered. "She works in a post office. You went there, stole people's credit cards, checks in the mail, anything you suspected had confidential information, and then you stole a person's identity." An unease shook my spine as another piece of the puzzle slid together. A piece Finn had delivered. "Bishop Fowler was a computer programmer. And my guess is Bishop had the connection to Evelyn Seacrest. Bishop told you how to do this, and then one of you killed him. I saw the skeleton in his house." I whipped my head back around to Brantley. "It was you, wasn't it? You somehow hooked up with him in order to learn...*right, Brantley?*" I asked, emphasizing his name. "Collin's your brother. I can tell by your sadistic smiles. What happened, Brantley?" I continued. "Did your mom kick you out of the house because you were too hard to get along with? Did Fowler take mercy on you and give you a home? And the drugs at Big Moby's, I'm guessing are a side job. It's been my experience that scum can't keep out of scumbag work."

Brantley scrunched his demented face up into a crazy grin. "Brilliant," he said.

Collin didn't laugh. Instead, he acted like he wanted to put a hole in my head the size of the national deficit. "You shouldn't have fed Tito Westbrook information, Darcy," he said.

Oh shiz...so they definitely knew what I'd been doing. "Why would you even want to hurt him or those other men anyway?" I asked. "You've got everything going for you. Looks, brains, position—"

Collin looked off in the distance, like a myriad of reasons existed to why he did the things he did—reasons he didn't have time to divulge. "Maybe everything I had going for me just wasn't enough," he finally said. "But I didn't want things to come to this. I liked you, Darcy. You're funny, and you don't take life too seriously. But when I heard you were showing around photos of Slapstick, Damon, and Brantley, I knew your mind must be piecing things together. I had Brantley tap into your Twitter account to see if we could throw you off. That didn't work, and then we took on your father, but he shut us down before the night was out. When Damon said you asked him about The Ghost, I tried to distract you by having Brantley ram Dylan's car. When that still didn't deter you, I lowered myself to made-up stories about Dylan and Brynn. I didn't want to think you'd be so stupid to continue with the behavior, so I even had Madison Flannery yank your chain."

"I suspected as much about Madison," I muttered, but God help me, he'd caused me to believe Dylan was a two-timer with his heart.

Collin gave me a shrug, like confessing his actions weren't a threat. An omen if I'd ever heard one. "Madison does what she's told, and her artistic fingers came in handy when duplicating signatures."

Remembering Slapstick and Damon lived with foster parents in the printing business, I asked, "Did Damon or Slapstick bring some printing knowledge to the table? Did they help you manufacture credit cards?" Collin had a brief moment where his face shocked-out. "You truly are smart," he said which I took as confirmation. "But that's your problem, Darcy. You just wouldn't go away. The final straw was when you used my phone to call Tito last time I was in here. All I had to do was hit redial and connect the dots you were still on the trail. Now you leave me no choice but to rid myself of the problem...just like I had to do with Nico Drake."

My body shook like a drop of water during an earthquake.

Nico's face flashed in my mind, and I never realized until then he was the creepy teenager with Brantley McCoy when he visited The Double-B a few weeks back. I should've recognized the mutual perv in him, but the fact he had an Abe Lincoln beard back then threw me. So either he or Brantley had dropped the credit cards and social security card I'd found. Had he been stabbed for it? Something else? Had he been lured to Bishop Fowler's and killed by Collin or Brantley?

Collin must've read my mind. "Madison told me Nico had a change of heart. He wanted to warn you. I don't usually get my hands dirty," he said icily. "But with Nico, it was a pleasure."

That meant Brantley had killed the others. I didn't have an extra breath to process the news. Collin had pretty much delivered my eulogy.

I prayed.

Prayed some more.

Then the lights snuffed out...

Now was my chance, but if I waited for the cavalry to arrive, God only knew how Heaven's wires got crossed. A red-flannel-pajama-clad Castro Belinski crashed through the back door like a battering ram. He huffed and puffed, yelling for me specifically as he scratched his bald head, flipping the switch on the lights.

His eyes misted with fear when he put two and two together. He barked out profanity, burped loud, and I swear, covered his privates doing the peepee dance. It might not have been exactly in that order, folks, but it was close. He then yelled, "Run, Walker...run!" while his feet pedaled like he rode a bicycle. Trouble was, it was a stationary bike. The man's bare feet didn't do anything more than burn a hole in the carpet.

The place boom-boom-boomed with his weight when he finally moved a couple of feet. By that time, d-bag Damon waved a knife in his face, threatening bodily harm of the permanent variety. Mr. B stopped dead in his tracks, like he teetered over a ledge, no bottom in sight.

Sweet Jesus, we'd all be DOA by morning.

Five minutes later, I sat back-to-back with Mr. B and our hands were duct-taped together, our feet also restrained. Rudi and Chichi were bound the same way.

Collin pitched a bag to Brantley. "Get the cans out man, and make it quick."

Collin was behind the vandalism locally and of Coach's car. He might not have punched the valve, but he was definitely in on it.

"So you like your spray cans, don't you?" I asked. Nothing but air. "Did you paint Nowacki's when you robbed it? The outside of Belinski's? Schomberg's? Coach Wallace's car?"

"My brother did," he admitted.

"Why? Did Coach make you angry or something?" His body tensed, but he still didn't answer. "So is there no legitimate reason for the vandalism, Collin? It's just something extra when you rob a place?"

Damon snagged a white can Brantley pitched in his direction, gave it a shake, and took a few swipes at the furniture. Brantley followed suit. Infuriated, Slapstick threw up both hands, kicking a nearby chair in frustration. "I'm leaving!" he snapped, gazing wide-eyed at the room. "Damon had told me about this guy called The Ghost, but I had no part or knowledge that it was Collin and these guys. Please, believe that, Darcy." With an odd expression to me, he jumped in front of Collin's vision and quietly corn-holed his knife across the floor in my direction. It landed silently at my bound hands.

Here's the thing I'd learned about situations like this. They could always get worse.

Collin reached underneath his hoodie and produced a 9mm gun, waving it at Slapstick with a threat. "The only way you're leaving this place is with your hands in the air or lying on a gurney. So chill."

Slapstick still made a move toward the door. Damon lunged with his knife. Slapstick pivoted at the exact wrong second, and Damon's knife sliced into his hoodie, leaving a bloody red gash in his gut at first strike. Slapstick immediately winced, but when Damon came at him again, Slapstick disabled him with a jaw thrust and punch to the gut.

Damon fell.

Brantley took his place.

My breath came out in fervid pants as I fingered the knife, flipped it around, and hoped and prayed I could cut through the tape like butter. Collin took aim, but Brantley and Slapstick were like a moving tornado on the ground. Not able to get a clear shot, Collin dropped the gun and nylon money bag and jumped on Slapstick's back, punching his head. While Slapstick was double-teamed, I felt a reluctant tear in the tape. With one big tug from Mr. B, my hands were free, and I quickly started slashing through the tape at my feet.

Slapstick roared.

Brantley cursed.

More pounding...more punching.

Tears welled in my eyes when I realized Slapstick would more than likely die. I didn't feel particularly soothed by the thought I'd probably get away. Nor did I feel particularly soothed by the thought the others would get away. Slapstick was my friend. He might've taken a wrong turn in coming to The Double-B, but he proved to be a friend when the crap hit the fan. Slapstick finally gained the upper hand and body-slammed Brantley to the ground—his head striking a chair. Brantley temporarily went night-night. Collin angrily slid down Slapstick's back, the exact moment I'd freed my feet. We both dove headfirst for the gun on the floor, but Collin came up with it, aiming the barrel at my head.

The shiz just got real.

"Wait!" I yelled, and let me tell you, people, anything seemed better than having a semi-automatic gun pointed between my eyes. Collin yanked me to my feet, his eyes locking on mine like we were two hungry scavengers fighting over the remains of a dead animal. He knew what *he* wanted, and I knew what *I* wanted.

Thing was, he had the gun...but I had the mouth.

I morphed from mild-mannered bookseller to a butt-kicking badass with negotiation skills. "Go out the back," I told him, jerking my head in that direction. "Mister Belinski's car is there. Take it and run, Collin."

His car wasn't parked there, but if I could get them to exit out the back, I could lock us all in and call the cops.

For a split second, it was like staring at Brantley McCoy. He mouthed, "Bang-bang," like Brantley had in the parking lot, right then using a real gun.

With the roar of a lion, Slapstick dove for Collin, sending both of them to the ground in a murderous rage. Slapstick desperately fought for his and all of our lives. Collin didn't care anymore. His face was one of complete and utter giving-over to the dark side. He'd lost his girl. He'd lost his anonymity, and his nice, little life as student council president was shot to heck and then some.

Blood droplets rained on the floor. Slapstick's body had taken a mortal shock. Still, he wailed on Collin to the point where I knew there'd be permanent brain damage if I didn't stop him. "Stop!" I yelled to Slapstick, but Slapstick punched away, striking out at all the things unfair in his life. As the gun jolted free, Brantley (back in the fight) scooped it up in a wince, and I went karate on his butt. Problem was, I flailed like a mofo drunk man. I pulled hair, ears, punched, and pounded. I braceleted my hands around his neck, trying to choke him into unconsciousness. My word, I even told him Collin got all the looks in the family (dumb move and made me sound even dumber). Nothing worked, but by God, my fear channeled into take-him-down mode, and I refused to be a bystander.

Freed by Mr. B, Chichi dropped to her knees, twisting at Brantley's legs.

Rudi jumped to her feet, tearing at Brantley's arms.

With a banshee yell, Brantley dislodged both, and they staggered back into one another and clonked heads, stunned. The gun toppled to the floor...I lunged for it...Mr. B beat me to the punch.

He grabbed the pistol in his pudgy hands and opened fire. A bullet busted a window...a filing cabinet...another sunk into what sounded like splintering wood. Sweet Lord, he was probably drunk because the gun hadn't hit the intended target one time. The sound of more gunshots ripped through my brain like I stood underneath the Liberty Bell when it rang. Momentarily rendered deaf, the ear-splitting pop-pop-pop had my adrenaline pumping around danger zone. I couldn't tell if I hurt all over or if I'd been shot.

Two more rounds left the gun's chamber.

Girls screamed.

In a twist of events, Brantley and Collin switched places with Brantley then kicking at Slapstick's legs. Slapstick dropped to all fours, trying to shield me from the gun Collin had wrestled away from Mr. B and had aimed again at my head. While I waited for death to come, a silver canister the size of a Coke can did a slow-roll up the aisle. After two seconds of blinking, a hard puff of white smoke hissed out its sides like steam. Each person in the room slowly began to cough, struggling to not go Rip Van Winkle. My lungs felt radioactive, my entire body burning and hacking at what I slowly concluded was some kind of knockout gas. Or nerve gas. Holy crap, my skin would probably melt off within seconds.

Slapstick ripped his bloodied hoodie off and shoved it over my mouth, trying his best to keep me from choking.

Mr. B fell first.

Rudi.

Followed by Chichi.

Collin grabbed the loot and stumbled for the front door. With a staggering deep cough, I turned my head to see a hawking body artfully striding toward me, like a warrior on a one-way suicide mission.

It was God—or Jesus—maybe it was Jason freaking Bourne. So immense he spanned the width of the aisle, he sported black fatigues, combat boots, and a faded, black cap so cool I'd steal it if I wasn't incapacitated. His black hair glowed like the blue of night, and his dark eyes punctuated a face that was Romanesque and noble. I'd guess him to be around forty years old, but he had one of those faces, which seemed to defy time, but those eyes—those eyes said they'd seen centuries of pain. My jaw dropped wide...it couldn't be. But everything in my churning gut told me it was the man from the yellow Dodge Charger.

I needed a minute...

Maybe two...

Thing was, he had no mask. How could he casually walk through sleeping gas without even a yawn? Giving me a nanosecond of his eyes, he moved faster than an X-15 fighter craft. Collin, Brantley, and a groggy Damon didn't even know what'd hit them. The collision sounded like the release of a cannon. Bodies flew. Grunted. Thumped. Landed in a pile like scrap wood someone intended to burn. Even if I'd sketched the thing out, nothing would've compared to the reality of what that man was capable of. He'd anticipated their moves before they even executed. My vision blurred when the action was over, nothing registering except Slapstick was out cold, Collin's leg had twisted awkwardly, Damon was belly-down and unconscious, and Brantley was sunny-side up, his face stuck in a wide-eyed stare.

He was dead. I was sure of it.

Struggling with consciousness, I heard footfalls and felt him kneel beside me. "Are you Jesus?" I choked.

Pushing the hair from my face, my hormones knocked on my hurting head how gorgeous he was. My type: tall, dark, handsome and so freaking deadly it was a turn-on. He threw his head back and laughed, wiping the tears that escaped my eyes. As much as I tried, I couldn't focus because brain fog was settling in.

"Can't say I've been compared to Jesus," he said, chuckling deeply. "Although I'm positive he wouldn't appreciate the comparison."

"Jaws?" I whispered through the sweatshirt, eyes still closed.

He gave an even lustier laugh, and while I reached for the scar

Jaws had on his hand, I was met with a strong grasp that was unmarred. "You are definitely one clever girl," he said and chuckled deeper, like he knew what I was doing. "But no, I'm not Jaws. Although, he's the one who sent out the S.O.S. Sorry about the gas, babe, but I've never seen a bigger cluster snafu in my entire life. This place looks like the backdrop to a bad dystopian novel. If I hadn't gassed everyone, God only knows what would've happened next."

It was definitely a moronathon. Troubling thing was, sleep was coming like a speeding bullet, and I didn't want to succumb without answers. "Why help *me*?" I whispered in a cough. "Jaws knew my mother. Did you?"

Dodge Charger continued to stroke my hair, his fingers going all the way to the scalp. A message laid there, but unfortunately I couldn't decipher the specifics. But he knew her. I felt it in his touch. He then bent down and dropped a chaste kiss on my forehead. "Jaws said he'd take care of you, babe. And he did. You're safe. The diversion I left for the 911 squad is probably clearing by now, so I've gotta bail. But I'm taking the evidence of me along. We're cool?"

The sector of my mind that commanded talking had ceased to work. The one that kept secrets, however, got the message loud and clear.

Keep my trap shut.

I fell asleep to a siren.

EPILOGUE: BENEATH YOUR BEAUTIFUL

$\mathcal{T}$ito had Charlotte Veronica Harper-Stark by the girl cojones, and Cookie didn't like the feeling. Getting my reward money—while remaining anonymous—had proven to be extremely difficult. Cookie was demanding a name. First off, Tito didn't have my name. And secondly, he knew me as Jester. I got the feeling giving $10 Gs to someone named Jester was a real government no-no. At my request, he had me on a conference call with the Prosecutor of Mack County as he so eloquently attempted to remind her what the word anonymous implied.

It didn't help matters that he ran the story that morning without her consent.

And it really didn't help that he mentioned the ten grand—again, without her consent.

Tito finished, "The Ghost was unmasked as Collin Lockhart, Student Council President at Valley High School, who my source corroborates as the real Ghost. He and two other males were arrested Friday night while attempting to rob Belinski's Book Store. A fourth suspect was found dead at the scene. He held three employees and the owner hostage at gunpoint. Lockhart confessed to my source that he killed a young man by the name of Nico Drake because he thought Nico was going to finger him as The Ghost. I've tied Collin's half-brother, Brantley McCoy, to the murder of Bishop Fowler, along with the illegal impersonation of a fictitious male named Eric Young. A lady named Evelyn Seacrest knew McCoy as Young. 'A nice young man who needed some love,' was her quote. She actually met McCoy at a church service, when his mother had kicked him out of the house, and told him Fowler had a room for rent. She can provide even more information, I'm sure. And give me some time, and I'll tie Lockhart and McCoy to a couple of other violent deaths of men just like me. McCoy also admitted he sold marijuana on the side as Big Moby. In fact, another Valley student named Madison Flannery was his delivery person, according to Slap-stick Wilson. And before the story ran this morning, I contacted an Officer Abbott to pay Madison a visit before she could jump town. I heard she is quite the artist, and I have a feeling she might be the one who forged my signature on some documents. Lockhart and McCoy also had a side hobby of vandalizing local storefronts. Everyone in my article has given police statements, Cookie."

Here was the great thing about the sequence of events from the night before. Each confession Collin and Brantley gave was only within *my* presence. Rudi and Chichi were in the back, play-by-playing the 911 operator and Dylan. Mr. B hadn't arrived yet. So when I phoned Tito with the scoop last night, my identity of Jester was, fingers-crossed, ironclad. If the other guys involved admitted what had been confessed, they'd admit their own knowledge. So as far as I could tell, Jester was still waving that flag of anonymity. But I was pushing it, folks. My deepest fear was I'd be doing the sitting duck thing months afterward and find Tito knocking on my door. The whole process made me think of a female last summer called Pixie. Pixie was Dylan's grandfather's informant. He was a vice detective in LA, and to the day, Lincoln Taylor still couldn't put a face to the name. I'd been rooting for him to pull off her proverbial mask. After what I'd gone through, I sort of rooted for her.

Collin and Damon were incarcerated. Slapstick was hooked up to an IV at University of Cincinnati Hospital. The first two had gone straight to jail. Slapstick's case, however, wasn't so cut and dry. His freedom would be hard sought because he one, had a knife; and two, hung with the wrong crowd. But Rudi, Chichi, Mr. B, and I were prepared to move heaven and earth to help him. He'd evidently spoken with Tito since being hospitalized. Otherwise Tito wouldn't possess the info about Madison. So the fact he cooperated with authorities was a sign in his favor. And Brantley? Brantley "fell" on the knife Damon stabbed Slapstick with. I reserved judgment on the particulars, and when the sleeping gas eventually cleared, everyone was so freaked out by the whole ordeal, no one mentioned mysterious smoke. And I'd take that detail to my cold, lonely grave.

Thirty minutes later, Cookie swore Tito would have his hands on ten thousand big ones before the end of the year. He'd hang onto it, and at my instruction would turn it over to me. We hadn't worked out details of the exchange, but I imagined it would involve Vinnie. Unbeknownst to Cookie (as well as Tito), I'd divide the money with Grumpy, Finn, Bean, Vinnie, and Slapstick. I went at the thing with equal parts ignorance and boredom, but since I'd found success, I felt it best to spread the green around. Christmas cheer and all that.

Now I just had to figure out where to hide ten grand from Murphy.

The man was an ex-bookie. He could sniff out money quicker than the IRS.

Thing was, the "end of the year" meant I still might not have cash by Christmas. Sigh. My only recourse would be to borrow money from Murphy and gradually pay him back.

Next came the issue of Coach Wallace's car. Collin fingered his brother. Story over. When I phoned Coach earlier, he offered a check for Services Rendered. Taking it didn't seem right, but I informed him he could close out his debt to me with a visit to Jojo. Once again, his response was silence. But then I heard a female's voice in the background I immediately recognized as Jojo's. Aww, that Christmas miracle felt good.

On a side note, Valley's Athletic Boosters had taken up a collection to get his car repainted. Dylan's father got him a deal for dirt-cheap, and since my karma bank could use a deposit, I'd donate money myself and consider the universe and me clear.

I padded upstairs and grabbed my iPhone, thumbing in the speed dial of the number Rookie and Red demand I call ASAP.

Rookie's annual Christmas party.

My presence was required.

With a plus-one.

Crap.

Because of the events from the night before, Dylan was still in the freaked part of freaked the way out. I could see his point. To say it'd been a violent few weeks was an understatement. Before I barely got "Hey," out of my mouth, his mouth jumped to fifth gear.

"I know we've talked until you're blue in the face, but there are a few things about last night that have been bothering me," he said. "Mainly, I'm overwhelmed with the number of people who have come in and out of your life right under my nose. Explain. Explain how this even happened."

Dylan was still having trouble with the Fab-Four, the crew from The Double-B. Well, I had no plans to date them—share a jail cell perhaps, but not date. To recap, police cruisers ran into a five-car pileup at the intersection three blocks away. No one was hurt, but if that was the diversion the man in the yellow Dodge Charger had spoken of, he had some majorly mad skills I needed to acquire. I'd wakened with an oxygen mask over my mouth and Dylan tenderly rubbing my hands with his thumbs. With the look of love on his face, in that moment, I would've given him absolutely anything.

My answer was more prolific than normal.

"It's who I am, D," was the explanation. "I told Coach I'd find out who trashed his ride. I fell into the identity theft stuff along the way because I ticked off the wrong people. I didn't know Collin was a possibility, nor did I know Brantley McCoy was his brother. In fact, Damon and Slapstick are better liars than I gave them credit for because I thought they smelled clean." See, that was the problem. That was a half-hearted attempt at the truth, but thank the Lord Dylan was more interested in other things than my integrity. How did I know that? In the past, he would've refused that explanation until he had a piece of my hide. At the moment, he was too concerned with getting a piece of my heart.

"Was there anything else on your mind?" he murmured.

Jesus, take the wheel...

"S-so will you, uh, go to Rookie's party with me?" I stuttered.

Dylan was silent.

Somebody. Kill. Me.

I then knew how the average guy felt when he got turned down after putting his heart and soul out there. I was positive I smelled like a donkey's ass because God knew I felt like one. I mean, it was last minute. That insinuated he was the last choice. But in all fairness, he'd asked me to the winter formal the freaking day of.

"Ah, two dates in one week," he murmured. "That spells relationship, but I must say you'd already promised Saturday night to me anyway. A promise I'd planned to remind you of in the next few breaths."

"Oh yeah, baby, but if I remember correctly that was under extreme bodily duress."

I slammed a hand over my mouth. Baby...I'd called him baby. What had crawled up in my tomboy tongue and sucked out my inner-bro?

"You're flirting," he murmured low in his throat.

The answer was yes...if I was stupid enough to admit it. And it sounded like Dylan had the whole thing planned from the start. He knew I'd ask because I'd already planned to see him anyway. He'd outsmarted me. "Are you going to make me beg?" I pouted. Oh, God, I'd beg. It was either Dylan or Vinnie, and Vinnie's Fu Manchu probably wouldn't fly with the hoity-toity crowd.

"No, sweetheart," he said, chuckling deeply. "I'm flattered you've asked, and as will always be the case, the answer is yes."

Yup, I started to hyperventilate. Put my head between my legs and prayed to the carpet gods I didn't eat the floor. Dylan murmured, "Breathe, sweetheart. It's a formal affair. Wear your red dress and new shoes. I'll dress accordingly because it's my understanding my parents are guests at Rookie's table. I'll pick you up at six-thirty."

———

Linen tablecloths draped the table and chairs. Red poinsettias served as a centerpiece. White china with gold edging laid in front of me with too many utensils and cups to count. I reminded myself to use them outside-in. As soon as we settled, Red gave me half a smile, unleashing her pearly whites on Dylan. "I'd like to apologize straight-up for what Darcy may or may not do tonight. I'm afraid this night will be a snore for Little Miss Crime Stoppers."

I snorted with a grin as Red and I had one of those mother-daughter moments where we both realized I'd never morph into the type of female textbooks said was ideal. We also had one of those moments where she informed me we'd converse later in private. I bet she'd feel differently if she knew I personally erased Cookie from her life.

As Rookie slid in beside her, he placed his arm around her chair, the gleam of his thick platinum wedding ring catching the light. He snuggled into Red for a quick peck on the cheek. Most men tried to hide their emotions. Rookie flaunted his. Red smilingly obliged, her actions not acknowledging they'd divorced a fourth time a year earlier. Her green eyes were the perfect complement to her emerald drop earrings and the perfect contrast to a strapless black velvet bustier gown no one—Rookie especially—could rip their eyes from.

After a lavish dinner, I took a sip of white chocolate latte and watched the couples file onto the dance floor, holding their loved ones tight, basking in a full stomach and the wintery feel of the room. Most had stopped by for holiday greetings to Rookie. I smiled as he proudly introduced me and acted unsurprised when comments were made on the similarities between Red and me. I came to the conclusion holidays brought out the stupid in people. Perhaps that was what'd been wrong with Dylan and me. The holiday spirit made us act ways—and even feel ways—we normally wouldn't.

As I contemplated the thought, I rapped my ruby-red stubby nails on the table, wishing like heck I had a plastic bag to suffocate myself with. Dylan put his cheek alongside mine, breathing in my ear. "Dance with me, sweetheart. I'm dying to get my arms around you."

Ditto...

Before I could protest, he lifted me up, taking my napkin out of my lap and depositing it in my seat. Kenny G's "White Christmas" seeped into my bones, and once mingled with the other attendees, I sulkily realized Dylan was by far the best looking young man in attendance. He was insufferably beautiful and irritatingly...unforgettable. He'd ditched his jacket, and my eyes lazily slid over his perfectly knotted tie and white fitted shirt. I knew the person beneath the clothes, and I could say without a doubt, his heart was more beautiful than the outer package.

Peering into his eyes, I blinked. "You're umm...."

Dylan inhaled in a sound of appreciation...even before the words left my lips. "You're the beauty here, but thank you," he murmured. "And I love the dress."

If anything, the dress was practical. My body was stiff with the beating it took, and the dress thankfully covered the bruises. The song transitioned into Percy Sledge's "When a Man Loves a Woman"...Rookie's favorite song. Rookie and Red slid out from behind the table along with Colton and Susan Taylor.

Time for the real couples to remind themselves why they were couples.

Dylan murmured, "You're quiet, Darc, and you've stopped moving your feet."

I snuggled into him, wishing I could never leave. "I almost fell asleep."

"Not the response Dylan Taylor was going for," he murmured and chuckled.

As always, I had an irrefutable desire to be close to him and molded myself even closer. "I meant it as a compliment," I said with an exhale. "You relax me, D. No one can seem to do that except you. When you're around, I don't worry about tomorrow."

"Watch yourself, sweetheart. You're going to make me fall in love with you."

———

I shivered from head to toe, the temp slightly teetering above freezing. The temperature between Dylan and me, however, said we were minutes from third-degree burns. Murphy and Marjorie had plans to close down the mall. Something he never let the six-year-old do, but Murphy received his bonus and was feelin' the love. During Rookie's party, I hadn't thought too much about being alone with Dylan, but considering the sexual tension between us, I should've. Add a lit Christmas tree and logs on the fire, and we'd tripled up on the trouble.

My hormones were waking up.

After Dylan got the fire raging, I immediately hit the sound system. Labrinth's "Beneath Your Beautiful" popped on. Before I could get all *hey, what do you want to do*, our eyes collided. A heat begging to consume us both was inside.

I stood about twenty feet away. When I felt the boiling emotion, I jumped even further back, scrambling up against the wall. I knocked over Murphy's nativity scene, briefly wondering if the Good News Angel thought our actions were a good thing or bad thing.

My God, that look...

First thing to come to mind was *lamb to the slaughter*. Dylan didn't seem normal, like he vacillated somewhere between man and beast. He stalked forward...and kept coming...and coming.

His grin grew big and naughty as he ripped his tie from his neck and unbuttoned the top button, letting the black silk tie flutter to the hardwood in front of us.

"Dylan, you need to start—stop it." I swallowed. "You're making me want to..."—I shook my head to clear it—"We can't..." My God, did I need a stun gun? "D? Say something." Next thing I knew, he closed the distance between us, backing me up against the wall. One leg slipped between my knees, successfully pinning me in the corner with no place to go but inside his arms.

Oh, rawr...rawr, rawr, rawr...

"Why are you doing this?" I whispered.

"You never begged."

"What?" I asked, confused.

"I wanted to kiss you so badly at the dance, but I must not have shown you how much I cared because you never begged."

My voice went MIA—my vocal chords shriveling up like a prune that needed to be trashed. My feelings ran deeper than the Mariana Trench, but by God, that wasn't a good idea. I wanted it too much. "Oh," I whispered as an answer. "This thing...between us...it can't happen."

Dylan looked at every part of my body except the eyes...up, down, side-to-side—lingering as if he tried to figure out which part he'd devour first. "Tell me why," he demanded, finally catching my gaze.

By God, I couldn't. "We've known each other too long," I used as an excuse.

"I interpret that as you think we'd be boring together."

"Yeah," I whispered.

He rubbed his nose against mine. "Anything else?"

"I like blondes." That made Dylan smile. "Geeky guys, not jocks," I added.

He rubbed his nose up against mine again. "The opposite of me."

"Totally un-alpha."

"Is that right?"

"Right." I breathed in my porn-star voice.

"Tell me why you think we *would* work," he coaxed.

My traitorous heart fell woefully short in its argument. I tentatively brought my hands up to his waist, my mouth opened, and against my better judgment, I released my soul. "Your smile is killer, but your heart is what makes mine beat every day. You're the concrete I stand on, Dylan. Always have been...always will be."

Dylan pulled back like he'd been scorched in a flame, giving one slow blink. "Jesus," he prayed, leaning his forehead into mine. "Conversations like this are what would make me lie down and die for you, Darcy. You're funny. Your face is gorgeous, but your soul...your soul is what slays me."

I thought he was done. In fact, I wished he was when the brevity of his next words hit me.

"Sweetheart, listen," he murmured softly. "Don't overthink us. For once, just fricking feel."

I shook like a leaf in the wind. "I'm afraid to feel," I gasped.

"Why?" he asked tenderly.

"Because of who I am. I'm not so sure you can handle...who I truly am."

At that Dylan stiffened, immediately going for eye contact. Something dark sparked in his gaze I didn't understand. "I know everything about you."

I could barely look him in the face, let alone say the truth. But here we were again—me truly being one way...him thinking I could be someone else. He placed his index finger under my chin, tipping it upward. "Not really," I said with a shrug, forced to look at him. "I use people, D. I used Ben as a science experiment to hold you off. I used Kyd Knoblecker last summer. I used Liam Woods last spring. They helped me in what I was trying to do at the time, but I also used them to see if I could make you jealous. Did I think they were cute? Sure, I'd be lying if I said they weren't, but I used their attraction to me for my own end."

Wow, talk about ripping off the Band-Aid. It felt good, but I wasn't so sure it felt good for Dylan. He took a good thirty seconds to mull over the admission. "So you think that makes you incapable of having a relationship?" he said, frowning with confusion.

Well, yeah.

I mean, shouldn't it?

Dylan moved in for the kill. "That excuse isn't good enough, sweetheart. I know full well who you are, and I wouldn't change one single thing. In fact, it would bore the life out of me if you'd change. Don't you want to experience what is yet unwritten?"

Um, wow...one heckuva pickup line. Trouble was, I knew he meant it.

A deadpan stare. "Maybe," I conceded.

Dylan's predator smile returned. "Give me a chance, Darc. *Please*," he added, whispering out the word please.

My hands traveled up to explore the planes of his chest, circling around behind his shoulder blades and back down to where they rested at his hips. I stared for a darn long time, enjoying each beautiful curve of his face. A strong yet tender jaw. Chiseled cheeks that grew more defined with a deep smile. Lips that only spoke words of encouragement. With a body that would rock anyone's world. Everything about him was intoxicating. Dylan Taylor left me breathless, and I wondered how in the world I could've missed what had been standing beside me for years.

I can't believe I am going to do this...

...say this.

Yet my mouth took over and unloaded the truth.

"When you got hurt," I said with a wince, "in the car accident," I paused, "I only saw reasons why this wouldn't work. Reasons that nearly got you and two of my best friends killed. I live with a lot of guilt, D. Guilt that comes from my mother and guilt over just... breathing. Guilt I prefer to not give power over me because if I do,

I can't function. But even though I build up walls, I'm still not right. Not really. I bite my nails. I'm an insomniac. I count crap when I'm nervous. But if I have a chance of being the person you think I am or I want to be, I know the chance only exists with you. I'm sorry I hurt you, Dylan—with anything I've done here lately or in the past. I want to apologize for the future because more is destined to come. I've given you my heart," I said exhaling. "Can you live with that?"

Dylan was on me so fast every ounce of air left my body.

His strong arms encased my waist, pulling us so close we toppled over as one body—spilling onto the floor. I felt his legs, chest, and hips straining against mine as though he literally tried to step inside my body.

Then he kissed me...

Oh. My. Word.

I'm making out with Dylan Taylor.

From the moment our lips met, I knew it wasn't a best friend thing. It felt carnal and powerful and awakened something I'd never felt possible.

Especially not with Dylan.

But then again...*only* with Dylan.

The kiss was tentative at first—as if I'd break—but then his mouth grew more fevered. He grabbed a handful of my hair and explored my cheeks...first the left, the right...and thank the Lord, found his way back to my lips. Dylan's kiss was the type that left no doubt as to what he wanted.

Me.

Any time. Any place.

Whenever he snapped his gorgeous, cocky fingers.

I gasped for air, attempting to crab walk backward in the search for O2.

Dylan grabbed my right shoe and yanked me toward him, his voice coming out in a lusty growl. "Oh, no, you don't."

"I'm just trying to breathe," I shakily inhaled.

"Oxygen is overrated," he murmured, his voice convulsing more than mine.

I wasn't so sure.

With Dylan's lips then at my neck, after a couple more minutes of holding hands with death, I made another fruitless move to sit up. We'd somehow worked our way from the edge of the stairs to the dining room table. I toppled over a chair. Dylan caught it in one hand, tossing it off to the side with a smacking crash. It nipped the base of the Christmas tree. The tree teetered like the Leaning Tower of Pisa and then came down in a tinging crash. The lights blinked off in two zaps. The star on the top flew across the room. A gingerbread man landed face down, and the gingerbread girl landed on top of him. The boom rattled a glass reindeer on a shelf. We both watched as it wobbled and fell to the hardwood, shattering into tiny little pieces.

"I'll replace that," he said in a breathy voice.

I'd been on all fours when I dove for the reindeer. Right then, I collapsed face down like I'd been shot with a rifle. My word, was that what a relationship with him would be like? We'd practically wrecked the place. I was worn out. Confused. Hormonally activated. Scared out of my ever lovin' mind. Dylan flipped me over, both arms in a push-up by my head, his eyes daring me to move.

His lips found mine again.

After several breathtaking minutes working at my lips, he moved to my hair and trailed down my neck to my collarbone until I moaned in complete and utter ecstasy. All right. I was a woman of opportunity, and it would be a crime to not take advantage of the situation.

At first I was nervous, thinking I'd do something that would turn him off, but then I figured I should YOLO the experience because it might be my last. My hands found his black hair and pulled and twisted to the point it had to have hurt. Tenderly moving my lips over his, I stopped searching for an answer to our muddied relationship. I didn't overthink the *what ifs* and *maybe we shouldn'ts*. All I thought was how unbelievably forbidden and predestined he tasted. I arched at every move his mouth made and answered each caress with equal passion. When Dylan kissed, he was freaking thorough...I didn't know where he began, and I ended.

All at once, he backed off and let me take more of the sweet taste he offered. And girl, did I make sure to take my fair share. I'd never really been given the reins to kiss someone...but when Dylan gave them to me, I took over in a horrifyingly violent manner. And yes, I apologize to anyone who has heart problems for that vivid description.

He murmured, "You're beautiful," and sucked my bottom lip into his, gently nibbling on its edge.

When I hooked my right leg around his hip and moaned, "Don't stop..."

He. Did.

Duuuuuuuude...

That was just wroooooonnnnnnng.

He fisted a handful of my hair in his hand, burying his face in my neck. Leaving my left hand at the small of his back, I put two fingers on my lips as if to cool them. "D," I mumbled, speaking behind them. Dylan's entire body shook. "Hey," I breathed, "are you all right?"

His passion slowly harnessed. And my heart took a free fall. Had he changed his mind so quickly? I recoiled defensively. Ah, shoot. He thought I was a good-time girl when frankly, I didn't even understand the good time. I did understand that why-buy-the-cow-when-you-can-get-the-milk-for-free thing better than anyone in the country. Murphy was from Kentucky. That was the unsaid slogan amongst parents and farmers. But right then, I might understand why some cultures worshipped the bovine.

I metaphorically placed my hand over my heart in a pledge. "D, I promise I'm not a milking cow, and I don't worship them either. I know that's bovine ignorance."

Dylan finally mumbled into my neck. "Sweetheart, give me a sec. I honestly wasn't prepared for your enthusiasm."

Oh. Okay. I could deal with that. Longing to touch him, I forced myself to remain still, afraid one quick move one way or another would erase what had gone down between us. Regardless of what he believed, I thought it was beautiful.

I sighed.

After a quick peck under my chin, he lifted his head with a gaze that I couldn't quite describe. It was somewhere else. When his eyes bled back into focus, he was drunk and drowsy on...*holy crap*.

It was desire.

He hadn't shaken because he was scared...or changed his mind. He'd shaken because he was holding himself back.

Dylan shakily set us both up and took my palm in his hand, placing it over his heart. It moved so hard and fast I could see his shirt jump up and down with each beat. "Feel this," he murmured. "This is why I waited so long for you, Darcy. I knew it would feel like this, and I wasn't going to let it slip away. Seriously, sweetheart, your kissing skills are off the charts. Some can't handle that sort of passion...I crave it."

Alriiiiiggggghtty then...

"Yeah," I said with a giggle. "I feel like I just ran a marathon."

My voice hiccupped all over the place.

The dimples made an appearance while Dylan ran his finger down my jaw. "That's love, sweetheart," he said, adding a soft wink. "It's going to ignite your insides every time I touch you. It's not going to be boring, or habitual, or predictable—"

"Or safe," I whispered.

"No," he quickly murmured. "That's where you're wrong. It's always going to be safe with me. I'm one of the good guys. I'd never hurt you."

I blurted out, "Kissing is an upgrade I underestimated. Can you at least tell me if I was any good?"

I ran both hands through my hookerfied hair, feeling like an absolute idiot. But my God, I was all ears. Wondering if he'd let me in on a trade secret that'd bring him to his knees.

I heard Dylan chuckle. No wonder...just cut out my tongue already.

"Trust me, sweetheart. I've never been so attracted to someone in my life. So yeah, it was good."

My fingers lingered on my lower lip, fighting back a smile. My mind couldn't unravel what'd happened let alone try to interpret Dylan was genuinely attracted to me.

Tunneling his fingers through my hair, he pulled me forward and gently placed a thumb in the dimple of my chin. "God, you're gorgeous."

My heart caught in my throat. "You ain't too shabby yourself," I whispered.

"Listen, I feel like I need to shoot straight here. I *just*..." he paused and inhaled deeply, "I just...*love you*," he finished with an exhale.

"Always," I added quickly. "Always, always, always."

He slowly shook his head from left to right. "Not like that. It's not our best friend love. I'm *in love* with you. I've loved you for years, but over the past year things changed for me. And in all honesty, I can't remember *not* having been in love with you."

I stop...take it all in...I'm stuck on shocked.

File that under *My Best Friend's On Drugs.*

Dylan grinned at my open-mouthed expression.

How in God's holy name was I supposed to respond to that? I know I should return the L-word phrase—because God knew I worshiped the ground he walked on—but the emotions struck me like a Kansas tornado. Dylan hugged a part of my soul that'd never been touched. That touch reminded me I'd loved and lost before too.

Dylan saw the panic, and I swear, he knew the source. "One thing at a time," he whispered. "I get you. I understand you. And I love you more than anything in my life."

Dylan's dimples had a way of making my discomfort vanish. While I slowly came to grips with his words, I couldn't fight the smile that enveloped my face. Darcy Winston Walker had a boyfriend. Dylan Michael Taylor held the title.

Eat that, all you haters!

The silence hung in the air like a question neither of us would ask...where did we go from here?

I wasn't sure of the chain of events, but we laid on the couch—Dylan, nothing but smiles, and me wondering why in the heck I'd just stripped myself of my single status...willingly. Somewhere between making it to the couch, the tree had been righted, the gingerbread ornaments rehung, popcorn had been popped, and both of us nursed a steaming hot cup of cocoa. "I have a couple of rules," he murmured, kissing the top of my head.

My popcorn took on the texture of wet potting soil. I started to cough. I didn't know—maybe I was crying. When Dylan pounded on my back, the noises dissolved into nervous giggles. Of course, Mr. Bossy Pants would have rules. I decided to look on things in a positive light. Everything had rules. Baseball had rules. Boxing had rules. War had rules. Relationships, I suppose, did too.

Pushing up on an elbow, I leaned in and braced my hand on his chest. Dylan kissed me once. Twice. Two more times. When I pulled back, he tunneled his fingers through the hair at my nape, deepening the connection once more. I moaned. Somebody help me, but I moaned like a darn mountain lion. "About those rules?" I grinned into his lips.

I could feel his smile against my mouth.

Tucked up under his arm, Dylan buried the fingers of his other hand in my hair. That felt so good I was pretty sure someone could set my hair on fire, and I wouldn't even care. "If this thing ever goes south," he murmured, "then you don't run. We stay up all night and duke it out until we're on the same page. It's a physical hurt when we don't get along, Darc, and I don't want any repeats. Please..." The hurt in his voice was palpable—I honest to God had no idea I could hurt him as much as he could hurt me. "When I lie down at night, I want to know that we're good."

"Kosher."

"Kosher," he agreed. "And I want you to quit thinking of me with other girls. There aren't any. There are no other relationships or hints of relationships. I'll be honest with you, and you be honest with me. But I can't explain what I don't know is bothering you. You've been tortured by things you've been hearing, and yet you've kept the bulk of those feelings to yourself. So you have to talk, sweetheart. That's a must."

The one thing I did mention to Dylan was that Collin admitted to making up stories about him and Brynn. Collin should count himself lucky he was in lockdown. Dylan tapped into his bloodlust when he heard and punched a wall. Thankfully, when Dylan asked for a "why," he accepted my reasoning that Collin was just a d-bag who wanted everyone to be unhappy. And thank God for that. The real "why" would show him a Darcy I wasn't ready for him to know.

Oh, he knew a little bit about my capabilities...but not the latest evolution of crazy.

"Pinky swear it to me," he murmured and grinned.

I giggled, waiting for him to run out of gas. *He* knew, and *I* knew I'd screw things up before the weekend was out. I pinky swore anyway, knowing insecurity would always plague me. Think about it. Dylan had curves and muscles in all the right places. I imagined half of mine and relied on the lords of voodoo to take care of the rest.

He tucked a stray hair behind my ear, slowly smiling. "So you're mine," he said.

"Yours."

"I can call tomorrow, and when I say 'I love you,' you know it means something more."

"Yeah."

"No more science experiments."

"Temporary insanity."

"We're exclusive."

"Facebook and Twitter official tonight," I said, grinning big.

"Saturday nights are booked through eternity."

They'd always been his, but I said, "Deal" anyway. I then added what I knew could be a huge obstacle if Dylan didn't appear to play things on the up-and-up. "And you're down with dealing with Murphy on a daily basis?" I said giggling.

Dylan was as sober as a judge. "I'm not a cheat, Darcy, and I never will be. Murphy and I will be fine."

"Well, no one has ever explained to him that stoning isn't PC anymore. He's stuck in the Dark Ages."

"Don't talk yourself out of this," he murmured. Both of us breathed for a beat, wondering how it would invariably change things. Dylan broke the standoff first. "How are you doing?" he murmured.

"I'm freaking out," I said with a giggle...then paused, turning the tables. "How are *you* doing?"

He threaded his fingers behind his neck and mischievously grinned. "I'm freaking awesome." I threw my head back and laughed. Typical. As usually blinding as his smile was, he had the look of the cat that swallowed the canary. Poor bird. It probably enjoyed being in his mouth. "I'm going to be selfish tonight and dwell on how this makes me feel, Darc. Tomorrow, I'll worry about you getting there."

"Considerate."

"I always am," he said with a wink. Dylan placed both his hands at the small of my back, pulling me tighter. "Now crawl on up here, and let me taste your mouth."

I'd never had a more appealing proposition...as in, EV-UH. My iPhone grumbled with the pop-pop-pop of gunshots, and as Dylan lazily nibbled away at my neck, I snagged it from the floor and read three texts I'd missed (imagine that).

The *Call me* was from Ben Ryan. He'd phoned, beside himself around noon, when he read the morning paper. Answering it seemed dumber than the relationship I'd just committed to. The following text included a picture of Vinnie's hand holding a black velvet engagement ring box with the caption: *She said yes*. Um, God help us...he'd still better be single. The third number registered as local, with an, *I need to see you, babe* message. Jaws, the sender. That one I'd answer before morning, regardless. As I held three other options in my left hand, I glanced back to Dylan's half-mast, drowsy eyes, and did what any red-blooded, American girl would do...I threw my phone across the floor and pounced on him like a hungry cat.

NOTE FROM THE AUTHOR

Thank you so much for reading 100 Proof Stud! If you read this book and enjoyed it, I'd be honored if you'd recommend it to other friends or readers' groups and leave a star rating at the retailer in which you purchased the book. Your words mean so much to authors and help other readers discover new worlds.

ABOUT THE AUTHOR

A.J. lives in Cincinnati with her husband, two daughters, an ADD dog, and a spoiled hamster burial site in her backyard. When she's not writing, she's reading, binge-watching the heck out of some show or eavesdropping-slash-creeping on those around her. And maybe searching the skies for aliens whenever the mood hits.

For more books and updates, connect with her on social media
and at:
https://www.ajlape.com

ALSO BY A. J. LAPE

DARCY WALKER
TEENAGE SLEUTH THRILLERS

Grade A Stupid

No Brainer

100 Proof Stud

DEFCON Darcy

Foolproof

DARCY WALKER INVESTIGATIONS

Side Hustle

Gut Check

Ride or Die

Medusa Effect

5 Pounds of Pressure

Heist & Seek

White Noise

RIVERA & GUTIERREZ SERIES

Vice

Vice Versa

Of Vice & Men

Vice or Consequences

ACKNOWLEDGMENTS

Thank you, Lord, for always being faithful; to my family and friends for your love and encouragement. Most notably authors Julie Cassar and CR Everett; my editing team of Jeff LaFerney, CR Everett, Debbie Brooks, Heather Mcguire, Justine Littleton, and Sheri Spell. Thank you for making me better; my Street Team for helping me keep Darcy's name alive on social media; Lindsee Baez and Kelley Grealis for answering endless fraud questions and dumbing things down when my moron side emerged; my fan club for naming the fictional band The Minstrel Cramps; and to the YA Ninjas, Secret Sisters, and bloggers for their friendship and social media shares.